DUSK
A CIRCLE OF NINE NOVEL

R.L. PARKER

Written by: R.L. Parker
Formatted by: R.L. Parker
https://rlparkerfantasy.com

Edited by: Kristina Parker
https://kpknitcraft.com

Visit the official website:
https://ayrelon.com

Published by Ayrelon Press
https://ayrelonpress.com

Art by: J.K. Pevahouse
http://jkpevahouse.com/

Paperback ISBN-13: 978-1-7366221-7-9

Hardcover ISBN-13: 978-1-7366221-8-6

E-book ISBN-13: 978-1-7366221-9-3

This novel is dedicated to **you**,
my cherished Reader.

You matter.

ABOUT THE ARTIST

John Kelly Pevahouse was born in Memphis, Tennessee, but grew up and still resides in Virginia. In 1987, at the age of 13, he began martial arts training. In 2003, a few years after reaching the level of instructor, he retired from martial arts for health reasons. Around this time, he began his first formal oil painting and drawing classes. He spent the next five years studying traditional methods and techniques that developed a base level of skill.

After a lengthy break, John Kelly re-emerged with his own style, using many mediums and techniques. Often using music as his muse, he creates original works. J.K.Pevahouse has always been influenced by film, television, pop culture, and Dungeon's & Dragons.

- - -

As an Author, I can say that John's art is very inspiring, and working alongside him is a joy. You can find his art at any of the links below. I highly recommend his works to anyone with a penchant for gothic, fantasy or dark arts in general. I have several of his pieces on my wall, and consider myself quite lucky to have him as my cover artist.

jkpevahouse.com

instagram.com/jkpevahouse

facebook.com/jkpevahouseart

TIMELINE / READING LIST

DUSK

A CIRCLE OF NINE NOVEL

R.L. PARKER

Chapter 1:
Catalyst

Ris'Uttyr, Caer'Nuun 17th, 575 of the 1st Era

VIOLET LIGHTNING streaked down from the dark, cloudless sky, surging forth from the magical weave that surrounded the world; bringing its power into view of even the weakest of the Elonesti Dominion's citizens. Normally invisible and inaccessible to most, it swelled into the visible spectrum like a glowing net made of lightning, stretching across the sky to the horizon. The display was brief, but frightening, and sent all manner of draconic creature fleeing for cover as far away from the point of impact as they could manage.

The magic descended upon the outstretched bone palm of a single figure, standing on the roof of a four story building at the northern edge of Nokara. Of all the beings Queen Mordessa could have selected to send north to the Talaani Empire, Lord Whun was the most terrifying to behold. He was completely aware of how his appearance made others feel, and had no qualms about leaning into that persona and leveraging it for his own purposes; it was an image he'd carefully curated, after all. He often had no need to show his true power, or cast any spells beyond simple conveniences. However, it was far beyond time to take action, and he was done waiting.

As he pulled the power he needed from the weave, the spectacle of his first spell in their presence had sent the citizens of Nokara fleeing in terror, scurrying through the streets below. Their flight suited him just fine. He was not concerned with their lives, or their safety, but he also bore them no ill will. They were inconsequential to his plans, but their absence would make his task easier to accomplish.

The white robes of the Ambassador of Baan'Sholaria would no longer suffice. In order to don his own robes, he had to summon the power to rip a hole in the fabric of reality and access the pocket dimension in which he'd stored them before accepting the Queen's assignment. As the power coalesced in his palm, he let his robes slide from his shoulders; little bits of silver and gold that adorned them clanking onto the slate tiles below his feet. His black skeleton glistened in the light of Ayrelon's two nighttime moons, Provoss and Aygos. The blue, purple and black runes etched into, and dancing across the surface of, his bones seemed to spring to life, as if thriving in the darkness that surrounded him.

A black heart hung suspended from rusted barbed wire at the center of his ribcage, bursting into purple flame as fresh air kissed its surface. He'd kept himself covered for too long, and decided in that instant that he'd never confine himself for their benefit again. He looked down at his ineffective legs, rendered useless long before he could remember. They hung motionless beneath his exposed hip bone, slightly akilter, with his feet curled feebly beneath them. He could have repaired himself at any time, had he chosen. However, that wouldn't have had the same visual impact as permanently levitating three feet above the floor, and floating from place to place in horrifying silence. Had his lower jaw still been attached, he would have smiled at the thought.

Still holding the power in his right hand, he extended his left palm toward the crumpled pile of robes on the floor and willed his jaw to return to him. Though he'd long ago chosen to keep his jaw concealed within hidden pockets, for the benefit of his counterparts among the Talaani, he saw no need to persist the ruse. The blackened jawbone burned through the cloth robes, floated upward, and clanked into his outstretched hand with an eerie echo, the smell of burnt linen filling the air in its wake.

Small bits of rusted barbed wire dangled from the two ends of the jaw, identical to the wires that held his black heart in place. Smiling to himself in his mind, he reached up and hooked the wire over his clavicles, then willed them to twist into place and hold fast, allowing the jaw to hang, teeth outward, at the top of his chest.

Lord Whun stretched his right arm to the side and pushed the violet powers into the air, spreading them outward in a slow spiral until the magical force became a ring encircling a black void. A crackling filled the air, the sound of cavern winds echoing far in the distance, calling out to him from beyond the mortal world. Without looking, he reached into the void and retrieved a crown rimmed with tall iron spikes, with an ornate embellishment on its front. As he placed the crown onto his head, the gray stone at the center of the adornment cracked and slid open like a pair of lids, revealing a large eye slightly obscured by a swirling purple haze. The eye blinked twice, sending waves of power rippling through Whun's head, neck and upper chest. He had missed the enhanced vision the crown granted much more than he'd thought. As ultraviolet, infrared and magical vision filled his sight, he questioned his past self's decision to hide the crown.

'*No more hiding,*' he thought determinedly.

He reached into the void one more time and retrieved his ancient robe. Made from black dragon skin, and adorned with black scale pauldrons and dragon tooth spikes, it was sure to raise the ire of the Talaanians. Their draconic overlords had long since vanished, and though he could not remember the war, he was certain to be accused of participating in their slaughter; an accusation he was confident was accurate.

Purple and black runes sprang to life across the robe's surface as he slipped his arms into the houppelande-style sleeves, and settled the inner shoulder pads over top his old joints. He reveled in the feeling as eons-old enchantments sprang to life at his touch, filling him with vigor, and making him far stronger and more durable than his skeletal enhancements alone could accomplish.

'*Never again,*' he decided as the power washed over him.

As he finished donning his robe, leaving the top half open to expose his heart and jaw, the void closed, and the sound of its presence blinked out of existence. It was time to reveal what the Talaani Empire was hiding. They'd carefully controlled what he saw, where he went, and who he met for decades. He had allowed them to as part of the game he'd been asked to play; determine their strength, and find out what they were hiding without raising their suspicions, or reigniting the war. Despite their best efforts, he'd discovered enough to know that one of their most protected secrets, which moved between the Dominions on an impossibly erratic schedule, was at the center of Nokara inside the Temple of Noktrusgodhen.

He could sense the hundred year cycle repeating. His Queen always grew more suspicious of the Talaani Empire whenever the patterns emerged. It was the reason she'd sent him as an ambassador, and quelling her fears was his primary mission. Everything inside the Elonesti Dominion that he could attribute to her concerns seemed centralized on the elusive guest they harbored within their temple. It was time to act, and diplomacy was guaranteed to be fruitless. He would have to use force. The game was over. His ruse had ended.

The dark of the night seemed to swirl and ripple in his wake as he drifted forward, off the side of the building, and slowly descended upon a cloud of black magic toward the street. A dozen Skaar ran toward him, brandishing twelve-foot-long spears in their humanoid hands, and snarling from their lizard-like, horned heads through ferociously fanged maws. They raced across the ground on their four hind legs, their serpentine tails writhing in the air behind them angrily. Rising six foot tall, and stretching nearly thirteen feet from snout to tail, they were far larger and stronger than Lord Whun could hope to be.

As he descended before them, coming to rest three feet above the ground, he peered at their leader through his lifeless, hollow eyes and laughed in their minds through the enchantment on his detached lower jaw. '*All this? For me? You shouldn't have.*'

He clenched his right fist in the air between them, grabbing hold of their skeletal structures with his magic. Several of them tried to move, to thrust their spears toward him and end his threat. Their muscles strained from the effort, flexing and swelling, tearing against the resistance from within as their joints refused to comply. With a wicked laugh that echoed through their minds, Whun thrust his hand open, causing their skeletons to shatter within them. The twelve draconic soldiers crumpled to the ground, most of them blacked out from shock, the rest writhing and hissing in agony.

Whun drifted over the horrid mass, continuing along his path without a care. He repeated the process twice more before reaching the temple, leaving three dozen or more Skaar all but dead on the road behind him. A gigantic stone dragon was perched atop the eighty foot tall, polished diorite building. Large columns descended from above, providing support at the corners for the great petrified dragon's massive front talons. He had seen the building from afar, but the guard had always kept him from approaching it. Seeing it up close put the sheer size of the dragons of old into perspective.

Though made of stone, the creature was as imposing as anything he could imagine. Standing upright on its fore and hind legs, its massive body and elongated neck held its head at an impressive sixty feet above its talons. Its wings were folded back, and its tail was coiled around its feet, so their exact dimensions were hard to deduce from his vantage point, but it appeared as if Noktrusgodhen had been over one hundred-twenty feet long, with a wingspan just as impressive.

'*It is no wonder Mordessa fears their return,*' he mused. He couldn't remember the war Mordessa often spoke of when they met. Some unknown event had taken the whole world's memories hundreds of years prior. It was such a significant anomaly to the eternal citizens of Dusk, they marked the years of their calendar with its occurrence as the starting point of all their recorded history. He'd spent most of his free time the past several hundred years seeking a solution to their great memory problem, only to find out after his arrival in the Talaani Empire that the affliction wasn't isolated to only their Kingdom.

He knew the Queen was being truthful when she spoke of an ancient war; just as he trusted her when she told him he'd been a part of it. Even still, he could not remember the war, which meant it had concluded before their calendar began. As powerful as he was, he couldn't fathom what it took to fight a nation such as the Talaani, when creatures such as the stone dragon looming above him filled the skies.

Whun had fallen victim to the true enemy of his people. Time. With so much at their disposal, it was quite common for them to get lost in thought without warning. He had allowed himself to be distracted by the statue of his Kingdom's ancient enemy, and during that distraction, two dozen Skalaani guards had spilled into the courtyard and surrounded him. Unlike their six-limbed Skaar counterparts, the Skalaani were bipedal, could reach up to nine feet in height, had broad shoulders, and were noticeably muscular. Their tails were shorter than a Skaar's, but deadly none-the-less. The only traits they shared were their lizard-like heads with a sharply fanged maw, two eyes facing forward, two eyes facing sideways, and the scaled, horned and spiked hide that covered their bodies. The ones charging toward him wore scale armor painted red, and brandished large serrated blades alongside blackened tower shields.

He didn't recognize them as members of the Elonesti Dominion, which prided itself on its magical prowess and intellectual pursuits. If he was correct, they were Guardians from the Fiirnasi Dominion, likely sent to protect whatever, or whomever, was hiding inside the temple. He'd learned a great deal about each Dominion's combat capabilities, and in those learnings he'd come to question one simple, but critical detail about Fiirnasi Guardians. They supposedly were chosen based on their magical resistance, and it was claimed they were immune to any attack spells the Elonesti magi could produce.

Whun was not an Elonesti magi, and he was happy to have an opportunity to put their legend to the test.

He pushed himself higher into the air on his cloud of black magic, rising twenty feet above his opponents; just in time for several to charge through the space he'd been occupying, the tips of their swords narrowly missing the trailing edge of his robe. He reached out both hands and clenched them, attempting to latch onto the Guardians' skeletons as he'd done with the Skaar.

His spell would not take hold.

Frustrated, he called down purple lightning from the sky and covered the courtyard in its destructive power. When the blinding light faded, and his normal vision could catch sight of the ground below, he saw the leader of the Guardians cackling back at him

5

defiantly, steam hissing across the surface of the Skalaani warriors' scales and weaponry.

Angered, Whun turned his focus to the equipment the warriors carried. He took hold of the scale armor, swords and shields with his mind and drew another pulse of energy from the weave. A wave of purple smoke rolled off of him, gathering on the surface of their weapons and armor, increasing their mass and crushing the Skalaani into the ground. As he hovered above them and held them in place, he reached down his right hand and swirled it through the air toward the courtyard. The limestone began to crack, falling away into a black void that was forming beneath them. The Skalaani panicked, frantically fighting to break free of his magical grip, and avoid tumbling into the nothingness below.

Just as his spell was nearly complete, a sudden gust of wind crashed into him from behind, and a pair of large talons ripped him from the sky. Purple energy sprang to life at the bidding of his robe's enchantments, shielding him from the impact of his attacker's massive claws and the ground below as it cast his shielded body from its grasp.

He floated back into the air, resuming his normal three-foot levitation, and looked for his new assailant. A Wyvern dropped to its talons at the center of the courtyard before him, its sixty foot wingspan blotting out all light from the moons and stars. It craned its fifteen foot neck and brought its maw within inches of Whun's chest, then issued a deep, resonating growl that shook the wall behind him.

'You aren't supposed to exist,' thought Whun, pushing his words into the creature's mind.

Instead of the fear the creature expected to smell, it could sense Whun's sheer determination washing over it like an icy chill when his thoughts entered its mind. It reared back almost instantly, preparing to strike Whun's chest and prevent him from casting whatever horrid spell he planned to use next, despite the searing pain that his robe's magic shielding would likely cause.

"Wait!" came a call from a human voice near the temple.

It was an older voice, and one Whun recognized. He turned to face its source as the wyvern pulled back, allowing the man to approach. 'You?'

"Not like this. There is a better way!" said the man, coming between Whun and the wyvern, his hands extended protectively.

Whun decided to give the man a chance to speak, relaxed the tension in his shoulders, and drifted a few feet back from his wyvern opponent.

'Is she listening?' thought the man, hoping Whun would hear.

'Not at present. Mordessa knows nothing of this event,' answered

Whun.

'Block her, so we might speak freely. Let me show you what we've been hiding, and why. It will all make sense!' offered the man.

Whun peered back with his lifeless eyes and gave pause, letting it be clear that he was hesitant to comply.

'The Noktulians have a way of restoring your memories. Isn't that what you want? Your greatest wish? Let them help you, and you'll know the truth of the war, and what your Queen has done. After that, if you still seek to destroy the Talaani, it's clear none here could stand against you. Though the great Tuldaxx means well, she has never fought a creature as powerful the great Lord Whun. Give us a chance to show you the truth. That is all that I ask,' thought the man.

Whun nodded and blocked Queen Mordessa's view of them with a single thought. He floated across the courtyard, past the Wyvern that shouldn't exist, beyond the frightened Fiirnasi Guardians, and followed the man who should have been dead into the temple, intent on learning the Talaani Empire's greatest secret.

MASTER NYR'TAHL stood in Tavyn's doorway, watching patiently as the young elf slid his dagger across the surface of a whetstone. "We can send a more experienced agent. It doesn't have to be you," he stated, crossing his arms.

"How does one gain experience then, if they are never sent into the field?" scoffed Tavyn.

"If her Majesty's story is accurate, you could be walking straight to your death," said Nyr'Tahl.

"Thanks for the vote of confidence, Master," sighed Tavyn. He sheathed his blade and stood, hands on hips, clearly displeased with their discourse.

"We usually send Purifiers after smaller targets first, young Tavyn. Zombies, a skeleton stumbling across the countryside, some witch out in a bog brewing poisons... never a Necromancer; especially not one capable of raising the dead as their first contract," said Nyr'Tahl.

"Well, I'm going. I found her out in the fields, barely clinging to life. I had to carry her back to Quaan'Shala. I kept watch over her while the healers saved her life. I performed the interview that gathered what little intelligence we have on this necromancer," barked Tavyn, getting more frustrated the longer he spoke.

"That's another reason not to send you. You're too attached to this, and I fear your emotions will win out over your training," said Nyr'Tahl.

"What am I going to do if I stay here?" challenged Tavyn. "You'll keep me on the guard rotation, scouting the southern savanna... for signs of what? Nothing has happened for hundreds of years. We don't get attacked. We don't even have any known enemies. Hell, most of Ayrelon probably doesn't even know Quaan'Shala exists. So, what are we scouting for? Why are we so terrified of what *might* come, when nothing comes?

"No. The one thing I can do is fight for the will of Ishnu, and I feel her will in my gut. This man in Amuer is evil, and what he attempted to do to our Princess is just a glimpse at his intent. I can handle him. I can handle fighting him far better than I can riding mindlessly through a savanna, night after night, especially if I've got to worry about some other Purifier doing the job in my stead!"

"We scout, and we guard, because Lord Dax'Vahr requires us to. It is he who instructs us, and guides us, in Ishnu's will. Not your gut. This isn't the Tavyn Order, is it? We are the Daxian Order," said Nyr'Tahl.

"Who among us have even seen Lord Dax'Vahr? I haven't. You haven't. Does he even exist?" asked Tavyn defiantly.

Nyr'Tahl salvaged what was left of his patience and calmed his tone as best he could, trying to defuse the situation. "Only the worthy meet him. You know that. If you can handle a Necromancer on your first mission as a Purifier, you'll prove your worth beyond a doubt. More likely, you'll end up dead, and we'll just send another Purifier anyway, but I will not stand in your way. I was only trying to give you an out."

"You'll be glad to be rid of my mouth, in either case," said Tavyn with a wry smile.

"Fine," sighed Nyr'Tahl, realizing Tavyn's determination. "Speak to Onala on your way out of the compound. She's been to Amuer several times, and can prepare you for what you'll encounter."

Tavyn paused briefly as he slipped past his master into the hall. "Sending me wasn't your idea, was it? It came from above."

"Princess Aelys is her father's favorite child, and heir to the throne. She asked for you by name," said Nyr'Tahl.

Tavyn nodded and continued on his way, gritting his teeth. The Princess was counting on him to be her savior, and prevent her assailant from hurting anyone else. She didn't know he was a new agent; that he'd only completed two small missions, and the trip to Amuer was going to be his first real contract. All she knew was he was there when she needed her, and had been at her side every second her personal guard would allow ever since. He ran the princess's words through his mind again as he walked, searching for any clue he might have missed.

"He drugged me, tied my hands, then led me through the

streets on what seemed like a very random path. I think he was trying to hide where he was taking me, or was waiting for the drugs to do their job and put me to sleep. Either way, it seemed to take ages. He stopped at one point and reached into his pocket to retrieve another vial of elixir. That's when I saw the small tome with Ishnu's sigil etched into the front, in gold," explained Princess Aelys.

"Is that when you got away?" asked Tavyn.

"Not quite. I yelled at him, demanding to know what he was doing with me. I told him my father wouldn't pay a ransom, and was more likely to destroy the city out of vengeance than give in to the demands of a kidnapper," she stated forcefully. Her face seemed to drain of blood at the memory, her fear threatening to take over even though the event had happened almost a month prior. "He didn't answer directly. He just stopped and asked, 'Don't you want to become one with Ishnu? To serve her in the purest form possible? I can give you that gift. You can take that gift back to your people.' That's when I broke away. The vial's cork was being stubborn, and he tried to use both hands to open it while keeping hold of my bonds. His grip loosened enough that I was able to rip the rope free and run," she explained.

"Do you remember where you were when that happened?" asked Tavyn.

"No. I'm sorry. I was completely lost. I ran in a straight line as fast as I could, and ended up in the Seventh District, near the Azure Courthouse. That's all I can remember. I could've gotten there from anywhere in the city," she said.

"I'm sorry to put you through this. Just one more question. Do you remember what he looks like?" asked Tavyn.

"No. His face was enveloped by the shadow cast by his cowl, and he'd used some sort of oil on his skin that made my night vision useless for discerning detail," she answered.

When the memory ended, Tavyn found himself standing outside Onala's office. He opened the door and stepped inside to find the old woman doing the same thing he'd always seen her doing; writing on a piece of parchment with a red-feathered quill.

"I've been expecting you," said Onala as Tavyn entered and pushed the door closed.

"I'm here for whatever wisdom you can share in regards to Amuer," said Tavyn, taking a seat in one of the two chairs across from her.

He always found the small office at the front of her residence to be quaint, if not eclectic. The Daxian Order's compound was carved into the rock at the side of a cliff, which meant most of the halls and chambers were simple, carved and smoothed stone. Onala had long ago covered her walls, floors and even the ceiling with planks of wood. The dark brown floor, reddish brown walls, and tan ceiling were unique in Quaan'Shala. He'd never seen the room's like, and yet it somehow made him feel at home.

Small shelves dotted the walls, holding books, knick-knacks, pots, and other belongings Onala chose to keep on display. Gaps between the shelves were filled with small potted plants, crude paintings, and little pieces of sculpted art. Onala had traveled extensively in her youth, and hints of her world experience were tantalizingly displayed in glimpses all around her.

"Amuer is a cesspool of human depravity and corruption," she said as she placed her quill down on a leather pad and looked up at him. "I assume you mean to travel there?"

"I must. Yes," said Tavyn.

"You'll find no pleasure in the trip, I assure you. I haven't been in some time, and I've no desire to return. I tried to warn Princess Aelys against going, but she insisted on the need for diplomacy with the Kingdom of Haern. 'Tis a pity what they allow to happen to political guests in their capital city," said Onala, shaking her head, sending her curly gray hair into an almost playful dance around her face.

"I'm going to hunt the man who tried to harm her. I just need an idea of what I'm walking into."

"As I said, it is a human place. There are a few dwarves, gnomes, orcs, plenty of half-breeds of this or that, and of course a great many elves of all kinds. Most of the elves are Dynar like us. Aelys wanted to form relations with Haern in an effort to protect our people there. I tried to assure her that they were all welcome to come live in Quaan'Shala, and chose to stay in Amuer despite their poor treatment in human lands, but... she wouldn't hear of it," said the old woman, once again shaking her head.

"Poor treatment?" asked Tavyn, raising an eyebrow. He had, of course, heard vague statements like that in the past, but no one had ever bothered to explain what they meant. He hoped that asking Onala in the context of his pending trip to Amuer would prompt a more thorough answer.

"Oh, aye. You'll see a great many people in Amuer with brown or black skin, but the majority of them will be Dynar. That, in and of itself, wouldn't be an issue, aside from the fact that it is widely known amongst the citizens of that 'great' city that we worship Ishnu, 'the goddess of death'. Since most of them have no interest in learning what that means, or what Ishnu truly embodies, any Dynar they see is shunned, cast down, or forced to become indentured servants just to feed themselves. A few do become successful, and the underground sure loves our racial propensity for stealth to aid them in their illicit nighttime activities, but by and large our kind suffer. Endlessly," said Onala.

"Then why do they stay? Why don't they come here and live in peace?" asked Tavyn.

"Any Dynar can live in Quaan'Shala, this is true," started Onala. "But one cannot *thrive* here. You live at the King's mercy. You fill a role. You do your part for our society and we provide for you in turn. All this is simple fact, and facts you grew up with, might I add. If you wanted to start your own business, though... that can't be accomplished in our great Kingdom without the King's approval, and backing. That means if you have any desire to be anything other than what the King decrees, you must leave and seek it elsewhere.

"Many have done so over the generations, and most never return. Some succeed, so the rest look up to their success, and it gives them hope. Children are born in those foreign lands, and they are raised in places like Amuer. To those children, the idea of Quaan'Shala is pure fantasy; a tale told to children to give them hope for some distant, far off land or an unattainable future. Many of them don't realize our Kingdom is real, because it sounds too idealistic when compared to their daily lives."

Tavyn found it hard to hide his distaste for what he was hearing. "So I'm heading into a city run by humans, where most of the populace is taller than me. The only elves there with black skin and hair are downtrodden and struggling to survive, have become voluntarily enslaved for the sake of basic necessities, or have joined the criminal underground and aren't to be trusted. That about sum it up?" asked Tavyn.

"Yes," said Onala. "I can tell by the look on your face that this upsets you. However, I must caution that the lives of our Amuer brethren are not yours to save. There are far too many, and most of them would not trust you enough to let you help them. Many missionaries depart from Quaan'Shala with hopes of luring those unfortunate souls back to our homeland, so they might live easier, potentially happier lives. Only a handful ever take them up on that offer. Of those that return, more than half eventually leave again... and go straight back to Amuer."

"Why?" asked Tavyn, more than a little shocked.

"Opportunity, and nothing more. Life may be hard for them in Amuer, but there is always a chance they might succeed; that the struggle will be worth it," explained Onala.

"I don't understand that mindset," sighed Tavyn.

"You have no need to. Your job is to hunt a man. So, go there and hunt. If you stay focused on that, you'll do fine. Walk in with a hardened heart, because if you don't, the treatment of our people will drive you mad," said Onala.

"Thank you, wise one," said Tavyn, gaining his feet.

"One last thing," said Onala.

Tavyn stopped halfway to the door and looked back at her.

"Some part of you might think that your birth parents are in Amuer, since you were orphaned and raised by the Order. Do not let that thought consume you. You will not find them there," said Onala.

"I haven't given them a second of thought, if I'm being honest. Most of the Daxian Order are orphans. I am of singular intent, worry not," said Tavyn.

Onala nodded her approval as Tavyn turned and left. As he exited the facility, his mind ran in circles around Onala's parting words. He hadn't given his birth parents any space in his mind for decades. Why had she mentioned it?

MORDESSA GROWLED and hissed in anger, sending tremors through her marble and obsidian ritual hall. Her crystal ball remained dark, despite all her efforts. She could not see into the mind of Lord Whun, and could not get sight of him by scouring Nokara from above. He had simply vanished from existence, leaving his white robes in a small pile atop the embassy at the northern edge of the city.

Two servants scrambled into the room, seeking to provide whatever aid their Queen might need. She spun to face them, towering above their human forms, her muscles tensed with seething rage.

"My Queen," uttered the braver of the two as they both dropped to their knees. "Might we offer assistance?"

"Bring me the Chancellor of Foreign Affairs," she hissed, her multi-layered voice echoing through the chamber.

"Yes, your Majesty!" answered the man as the pair stood and made a hasty retreat.

She paced for a short time, her cloven hooves cracking against the marble floor rhythmically.

"This is ill timed, Whun," she growled to no one in particular. "The cycle has emerged. The Caier are being reborn. The signs are stronger than they've ever been, and you choose *now* to rebel?"

She grabbed her chair and threw it across the room, sending it violently crashing into the far wall.

"If they return to the Talaani Empire and wake their masters, I will be forced to rend the north to ash. Is that what you wish? Their absence will weaken me, and as a result all of Dusk. Is that your desire? You seek a weakened Queen? Perhaps you seek the throne for yourself?" she challenged angrily.

"I can't look for you myself. You have masked your presence from me, and would sense me coming. I must rely on unreliable agents; something you *know* I detest. You will feel my wrath, Whun. I do not take betrayal lightly."

After a time, the Chancellor visited her chamber long enough to receive his orders, then left her in peace. When she was calm enough to proceed, she returned to her crystal ball with renewed focus. She had to find the Caier.

Whun's betrayal would have to be dealt with at a later time.

TAVYN'S JOURNEY to the Kingdom of Haern was fairly uneventful, though long. The Daxian Order had supplied him with a horse specially bred and enchanted to ride great lengths without the need to rest. Even with the ability to make use of almost the entirety of Ayrelon's twenty-eight hour day, his trip to the Shattered Coast in the south took nearly two weeks, and coincided with the depletion of his meager supplies. A side benefit to the constant nature of his travel was his lack of need for any form of long duration camping, which removed a great deal of the risk in him traveling alone.

The savanna was home to several tribes of nomadic Tryn elves. They were quite capable of keeping their lands clear of foul creatures such as goblins, hobgoblins, and less-discerning human bandits. Even still, there was always the risk of attack from groups the Tryn hadn't discovered and taken care of. It was, therefore, a pleasant surprise to have made it through the entire savanna without issue. He made a point to wave and nod his thanks whenever the red haired, olive skinned elves came into view, no matter the distance. After all, if he could see them, he was sure they'd already been watching him for some time.

Once he reached the coast, his journey took him east along the rocky shore. The Shattered Coast got its name from both its harsh terrain, and the seemingly endless string of islands and jagged rocks that jutted through the rolling waves. Even with the myriad difficulties nature presented, countless fishing villages lined the coast, each with long piers built far enough out into the waters to allow for safe harbor.

Tavyn did not use any of the settlements for shelter during the final weeks of his ride to Amuer, but found a routine need to stop and purchase food and water, for both himself and his mount. The people seemed nice enough at first; made tough by their environment, but still welcoming to visitors, and thankful to make easy coin as he passed through. The closer he drew to Haern, the more self absorbed, dismissive or apprehensive they seemed to be. By the time he reached the outskirts of Haern's territories, he found himself so distrusted by locals that he had to find and pay intermediaries to go shop on his behalf. What troubled him about that need was how easy it was to meet. The streets seemed more and more littered with homeless, beggars and malnourished orphans the closer he got to Amuer.

He had to keep reminding himself of Onala's words of advice as he rode. The people were not his concern. Whether they be human, elf, gnome, dwarf, man, woman or child... he couldn't save them all. Who was he to choose which ones to save? Who was to say they'd have taken his help? No, it was best to stay focused on his mission, and offer his help by way of paying for simple services. In that context, they were more than happy to accept his coin in trade for small favors. He got his food, and they had the coin to buy some of their own. It was the best he could do, even if it felt wrong to see so many people struggling to survive and take no action to save them.

When he crested the final hill before Amuer and the city came into view, he was instantly overwhelmed. All of his life experiences had been either out in nature, or in the ravine-side settlements that comprised Quaan'Shala. To him, the Dynar city that stretched across the open air, suspended between cliffs over the Arashyvi river, was a very large community. Compared to the city that stretched out before him, it may as well have been another fishing village.

Half a day later, as the city's four and five story buildings and their seemingly random construction materials loomed over him, he was nearly overcome with a strange sense of claustrophobia. Rope spanned between the buildings, weighted down with wet laundry. People crowded the streets, rushing to and fro with purpose, lazily conversing, or pleading for coin from passers by. It was unlike anything he'd ever seen. Most importantly to him at that moment, there seemed to be no room for him to navigate the streets on horseback. The few horses, and oxen, that he had seen entering or exiting the city were pulling wagons and carriages; none of which were moving quickly. In fact, most seemed to be stuck on the road at various points, yelling at one another as some tried to slip around others that were loading or unloading cargo without a care for anyone they might be inconveniencing.

Sighing in both frustration and anxiety, he slid from his saddle and scanned the area for a stable to sell his horse. *Now I know why Master Nyr'Tahl suggested I free myself of my mount and use the coin to fund my hunt,* he thought.

After finding a stable and spending the better part of the remaining daylight haggling for a better price on a Dynar-bred mare, he set off into the city on foot to learn his way around, and start the hunt.

How am I going to find one person in this sea of madness without so much as a description of their appearance?

CHAPTER 2:
OMENS

Ris'Uttyr, Amaethur 11th, 575 of the 1st Era

THE NARROW streets and alleys of the Scarlet Quarter always seemed to grow their most active just before sunset; merchants hurrying to close their shops before night, skittish citizens scurrying home as quickly as they could weave through the crowd, and denizens of the night slipping out of their hiding places into the gloaming. It was the perfect time to get lost among the masses and scour the city for one's quarry without being noticed.

Tavyn was beyond frustrated. He'd been in Amuer for nearly six months. The contract should have been simple; travel to Amuer, search for the Necromancer, and end his life. Onala's description of the city hadn't done justice to just how corrupt Amuer had become, or how quick its citizens were to turn a blind eye. Every moment he spent in the capital of the Kingdom of Haern made him want to burn the entire place to the ground and let nature reclaim the lands for its own purposes. He found himself fuming at the thought as he weaved around yet another filth-covered beggar and ducked into one of the countless offal-drenched alleys that peppered the city's sixth district. So commonplace was the ambient stench that he found his nose growing blind to it, and often wondered if he would recognize fresh air if ever confronted with it.

It seemed that every week he spent in the city, another young girl went missing. He'd hear about them from concerned citizens through rumors that seemed to spread like wildfire, through the contacts he'd made in various underground organizations, and official notices whenever the victim was a child of someone deemed important. He'd made a point not to try to count the number of victims his quarry had accumulated, because he knew the answer would be far too disheartening, and he couldn't afford the time to cope with his own failings. Not yet.

The order should have sent a team of us. First thing I'm demanding when I get back is they abolish their rule of one agent per mission. This city is too big for just one of us to scour, he lamented.

He'd put off searching the Scarlet Quarter for as long as he could; mostly due to its horrid condition, but also because it seemed too obvious a place to find the unspeakable evil he sought. Each of the districts had their own dark side, but none had been as blatantly obvious as the piles of refuse he deftly dodged on his way through the lower sixth. He was below sea level, in a section of the city that had once been an underground aging and storage complex for the largest distillery in southern Gargoa. It had long since been destroyed by a hurricane and the enormous tidal surge that accompanied it.

Small, cheaply constructed hovels had been laid across planks to cover the smaller openings at ground level, and barely-stable boards and beams had been placed across the larger gaps to create make-shift roads. Most of the construction in that neighborhood of the district had been accomplished using the splintered fragments of the distillery's massive warehouse; all of which bore remnants of the building's original bright red paint, giving the area its name. Beneath the ramshackle streets and shacks lay a large complex of granite, concrete and carved limestone chambers, each claimed by the least scrupulous residents of the district.

Thin beams of the day's failing light broke through the cracks and seams in the false road above, casting an eerie, dull glow into the dark halls beneath. Openings lined the walls; some obscured by thin sheets of tattered cloth, loosely flitting in a rancid breeze; others by planks of half-rotted wood, slid into place by their nervous occupants upon seeing a dark-elven man approaching. With black skin, black hair, angular features, a muscular physique and black leather armor that allowed him to traverse through shadows easily, Tavyn knew that his appearance was fairly imposing in the right situation, and wore that impression like a cloak as he traversed the maze en-route to his destination.

He'd walked the halls for several nights in a row, seeking entrance to the seventh district's sewage system. After finding what he sought just before dawn the night prior, he'd returned with tools to help him gain entry, and allowed them to clank eerily as he made what he hoped to be his final trek through the complex. After months of searching above ground, he had found nothing that would lead him to his prey.

Whoever the necromancer was, they were highly skilled in the art of secrecy if nothing else. Though Princess Aelys had escaped and drawn the attention of the Daxian Order, there were no clues across the entire city that would lead an agent such as Tavyn to the abomination's laboratory. To say that the hunt had been an effort in futility would have been an understatement, and he was sure that his last report to the Order must have made him sound like a madman.

The last place left for him to check was the one he'd been least interested in entering; much for the same reasons he'd avoided the Scarlet Quarter. He'd been searching for so long that he'd been forced to take contracts for one of the many gangs in Amuer, just to make enough coin to secure room and board. Working those contracts had caused further delays in his investigation, resulting in more innocent lives lost to the perpetrator, and several increasingly heated messages from his commander back in Quaan'Shala. Their patience had worn as thin as the soles of his boots, and try as he might, he still had nothing to show for his efforts.

When he finally reached the entrance to the sewers, the natural light had faded from the sky above. New iron bars blocked entry to the underground cesspool beyond, but allowed a constant stream of human waste to flow freely into the halls of the Scarlet Quarter. What should have been hailed as a marvel of engineering did nothing but feed noble shit directly onto the floors of those they viewed as their lessors. As he pried at the bars with a three foot long crowbar, he felt anger welling up within him at the audacity of the city's ruling council for allowing such a thing to take place.

While the bars, and the bolts that held them fast, seemed freshly installed, the surface to which they were mounted wasn't nearly as stalwart. It only took a few minutes for him to chip away the crumbling, water-logged limestone that lined the outer wall surrounding the opening. Once he created enough space to fit the crowbar between the stone and iron, he wedged it in and pried outward. The wall crumbled away after a few minutes, breaking the bolt free. He repeated the process a few more times, freeing each bolt on the right side of the grate, then dropped the crowbar and grabbed the right edge with both hands. Gripping firmly, he put his right foot on the wall and pushed to give himself leverage, then raised his left foot up beside it. With all the strength in his arms, legs and back, he pried the grate away from the wall, the left side's bolts cracking and grinding on the stone in disagreement.

After a few moments, the grate broke free and went tumbling into the street. Chunks of limestone broke away from the left side of the opening and flew into the sewer, splashing through putrid puddles and narrowly missing Tavyn's face as he crashed to the ground on his left side. With a grunt and a sigh, he got to his feet

19

and gave a long, sullen stare at his feces-caked clothing.

His disgust with the city at a new high, Tavyn stepped into the five-and-a-half foot sewage drain, just a few inches taller than he; which had clearly been constructed by elves like him, most likely as forced labor under their human masters.

PROVOSS, AND the slightly smaller moon Aygos, seemed to sparkle intermittently; their light dancing and playing across the sky as they slowly crossed the heavens on their nightly journey. Mina reached her hand upward and imagined she was touching Aygos, pushing it closer to Provoss, so that it could join its brother and they could enjoy a nice evening among the stars. Lying on her back atop the grass, she giggled at the childishness of the idea that someone could affect the moons, and the joy imagining it had brought her.

"What are you laughing at now?" asked Eros. His voice was playfully inquisitive, a stark contrast to the terse, oft-judgmental feedback she usually received from her guardian, Ahm.

"Nothing," she said, letting her arm flop down atop her chest. "Just being silly is all. I don't get to be silly, very often."

"You don't get to be *anything* very often," he sighed. "I wish I could take you away from this place."

"They might let *you* leave, but not me. I'm stuck here."

"If you decline Ascension, they have to let you leave. It's the law."

"Only for citizens. Like I told you, the law doesn't know I exist. Ahm has kept me hidden my entire life," she lamented.

Eros rolled onto his side and gently placed his fingers on Mina's cheek, then nudged her face toward him. He stared into her crystal blue eyes in silence for a moment while brushing her black hair off her cheek. "You shouldn't be forced to live in hiding. The danger can't be as bad as he says. After all, you sneak out to meet with me and nobody seems to care. So what's stopping us from just boarding a ship and sailing to Gargoa? We could live there in peace, far away from this place," he said. He leaned in and kissed her softly on the forehead, then resumed his position. "I'll tend our farm. We'll have crops, sheep... maybe a couple cows and some chickens."

"What would I do?" she asked playfully.

"You'll fight off the bandits while I cower in the corner of our kitchen brandishing a rolling pin. Clearly," he teased.

"Oh, come on," she scoffed.

"Hey, you're the strong one between us. Besides... they'd never see it coming," he laughed. "A beautiful, five-and-a-half foot tall, blue eyed, raven-haired woman strolling up the path with a sword, wearing nothing at all? They'd be so distracted they'd kill themselves trying to dismount their horses."

"Why would I be naked? Is this the kind of thing you fantasize about? Me, naked with a sword?"

"Not so much with the sword, if I'm being honest."

"Uh huh," she said sarcastically.

"All I'm sayin' is, it's gotta be better than here."

"So you're willing to decline Ascension and give up your chance at becoming an immortal Unliving just to drag me to another continent? All to see me naked with a sword?"

"A man's gotta do what a man's gotta do, you know?" he teased.

"Shut up and lay back down, ya dolt," she laughed.

Eros did as he was told and looked up at the stars. She rolled over to join him with her head on his chest, an arm wrapped around his waist.

"I love you, Mina. You know that, don't you? I would really do anything for you."

"I know," she sighed as she closed her eyes and nestled into his embrace. She listened for a short time to his heartbeat, and slowly let the sound carry her to the edge of sleep. "Eros?"

"I'm still awake," he answered.

"Do you think people miss this after they ascend?" asked Mina.

"Miss what?" asked Eros.

"Listening to their lover's heartbeat? Or even hearing their breath?" Mina clarified.

"Maybe? I mean, the undead Xxrandites might, but the unliving Ishnites' bodies aren't actually dead, so they could still enjoy cuddling like this," said Eros.

"It's not the same. They sound hollow... unnatural. Besides, there's just something about them," she said, avoiding the truth. Ahm had forbidden her from ever admitting to anyone that she could see spirits, and thus, the magically re-attached souls of the Unliving shimmering atop their flesh. It was a gift that Queen Mordessa feared, and had outlawed.

"So I shouldn't ascend, is what you're saying? I wouldn't want you to see me differently and ruin our fancy evenings out on the town. I mean, the wait staff here sucks, and there's no food to speak of, but I like its ambiance all the same."

"No, not at all," she said, ignoring his jest. "You do what you feel is right. That's a decision only you can make, and I'll love you either way... even when you start to grow distant from reality."

"Well, if you can't leave with me, why don't you at least ascend and marry me?" asked Eros.

"We'll see. I'm not sure I can do that either. Besides, who says I serve Ishnu and not Xxrandus? Maybe when I ascend I'll become a Lich. No, I just want to love you right here, right now, while I can. So, stop squirming and let me listen to you as you are!"

"Are you just going to ignore me haphazardly proposing marriage?" Eros asked.

"That wasn't a real proposal, so yes," she said with a slight nod of her head for emphasis.

"A real proposal?" he asked, tilting his head to look down at her.

"Did you ask Ahm for my hand? Are you on one knee? Do you have a talisman of Ishnu to present with your family crest at her feet?" she asked in jest. She didn't really care about such things, and knew that he was fully aware of her stance on tradition, but she couldn't resist a chance to tease him.

"Ahm, Ahm, Ahm. In one sentence he's your captor, in another he's your father. Either way, that man's name is constantly on your lips," he sighed.

"Maybe I'll marry *him*, then," she teased.

Eros tickled her sides with a fake grimace on his face, pretending to be angry. Mina giggled, squirmed and jumped atop him, pinning his hands by his side with her own. She was indeed stronger than him, and he seemed to enjoy making her prove it.

After a short bit of laughter, she slid back down into his arms and planted a brief kiss on his lips before resuming her position on his chest.

MOST OF the convex, concrete walls of the sewage system seemed clean, as if they'd recently been scrubbed. The lower portion was covered in a thin, green slime directly at the murky water's edge, making Tavyn's footing tenuous at best, unless he trod directly in the filth that flowed through the center.

His anger grew at the idea that his brother and sister elves were being forced to serve as cheap labor for the construction and cleaning of such atrocities. He was inspired to hunt the men, or women, who'd approved the city plans and executed the contract that created the sewers for the seventh district. So deep was that motivation he nearly missed an unclean tunnel jutting abruptly southward from his path.

The walls of the abnormally dark passage were covered in the same green moss that only hinted at growth along the rest of the sewer. No water flowed at its base, which was instead covered with all manner of brown and black debris. Household waste, leaves, branches, rocks and various bits of broken goods lie strewn about the bottom of the tube, hinting at both disuse and lack of attention by whomever cleaned the other sections of the system. It was a strange corridor to be sure, but was made quite a bit creepier when viewed by a Dynar elf in the dark of night.

The beams of light that found their way down through the small hole in the ceiling glowed bright purple, and seemed to dance and play across the detritus on the floor of the corridor. Algae and moss glowed dimly, radiating faint violet hues beneath, behind and around the debris; casting eerie shadows that amplified the unease he'd been feeling since he entered the sewers. The scene made him feel as if he was about to be attacked by an unseen force at any moment.

Come on, Tav, they trained you for this, he reassured himself. *You're an assassin. You hunt Necromancers and the undead. What would Dax'Vahr think if you let this hallway get under your skin?*

Tavyn knelt at the entrance to the obstructed pipe. He studied the ground for signs of passage, but none seemed obvious; at least not near where he stood. A few yards down the pipe, he spotted a large, flat stone. It was coarse in texture, likely to provide a slip-proof footing. Above the stone was a small hole in the pipe, and a barely visible piece of rope dangling from overhead. Small stones of similar style seemed to lead off into the distance from that point, allowing someone to drop down from above and head south without the need to touch any of the sewage passing through the rest of the system.

He stood and leaned into the opening to check for places he could step. With the rope dangling so far up the tube overhead, he was certain that whomever used this section of pipe wasn't there at the moment. There was also no way to know for sure if he'd actually found the secret laboratory's entrance, or if this was someone else's doing entirely. Without knowing for certain, he needed to leave as little evidence of his passing as he could, and that meant treading very carefully.

After a moment of contemplation, he made his way toward the landing stone as best he could, trying to disturb as little of the make-shift dam as possible. He stepped onto a thick piece of branch, then carefully shifted his weight and brought his body across. Next, he stretched his left foot over to a small rock and tested his weight. The rock slipped a little, then wedged against another and settled into a firm position at a slight angle. He quickly sucked in a bit of air through his teeth, held his breath, lunged his weight toward the rock, then leapt off that foot toward the landing stone.

The balls of Tavyn's feet landed on the edge of the stone, his heels hanging over the moss-coated debris precariously. While he knew there was no real danger had he missed the jump, his heart was racing none-the-less, as if his life hinged on his success. He stepped fully onto the stone and leaned over, hands on knees, to settle his heartbeat and steady his breathing. The obstructed section of pipe smelled a little less rancid than the rest, but not by much, and he instantly regretted the deep breaths he was taking.

AFTER FOLLOWING the path of stones—which had clearly been spaced for a human's stride—Tavyn found himself standing on a landing before a large wooden door, a wooden bar spanning its width.

That's... odd, he mused.

He lifted the beam out of its cradles as quietly as he could, then set it aside. With his right hand gripping the dagger at the small of his back, he gently pulled on the handle. The door creaked faintly on its hinges, but no sounds of alarm rang out from within. Content that he hadn't alerted anyone, he hefted the beam again and walked inside with it, lest someone bar his escape.

Several feet inside the small hallway beyond, he found an alcove full of cleaning supplies, tarps and other odds and ends. He stashed the beam amidst a collection of brooms and mops as quietly as he could, and covered the lot of them with one of the tarps haphazardly, to make it appear as if nothing was amiss. The task complete, he returned his attention to the small hallway and whatever lay beyond.

The hall was just large enough for a shorter than average human to traverse without ducking. Sprigs of sage and lavender lined both sides of the hall, hanging from bits of twine that had been strung down its length across several tiny, rusted nails. The florals provided an odor barrier to the nastiness of the sewage-laden entry, and seemed to be doing their job... except that the underlying smell of offal was slowly being replaced with the stench of rot as he walked.

At the far end of the hall, several bundles of sage had been hung across the opening that led into the room beyond. He stopped for a moment in front of the make-shift curtain and listened for any signs of movement. No sound came to him from in front or behind, not even the slow trickle of septic water moving through the sewers he'd entered through. His breathing suddenly felt unreasonably loud, even though he was sure no one was nearby to hear it. Holding his breath, he reached both hands up to part the sage and walked into the room. The sound of dry stems and leaves knocking and rubbing against each other seemed to echo off the walls of both the room and hall, sending chills across his skin and amplifying that all too familiar sinking feeling that had been growing in his gut.

No sooner had the first of his feet stepped onto the stone floor of the small room than a pair of gurgling, guttural voices sprang to life a few feet to his right, accompanied by the rattling of chains, and the squish of oozing flesh.

THE COOL night air, gentle breeze and calming sound of distant crickets chirping lulled Mina to sleep as her breathing fell into rhythm with Eros' heartbeat. The black that normally awaited behind her closed eyes was disrupted almost immediately by a swirl of purple hues, spiraling at the center of her vision and spreading to fill the darkness like sentient wisps of smoke. As the violet tones filled her vision, they began to fade, leaving speckles of clarity in their wake and revealing a distant scene.

A pair of large cloven hooves strode determinedly across a highly polished marble floor. The sound of their impact sent chills through Mina's spine, as if they were occurring directly beside her. The digitigrade legs attached to the hooves were long and slender, their leathery flesh rippling with muscular definition yet strangely alluring in their physique. Though distinctly feminine, the woman who owned the legs was unlike anything Mina had seen before. She towered over the two men that had come to see her, rising several feet above the tallest of them.

Her skin was silvery white, with streaks of black accentuating her musculature, and dark, talon-like nails that she clicked in rhythm with her steps. She kept a pair of large black wings tucked back to avoid hitting the walls of the chamber. Her neck was bent forward at an awkward angle in a feeble attempt to keep the black horns atop her head from scraping the ceiling as she walked, which they periodically did, leaving small scratches and grooves in the stone to mark her passage. The myriad small scars across its surface indicated she visited the chamber often.

Pointed, silvery, elven ears jutted out from the black locks that trailed down from her head, which bounced and swayed as she moved. Her face was ringed with a faint tinge of blue, green and purple energies that seemed to swirl beneath her flesh; barely visible through her nearly translucent skin. Her spiked brow furrowed as she came to a stop before the men, her three serpentine tails whipping about angrily behind her. She was not pleased, and made no effort to hide her disposition.

"The apex of the Cycle draws nigh, yet you interrupt my

preparations... and with what? More displeasing news? Unless you've designs which could aid my efforts, have found Lord Whun, or you've identified our targets, I suggest you leave before the rest of my patience wanes," she growled. Her voice echoed throughout the chamber in multiple tones, as if several voices were speaking at once. One of them sounded soft and silky, as would be expected from an elf woman. Another sounded harsh, guttural and deep, as would be expected of an overly large male. Behind them both was a layer of airiness, an audible shimmer as if her words were being spoken through some form of veil and it was reacting to the volume of her tones.

"Your majesty, the Minister of Defense is refusing to cooperate. We came to beseech you to intervene," muttered the smaller of the two men. His robes held the sigil of Chancellor of Foreign Affairs.

"You waste my time with such trivialities? You've had months to prove your worth!" roared the creature. She clenched her right fist in the air between them angrily, purple flames flitting to life across the surface of her eyes. The man crumpled into a ball with a horrid crunch in midair, then fell to the ground with a pulpy squish, his body rendered into a gooey mush. The other man straightened and bowed as his face went stark white. "I trust that you've more sense than your predecessor, Chancellor," she snarled, promoting the survivor on the spot.

"Yes, your majesty. I will tend to the matter myself!" he barked sharply.

"See that you do," she said. "If I must get involved, why do I need *you*?" she asked as she turned and left the room. Servants rushed into the chamber in her wake, carrying shovels and buckets. As they scurried into position, the other man fled as quickly as the robes of his station would allow.

Mina woke as the vision ended, her adrenaline coursing, then lurched abruptly upright, leaned away from Eros, and vomited.

EROS LURCHED into a seated position in response to Mina's heaving. He reached over and rubbed her back reassuringly, saying, "Another nightmare, love?"

She accepted the handkerchief he offered and dabbed the remnants of her evening meal from her lips. Sorrow and horror in her eyes, she shifted her position so she could face him before answering. "They come almost nightly, now. I... I don't think they're nightmares anymore, though. They're too real."

"Visions, then?" he asked.

She nodded sheepishly.

"Of what?" he asked with more concern in his voice than she liked to hear.

"I keep getting glimpses of things through another woman's eyes. A very tall and powerful woman. Tonight, though, I saw her as if I were watching through someone or something else," she said.

"That's... strange," he said.

"Usually I'm watching through her eyes as she whispers incantations, or studies far-off places in a crystal ball," she said.

"What do you see in the crystal ball?" he asked.

"Nothing. I can't see what it is that she's looking at, just a swirl of magical energies, but she seems very intent on whatever she's seeing. She's searching for someone, I think. She talked about it tonight, briefly," she explained. "When I've had the visions in the past, I can feel the magic pulsing through her, as if it were moving through me. It's exhilarating in the moment, but when I wake I somehow feel simultaneously abandoned, terrified and... like I'm going through withdrawals. So, the dreams have never really been nightmares, in the truest sense," she admitted.

"Then why do you–" he started.

"It's easier to just let you think it's a nightmare when I wake in a cold sweat, trembling. Isn't it? I mean... would *you* want to explain that you're detoxing from a power you don't even possess, but yearn for; yearning for something that you only experience in your dreams?" she asked.

"I suppose not," he admitted. He slid forward and grabbed her hands out of her lap, then kissed the knuckles of her right hand. "I'm here, love. You won't scare me away."

"When I'm in those dreams, I feel like I could pull the entire city down if the urge struck; rip the entire continent in two. Moreover, *she* knows she could do those things, and revels in it. The feeling is unlike anything I've ever felt, and I couldn't give it justice with my words no matter how hard I tried. In those moments, I don't want to be anywhere else, or be with anyone else. All that matters is the power, and I think that's all that matters to her. Maybe I'm feeling what she feels? Maybe there's some connection between us? I... I just don't know. All I know is, when I wake up I'm in knots; part of me wants to go back and feel the power, the rest of me is terrified that I'm so willing to give up control of myself just to get a taste of whatever that woman's got," she said as the color slowly drained from her face.

"I understand. I don't know how I'd react to such stimuli. When I use the priestly magic of our order, I feel a rush as the power courses through me. I've often wondered if a mage feels that same thing at all times, since they store the power to cast spells within them rather than channeling as we do," he said calmly as he gripped her hands more firmly, trying to reassure her.

"Well... I don't know how it happened, or why, but tonight I wasn't living through her. I was watching. She's horrific, and I don't know whether that's because she was born that way, or if the power she wields twisted her body into something different. All I know for certain is that she's absolutely terrifying to behold, and what she did," said Mina, her voice wavering more and more as she continued. Tears welled up in her eyes, and her hands began to shake.

"Can you describe her?" he asked as he pulled her into his chest.

"She must be at least twelve feet tall. She has black horns, hair and wings, silvery skin with black streaks along her muscles, strange legs with cloven feet, and small spikes where her eyebrows should be," explained Mina between gasps. She was nearly hyperventilating just thinking about the woman.

"Are you certain?" asked Eros, gently pushing her shoulders back so he could look her in the eyes.

"Yes. Why?" she said, pulling her hands away from him.

"You just described Queen Mordessa," said Eros.

"*What?*" gasped Mina.

TWO CREATURES thrust their chests toward Tavyn from the wall to his right, each bound at the neck, biceps, wrists and waist with thick chains and shackles. The first was as small as an elf, but so thoroughly rotted that it was hard to discern what he or she might have been when they were still alive. More than half its face was gone, having rotted away and fallen off in clumps, exposing the bone underneath. Little flaps of flesh around its gnashing teeth fluttered in and out as it strained to pull in breaths for the explicit purpose of hissing and growling at its potential meal. The second zombie was less desiccated than the first, but still unrecognizable due to decay.

Beside the putrid pair was a nearly emaciated woman, stripped bare and shackled an untold number of days or weeks prior. Her red hair, caked with sweat and zombie spittle, hung forward over her slumped head, obscuring her face. Her chest moved almost imperceptibly as her body struggled to hang on, barely able to breathe in her weakened state. The poor woman's skin seemed covered with mild sores; destined to grow into lesions and burst in the coming days. Through the din of zombie hisses, grunts and growls, Tavyn thought he could make out a faint whimper coming from the woman as she finally exhaled.

With newfound fervor, Tavyn drew his twin blades from their sheathes and lunged toward the undead. He leapt into the air just before he arrived and drove his blades into the crown of their skulls as he descended. As he landed, his smaller stature, and momentum, ripped the daggers downward with great force, rupturing the creatures' necks and nearly severing their heads as their flesh fought against the iron shackles that bound them. Thick ooze gushed forth from the wounds as he yanked against his daggers to pull them free, plopping to the ground at their feet, spattering up his arms and speckling the sides of his face.

He slid the blades across his thighs to wipe them off, then sheathed them and moved over to the woman. Now that the room was silent, he could hear the harshness of her breathing and the faint whimper as she exhaled. He wasn't sure if she was cognizant of his presence, or if her whimpering had become a subconscious act after what seemed like weeks or months of agony. It was clear she hadn't been fed in quite some time, and the skin surrounding the iron that bound her had long-since worn away from friction, and seemingly given up its attempts to bleed and scab over.

"Miss? Are you awake? Can you hear me?" he asked, placing his hands on her cheeks and raising her head to look her in the eye. She was half elven, half human, and slightly taller than he. Her skin was clammy and cool to the touch, and under any other circumstances, he would have yanked his hands away instinctively. There was an almost tacky consistency to the thin layer of moisture that covered her. Combined with the smells in the room, and the horrid goo that peppered his forearms, it was all he could do to resist vomiting in that moment.

"S... s..." she muttered, attempting to speak.

"Take your time. I," he said as he looked to his sides quickly, "I don't see a key nearby, but I can't let your head go to search just yet. I don't think you can speak if I do. Just... hang on, okay? I'm going to get you out of here." He repositioned his left hand to the woman's forehead as she continued her attempts to form a complete word. With his right, he dug into a pocket on his hip and retrieved a small vial of purple liquid. He uncorked the vial with his teeth, spit the cork to his right, and tipped the drink to the woman's lips. "This isn't going to heal you completely, but it might help with the pain and give you a short burst of energy. Can you tell me your name?"

He waited for a moment as the fluids washed across the woman's tongue and down her throat of their own accord. After a few seconds, she gulped air and whispered, "Ss... save her."

"Save who?" he asked, whipping his head around. He couldn't see anyone else in the room.

"Save *her*! K... kill me!" said the woman firmly. Her bloodshot eyes opened almost instantly and locked onto his. A chill ran down his spine. "Save *her*! Kill *me*!" she yelled with greater intensity. Her demands were accentuated by an involuntary, guttural hiss.

"Fuck!" grumbled Tavyn. He released the woman's head. Her voice gurgled under the weight of her neck against the shackles as she struggled to repeat the same two phrases. Fighting back against the unease in his gut, he drew his daggers and drove their blades into the top of the poor woman's skull.

"I CAN'T be absolutely certain, because she doesn't sit on a throne, attend public functions, or anything of the sort. However, by all the accounts I've read or heard, you just described our Queen," said Eros.

"She... that thing? It rules us?" gasped Mina.

"You do know who Queen Mordessa is, don't you? Ahm is teaching you down there, isn't he?" asked Eros, puzzled.

"Of course I've heard of the Queen, but the only description I've ever read or heard simply calls her 'Demonic' or 'Sylvani'. Without ever seen pictures of that, or one in person, how would I know what those terms meant?" answered Mina.

"Ahm really has done a number on you," sighed Eros as he gently stroked her cheek with the back of his fingers.

"Ahm? Does everyone in Dusk know what she looks like except me? Or is it that you expected me to know, because you expected more from his training?" she challenged.

"Considering he's Minister of Defense, I guarantee he's spent quite a lot of time in her presence. But then, maybe he didn't give you details because he knew they'd scare you?" offered Eros. "Either way, my master claims he met with her when he was appointed to his station. Your description fits his fairly accurately. She doesn't meet with many people, so seeing her is usually regarded as something of an honor."

"Why would we follow a creature like her?" said Mina as her skin went pale. She couldn't believe what she was hearing, after what she'd seen and the power she'd felt.

Eros was taken aback and sat for a moment in silence. "I, um. I mean, I guess when you're raised with tales of her and how she built Baan'Sholaria, you learn to never question it."

"There's no way," gasped Mina. "No way! She'd have to be hundreds upon hundreds of years old!"

"There are centuries old liches walking our streets, and you question *her* longevity?" teased Eros.

"She isn't an unliving Ishnite, nor is she an undead Xxrandite. So, how is she still alive if she was around to build our kingdom?"

challenged Mina.

"Do you know the lifespan of a creature like her? I don't," scoffed Eros. "Besides, if she has the kind of power you describe feeling, who's to say how old she is or isn't? And of course, she isn't an Ishnite or a Xxrandite. According to legend, she's both. The one and only Forsaken, so named because the gods fear her and have forsaken her, leaving her to her own fate."

"Well, she's not unliving, and she wasn't rotting. So, I still say she's neither," said Mina forcefully. Her face flushed with color as she stood, her anger clearly visible on her face. She couldn't understand why he was arguing with her.

"How could you know if she was unliving?" asked Eros.

A chill washed over Mina. She'd spoken out of turn. Ahm had warned her not to let anyone know she was able to see the detached souls of the unliving, lest it reveal her as a Touched and make her a target. *'Mordessa fears the Touched, and any hint that one might be Forsaken. You must hide who you are,'* he'd instructed.

"It just didn't... feel like she was. I was inside her throughout multiple dreams. She felt normal; very, very powerful, but still normal... still *alive*," said Mina.

"Well, I'm telling you that you're wrong. I'm sorry, I know that's not what you want to hear, but they've been teaching these facts all over the Kingdom for as long as it has existed. People swear by it, live by it... die by it. We follow her because she bridges the gap between the two religions and their followers. Without her, there would be chaos... even war," said Eros, standing to join her.

"I need to go," said Mina as she turned back toward the city.

"Don't go," sighed Eros, reaching for her hands.

Mina yanked her hands away with an involuntary cringe and backed away. "I need to get back before Ahm wakes. He's been testy lately and I don't want to risk getting caught and riling him up."

"I don't think anything riles that man up. He's round-the-clock stoic. However, you do what you feel is right. I just hate to see us parting like this," he explained as she jogged away. Once she was out of sight, he kicked a tuft of grass in frustration and crossed his arms. "Good work, Eros. Fine fucking job."

TAVYN BACKED away from the poor woman in disgust, his daggers dripping with her blood and cranial fluid. He didn't bother to wipe them clean or stow them, but instead focused his mind immediately on following the first of her instructions; *'Save her.'*

The rest of the room was clear, save for a few small tables and shelves along the outer walls. Another doorway led further south on the far side of the room, tucked back into a corner and obscured by two large bookshelves. He made his way toward it as silently as possible, even though he wasn't sure it mattered after what had just transpired.

Beyond the door was a room shaped like a large half circle. The walls immediately to his right and left stretched out eight feet before they turned and curved around the rest of the room. Each of the flat walls had a large work surface with shelves and hooks above to store laboratory equipment, most of which were in disrepair. The curved walls encircled a single, padded table to which a small elven woman was tightly bound.

Her feet kicked against the leather straps that held her fast, trying desperately to get Tavyn's attention and escape the necromancer's chamber. She continued to squirm frantically as he approached, daggers still in hand, her red hair jostling about as she strained against the leather strap across her forehead, and the gag wedged into her mouth. She calmed briefly when she caught sight of his steel blades, but quickly resumed when she saw him reaching for her bonds.

"Easy. Easy, now. If I'm going to cut you free, I can't have you squirming. Okay? Just lay still. I'll have you out of here in no time," he said through a forced smile. He was trying to be reassuring, but nothing about the scenario made smiling easy. He was angry beyond reason. His nerves were shot and holding his hand steady enough to cut through her leather shackles was far harder than it should have been.

As he cut her hands free, she immediately reached for the buckles that remained. She was so frantic that Tavyn backed off out of concern that he might cut her. He turned away from her for a moment and found a cloth to clean his blades, then carefully sheathed them once more. Before he turned back to face her, he looked about the room and found a sheet. After grabbing it, he came back to her side and presented it to her, so she could cover herself if she chose to.

"Th... thank you," she whispered, extending her jaw at funny angles as she spoke. She hadn't been able to talk for quite some time, and the muscles and joints in her face were stiff from disuse. "We have to go. Now," she urged.

"I will get you out of here, but I came to kill the man who took you captive. Do you know who he is? Is he due back soon? I could just-" started Tavyn.

"Please! He didn't come last night, so he'll be here soon! This is the worst place to fight him. All his reagents are in this laboratory! *We have to go!*" she pleaded.

"I'm all for getting you out of here, but I have to be able to track this asshole down outside if I can't fight him here. So, if you have any hints as to who he might be, that would be very helpful," said Tavyn.

The woman slid off the table, wrapped the sheet around herself and started making her way to the exit. Her right leg kept giving out as she moved, nearly toppling her several times before she reached the door. Tavyn rushed to her side and offered to hold her up, but she stopped and looked into his eyes, then nodded toward the table along the wall behind him.

"His... his journal is in the drawer," she said. Her voice was trembling, and she seemed to be on the verge of passing out.

Tavyn left her where she stood for a moment and rushed over to the drawer. It slid open with a metallic thunk, several scalpels, quills and small metal tools toppling over one another as it came to a stop. He dug through the pile for a moment and found a small, leather-bound journal tied shut with a piece of twine. He didn't bother to look through its contents, but instead pocketed the small tome and returned to the man's captive.

"Thank you. The book should help. Let's get you to a healer," he said as he offered her his arm.

"No!" she gasped, shaking her head.

"Why not?" he asked.

"He... he'll find me," she whimpered.

"Well, you need healing. I mean, I could take you to The Bones, but they aren't the most savory bunch," he said.

She nodded her agreement without a word, leaned into his side, and started shambling forward. He wrapped his arm around her and kept her steady.

"You were quick to agree to that. Do you know members of that gang?" he asked.

She shook her head no.

"Is it because they're different from him?" he asked.

She nodded yes.

"Is he a nobleman?" he asked. She didn't respond. "Is he from the seventh district?"

She nodded yes more vigorously.

"Does he wear the robes of a councilman? Is he a politician?" he asked.

"I think so," she whimpered. "Yes."

As they made their way into the sage-lined hall, he changed positions to walk behind her, placing his hands on her waist for stability. She leaned her right hand on the wall as they moved.

"Is he human?" he asked.

"Yes. Tall. Very plain," she said. Her confidence seemed to be returning, albeit slightly, as they neared her freedom.

"Thank you, you've been very helpful. Be careful up ahead, okay? The stepping stones are slippery and I don't want you to fall, cut yourself and get sewage in the wound."

"Okay," she whimpered.

After a few minutes of struggle with her footing, and her anxiety escalating with each passing moment, Tavyn finally picked the poor woman up and carried her in his arms through the debris-filled tunnel. Once they were clear of the mess, he lowered her back down to her feet and walked in the offal-laden waters of the remaining tunnels so that she could lean on him and stay out of it.

There was a small crowd gathered around the entrance to the tunnel, studying the bars and broken bits of wall. They cleared a path when they saw Tavyn and the young woman approaching, whispering amongst themselves and pointing at the pair.

"I need clothes for her! Now!" barked Tavyn forcefully. His armor and weapons were enough to send the impoverished bystanders into a flurry of activity. Several of them raced off to find what they could.

"Hannah," she offered timidly.

"Let's get you cleaned up, Hannah. We've got to cross the city, and we can't have everyone staring at you," he said.

When a pair of older women returned and presented a few scraps of clothing, Tavyn tossed them a few silver coins and led Hannah into one of the nearby residences. He blocked the door from outside while she got dressed, then presented a silver to each of the bystanders. "Tell no one you saw us." Each person nodded their agreement as they took a coin and walked away.

Before long, Tavyn and Hannah were crossing the city toward the docks.

LORD WHUN woke on a small stone table. It had been eons since he last slept, and while it had been involuntarily induced, he found himself yearning for the experience to continue. According to his normal vision, the room was pitch black; not a single source of light was present in any form, not even an unlit candle. To his extended, magical vision the room was awash with glowing runes in a myriad of colors. They shone so brightly, in fact, that he had to fight back the urge to shield his crown's magical eye, which wouldn't have helped anyway.

He had no idea how long he'd been asleep. Recovering several thousand years of veiled memories had taken a lot out of him, and his undead body took much longer to recover than either he or his hosts had anticipated. Now that he was awake, and his full memories had been restored, he could see the patterns clearly. Their time was drawing short, and he needed to get the pieces into place if he planned to stand up against their enemy; to free Xxulrathia from Mordessa's tyrannical rule.

It was time her curse ended.

Everything was clear to him at that moment. His memories had returned in full, and he knew beyond question what he'd done in the past, what he'd helped Mordessa to do, and that everything that was happening across Xxulrathia was ultimately his fault. He had freed her from her prison, and helped her gain power. At over a thousand years old when he found her, he'd long since walked away from his desire to rule the land. He'd accomplished it, experienced it, and decided it wasn't his place in the world. Ruling others meant having to care for them, or at least that's what he'd grown to accept. He lacked the capacity to care for others. They were beneath him, and wholly inconsequential to his own existence.

What Mordessa had done, though, was unacceptable. She'd used him, and gained power through unforgivable deception. She'd committed acts he could not abide; done things he would not have approved of, had he been aware of her intentions. Worst of all, she seemed intent on maintaining her position, and thus her control of an entire continent, through deception, genocide, and worse.

He would not stand for it. She would meet her end.

Whun rose from the stone table and drifted from the room, seeking the Noktulian priests who had returned his memories to him through great sacrifice in a ritual he would not have thought to devise. Though weaker than he, they had insight, and memories he would need to forge a plan of attack. His power, as extreme as it might be, was nothing in the face of Mordessa at her full strength. He had to find a way to strip her of that power in order to confront her, and that meant dethroning a would-be god.

It was just the sort of challenge he craved.

CHAPTER 3:
PREY

Ris'Enliss, Amaethur 12th, 575 of the 1st Era

MINA AND Eros often met on the southeastern edge of the city. They'd picked a spot behind a dilapidated building next to the outer wall, near a path that led up the cliffs overlooking the fishing villages that lined the shores of the Hystari ocean. From there, they would walk together to a small patch of ground near the edge of the cliffs, tucked back from the path behind shrubs and saplings. Their walk to the overlook on any given night was spent in deep conversation, to the point that neither of them paid much attention to the beauty that lie all around them. The trip back to the city the following morning was, more often than not, similarly filled with distraction.

In fact, Mina couldn't recall ever walking home completely alone. Ever since the first night she'd snuck out—and collided with poor Eros haphazardly on the street—she'd been so wrapped up in everything 'him' that she'd forgotten to do what she'd originally snuck out to do: see the world around her.

She paid more attention to her surroundings on the way back toward the city that night; the sound of the dirt shifting under her booted feet, the gentle rustle of tall grass and brush on the sides of the path, crickets singing faint melodies that only they could understand. As she crested the final hill of the descent, the city came into view. She stopped for a moment to take it in. The path wound down the side of the hill before her like a brown snake fading into the distance. Directly below the hill stood the familiar wall, its dark stone covered in stubborn green ivy. Beyond the wall sprawled the largest single city on all of Ayrelon, at least according to Ahm's teachings. Black stone towers, spires and multi-story buildings poked up sporadically amidst a sea of dark wooden houses for as far as her eyes could see.

The buildings in that section of the city seemed haphazardly placed, with no regard for strategic planning. Roads wove between them at confusing intervals, growing wider and thinner as the homes, businesses and churches would allow. Considering its size, she wondered how anyone could learn their way around the whole of it. Thankfully for the citizens of Dusk, time was not their enemy.

She began her descent along the winding path, thinking about the sheer size of the city, which she could only see a portion of from the top of the hill. It was a good distraction from the frustration of her conversation with Eros, and the fear of Mordessa that kept creeping into the back of her mind. It was hard to fathom just how large the city was, even though she'd been taught about it at great length. She had no concept of how long a mile was, let alone the distance seven-hundred-forty-three of them would cover. Yet she knew that was the measured circumference of the unified city of Dusk; the whole of the Kingdom for all intents and purposes.

Those who lived outside the city's walls were either selected to remain living, or had refused Ascension, but successfully leveraged the value of their trade to prevent exile. The outside world only ever interacted with those stationed in small villages along the shore. Villages that were nothing more than fronts acting as trade hubs, hiding the true nature of the Kingdom behind a ring of hills, mountains, and ivy-covered walls.

Trade was important to the residents of Dusk. They'd long ago exhausted their own supplies of precious metals, gems, crystals, and many of the alchemical ingredients they used daily. That was to say nothing of materials such as cotton, leather, and linen which they still produced, but at insufficient volumes. With tens of millions of residents, the sheer numbers were mind-boggling, even though Ahm made sure she heard them routinely. The only singular good they produced at high volume was wool, but it was barely enough to allow for trade.

However, since more than half the residents of Dusk didn't need to eat or drink, such things had quickly become the primary goods traded with outsiders. A large majority of the residents of Baan'Sholaria, both inside and outside the walls, worked specifically to produce foodstuffs they would never consume. Fertilizers, seed, root vegetables, preserved goods, salted meats, and more alcoholic beverages than she could count. Ships docked daily at the numerous ports that dotted the coast, and none of them left with empty holds. All the Kingdom had to do was produce enough food to feed everyone, even though they only fed approximately two-fifths of them, and it would always remain wealthy.

Several sections of the enormous city specialized in the production of a particular good. Coastal villages handled trade, fishing, farming and harvesting. In a Kingdom that spanned such great distances, and the nearly Kingdom-sized city of Dusk and its navigational nuances, there was one invention that allowed everything to function like a well-oiled machine. According to Ahm, Dusk was the only place in the world where such a marvel could be found. It was the first thing she snuck out to see, and the thing that had occupied most of her time outside the Cryx until she'd met Eros. Standing at the rusted, half-fallen gate at the end of the path, it was the one thing left to look forward to on the trip back to her bed.

The well-educated called it the Grand Subterranean Conveyance, or simply the GSC. Some Unliving citizens, who would never be forced to work it, referred to it as the Dead-Line, or the DL. However, to most of the citizens, it was known as the Flute Tube, or just the Flute. When she'd expressed how cute she thought the name was, and how it was the first thing she'd raced out of the Cryx to witness with her own eyes, Eros had barely been able to contain his laughter. The 'Screamer', as he told her the younger generation had nicknamed it, wasn't 'worth the trouble' as far as he was concerned. It was a non-thing; something to be taken for granted. She disagreed. Not only was it the most magnificent thing about living in Dusk, nothing was written about how it had been constructed, or by whom. It simply existed, and the whole Kingdom made use of it. Those facts fascinated her beyond measure.

The Flute sprawled across the entirety of the Kingdom like a gigantic spider web. It had been built beneath the city, long before many of the buildings had been erected, or streets had been paved. While the layout of blocks and streets at surface level didn't appear to have any rhyme or reason, there was one constant no matter where one found themself in Baan'Sholaria; one was never too far from a Flute station. In fact, from the little of the city she'd been able to see from above, buildings seemed to cluster around each station like the pedals of a flower, blossoming outward from various points dotted across the landscape, colliding and swirling where clusters met.

She usually made it back to the Flute with only a few minutes to spare. Her room in the Cryx was located over a hundred miles away from her meeting spot with Eros. On foot, on the surface, she'd never make the trip in a single day, let alone a single night. The Flute made it possible for her evening escapades to fit within the span of a single evening, and with it she would never get to spend time in his arms, or lay upon matted, dew-kissed grass and study the stars. That, if nothing else, made the Flute one of her favorite things.

Descending the steps into the station always filled her with a sense of wonder. Twice she'd ridden down in the cargo lift, just to see what it was like. There hadn't been any crates going up or down on those evenings, and Rusty Tom, as she called him, had been in a playful mood. He hadn't been at the lift since that last trip down. She didn't know why, or where he'd gone, but she always looked for him. He was unlike most of the workers on the Flute, still covered in rusted scale armor from his soldering days, so many hundreds of years past. Like the rest of those stations on the Flute, he was a mindless undead that had long ago lost his capacity for cognitive thought and had been put to use for the benefit of the city.

The process saddened her to think about. Being bolted to a surface, a seat, or a pole, and enchanted to perform a single task for the rest of your days, seemed horrific. Ahm's teachings claimed that people volunteered for such positions whenever their time came, and that their families were well compensated. Even though Eros had confirmed the details, she still felt it was wrong to treat a person that way. Perhaps she had a unique point of view after being forced to stay hidden in Ahm's workshop in the Cryx her entire life. Maybe she was simply naïve. After all, she had no way of knowing if the Flute-bound had emotions, or regretted their choices. One thing she was certain of was that she could see the fear in the eyes of those who were near to their end, or at least that's what her mind convinced her she was seeing.

Shaking off the sudden sadness, she focused her gaze on the three-railed tracks of the Flute. The two outer rails supported the wheels of the many carts pulled by a conductor. The center rail, glowing bright blue, provided the magical energies that made it all work. A center wheel jutted down from the bottom of each conductor's pod, draining just enough magic off the luminous rail to make their pod move, which in turn pulled the cars along behind them. Their pods had but one lever, and its only function was to raise and lower that center wheel. Raising it caused the pod's brakes to engage and removed the pod's source of power. Lowering it released the brakes and connected the power. It was as simple a device as she could fathom, and yet so critical to the success of the Kingdom.

No cars were in the station when she entered, neither were any awaiting passengers or shipments. She'd never ridden the Flute mid-way through the night, only early in the evening or just before dawn. Considering that more than half the population of Dusk didn't sleep, she found it odd to be alone on the platform, regardless of the time of day. There was, of course, no way for her to know for certain the accuracy of her assessment. Ahm often reminded her to ignore her flights of fancy and focus on the task at hand.

A deep, crunching sound echoed off the walls to her right, accompanied by a glimpse of shadow moving in her peripheral vision. She spun her head to face the disturbance, but couldn't see anything that could have caused the noise or movement. Tingling ran up her spine and a cold chill washed over her skin as her mind raced, trying to decide if Mordessa could have made it all the way to Flute Station three-nineteen, and whether the sound she'd heard had indeed been hoof on stone.

She took a step toward the dark recess between the shipping lift and the stairs just as the eerie whistle of a Flute train broke the silence in the distance. With a sigh of relief, she turned back to the rail and waited patiently as the cars approached, the rumble of heavy, iron wheels providing a bass undertone to the high-pitched whine of wind passing through the skeletal conductor. The orchestra was soon joined by the grinding squeal of iron on iron as brakes pressed onto wheels and the carts slowed to a stop before her.

"Good to see you again, Marcus," Mina said to the conductor as he passed. All his flesh lost long ago, he had no lungs to fill with air, no throat or lips with which to form words, and a distinct lack of brain function remaining with which to form a response. Instead, he clacked his blackened teeth together and slightly nodded his head. It was a conditioned response—a simple acknowledgment of the greeting he received from a passenger—but to Mina it was a sign that somewhere, deep down, the skeleton could hear her, understand her, and appreciate her kindness.

Mina took a seat in the first cart while she waited. Each passenger cart could hold up to six people, seated side by side in rows of three. There were no other persons riding that particular Flute that evening, which again struck her as odd. Several cars were carrying goods, but they took little time to disembark. The train would be on its way in no time, and she couldn't wait to feel the rush of wind on her face.

Skeletons in various stages of decay reached over from their positions and released the latch on their cars. The outer side of each dropped to the stone ledge beside the rails, creating ramps for the goods within to be wheeled out. Each load had been placed on the standard shipping carts used on the Flute, which made it easy for the skeletal custodians to roll their shipments through the side of the cars and down the metal exit ramps. Once through, they all turned and lifted the sides of the cars back into place, returned the latches to their closed positions, and stepped back from the Flute.

The entire affair lasted less than a minute, its events playing out like a well-choreographed dance. Mina couldn't help but marvel at the efficiency of the Flute, even though she felt pangs of sadness when she considered that each of the skeletal workers that made the process flow so flawlessly had once been a human, elf, dwarf, gnome, or some other sentient, bipedal being. Just as always, the

41

thoughts of their past selves threatened to overtake her mind. She was saved at the last moment by the train departing the station, and the wind caused by its movement playing a song for her as it passed through the conductor one car ahead.

She closed her eyes and let herself get lost in Marcus's particular tones. Each of the conductors sounded unique, and each had a small, glowing sigil carved into their forehead to indicate who they had been in their former lives. Every time she'd ridden with Marcus, the surrounding cars had been full of passengers, shipments, or both. She'd never had a chance to hear Marcus's tone clearly, unspoiled by the sound of others nearby. At times, riding the Flute was torturous for the passenger, if they still had capable ears. However, there was a certain beauty in the sound of a conductor, she decided. It made each and every train a unique experience.

If one wanted to be inspired towards anger, they need only ride with Landris. His tones were, unfortunately, very dark and grating. By contrast, riding with Hareth could make one feel jovial, for no particular reason at all. Marcus's song, apparently, inspired complete and utter calm. Now that she was able to hear his tones clearly, she decided that Marcus was her favorite of them all.

"FENIX! WHERE'S Hain?" called Tavyn.

As they rounded the corner, and the docks came into view, they saw a man leaning against a lantern post, smoking a pipe. He wore the standard black leather armor and white sash of a member of The Bones. Tavyn recognized him as they drew closer and called out, hoping he knew where the gang's healer had gone.

Fenix looked up to see Tavyn approaching, a young girl limping along beside him, her arm over his shoulder. "Have a little too much fun, did ye?" he joked.

"No questions. I just need Hain," declared Tavyn as he came to a stop in front of Fenix.

"You don't do enough work for us to go 'round making demands," said Fenix.

Tavyn glared at Fenix as if he forgot who he was talking to. He'd beaten Fenix in duels many, many times in paid matches for the gang's entertainment. "You wanna do this? Now?"

"Got no better time in mind," said Fenix as he tapped the ash out of his pipe and slipped it into his belt pouch.

"Listen, you egotistical fuck, you know why I'm in Amuer. I told you and the rest of The Bones just as soon as I was sure none of you were the perpetrator," said Tavyn.

"You gonna go on about that necromancer bullshit again, mister holier-than-thou?" growled Fenix as he stepped away from the pole he'd been leaning on and approached Tavyn.

"I found his lair, you ignorant bastard! Hannah, here, was chained to a table in his lab and he was about to kill her and turn her into a zombie!" explained Tavyn.

"He speaks true, my lord," whimpered Hannah, her voice barely above a whisper.

"Oh, fuck. No... you're crazy. That shit doesn't happen," stammered Fenix in disbelief.

"It does, and that's why the Daxian Order sent me... to handle it. So, take her to Hain, please, so I can go fucking handle it!"

"Nah, take her to the Guard, Tav... let them deal with this mess. We don't wanna get involved in this shit!" argued Fenix.

"The fucker is a nobleman, Fen; a councilman. You think the Guard is going to take *our* word for it that he's killing young girls from all over town? Young girls from poor districts they don't give a damn about? They dump literal shit on people like us, Fen. Besides, how do you think the Guard would go after this man if they even believed me? Full frontal assault like gods-damned morons. You know it. I know it. Hell, fucking Hannah knows it. You don't go after a guy like this out in the open with the law at your back. You do that, you lose. Every time. That's why I exist. That's why I was trained to do what I do. So, take Hannah to Hain while I go deal with this bastard how he least expects it," said Tavyn.

"How will you know it's him?" asked Fenix as he shouldered Hannah's weight.

"If I hurry, I should catch him scurrying away from his lair, freaked out that he's been caught. Barring that, I have his journal, thanks to Hannah," he explained, flashing the book for Fenix to see.

"You gonna share the bounty with The Bones?" asked Fenix.

"There's no bounty to be had," sighed Tavyn. "As I told you before, this is a right versus wrong thing, not a financial opportunity. Feel free to claim the glory, though. The Daxian Order would rather not have the citizens of Amuer running around, singing their praises," said Tavyn.

"That's why you got us involved, aint it?" asked Fenix.

"Now you're getting it," smiled Tavyn. "I do the work. You get the credit for saving the women of Amuer, and all the street cred that goes with it."

"Fine, but Hain's gonna want coin to heal this girl," said Fenix.

"My stash is with the rest, in the Bones' hideout. Take it," said Tavyn.

Fenix nodded and took Hannah to find Hain.

HAD MINA walked from her spot with Eros back to her home in the Cryx, it would have taken her several days to arrive. She wasn't sure of the exact distance between the two points, especially considering the layout of streets and the density of foot traffic that might be present to slow her progress. She was, however, keenly aware of how fast the Flute traveled, because Ahm had made it a part of his lessons.

Powered by an unknown magical force, the lead car in any Flute could travel upwards of ninety miles per hour. With the weight of the cars they pulled behind them, in addition to any passengers and cargo, they were typically slowed to around seventy miles per hour. Her ride to and from her evenings with Eros typically took just under two and a half hours, with a few five-minute stops along the route. On a given night out, if Ahm left his laboratory early enough, she could travel to meet up with Eros, spend four or five hours in his company, and still be home before sunrise.

On that particular evening, due to their untimely disagreement, she'd arrived back at station forty-nine several hours ahead of schedule. This afforded her a rare opportunity to wander the streets and see more of the world directly above and around the Cryx without the distraction of being near Eros. Her mind, however, seemed to have other plans.

As she ascended the steps toward street level, her thoughts kept involuntarily switching between the argument she'd had with her boyfriend and the vision she'd seen of Mordessa. No matter how hard she tried, she couldn't keep both of them away at the same time. As a consequence, she was getting more and more frustrated with herself at every step.

It's a lack of sleep. It's gotta be lack of sleep. I've been surviving on one hour naps ever since I met Eros... a month ago? Or was it two? she thought. Her inner debate had been enough to forestall the inevitable mental onslaught for a time, but it also served to distract her from her surroundings. Just as she was debating how long she'd known Eros, she caught a glimpse of something tall, white-skinned, with black, leathery wings moving in an alley to her right. She involuntarily jumped and squealed, expecting Mordessa to burst out of the shadows and grab her violently. Not only was nothing in the alley when she spun toward it, she somehow managed to trip over a Xxrandite's dog in the process.

"Oh my gods, I'm so sorry," she blurted as she landed on her rump, the poor creature's bones clacking horribly as it crumpled to the ground beneath her calves and struggled to regain its feet. The tiny canine was extremely far gone, but its owner was apparently very rich. Paying for enchantments to re-bind and animate bone that had otherwise lost the ability to function properly due to the absence of muscle fibers was not a cheap endeavor. Buying such a service for a comfort animal was something she couldn't fathom happening, yet there it stood, a dog with a fully exposed skeletal structure, and little-if-any soft tissue remaining; blackened bones glowing blue with runes, which pulsed brighter whenever the nearby joints flexed. It belted a faint, hollow bark in her direction as it trotted back into position a few feet behind its master; a master that had thankfully missed the altercation entirely.

She got to her feet after the dog left her presence and brushed herself clean with a sigh before standing upright. The dog's master was a levitating lich; ancient enough to have lost its legs to rot, but powerful enough for that to have no impact on its mobility. A chill ran down her spine at the thought of upsetting a being so powerful over something as trivial as not watching where she was going.

With renewed focus on where she was stepping, she resumed her walk back toward the Cryx and decided to forgo any sightseeing for the rest of the evening. Eros's unintentional badgering seeped back into her mind. She found herself arguing as much with her own brain for insisting she rehash the argument, as she was with him in her mind for daring to challenge her observations. Even though she knew he hadn't meant any ill will, and was simply trying to educate her, the sheer nerve of him to take such a tone with her and be so crass was upsetting.

A shadow moved at the edge of her vision again, this time in the shape of large, blackened horns on a creature far taller than even the floating lich's head had been. She once again involuntarily lurched in response, seeking to dodge an attack which wasn't coming. Frustrated with her brain, she growled, "By Ishnu, can you please *stop!*"

"I'm sorry, miss," said a shambling merchant. "I'll do better." His voice was airy and strained, having taken a great deal of effort to produce.

She glanced over at the man briefly. The flesh on the left side of his torso was almost completely missing, and only a third of the muscles on his neck remained intact. He was a Xxrandite, and would soon decay beyond usefulness on the surface. The poor man was a Cryx-Bound, and likely terrified of being noticed and considered a burden before his time.

"Not you, kind sir, my brain. It's doing funny things today," she said, her hands instinctively mimicking like she was about to claw at her own mind.

"It can be like that at times," he wheezed with a chuckle, his left lung visibly inflating each time he pushed himself to speak.

"Yes. Yes, it can," she said with a sigh as she hastened away. "Have a splendid dawn, good sir. May Xxrandus bless you," she concluded with a slight curtsy. *Best to leave a good impression wherever I can tonight. Gods know I'm putting on a scene otherwise,* she sighed to herself.

For the rest of her walk to the Cryx, Mina focused her mind on counting the cracks in the pavement beneath her feet. It was the only way she could think of to keep the other thoughts at bay long enough to make it home without drawing attention to herself. As she reached the hole cover at the back of a dark, thin alley, she sighed in relief that her mental exercise had worked. Without another thought, she knelt down and lifted the heavy metal cover out of the way and stepped down onto the ladder below. Once she was inside far enough, she reached up and pulled the cover back into position over her head, then began her twenty-minute descent into the darkness below.

The Cryx was the enormous, unlit void beneath the former capital city of the god Xxrandus, which had been pulled out of the sky by gargantuan iron chains long before recorded history. Or at least, that was the explanation Ahm had given her. Nobody was sure what to believe, other than their attempts at deciphering what little evidence they could find; evidence such as the gigantic iron chain links that seemed to clamp onto the edges of the crevice that encircled the entire royal district at the center of Dusk, and the fact that they disappeared into a void in the surrounding walls just beneath ground, riding atop what appeared to be twenty-story-tall iron cogs.

It was hard to question the massive iron constructs, or their apparent purpose. At the end of the day, however, no living soul could prove such theories for certain. Ultimately, the cause of the city's construction was irrelevant to their modern situation. Citizens lived on the surface, eventually Ascended to either unlife or undeath. Once they depleted their usefulness, they were sent to serve in the Cryx by means of magically controlled enslavement. Mina was far too familiar with that final state of affairs, considering Ahm's chosen location for his laboratories and offices, and thus the required location for her secret sleeping and living quarters. She'd grown up around society's cast-offs; those pushed beneath ground as unworthy, no-longer-valuable, and, worst of all, forgotten. She felt for them, and constantly wished there was something she could do on their behalf. That's why she named the nameless, greeted the formless, and went out of her way to be polite to the Cryx-bound.

She was minutes from her bed by the time those recurring thoughts tickled the back of her mind once more. Soon her night would end, and she'd get some much needed rest before Ahm's plans for the day took control. She wasn't sure when she'd make it out to see Eros again, or if their argument would be the last thing they ever said to one another. She hoped beyond hope that he wouldn't accept Ascension before seeing her at least one more time. Her feet touched the stone floor of the Cryx with an echo as a tear of regret cascaded down her cheek.

IT TOOK several hours for Tavyn to work his way back through the sixth district toward the seventh. The air was noticeably more pleasant just a few feet inside its boundaries, and the stench of his own clothes quickly became apparent. He ducked into the first alley he could find to avail himself of any standing water. To his relief, there was a barrel full of rainwater only a few yards away, and he was able to wash most of the surface filth off himself with relative ease. The underlying stink remained, but from a distance, none would be the wiser. That was all that mattered to him. True cleanliness could come later.

He did his best to approximate where the sewer entrance might be that contained the dangling rope. It was impossible to determine its exact position without a precise series of maps, and quite a lot more navigational experience than he had, but he was able to follow roughly the same series of turns he'd made underground by following the paths and intersections on the streets above. More importantly, he tried to keep himself between the overall section of town he assumed he'd been underneath prior, and the court district further in toward the center of Amuer. He figured if the man went down to his lair and saw his victim had been set free, he'd scurry past on his way back to the relative safety of his residence.

It didn't take long for his assumption to pay off. Not long after his gut told him he'd found the correct route, a medium-sized human male with a very plain face and wearing court robes rushed out of an alley, looking over his shoulder with a great deal of concern on his face. He charged headlong, at nearly a jog, through a crowd of celebrating clergymen and judicial scribes, seemingly unconcerned with their cries of disagreement.

Within a few seconds, he'd disappeared around a corner, heading straight for the condominium district allocated for mid-ranked court officials. He was heading home, and whoever he was watching out for wasn't someone he expected to be a resident of the district. Tavyn was certain he had found his man.

He raced down the far side of the street toward the corner and watched from a distance as the man continued onward. Not following him directly was a calculated risk. The man could easily slip away, or turn another corner and enter any number of buildings. Tavyn decided to trust his gut, and his gut was telling him the man lived close by; close enough to escape his lair and disappear in a hurry if his activities were ever found out. His gut paid off. The man nearly broke out into a full run before reaching the fourth building along the main street of the housing complex, and burst through its front doors like his life depended on it. Tavyn nodded his success. Knowing the building was enough to get the job done. First, he wanted to verify his suspicions.

With a quick clap of his hands in self congratulation, he spun on his heel and calmly made his way to the alley he'd seen the man escape. Near the back of the alley lay a manhole cover, haphazardly placed into its seat, with several scrape marks scoring the pavement above. He lifted one edge of the cover, as calmly and quietly as he could, and peered underneath to find a coiled bit of rope clumsily draped over the top rung of the not-quite-long-enough metal ladder built into the tunnel's northern side. Down below, he could make out a flat, dry expanse of stone, just barely close enough to discern with his elvish night vision. Content he'd indeed found the right man, he carefully lowered the cover back into position, intent on making as little noise as possible.

"This ends tonight," he declared under his breath as he stood.

THE HOUSING district was composed of three dozen four and five story brick buildings, all identical in architectural style and artistic theme. The residences therein were nearly identical to one another, having few details that might indicate an occupant's rank or position within the courts. Great care had been taken to obscure, or outright avoid, any impression of the residents' stature. So much so that once one knew the layout of any given condominium, none of them would bear any surprises.

It was the only part of town constructed from baked red brick. It was a technique considered unusual for Amuer, and had been brought to it from lands far away. In fact, most of the construction materials and techniques used throughout the neighborhood were considered quite elegant by city council-members, if for no other reason than their uniqueness in the Kingdom of Haern. To Tavyn, the sameness that persisted from building to building resulted in nothing more than an eyesore that he couldn't wait to be done with.

The residents of the Sixth referred to the Council Heights as 'Brick City', both to denote the section's appearance, and the presumed mental capacity of its residents; often considered 'talking bricks' by most residents of Amuer. One of the reasons Tavyn avoided Brick City in his investigations was his assumption that the citizens were correct; anyone dumb enough to serve on the council and make such poor decisions would be too uneducated to bear the knowledge of such a learned magical art as necromancy. He sighed at his ignorance and arrogance as he entered the courtyard of a nearby building.

Tavyn slowly traversed the outer edge of the courtyard between the third building on the main road, and the building behind it on the secondary road. He studied the windows intently, seeking an apartment that might be vacant. Finding no obvious signs of vacancy from the exterior, he chose instead to seek one whose windows were entirely dark; devoid of any interior light from any source. At that time of night, that was a much easier task.

He selected the apartment directly opposite the main road on the third floor and approached the rear of the building to begin his climb. Several artistic ledges and small sculptures lined the top of each floor, allowing for easy hand and toe holds during his ascent. The expanse between those holds was easy enough to scale if he stayed at the outer corners of the building and made use of the downspouts that brought rainwater safely down from the roof. Thankfully, the spout on the rightmost rear corner was barely visible through the overly large oak tree that grew in the courtyard, allowing him to climb with relative ease and little risk of being seen.

Once he reached the third floor, he scaled horizontally toward the balcony of his chosen condominium's central living space. With his feet firmly planted on the railing, he lowered himself onto the balcony and crouched as low as he could. A sliding door made of teak blocked entry into the home, but it was not barred from the inside as it should have been. A few silent steps inside revealed that he had, indeed, selected a vacant apartment. With a sigh of relief, he explored the residence to learn its floor plan, in preparation for his attack on the horrid necromancer's home. He wanted as few surprises as possible for the coming fight. Knowing his entrances, exits and any potential hiding spots would be critical to his success.

After learning all that he could, he made his way back to the balcony and climbed the rest of the way to the roof. All he had to do was determine which floor of the neighboring building the man lived on, and he could make his move. He settled in for what would possibly be several days of waiting and watching.

A SHORT while later, candlelight illuminated a pair of the windows on the building's third floor. It seemed to drift around the room for a short time, then became stationary. From what he recalled of the apartment he'd just studied, he discerned that the lit room was the master bedchamber. It was nearly midnight, and he felt confident assuming most of the building's residents had already gone to sleep for the night. If his assumption was correct, any sign of candlelight was a strong indication he'd found his target's home.

He lowered himself, as carefully and silently as he could, to the balcony across from the window. When he reached the railing, he leaned out as far as possible and focused his eyes to see normal light spectrums, lest the brightness of the candle disrupt his vision. Two figures were standing in the doorway to the room, heatedly arguing in hushed tones. The one furthest inside the room had long hair and wore a long white gown. She was angry, and talking with her hands, which made the candle shake around so much it almost went out several times.

The other figure, slightly bulkier and shorter than her, seemed to be trying his best to calm her down. He opened his arms down low, submissively, in what Tavyn could only assume was a gesture requesting her forgiveness. She waved him off with her free hand while turning into the room and shaking her head. Tavyn ducked back instinctively as her movement brought her face around, hoping she hadn't caught sight of him across the alley.

Maintaining his subservient mannerisms, the man entered the room and persisted his request for forgiveness. She placed her left hand to her forehead, seemed to mutter something relatively calmly, then sat her candle on a small table at the foot of the bed. They embraced for a moment before she pushed his shoulders away. She looked him in the eye and said something firmly, to which he nodded, then she retrieved the candle and made her way to the far side of the bed. He waited as she slipped under the covers, handed her a book from the bedside table, moved the candle right next to her face, and leaned in to kiss her forehead.

It was him. The moment was brief, but his face had entered the candlelight just long enough to identify him properly. As the man left his wife in bed and exited the room, quietly closing the door behind himself, Tavyn turned and climbed back to the ground. He slipped through the shadows, avoiding the lantern light creeping in from the street, and started his climb up the downspout at the rear of the building.

When he reached the decorative trim between the second and third floor, he scaled sideways along the seam on his fingertips, stopping under the far side of the necromancer's master bedroom windows. With the balcony to his left, and windows to his right, he raised himself up precariously using the slight protrusion of brick faces around the window so that he could wedge the toes of his boots on the lip above the decorative seam. He managed to find a single, reliable handhold higher up for his left hand, and gripped the outer edge of the window with his right to create enough leverage to stabilize his position. Content that he wouldn't fall, at least for a short time, he leaned his head closer to the window and waited to catch sight of the man again.

The last thing he wanted was for a powerful necromancer to see him coming, and have time to cast a spell. One of the most important tactics he'd been taught was to never, ever, let his quarry react.

Ris'Enliss, Amaethur 12th, 575 of the 1st Era

'We are assassins. We attack when our opponents least expect it, in a time and place of our choosing. We do not fight face to face, for if we do, we lose. Make no mistake, our targets are some of the most capable and horrifying creatures on Ayrelon. I don't care how skilled you think you are. Do not fight face to face with a man who can raise the dead. There is no victory to be had from such folly. Take them when they aren't aware you exist, ideally while they're sleeping.'

Master Nyr'Thal's words echoed in his mind as he clung to the wall. This was his first contract for the Daxian Order, and only his third mission. He'd already spent far too long investigating what Nyr'Thal told him would be a simple contract. Coupled with his desire to prevent further loss of innocent life, his impatience was threatening to get the better of him. At the same time, he could feel the hot ball of anxiety forming in his chest, sending random chills down the core of his limbs. He did his best to calm his emotions, lest his hands start to tremble and he lose his grip.

Necromancer or not—no matter how strongly he knew the man deserved to die—Tavyn had never assassinated anyone, or taken a life in combat. In fact, the only person he'd ever killed was the poor woman bound to the wall in the laboratory, and she had pleaded with him to do it to prevent her horrid fate. He could feel the small, but growing, pangs of guilt at the back of his mind for that act. Had he acted too quickly? Was there another way he could have saved her?

He shook his head out of frustration and drove the thoughts away by focusing on the room behind the window. His quarry was somewhere inside, and it was critical for the man to die. Adjusting his grip, he settled in for however long it would take to wait for the man to join his wife in bed.

CHAPTER 4:
CALAMITY

Ris'Enliss, Amaethur 12th, 575 of the 1st Era

WHUN HAD hovered at the center of the temple's ritual chamber ever since he woke, staring into a crystal ball that he'd retrieved from a black portal, much to the surprise of the Noktulian priests in his company. Frustrated with his lack of progress, he let the orb drop into his outstretched hand with a clank and slipped it into one of the many hidden pockets of his robe.

'I *will try again another time,*' he said with his mind, sending it echoing into theirs.

"Do you require rest? Sustenance?" inquired the head priest out of kindness, knowing full well the answer to both questions was no.

Whun chose to ignore the priest's pleasantries. '*I will meditate on our course of action, and see if I can learn anything further from your hidden guest before I-*'

His thoughts were cut short as a burst of energy flooded into Ayrelon's magical weave. As a creature whose existence was directly bound by the magic within the leylines that spanned the world, Whun felt the surge pass through him with unmistakable effect. In the same instant his spine tingled, his exposed bones felt a deathly chill, and the core of his being felt hot enough to melt iron.

'What is this?' he thought.

Focusing his crown's vision on magical sight, he looked through the stone floors, ceilings and walls to the sky beyond, seeking the wave of power so he could trace its ripples back to their source. The magical net of power that enveloped the world fluttered as if being blown by a strong wind, the source of its motion seeming to come from far to the west.

He quickly retrieved his crystal ball and tossed it back into the air before him, causing it to levitate mere inches from his face as it had before. Closing his physical eyes, he peered into it with his crown, and focused its clairvoyant powers onto the weave. Pushing the scene across the sky, he followed the ripples west to their epicenter.

Standing amidst the debris of a shattered port town was a young woman surrounded by piles of dark ash. As purple, black, green and blue magic dissipated in the air around her, she seemed to regain her composure, easing the tension in her shoulders, neck and spine. Her body aged almost instantly, settling into the form of an unbelievably old woman. She reached down and grabbed the leg of a broken table and proceeded south, using it as a cane and muttering to herself about Mordechai; a name he recognized from his distant memories.

Whun chose not to follow her departure with his scrying. Whatever powers she'd unleashed, though clearly far beyond his own, were of little concern in that moment. What he could see pulsing below the detritus was far more troubling. Extra-planar power surged into the mines far below the city, as if an ancient evil had been unleashed. It was an ancient evil that felt very familiar; one that Mordessa would certainly detect, and seek to harness for her own purposes.

'Her sister has been freed,' thought Whun to the priests.

"How? By whom? For what purpose?" rattled the head priest as fast as its lips would comply.

'How is a problem for another time, and the whom is irrelevant. Both sisters have a mastery of soul magic unlike any power we are capable of attaining. I must watch to see if they seek to reunite, or if their ancient rivalry still stands. The two of them combined are a force we cannot overcome, no matter the plan or participants. However, Siscci's return has brought with it a wave of power that has broken the seal between life and death in that part of the world... at least for a time. If I am correct, we might find a Caier in those lands, thanks in part to this event. If one is present, they should grow stronger due to the weakened boundary, and their greater power will make them easier to discover,' explained Whun.

"We will leave you to your observations, Lord Whun. We've preparations to make, if we are to lure the Caier here from lands so far away," said the priest.

Whun ignored the priest's response. He was too focused on the creature crawling from its hardened obsidian tomb halfway around the world to pay the mortals by his side any mind.

TAVYN WAITED so long his fingers felt like they were about to lose their strength. He didn't know how much time had passed, but he was certain he couldn't wait for much longer. Regardless of the risk, he couldn't continue clinging to the wall. He looked to his left and couldn't see any light coming through the balcony window. Perhaps, if he was lucky, the necromancer would be so confident in the safety of his third-floor residence that he'd dismiss any need to bar the sliding door.

He leaned left and crossed his right hand over to take the place of his left. Blood rushed into his left-hand fingers as he released his grip, causing his knuckles to ache and the skin to tingle. He shook it briefly before reaching for the railing, then climbed over as quietly as he could. A sense of dread washed over him at the thought he'd have to climb back out if he found the door locked.

Pressing his ear to the door, he listened for a few seconds for any movement within before trying the door. It didn't budge. The window beside the door was a single piece of solid glass, not designed to open. He took a few moments to rest his hands before resigning himself to climbing back out onto the side of the building. There was no movement visible through the balcony window, and no way he could see into the bedroom from his position. He had to climb back out, whether he liked it or not, but he couldn't just cling to the wall and wait. Even if it was the least optimal decision in regards to stealth, he had to gain entry to the bedroom, even if the man hadn't gone to bed yet.

Angry at his circumstances, he hefted himself back over the rail and resumed his position on the wall. To make his grip easier to maintain, he moved beneath the window and grabbed the lower sill with both hands, then lifted himself up to study the near side of the room, opposite the bed. A pair of high-backed chairs stood in the nearest corner, angled toward each other around a small tea table. He decided his best option was to get into the room quickly and hide behind those chairs to wait for his prey.

Moving as slowly as possible, he retrieved a very thin piece of metal from a pocket along his thigh. It was four inches long and almost an inch wide, but as thin as a sheet of parchment. He reached up and carefully slid it between the left and right halves of the left window, then applied gentle pressure to the locking mechanism. The latch popped up and to the right with a barely audible click as his tool pushed against it.

He returned the tool to its pocket and retrieved the curved dagger from the small of his back, then wedged its tip into the bottom right edge of the right window pane. With a gentle tug, he pulled the pane outward an eighth of an inch, then stopped. After returning the blade to its sheath, he slowly opened the right pane, then the left, and lifted himself inside.

As his muscles once again sighed in relief, he quickly turned back to the window, closed and latched it, then made his way behind the seating area. While his new position was certainly better than risking a fall to his death, he was at far greater risk of being seen whenever the man finally entered the room. Furthermore, his wife's gentle snoring at the far side of the room had a lulling effect he was completely unprepared to contend with. He hadn't properly rested in over a week, and while elves normally didn't need much more than a few hours of meditation, he could feel his consciousness slowly drifting toward a deep, deep sleep at the sound of her slumber.

Nearly an hour later, the door to the bedchamber slowly swung open as the necromancer entered. He kept his eyes focused on his wife, trying to assess if he'd woken her. He turned back to the door and eased it shut with both hands, slowly releasing the handle after it was closed to prevent the typical click of its bolt. He seemed about as normal as a man could look, as far as humans were concerned. His face was very unimposing, if not distinctly average. There was nothing remarkable about his features, and no reason to give a man like him a second glance on the street. To anyone observing his behavior in the room that night, he appeared to be a loving, attentive husband and nothing more. That was his trick; he hid in plain sight. No one had any reason to make assumptions about his motivations, because there was nothing out of the ordinary about his appearance or actions.

His house coat was nicer than those of a normal citizen, but did not speak of his wealth. Even still, he spent an inordinate amount of time carefully releasing each button from its hole, and draping the coat over the rail at the foot of his bed. He even spent a few moments gently stroking wrinkles out of the coat, as if he were quite intent on persisting in his facade of walking the line between wealthy and average.

The man's shoes were no different; well cared for, neither expensive nor cheap, and suitable for either the Parliament floor or a street near the docks. Any dirt they collected was cleaned off nightly, as evident by the length of time the insufferable man spent quietly stroking them with a soft-bristled brush as he sat on the foot of his bed.

Once he was satisfied with the state of his footwear, he placed them in their precise position under the edge of the bed and stood facing the armoire. The old wooden doors opened without a sound, indicating he was as attentive to the maintenance of his furniture as he was to his wardrobe. The hinges were well oiled, likely to prevent him from waking his wife when he accessed it.

Tavyn continued to watch—his patience waning—as the man methodically removed his white shirt, one button at a time, and slipped a nightshirt over his head. He then removed a leather belt from his waist, taking care not to drop a leather pouch attached at his front right hip. He paused for a moment and opened the supple pouch, producing a small leather book. Tavyn couldn't see the book's ornate cover very clearly, but it seemed exquisitely detailed from his point of view.

"They can't stop me," he whispered as he ran his fingers over the cover, following lines of runes with his fingertips. After a few seconds, he tucked the book back into its pouch, cinched the bag closed, and placed it in the armoire. He then removed and neatly folded his pants, placing them atop the pouch as if to protect it from dust, or conceal it from his wife.

Finally ready for bed, he walked to his wife's side on the balls of his feet. He gently brushed the hair out of her face, leaned over and kissed her forehead before retrieving her candle and walking back to his own side. With the candle resting on his nightstand, he climbed into bed and carefully adjusted the blankets to ensure there were no wrinkles atop him, then leaned over and blew the candle out.

Tavyn waited until the man's breathing calmed and then counted to four hundred. He wanted to be sure his prey was fully asleep before taking action. As he finally crept toward the bed, he drew his curved dagger and held it with the blade pointed downward, then positioned the tip just under the man's chin. With a quick flick of his wrist, the blade sliced deep into the man's throat, severing his jugular and carotid in one smooth motion. His victim woke instantly, gasping for breath and drowning in his own blood.

The sudden commotion, and warm spatter of blood, woke the man's wife. She rolled toward her husband and whipped her head around just in time to see the Dynar assassin rise upright, dagger in hand. She screamed louder than Tavyn had ever heard anyone scream. His blood went cold, and a chill ran down his spine. There was no way the building's guards had missed her outcry.

Footsteps echoed down the hall, heading toward the master bedroom. Tavyn briefly considered going for the window, but their home was too far above the street, and the tiny cracks he'd used to climb his way in wouldn't serve for a quick escape. He suddenly realized he'd planned very poorly. After such a long search for the necromancer, he'd acted too hastily. He also needed to retrieve the book from the armoire, and the man's wife was reaching for him. She was sure to disrupt his efforts if he went for the tome.

He leapt onto the bed and lunged for her, all the while arguing with himself about what to do about the situation. She drove her hands upward to deflect him and caught her left wrist on his curved blade in the process, gashing her forearm open from palm to elbow. Her wailing somehow increased in volume.

She flailed her left arm, attempting to knock his weapon away—splattering blood in every direction for her efforts—while simultaneously trying to push his chest away with her right. In order to get his hand to her mouth—which had been his original intent—he had to get inside her reach, and that meant putting himself in a position where she could latch on, and trap him. In a moment of panic, he thrust his dagger downward, burying it deep into the flesh of her abdomen. He instantly regretted the attack and tried to pull it free, but the curved tip was lodged behind her sternum.

He hadn't entered with the intention of killing the man's wife. She was innocent; completely unaware of her husband's secret second life. With the tragic turn of events, leaving her alive was no longer an option. She'd seen his face, and he'd already mortally wounded her, even if accidentally. The best he could do at that moment was to put her out of her misery.

After pushing the dagger toward the bed, he was able to pull it toward her feet and remove it from her ribcage, effectively gutting her in the process. With one final motion, he drove the dagger into the woman's throat, cutting off her air supply and hastening her impending death. Distraught at what he'd done, and dangerously close to succumbing to the growing sense of dread within him, he backed off the foot of the bed, his eyes firmly locked on the horrid scene he'd caused.

In those disastrous few moments, he'd completely forgotten about the approaching footsteps. He broke free of the horror just as they suddenly stopped behind him. Whoever it was had arrived. He spun frantically, desperately taking action to defend himself from what he assumed to be a guard. Expecting the assailant to be an adult human, he ducked low as he spun and drove his dagger outward, hoping to take any guard out at the knees and dodge their incoming attack.

The last of his composure left when his maneuver ended. Standing before him, no taller than he was while kneeling, was the couple's young daughter... and his dagger was buried deep in her chest.

"Ishnu, forgive me," he muttered. The girl's eyes went wide. She reached for her mother and father, but only managed to squeak in pain before falling over.

Tavyn stood, horrified. He ran for the door, desperate to get away from the scene, and made it to the foyer before he realized he was running. It wasn't until his hand touched the latch that he remembered the necromancer's book.

He swallowed hard and ran back for the pouch in the armoire, averting his eyes from the slaughtered family as best he could. With the pouch in hand, he ran for the exit again, and finally found himself in the hallway of the fourth floor. Four families lived on each floor of the building, and the sound of movement was coming from all of them.

The wife's screams had woken everyone, it seemed, and his own thunderous flight across their floor had confirmed their suspicions. There he was, standing in a lantern-lit hallway on the top floor of a residential building, dressed in black, covered in blood, and wholly out of place in every way imaginable. He pushed aside the panic as best he could, tucked the small pouch into the folds of his shirt, and made his way toward the stairs.

The center of the building was an open chamber leading from the ground floor to the roof. Each level was rimmed with railing, with only one opening leading into the staircase beyond. As he reached the opening, several citizens spilled into the hallways and ran toward the railing. Cries of alarm rang out behind him, as several men in bed robes watched his descent and called for guards.

When he reached the second-to-last landing before the second floor, two guards rounded the corner and rushed toward him. He reached instinctively for the curved dagger at the small of his back, but it was missing. That was when he realized he'd left it buried in the chest of his quarry's small child. Panicked, and with few options at his disposal, he ducked to the floor, then leaped as forcefully as he could up and over the guards as they ascended the final few stairs toward him.

Tavyn barely cleared the guards' heads before crashing to the floor on the landing below with a violent thud. He shook off the pain and rolled to his feet as they turned and clamored down the final few flights as quickly as his body would allow.

Two more guards stood in the lobby on the first floor, poised for attack. They stepped toward him as he rounded the corner. He closed the distance as fast as his legs could move. Just before they collided, he dropped to his knees and slid beneath their thrusting spears, ending his momentum with his fist buried deep into the groin of the guard on the right.

He stood quickly, driving his shoulder into the same guard's gut and spun to the right, pushing the guard into his comrade. Before they could recover, Tavyn was out in the streets and barreling toward the Capital District. While he knew that route would take him through the highest density of city guards, his ultimate goal was to reach The Bones' hideout on the docks, and he couldn't risk them following him directly there.

The only people working in the Capital District at that time of night, besides guards, were cleaning and cooking staff. His plan had always been to take advantage of the near-chaos that consumed the alleys between Parliament and the four High Court buildings if his actions were discovered. He was upset that it had become a necessity, and even more upset that he'd taken unplanned, innocent lives. However, he felt a slight comfort in the fact that he'd at *least* gotten that part of his planning correct.

As he wove through the expected throng of night workers, carts, baskets, and crates behind the Parliament building, he removed his layered over shirt and tossed it aside, taking care to maintain a grip on the tome pouch as he moved. He continued the process and took short breaks to remove a piece of his black leather clothing whenever he felt safe enough to do so. By the time he reached the end of the alley, he was left wearing the simple brown shirt and braes of a dock worker. All that was left was to wash the blood and ash off of his face and hands.

Tavyn ducked behind a crate at the end of the alley and waited while a few guards ran past, then quickly crossed the street and ducked into the back alleys of the decrepit Sixth District. Once there, he checked alley after alley, seeking a rain barrel. They were the only regular source of clean drinking water for the local residents, who mostly lived on the streets, so his search didn't take long to find one that was full enough he could reach its contents without a drinking ladle.

He washed his face and hands hurriedly, trying to keep his filth from falling back inside the barrel as best he could. Once complete, he dried his face on his sleeves and walked as calmly as he could through the Sixth District and into the Fifth, making his way slowly toward the docks.

By the time he reached the row of shops at the center of the Fifth District, most of the street dwellers had been awakened by cries of alarm, and the stalking of city guards. It was a scene not often witnessed outside the Capital District, as most crimes in the outer districts were seemingly ignored. However, talk of a child murderer running the streets had spread from guards to common citizens, and was being spoken in semi-hushed tones all around him as he moved. Some of the poor seemed elated that a noble family had finally gotten what they deserved. Others were horrified at the death of a child, and the senseless loss of life.

His panic had given way to overwhelming guilt. He was trained to kill, but only when his target was considered an abomination in the eyes of Ishnu. That only accounted for one of his three victims; the other two would be his undoing, he was certain. While Ishnu was a goddess of death, none of her teachings encouraged the unnatural, untimely loss of life. Rather, she revered the cycle of life, and how death was a beautiful contribution to the birth of something new. Death was something to be celebrated, instead of feared. In all her teachings, murder was the most heinous crime... even if it was accidental. He'd just broken Ishnu's greatest law, and sullied the name of the Daxian Order.

There's no way I can return home. I must atone for my actions in the eyes of Ishnu. Until I do, I am lost, he lamented.

Tavyn stopped and leaned against a wall with his head down. Horrific visions of the laboratory and the master bedroom flooded his mind. He tried to push them aside and focus on the image of Ishnu, and enter a state of prayer. The task was nearly impossible.

Please forgive me, oh great Ishnu. Help me find a way to re-earn thy trust. Guide those innocent souls to the afterlife with honor, and put them in a place of glory. They knew not what he was doing, and should not be held accountable for the lives he destroyed. Neither should they suffer for my mistakes.

With his prayer complete, he resumed his walk and eventually found his way to the docks.

FENIX WAS leaning against the same post when Tavyn rounded the corner to the docks. As soon as he noticed him approaching, he thrust himself off the post and started marching angrily toward the dark elf.

"Was it you?" demanded Fenix, his bushy black brow creased in anger.

"Was what me?" asked Tavyn, pretending he didn't know.

"Did you kill a whole fucking family?" demanded Fenix, coming to a stop and block Tavyn's path.

"Not intentionally," admitted Tavyn.

"How do you 'not intentionally' kill a fucking child, Tav?" growled Fenix as he drew his dagger.

"Her father was a necromancer. He was the one who killed all those young girls. So, I went in to kill him. Then his wife woke and became a problem, and their daughter ran up behind me without warning," explained Tavyn.

"Oh, well, why didn't you fucking say so, eh? That makes it all better!" yelled Fenix as he lunged toward Tavyn's torso.

Tavyn caught Fenix's wrist and pushed it high above his head, bracing the man's weapon out of harm's way. "It was unfortunate and unintentional, Fen! Stop, I'm completely unarmed!"

"So was she!" blurted Fenix.

"I thought she was a guard running up behind me, ducked, spun and stabbed toward what should have been their knee. It wasn't supposed to be a little girl, Fen!" yelled Tavyn defensively. While he put on his show of strength for Fenix's sake, his heart was aching and his stomach was in knots.

Fenix dropped his dagger and backed away, still angry but conflicted. "The Bones don't kill, Tav. We never kill. We'll shake someone down, steal, or force people to pay debts, but we don't kill. Not ever. Not even you, Tav. Not even for this," he growled.

"It was an accident. I'll find a way to pay my penance."

"That's between you and your god. Get the fuck out of my city," demanded Fenix. "No... Bones don't kill, but if any of us ever see you again, we're going to break that rule."

Tavyn sulked his way into the docks, seeking a ship he might pay for passage. He had very few coins left to his name, but he'd somehow have to make the situation work. Word of his contract's outcome would reach Quaan'Shala eventually and he would be exiled. If he was there when word arrived, he was sure to be executed. As much as he'd lost his will to live, he feared what might await him in the afterlife if he didn't find a way to atone before his end came.

He found a spot near the water, on the other side of a huge pile of crates, and slid to the ground to wait for the crews of the nearby ships to start their morning routine. He didn't want to risk sneaking aboard one and being caught, to say nothing of the fact he was starving and would likely succumb to weakness before they reached the next port.

Once the sun was high enough in the sky, and ships started bustling with activity, he approached each one by one and inquired about paying for passage. As he expected, they one by one told him where he could stick his coin.

"Pardon, good sir, but might I speak with your captain?" he asked as he ascended the only remaining gang plan on the dock.

"We ain't got no captain, lad," answered the burly, shirtless man.

"Stop fuckin with him, Tash, and go get the Lord," interrupted an even huskier, shirtless man. He smiled down at Tavyn with a nearly toothless grin in a failed attempt to be reassuring.

After a few minutes, a very well groomed, bearded man approached the railing in a highly polished suit of scale armor. It wasn't the kind of garb Tavyn expected to see on a sea-faring vessel, let alone such a highly manicured man.

"I am Siege Lord Branforth, about as close to a 'Captain' as you're going to get among my crew. What can I do for you? Did we leave something on the dock?" he asked, peering around at the nearby crates.

"No, my Lord. I am seeking passage out of this hellhole. I'll pay all the coin I have and work for the rest. I'll do whatever it takes. I just can't stay here... so it's your ship, or I start swimming," said Tavyn.

"You're pretty well spoken for someone dressed like a common sewer rat," said Branforth.

"I'm not from Amuer, Lord," said Tavyn.

"Where then... Quon Shall... sha-" started Branforth.

"Quaan'Shala, Lord, and... yes," answered Tavyn.

"We're sailing north to Algona, near the border of Tellrindos. We aren't making any stops along the way. You'll be at sea with us for weeks, and the work is neither fun, nor glorious," said Branforth.

"That is fine, Lord. The further I am from this place, the better," agreed Tavyn.

"Then welcome aboard The Eagle's Ire, lad. We've no need of your coin, but I'm sure Tash wouldn't mind you swabbing the deck for him, or washing the head," said Branforth.

Tash chuckled at the thought.

"Whatever you need done. If I can do it, or learn it, I'm your man," said Tavyn as he ascended the plank.

"That's what I like to hear, lad," said Branforth, clapping him on the shoulder. "The other half of your payment is telling me everything you know about Quaan'Shala."

Tavyn perked up and spun to face him, unsure if he was serious.

"I am Siege Lord for Velarus Orlandis Vaelin, Lord and ruler of the territory and former Tellrindosian fiefdom of Algona. My job is to know our enemies, how to defend against them, and how to lay siege to them... should it come to that."

"Is Quaan'Shala your enemy?" asked Tavyn, suddenly concerned.

"Not in the slightest, lad. We can't even pronounce its name properly," he quipped. Several sailors laughed around them. "It's called being prepared, and that's all I'm asking you to do for me: provide information so I can be prepared."

"Very well," agreed Tavyn. "Though I think it's far more likely that you'd find enemies in Haern than Quaan'Shala, and I've learned much about the wretched place during my stay in their capital," he added.

"I like you already," smiled Branforth. "No work today, lad. You'll be too busy getting your sea legs, anyway. Why don't you join me in my cabin, and we'll have a nice little chat."

"Aye, Lord," said Tavyn with a nod.

Just as Branforth predicted, Tavyn spent most of the evening doubled over the railing, losing his stomach's contents into the sea.

CHAPTER 5:
TENTATION

Ris'Enliss, Amaethur 12th, 575 of the 1st Era

AHM ARRIVED early that morning. On any given day, he didn't arrive until several hours after sunrise, once he'd finished his morning meal and tended to any pressing Ministry affairs. It was sheer luck, or fate, that had brought Mina home early the night before, and she counted herself very lucky regardless of the horrid vision she'd seen, and the argument she'd had with Eros.

When Advan entered the room to wake her, at Ahm's bidding, he seemed apologetic for disturbing her. He was aware she'd been sneaking out each night, and had in fact inspired her to seek her freedom. However, he knew that meant she was surviving on very little rest, and needed her sleep. He'd been relieved to see her return home earlier than normal, but like Mina, had been completely unaware of Ahm's plans to get an early start on the day.

"Sorry, Mina," said Advan as he opened her door while knocking. "Master Ahm has arrived and requests your presence," he finished with a sympathetic smile.

He was an Ishnite, and thus unliving rather than undead. Their kind didn't decay into nothingness the same way Xxrandites did, but their lives were not infinite. His body was stiff and seemed to argue with his every intention, fighting back with severe old age and hints of rigor mortis. It was common among Ishnites of extreme age, and much like the plight of elder Xxrandites usually relegated them to magical servitude in the depths of the Cryx. The Ascension process was extremely effective at prolonging their lifespans, but as the powers that kept them alive grew close to depletion, their bodies were slowly subjected to an extended version of the stages of degradation a common corpse would experience. Once an Ishnite showed signs of rigor mortis, they were rushed off to the final stage of their existence.

Advan, however, was given special treatment by Ahm, because of how close they'd grown after centuries of service alongside one another. His physical limitations had increased over recent years, and he was no longer able to perform all the duties he once had, but Ahm had given no hints of terminating the man's employment. The slight curling of his lips and almost imperceptible raising of an eyebrow was all he could muster to show how he felt about having to wake Mina early, but it was enough that she could easily see he didn't enjoy doing it.

She climbed out of bed without argument, despite her discomfort, walked over and gave Advan a hug of reassurance. He'd stopped smiling some time ago, or at least had told his face to rest. Everything he did seemed to drag out like a strange echo. His lips were still curled into that feeble smile several minutes later when his eyes finally registered the fact that she'd long since departed her bedchamber. With a sigh that lasted ten times longer than he intended, he turned and closed the door behind himself as he returned to his other duties.

"You're here early," said Mina as she entered Ahm's office. He looked up from a large sheet of parchment, covered in blue ink; the same parchment he'd had in front of him for the last several weeks.

"I am. There will be no lessons today. Instead, we will be performing an experiment," said Ahm. Somehow he was far older than Advan, yet still looked full of youth. If she didn't know any better, and were passing him on the street, she'd have assumed he was only a few years older than Eros. She wasn't sure whether to attribute that to his magical abilities, or some unknown benefit of his station, but it was something that had always intrigued her. Some part of her still found it hard to believe his claim that he was older than the Kingdom. With his brilliant blonde hair and crystal blue eyes, he was a stark contrast to all the darkness that surrounded them.

"So I'm finally worthy of seeing what you've been working on?" she teased with a smirk.

"Worthy? Probably not," he joked. "It's ready, though, and you're to be my pilot," he answered as he stood.

"Pilot?" she gasped.

"Yes. Pilot," he answered.

"So all this time you've been, what, staring at engineering diagrams for a boat? In the Cryx? Way underground, and far removed from a single body of water?" she asked.

"Who said anything about water?" he asked, smirking pridefully.

"Oh, now I'm intrigued!" she chirped.

"Well, let's get to it then, shall we?" he said as he rounded the desk.

She fell in behind him and matched his stride, completely oblivious to where they were walking in her excitement. "Am I going to drive a Flute? But... I guess it wouldn't *be* a flute if I drove one, because wind can't pass through my bones."

"Stop," sighed Ahm.

"Oh, I know! It's *like* a Flute but it moves on the surface somehow. But... how will it draw power? Is that... is that diagram some kind of magical battery?" she asked.

Ahm stopped and turned toward her. "Look, I love that you're excited, but you're just going to have to wait a *few more seconds* and this will all make sense. Why couldn't you be this happy to learn our politics, or about Ishnu, or Xxrandus? To think, all I had to do was walk around with some mysterious parchment that I wouldn't let you see for a while and you'd get all giddy at the chance to learn what I'd been hiding. Maybe I should have hidden more from you, as I raised you."

"Nah, that's not it. You said 'pilot'. I get to be a pilot," she said, smiling wider than she ever had.

Ahm sighed and resumed his walk, shaking his head. "Here I was worried I'd have to convince you. What I'm asking you to do is quite risky, after all."

"I don't care. I get to be a pilot!"

A few minutes later, Ahm stopped in front of a set of double iron doors that Mina had never seen. She hadn't been paying attention to where they were walking, but instead had been fantasizing about all the different things she could imagine piloting, her eyes affixed to the roll of paper tucked under Ahm's right arm.

He snapped his finger twice to break her out of her train of thought and draw her attention. When she blinked up at him, and finally met his gaze, he explained, "This might seem like a fun adventure to you, but I assure you this is no game. This isn't 'Father Ahm' talking to you right now. This is 'Defense Minister Ahm Stonehawk', got it?"

"Yes," she said, bouncing up and down slightly on the balls of her feet, her hands clasped before her impatiently.

"What I've been engineering is a machine that could help us

fight back, should the Talaani Empire ever regain their strength and come after us," explained Ahm.

"Okay," she said, as her joy slowly faded.

"This is official business, and I've had to do it in secret because the rest of the ministries consider my work a waste of time. So, we have to be careful that no one finds out about this, understood?"

"No one knows about me, so how could they possibly know about whatever this is?" she said, waving her hand at the doors behind him.

"Because," he started as he turned toward the doors and grabbed the handles, "I don't want you to get too excited if this works," he continued as pulled the doors open, "and fly it to the surface," he finished as the device came into view.

"By Ishnu's will! Is it real?" gasped Mina.

"Very real," grinned Ahm.

Perched at the center of the chamber beyond the doors was something Mina could only describe as an enormous iron raven. Its wings splayed out to its sides, covered in feather-shaped, thin sheets of blackened, rune-covered steel. Square, runed tubing made up the bulk of its framing, with gears, pulleys, cables and rods laid out in a confusing array of mechanical wonder, all shaped to look like, and if Ahm's theories were correct, function like a bird.

The runes that covered its surface were exquisitely precise and pulsed a faint blue, like its heart was beating. At the top of the bird's body, near the front, was what appeared to be an inset saddle, of sorts, with slots for the pilot's legs to extend down across the sides, and leather straps for securing the rider in place. She stepped up into the stirrup to look inside, where half a dozen handles poked up out of the machine's false head.

"One thing we've got an infinite supply of in Dusk is time. As a result, we have endless tomes of knowledge about an unreasonable number of topics, just lying around ready to be studied because someone got bored enough to document one trivial thing or another. One such topic happens to be birds; specifically the raven. It's the most common bird found in our lands, so that's not surprising in the least. What is worth noting is that Lord Hapshren was exquisitely detailed in his accounting of how their bodies worked, and the mechanics of how they flew.

"It's all very pointless knowledge in the grand scheme of things, and Hapshren was shunned by the Ministry of Science for 'wasting his time' going to such lengths on the subject. They didn't know, and he of course could have no clue, that what he was actually *doing* was laying the groundwork for a device such as this," explained Ahm.

"This is wonderful!" she said, running her fingertips along a line of runes.

"Should the dragons ever return to their subjects in the Talaani Empire, and should they rise up against Baan'Sholaria, we would be faced with the prospect of battling opponents who can not only fly, but attack us while doing so. Now, I don't presume that this machine, in its current form, could necessarily help us to fight back against them... at least, not yet. It could, however, give us a fighting chance once we perfect it... providing, of course, that it works in the first place," said Ahm.

"How did you come up with this?" she gasped, turning to face him.

"In truth, I didn't. At least, not by myself. Before you were born, there was a heated debate before the Queen between the ministers of that time. I was merely the High Priest of the temple Kesh back then, and only served as an adviser to Lord Palrin, the Minister of Defense. The meeting was only supposed to be the typical, yearly budgetary discussions, but Palrin was adamant that his funding needed to be tripled because he sensed an imminent threat from the north. As you can imagine, this did not go over well," said Ahm.

"No, I expect not," agreed Mina as she tried to imagine Mordessa taking Palrin's declarations kindly.

"The Queen, quite expectedly, put the man in his place, both verbally and physically. It was that altercation which caused my promotion to Minister of Defense, because I was the only one of his advisers that didn't openly support his efforts. Most importantly to this," he said, indicating the flying machine, "is something she said while berating him. 'You sound like the fools of old and their flying machines,' which struck us all as odd, because we'd never heard of such a thing.

"However, since no living soul has any memory of our Kingdom's past, and only knows what the Queen has shared with us, we've been conditioned to take her words as truth. I was left, therefore, to trust her outburst and take it for what it was. That meant accepting the reality that flying machines were not only possible, but had existed at some point in our past," said Ahm.

"So you set out to make them real," said Mina with a smirk.

"Indeed," said Ahm. "I was able to design the frame, outer shell, and overall shape of the machine based solely on Lord Hapshren's drawings. The mechanics of how to make them move properly, that was another thing entirely. Advan was a brilliant engineer in his youth, and contributed a great deal to the ongoing maintenance and enhancements of the Flute system you've heard so much about," explained Ahm.

"That's why you keep him around!" gasped Mina.

"It's part of the reason, yes. He and I worked in secret for years, designing different mechanisms to make the wings move and flex as if this device were a living, breathing raven. His mental faculties slowed enough in recent years that our progress was stalled, and then you came into our lives and distractions took hold. However, since you've been sneaking out at night, I chose to let you believe you were getting away with it, and spend that time working on my machine," said Ahm, his arms crossed in frustration.

Mina felt a cold chill run down her spine. She stammered, struggling to find the right words, but eventually gave up and sulked.

"It's not like I didn't see it coming, Mina. I keep you here to keep you safe, not to make you my prisoner. I knew you'd eventually seek your freedom. I just hoped I'd put enough fear in you by then that you'd be smart about it. By all appearances, you have been thus far," said Ahm. "Nobody's come to my door searching for you, and that's what matters... well, aside from my trust," he scolded.

"I didn't mean to hurt your trust, I just had to see... the world!" gasped Mina in frustration, the tear on her cheek revealing her sadness.

"Why do I keep you here?" asked Ahm.

"You know why!" belted Mina as more tears joined the first.

"I want to hear it from you," said Ahm.

"Because I'm not supposed to exist! I wasn't supposed to be born, and my mother was a criminal, and they'd kill me if they found me!" said Mina.

"That's an oversimplified version of what I told you, but basically true. Do you know what it means, though? Have you figured it out by now?" asked Ahm.

"No. I've always been so frustrated with what I thought you were doing to me that I didn't really spend the time to consider. I *believe* you when you say you're protecting me, but to go to these lengths just doesn't make sense to me. I mean, so *what* if I can see spirits? Why does that matter?" grunted Mina.

"Seeing spirits makes you a Touched, which is indeed something Mordessa fears. Any Touched that are discovered disappear never seen again. Being a Touched is easy enough to hide, though. What you are is much harder to disguise," said Ahm.

"Then why don't you just tell me?" sighed Mina. "What's so *wrong* with me?"

"You are, for lack of a better term, a Forsaken," said Ahm.

"That's what Eros called Mordessa," said Mina as she suddenly fell eerily calm.

"Your mother wasn't so much a criminal as she was Unliving. Your father was Undead. They were both forced, by their families, to take Ascension and tried to sneak away together, which led to your conception. Not only should you never have been born, your mother's pregnancy shouldn't have been possible. You aren't supposed to exist. You can't Ascend as an Ishnite, because your soul is already in the same state we cause through Ascension. You can't become Undead like Xxrandites, because that requires trapping your soul in a phylactery through a very special ritual, and your soul was already born bound to something in a similar way," explained Ahm.

"Bound to what?" asked Mina.

"The Aggripha. The literal and figurative heart of our Kingdom. The very thing that allows us to ascend. It imbues the Ascension rituals of both sects, powers the Flute, and a great many things around the Kingdom. Only certain things can tap into its power; specially enchanted devices, the rituals Mordessa created, and Mordessa herself," said Ahm.

"And me?" asked Mina.

"Quite possibly. That remains to be seen, but my theory says yes," said Ahm. "The sheer possibility that you *could* tap into the Aggripha's power makes you a potential threat to Mordessa's rule."

"Oh, like there's some prophecy that says a Forsaken will overthrow her, or something?" scoffed Mina.

"There is," said Ahm.

"What?" asked Mina, her eyes wide in shock.

"I don't put much stock into prophecies. If I did, I'd have killed you when you were born, like my duty as the Minister of Defense dictates. There are prophecies for everything. As I said, the one thing we're never short of in Dusk is time, and that means way too many people have way too much of it on their hands. Some of them seem to do nothing with it but sit around making up prophecies for every little thing under the sun. It's a path toward madness, really," said Ahm. "However, at the end of the day, it's not safe for Mordessa to discover you exist, so I've kept you hidden."

"And you want me to pilot this device too, apparently," said Mina. "That's going to put me at risk, isn't it?"

"I don't really have a choice if I want it to work. It still might not. Everything depends on your connection to the Aggripha, because that's what supplies the power to make it fly. It's far too heavy to do so on its own, regardless of how accurately it mimics a bird's shape."

"And that's why you finally told me the truth," sighed Mina with a grimace.

"What good would it have done for you to know those finer details sooner? I didn't lie to you, I just didn't share everything. I wanted you to grow up with as close to a normal childhood as possible, all things considered. I'd like to think I did a damned good job at that, I might add," scowled Ahm.

"Fine. Let's get it over with," belted Mina as she stormed past him defiantly.

"Mina Llanthor, you will calm yourself before you proceed, or this is going to escalate in a manner you least prefer," commanded Ahm.

He never used her full name unless he was truly angry. She stopped cold, taken aback by his sudden shift in tone.

"You dare hold anger toward me for not volunteering knowledge to you that you did not need to know, while lying boldly in my face for the past nine and a half weeks about sneaking out to meet a boy near the slopes of Bidlesh Village? I did what I did for your benefit, not mine. You did what you did out of selfishness. I can chalk that up as typical teen angst and rebellion, but I will *not* be talked down to by the young girl I only saved by putting my own eternal existence at risk. What do you think would happen to me the moment they were done with you? Kind words? A quaint little slap on the wrist?" belted Ahm. He did little to hide his anger.

"I'm sorry, father," said Mina as she turned to face him.

"Now, then," sighed Ahm, noticeably calmer, "let's sit and have some tea while we both calm down, shall we?"

"Yes," agreed Mina.

She walked to the table by the door and sat while Ahm fetched the tea. They'd never argued like that, and she was shaken because of it. *Perhaps I'm angry at Ahm for nothing? Am I wrong to feel trapped?* She sighed at her uncertainty and let her emotions take over again. Fresh tears glistened upon her cheek when he returned.

"I'm sorry, Mina, I should never have yelled at you," said Ahm as he poured their drinks. "I've put a lot on the line to keep you safe, but that's no excuse for making you feel this way. I never wanted you to be trapped down here this long. Everything you're feeling is my fault, and I can't take that back or make it go away," he said as he sat. "You were too young to know at the time, but I spent the first ten years of your life looking for a way to mask what you were, so you could go and live a normal life. I even took you with me to visit Lord Whun at his embassy in the Talaani Empire when you were nine, but your attachment to the Aggripha didn't fade. Otherwise, I could have found you a home in Gargoa.

"Truth is, I don't really understand how or why you exist, or what your connection to the Aggripha means. Hells, I didn't even know how strong your bond was until you turned sixteen last year," said Ahm.

"Why then?" she asked, perking up.

"The night you became a woman, when you were in pain, balled up on your bed? Remember, I came to your side, brought you tea, and raced off to find a potion to relieve the pain?" he asked.

"I do. You were gone so long, by the time you returned I felt fine," she said.

"But I wasn't gone that long at all. In fact, I was only gone a few brief seconds," he said.

"What? It felt like forever," she said.

"I exited your room and immediately stopped in the hallway. The ground was glowing, pulsing with blue magic that streaked toward your bed. I turned back into your room and it shot up into your body faster than I could respond," said Ahm.

"What?" gasped Mina.

"It was the Aggripha. You instinctively drew power from it to heal yourself and end your monthly cycle early. Which, by the way, is one hell of a trick. If we could bottle that and ship it worldwide, we'd be infinitely wealthy," said Ahm.

Mina couldn't help but chuckle.

"Women the world over would hail you as a hero. We could call it Mina's Brew," he teased.

"Okay, you can stop," said Mina.

"The point is, you healed yourself of a normal bodily function because it was causing you extreme discomfort, even though a healing potion or spell would have only dulled your pain. Not only that, you did it through your connection to a source of magic you didn't know existed, and you accomplished it instinctively," said Ahm. "That, or the Aggripha is sentient and did it on your behalf, which is slightly more concerning, and thankfully less believable."

"So it's not that you hid everything from me my entire life... but you were learning as I went along," realized Mina.

"That is correct," agreed Ahm.

"I think I'm calm enough now," said Mina.

"Right," he said as he rubbed his hands together. "Let's go over the finer points of the control system, shall we?"

AHM SPENT the better part of an hour explaining how Advan had designed the controls to function. Each lever had a precise function, and a certain range of movement forward, backward, or to the sides. "If you can learn and master these controls, you should be able to make the machine perform all the same movements a raven is capable of. Flying up, down, tilting to turn left, or right, moving forward through the air by thrusting its wings, gliding, and even slowing to a stop and landing," he added.

"There's a lot going on here, Ahm. My hands have to be in like... six places at once," she said as she stared down at the controls. "How is this even supposed to be possible?"

"Let's just try to get it off the ground today, okay? Nothing fancy. No actual flight. Just see if you can get the Aggripha to power it and make it weightless, like we discussed. It should lift off the ground a bit, and then you can set it right back down. No risks, okay?" asked Ahm.

"Yeah, I was pretending I wouldn't have to do that part. I have no clue how to do it. Do I close my eyes and focus? Chant some mystical phrases? Maybe I have to tell her she's a 'pretty bird' and stroke her wings?" she teased with a smirk.

"The lever on the far right, Mina, which I just explained the purpose of. Were you listening?" asked Ahm.

"You just dumped a decade's worth of knowledge about a strange device on me all at once. You're going to have to repeat a few things," she sighed.

"Fine, fine. When you push that lever forward, it's supposed to connect two iron bars at the center of the device, which are each covered in runes that comprise half of a very particular spell. When the rods touch, the spell inscriptions join and it becomes whole. It's a slightly modified version of the same spell that powers the Flute. When that system has to be taken offline for whatever reason, only Mordessa can turn it back on... by connecting a spell in a very similar fashion to this device," said Ahm.

"So when *you* push the lever to connect those rods, it completes the spell, but because you aren't able to draw power from the Aggripha, nothing happens?" asked Mina.

"Precisely," he answered.

"That means if I'm as connected to the Aggripha as you theorize I am, when I push the lever forward, it'll complete the spell but *actually* work, send magical power through the device, and cause it to lift off the ground?" she asked, seeking confirmation.

"Indeed," he said with a smile.

"Fine. Back up and let me see if this thing works. When it doesn't, and you see that I'm not bound to the Aggripha like you think, then maybe you'll let me spend time on the surface during daylight, yes?" she asked.

"Fine. Yes. If that's the case, I'll let you roam free. Hells, I'll even rent you an apartment near Bidlesh," he offered.

With a nod of agreement, she settled fully into her seat and cautiously reached for the lever. As she pushed it forward, she cringed in anticipation of a surge of raw energy. To the surprise of both of them, nothing seemed to happen. She was about to point out how wrong his theories were when the runes all across the mechanical bird erupted into blue flame, and the creaking of steel and iron filled the test chamber.

Ahm took an involuntary step back as the metallic bird lifted off the floor, a low thrum resonating through the room as magical energies swelled and surged within the device's inner mechanisms.

Mina looked back at Ahm with a mixture of elation and fear washing across her face. She could feel the iron and steel beneath her rump, pressed firmly between her legs, but her gut simultaneously felt as if she was falling backward uncontrollably. She lurched forward and grabbed at the controls, fearful that she was about to crash backward, not realizing that the feeling was only in her mind, and that the bird had levitated off the ground and was completely stationary.

Ahm jumped forward and yelled, "No," just as her hands pressed against two of the levers. He hadn't been fast enough.

The great mechanical bird spun to the left and dove beak-first into the granite floor, toppling over itself and throwing Mina across the room. She hadn't expected to be steering the device, and hadn't bothered to strap herself into the seat. Her exit from the device was so abrupt, and forceful, that her impact against the controls as she went past dislodged the power lever, and forced the device to cut off. It landed top-down on the hard granite floor, damaging many of its components in the process.

Ahm rushed to Mina's side. She'd landed face-first on the unforgiving granite and slid several feet before crumpling into a ball against the far wall of the room. Her head, face and neck were severely injured, blood pouring everywhere faster than Ahm could summon his spells. As his healing magics began their work, blue energy coursed across the ground and surged up from below, rushing through her body like a great wind.

The power knocked Ahm backward and lifted Mina off the ground for a few seconds before she slowly came to a rest a few feet from where she'd started. He raced back to her side, but there didn't seem to be anything he could do. Her wounds appeared to be completely healed, and she was breathing, but no matter what he did, he couldn't seem to wake her.

Distraught at his inability to help her, and deeply angered at his insistence she pilot the device, he called out for Advan and settled onto the floor, her head in his lap, to wait for his belabored servant to arrive.

AFTER WATCHING events unfold for several days without moving, Whun finally relaxed his shoulders and let the tension in his magically bound joints ease. Visions of the far off land faded from view in the crystal ball, as the demonic creature on the other end was finally overcome. He let the orb drop into his bony palm and pocketed it before even opening his physical eyes and taking note of who was in the room with him.

"Is the sister going to be a problem, Lord?" asked the head priest.

'She never regained her full strength, and was bested by a young girl, of all things,' answered Whun. His face would have contorted into mild surprise, had he the muscles and skin left with which to produce such a reaction.

"Have you found the Caier? We have searched ourselves and are no closer to f-" started the priest.

'I have sensed one near the area I was watching, but have not been able to pinpoint its location as of yet. Now that the demon is no longer a concern, I will focus all my energies on the pursuit of it... once I rest,' explained Whun.

"We thought you did not rest," said the priest.

'Not for the sake of my body, no. I have, however, expended a great deal of magic these past few days. Even a lich cannot cast spells indefinitely. I must meditate and rest my mind. I must return to full strength, if I am to find the Caier.'

"Very well, Lord. Let us prepare a chamber for you," said the priest.

'There is no need. I will stay here. I have already masked this room from Mordessa's sight,' said Whun.

Nodding their agreement, the priests left and sealed the chamber.

Whun lowered to the floor, releasing the levitation spell that held him aloft. He allowed his body to crumple into a pile of bones, his skull resting on top. With one last spell of his own, he caused the walls and door to fuse together, preventing anyone from entering until he reversed his spell. Exhausted beyond reason, he accepted the darkness into his mind, and allowed himself to fade from existence for a time.

CHAPTER 6:
PROCUREMENT
Ris'Enliss, Ahr'Antaerwyn 6th, 575 of the 1st Era

THE GNOMES of Algona were an odd bunch, and she was absolutely convinced her family was the worst of the lot. At any point, any of her gnomish brethren could have joined human society, moved into any one of the numerous cities available, and contributed to the betterment of their mutual existence. Was that the way of her people? Was that even an option in their tiny little heads? Without a doubt, her answer to both unasked questions was a deep and resounding 'no'.

For some unknown reason, they chose instead to cluster in roving bands of homeless vagabonds and miscreants, wearing brightly colored, mismatched clothes and making a scene every time they crossed paths with normal people. It was as if they all had a meeting one day, a hundred years prior, and decided, 'Hey, let's be as unlikable as possible!'

Maybe that was their defense mechanism, or some misguided form of retaliation against nature for making them so short and pudgy? She'd spent the better part of the past two decades trying to convince innocent bystanders and witnesses that, 'I'm not like them,' and apologizing profusely for how poorly her family behaved in public. For some reason, no matter how much trouble they got into, they just couldn't respect the lives of others, or personal boundaries, or the rule of law. After all, those laws were human, and didn't apply to gnomes, or so her father loved to claim.

There was nothing surprising about Lord Vaelin signing a law from his throne in Gusarski Cove that gave towns the right to kick gnomish vagrants off their land. Just as there was nothing surprising about her entire family making the nearly unanimous decision to move north to Tellrindos in response... and etch rude symbols into trees, roads and signs on their way out.

Thankfully, she'd earned enough of a reputation for herself to stand out from the rest, and be accepted into Menshe and the surrounding villages. It was already cold enough in Algona, and she detested cold weather. She had no interest in moving north, even if that meant she'd be the only gnome left standing in Algona. Maybe she'd earn some good, honest money and pay her way south, where it was warm and nice, and she could rub her toes in the sand on a sunny beach some day.

If the man she was sitting next to was telling the truth, there were gnomes everywhere across the Gargoa, and most of them were nothing like the crazy ones she grew up with. As she sat there, sharing an ale, and hearing tales of gnomish explorers, and gnomish inventions the man had seen in the south, she let her mind wander with visions of what it might be like to someday meet those people, and see those things.

As she slid his coin purse deftly off his waist with a flick of her wrist and a wriggle of her index finger, she smiled blankly up into his eyes and said, "Oh how I wish to travel as you have," in her sweetest, most alluring voice.

He perked up at her response, and began to regale her with details on precisely how she could earn enough money to travel, and where she could go to seek safe passage to the lands along the Shattered Coast, just west of the Kingdom of Haern. She couldn't imagine that a man who barely knew her could be so open and caring, freely giving her advice she hadn't asked for, and providing ample distraction with which she could avail herself of his hard-earned wages.

"I think I do okay for myself," she quipped with a smile, reaching into his coin purse tucked under her waistband and producing a coin to cover the cost of his next ale. She nodded at the bartender and slid the man's coin across the bar dramatically, adding, "his next round is on me."

"Oh, you don't have to do that," he countered, shocked that she would offer to pay for a hardworking man's froth.

"Trust me, you earned it. I'm off to set your plans in motion. I'll be a world traveler the next time you see me. The least I could do is buy you a drink in thanks," she chimed as she slid off the bar stool and dropped to the ground. He almost didn't notice how she ducked her little head to avoid hitting it on the seat on her way down. At the very least, he was kind enough not to mention it.

"I didn't catch your name," he called as she walked away.

"Breela, love. You can call me Breela," she answered with her sister's name.

She stepped outside shortly afterward, and got assaulted almost immediately with a cold gust of air. Winter had arrived, and she had precious little time to move south before snow began to fall, if that's what she planned on doing. With the rest of the gnomish population vacating the area, there was a lot of potential coin free for the taking, with little to no competition left in the game. Everyone loved her sweet little smile so much, it was all a little too easy.

It was her policy never to steal from locals; especially those that lived directly in Menshe. The city was unreasonably small for how important it was to regional travel. Why more folk didn't settle down within its borders and build businesses that catered to wandering merchants and would-be explorers was far beyond her capacity to understand. Far be it from her to turn away the small fortune she could earn in their stead. She knew it would all eventually catch up to her, but she planned to take advantage of the situation for as long as she could manage.

She rented a room at a small cottage just north of town proper, nestled into a copse of trees that seemed to have decided it was too good for the literal forest a few hundred feet away. It was a quaint little place, owned by a very old lady named Nance, who was unfathomably nice to wayward wanderers and misplaced miscreants. She grew her own crops, and only asked for the tiniest bit of help in her efforts. Each of her seven tenants paid her one silver per month for room and board. Even though they had to share two rooms, and often argued about whose turn it was to sleep near Snoring Bill, her rates couldn't be beat anywhere within a week's travel.

Life was just about as good as she could have pictured it... right up until that moment. As she trudged toward Nance's cute little remote cabin, a dark figure came into view off to the side of the path, near the trees. She could handle herself in a fight, if it came down to it, and couldn't recall burgling from any creepy, dark figures in recent days, so the sight of it was more shocking than concerning. Even still, the closer she drew, the more she realized that whoever the dark figure was, they were standing along the path with the explicit intent of awaiting her arrival.

Not one to walk headlong into danger, she turned on her heel to march determinedly back toward Menshe as if she'd simply forgotten something, and hadn't seen the figure there at all. Just as her face came in line with her newly chosen walking direction, the dark figure materialized directly in front of her, so close she could smell the ashy, sulfuric stench of its robes.

She took an involuntary step back out of reflex, stumbled, and landed promptly on her rump with an audible, "Oof!"

"I don't mean to startle, young one, but I have need of your services," said the old woman. The skin on her face seemed like it was far too weak to hang on and would soon fall to the ground. She was ancient, by any measure, and far more frightening up close than she'd been from far away. The table leg she was using as a cane seemed completely out of place in her hand, and brought a bit of levity to the situation in the eyes of the gnome.

"How did you do that?" asked the gnome, more concerned with the strange woman's mode of travel than her appearance.

"Oh, I have my ways. While those ways can get me to many places, they won't allow me to enter into places I have never seen, or obtain the object that I seek. That is where you come in, my dear, and I will pay you handsomely for your assistance," she said.

"Look, I don't know who you think I am, but I don't go around stealing, so whoever sent you to find me is clearly wrong and owes you an apology," said the gnome as she got to her feet.

"Little Gnately Migglesmythe, I know very well who you are. Your mother is very proud of the woman you've become, and was adamant that you were not only the best thief in Algona, but in your family as well," said the woman.

"That doesn't sound like mom at all," laughed Gnately. "Besides, she's long gone. Passed away more than ten years ago."

"I know your name, and still you challenge me? She's no more than a few miles south of Tellrindos, last I saw her; arguing with your father about whether she *really* wanted to move that far north, or head to Uldenheim instead."

"Yeah, that sounds more like her," nodded Gnately.

"Coincidentally, they chose Uldenheim, but I'm not here to discuss your family business. I am here because I need a map; a very particular map, which marks the possible locations of a very particular thing," said the old woman.

"What thing?" asked Gnately, her curiosity piqued.

"Oh, nothing for someone like you to trifle with. Just a large, black tower made from a single piece of stone that some say appears and disappears at different locations across the land of its own accord."

"Oh, you mean the Obsidian Spire!" gasped Gnately.

"You've heard of it?" asked the old woman.

"No," answered Gnately firmly as she turned to walk to the cabin. The old woman materialized in front of her again.

"It goes by many names, and Obsidian Spire is indeed one of them, strangely enough. Regardless, I care not if you know the thing I seek, only that you can acquire the map that I need to find it," said the woman.

"Fine. How much?" asked Gnately.

"Is it really coin that you're after?" asked the old woman.

"Yes?" said Gnately, intrigued that the woman would think otherwise.

"Well, if that's the case, this will be cheaper than I thought," chuckled the woman.

"Fine, what *should* I be asking for?" asked Gnately.

"This stone," said the woman as she produced a small, highly polished pink and white stone in the palm of her right hand.

"What on Ayrelon would I do with a pebble?" gasped Gnately.

"Nothing now, but it will be quite useful in your future," assured the woman.

"Fine. I'll do the job, and take your little polished pebble, but I want ten gold as well," declared Gnately. "Five up front, five after the job is complete."

"What's the current conversion rate between gold and silver, young one?"

"Why? Do you need to pay in silver?"

"Oh no, not at all. I have gold. It's just that I'm remembering too many timelines right now, and can't be sure which reality I'm in."

Gnately looked at the woman like she'd just grown seven heads.

"Never you mind. Ten gold it is," she said, waving off Gnately's concern.

"Um... okay? It's three hundred and fifty to one, in Algona, but only if the coins are Tellrindosian. Haern coins are worth far less unless you melt them down," said Gnately as she came to her senses.

"Just the information I needed. Here's your down payment to get you started," she said as she offered five gold coins. "The map I need should be in the possession of the Lord of Dereign Hold."

"Thanks," said Gnately as she took them. "Hey, um... since you're all mysterious and can go all over the place whenever you want, how do I find you when the job is done?"

"Just look into the shadows and call my name. I'll be listening."

"What name would that be?" she asked.

"Nightweaver," said the woman as she faded into nothingness.

"Okay, what the fuck just happened?" Gnately asked no one in particular.

She didn't enjoy the rest of her walk home, as her mind raced with all the possible ways the job could end poorly. Neither did she enjoy lying awake all night to the sounds of Snoring Bill as she tried to think of a way to get into Dereign Hold without being caught.

GNATELY FELT more than a little out of place in her present company. She sat atop a stack of books piled onto a chair, kicking her feet mindlessly as she fidgeted with her far-too-large mug of ale, peering around the crowded courtyard. *Yep... definitely don't belong here*, she thought as she hefted the mug in both hands and took a frothy sip.

The occupants of Dereign Hold were celebrating the end of another relatively peaceful year in Algona, and had invited a group of soldiers from nearby Ulthran. In the midst of all the comings and goings through nearby Menshe, she'd managed to sneak herself in under the guise of being a servant of one very drunk ambassador from Uldenheim, who was happily snoring away in an ale-induced haze, slumped over the table across from her. None of the other guests were aware that she'd been the cause of his intoxication, and that suited her just fine.

It'd been two weeks since she took the job from Nightweaver, and had been hard at work trying to find a legitimate reason to gain entry to Dereign Hold ever since. It hadn't been easy, considering she had no chance at all of passing herself off as a guard. She had briefly considered trying to disguise herself as one of the guards' children, and pretending to be lost and injured, but her girth finally dissuaded her. More to the point, the size of children's clothing sold in Menshe's only clothing store made the ploy impossible.

She'd never been inside a Keep, and for some reason had always expected more from the experience. The party raged in the courtyard, surrounded on three sides by a wooden fence made from spiked logs, lashed together and buried a few feet into the ground. To the rear of the complex stood a wide stone tower no more than three human stories tall. The only other buildings were a small wooden barracks, and a poorly maintained stable capable of holding no more than six horses. After seeing the fortifications in person, she had to wonder why she'd bothered with such an elaborate plan to gain entry... she could have snuck in without the ruse and saved herself some trouble.

With the party all around her, she was forced to either find a way to sneak into the tower unseen, or wait until most, if not all, of the guests passed out, like her supposed 'Master' had done shortly after their arrival. Things being as they were, she was most thankful that none of the other soldiers had taken Sir Ganreth seriously when he kept randomly turning to her and asking, 'Who are you, again?' A simple smile and playful, 'oh stop,' had made his question seem like a familiar joke between old friends, and thankfully, no one became the wiser.

She wasn't sure how long she would have to wait. It was rare for the soldiers garrisoned in Dereign to make their way to Menshe, and even rarer for them to visit the small town's single tavern in search of drink. It was even rarer still that old Mr. Dohniger would let her wait tables or tend bar; those nights were usually reserved for when he'd had too much of his own ale to do the job without toppling. She had, therefore, had little opportunity to serve the soldiers ale, or witness their tolerance for herself.

"And what's your name, little one?" barked a gruff, middle-aged man as he thumped his half-empty mug onto the table. More than a little of his ale sloshed out of the cup onto his hand as it landed, but he didn't seem to notice, or care.

"Gnately, my Lord," she answered, her voice sounding very tiny amidst the din.

"Good to meet you, Natelly," he said, finishing his sentence with a choked-back hiccup.

"No, Guh-nat-elly. It starts with a G," she corrected, trying to sound as playful as she could.

"Oh, well, *pardon me*, lass," he joked before knocking back another swig of his ale. He then pointed his mug at the man passed out before her and asked, "this yours?"

"Sir Ganreth has had a rough week, and couldn't resist relieving his stress earlier today. I'm not sure he even realizes we arrived at this wonderful party, but gods know he deserves a break," she said with a nod to accentuate her point.

"That right? You carry him here on your own, did ya?"

"His carriage did, ya *dolt*. I'm barely big enough to pick up this ale, as you can clearly see," she said as she hefted it.

"All that drink for little ole you, eh? I think you'll drown before you finish it," he said with a laugh.

"Oh, aye! But I'll do my best to try, all the same."

"Yeah? You had a rough week too? Peaceful as the land's been, I can't fathom what stress *poor Sir Ganreth* could've been through," he said mockingly.

"Well, it's none of my business—I mean, I only tend to him when he travels—but it seems to me his wife's been seeing someone else. It's quite the talk in Uldenheim, and the poor man only found out a few days ago."

"That's a shame," said the man. He raised his mug in a toast of sympathy to the passed out Lord, then tossed the empty vessel onto the table, sending it skittering across and to the ground on the other side.

"Rumors say her mister was someone from Dereign, right here among the lot of you." She was usually quite adept at fabricating tales out of nowhere, but was beginning to wonder if she wasn't taking things a bit too far. *It's too late to take it back now. I've got to see where this goes, I guess.*

"What's that?"

"Aye. It's a pity, really. You all seem a nice lot. That's why he traveled all the way here from Uldenheim, though; to confront the man."

"He say who it was?" His brow wrinkled in what seemed to be a mixture of anger and frustration.

"Didn't mention a name to me, I'm afraid. Like I said, it's not really my business. I don't think he was aware that I knew. He brought me along to tend his clothes and make him meals on the road, nothing more."

"My brother's wife ran off with a man from Faerenia, the lousy wench. It ain't right what people do at times. He's off serving our Lord, and she sees fit to take to bed with some silver-tongued fop in a fancy tunic? If I'd gotten my hands on that prick," he said, letting his words trail off. His face contorted in anger at the thought, and his ale was getting the better of him. He took a moment to stare off into the distance, as if leering at the culprit, and barely broke out of his thoughts in time to wipe a bit of drool from his lower lip. "Sorry, lass, ain't no man should have to go through that."

"Oh, I agree. Look," she said, sliding her ale toward him, "you need this more than I do. This is a celebration! Your garrison held the fort for a full year without being attacked or overrun. You shouldn't be troubled by the poor decisions of a man with no scruples."

He took the mug and nodded while she talked, then gave her a confused glance. "Scruples?"

She rolled her eyes and laughed ever-so-slightly. "Yes, 'scruples'. That little thing at the back of your mind that warns you when you're about to do something stupid, or wrong?"

"Ah, right," he said, nodding. He took a long draw of her ale, wiped his mouth and nodded again. "Yeah, man ain't got no scruples if he lies with another man's wife. Especially one from Ulthran. They're our brothers... that shit could start a war."

"Aye, it could. Especially since Sir Ganreth is an Ulthran ambassador."

The man went stark white. "We have to find the fucker! Fast!

Before he wakes!"

"You think?"

"Aye!" he drank another mouthful of ale, slammed the mug onto the table and turned to face the rest of the party. As he started yelling accusations at random men about the crowd, the minstrels stopped playing, and the little gnome girl slid off the pile of books, down out of the chair and into the sea of hips and legs.

Gnately acquired two boot daggers from random soldiers as she weaved among the crowd, too short and quiet for anyone to notice with all the arguing going on behind her. She slid the daggers behind her belt, one at each side, and worked her way toward the large door of the Keep. She looked back at the bottom of the stairs and watched for a moment as the crowd surged toward the burly man, throwing accusations of infidelity and dishonorable conduct. With a chuckle at her cleverness, she turned and ascended the steps.

The door was quite large; far bigger than a human needed it to be, as far as she was concerned. Inset into the bottom of the door, however, was a much smaller one, which she assumed existed for the benefit of their hounds. She let out a very faint, playful 'yip', then got down on her knees and pushed her way through while stifling a laugh.

Once inside, she stood and took note of her surroundings. The entire first floor of the building was one large chamber. It was filled with tables and chairs in the center, while shelves, crates, and barrels lined most of the walls. At the center of the far wall was a great hearth, its fire raging. Lanterns hung from small hooks at intervals on each wall, and several banners and flags filled the gaps between them.

On the far left was a set of wooden stairs leading up to the next level. The opposite side had a similar railing, indicating that there was a route down to rooms below ground. She was intrigued by the discovery of a basement level. Either Nightweaver hadn't known that detail, or had decided it wasn't relevant enough to share.

Well, she did say I would find the map in the commander's possession, and commanders usually reside on the top floor. Maybe she didn't feel the basement was important.

With a shrug, she turned toward the stairs on the left and walked toward them, her palms resting on the pommels of her new daggers. She stopped just shy of the stairs, a little off to the side, and leaned in to look up at them. There didn't seem to be anyone in view, or anyone's shadows moving along the wall from her vantage point. After a few seconds, she proceeded up the stairs, hunched over slightly, next to the rail.

She stopped again before reaching the top, just high enough to stand up and look through the railing. The second floor had a central hallway that ran the entire width of the building and led to another set of stairs on the far side. The walls to the left and right contained several doors, which she assumed were bed chambers for higher-ranking officials, or set aside for important visitors.

Gnately continued onto the second floor and crept as quietly as she could to the far side. She didn't know if anyone was trying to sleep in one of the rooms on that level, and didn't want to risk finding out. Once she reached the other set of stairs, she ascended them in the same manner as before.

The stairs let out into a small audience chamber on the top floor. Padded leather chairs sat in a small circle atop a collection of animal furs, all surrounding a small round table carved from the trunk of a very large tree. The walls around the chamber were lined with lanterns and tapestries, each depicting a portion of the history of Algona. The middle of the far wall opened into a hallway.

She made her way around the room, avoiding the soft fur rugs so as not to leave her tiny footprints impressed upon them. In the hallway, there was one door on the left, one on the right, and a set of double doors at the far end.

The first door was plain and hung an inch above the floor. Its bottom edge was chipped and worn from being frequently kicked with booted feet. She knelt down and reached her hand toward the thin opening, and could feel a slight breeze coming in through the room's window. The faint rush of air smelled of oils and burned herbs. *That must be the commander's prayer room*, she decided.

The door across the hall hung similarly, but furs were rolled around its bottom edge and affixed to the door with hooked nails. They provided an extra seal for the door, to help reduce noise and airflow between the interior and the rest of the floor. *And that must be his bedchamber*, she surmised.

Her quick inspection confirmed the obvious; the room at the end of the hall was the commander's office. She made her way over and studied the latch. There was a small keyhole under the right handle, but the left was bare. The doors didn't seal completely in the middle, and she could see a thin stream of moonlight coming through the thin gap. A small bar crossed the gap behind the door, at about the same height as the keyhole.

The locking mechanism is on the back of the door, she surmised. *That means the lock is too far back from the front of the door for my picks to reach*, she sighed. Frustrated, she walked back to the prayer chamber door and stood facing it. She closed her eyes and thought about her journey through the building and the placement of the door in front of her. After a few moments, she opened her eyes and nodded, sure that the room beyond was at the back of the Keep and wasn't visible from the courtyard below.

She tried the latch on the door, and it opened easily. *Yeah, why would you lock a prayer chamber*, she chuckled. There were two windows at the back of the room, each a few feet off the floor. Both were framed in wood, enclosing panes of glass. They hung from hinges to allow them to swing outward, so that the room could be aired out after prayer concluded. Neither of the windows sealed properly, nor did they lock.

Gnately closed the door behind her and moved over to the window on the right, closest to the commander's office. She pushed the window open and stood on her toes, looking for a ledge or any other way to cross between windows. The exterior wall was perfectly flat, all the way to the ground. Frustrated, she dropped back onto her heels with a sigh.

Even though she was certain it wouldn't work, she made her way back to the double doors and retrieved her picks to try the lock. As she expected, the picks were too short to reach the locking mechanism behind the door. She grunted in frustration as she pocketed the picks and turned to leave, defeated.

"Nightweaver's not gonna like this," she muttered under her breath.

The hallway suddenly grew brighter, as if the shadows were fading from existence and the only thing nature could do was flood the area with more light. A faint hissing sound filled the air, echoing ever-so-slightly off the walls. Gnately squinted her eyes and lifted her hands in front of them out of reflex, to shield them from the intense glow. When the bright light faded and she opened her eyes again, Nightweaver was standing in front of her, calmly gripping her table-leg cane.

"H... How?" gasped Gnately, her voice quivering with hints of fear.

"I only needed your eyes, my dear. I cannot travel to a place if I've never seen it. Now, step aside," she urged with a wave of her ancient hand.

The woman's appearance was still as off-putting as it had been the last time Gnately had seen her. A long mop of mottled gray hair hung loosely atop her unreasonably old face. Her hunched back and stiff knees forced her to use a cane to walk, and for some reason, the old hag had selected a table leg for such a purpose. There was something terrifying about her presence, as if she shouldn't exist and was holding the cycle of life at bay by sheer force of will.

Gnately took a step back and made room for the old woman to pass. Her dirty black robe dragged the floor behind her sickeningly, clumped with mud, some kind of dark ash, and bits of hair. When she reached the double doors, she shifted the make-shift cane into her left hand and raised her right to touch them. She closed her eyes and began muttering something very faintly in a language Gnately couldn't understand, then abruptly took a step back.

The wood of the doors began to age extremely quickly before their eyes, and appeared as if they were being eaten away like a log lying on the forest floor for countless years. The locking mechanism fell to the floor with a clank, followed quickly by the handles, key mechanism and nails. After a few seconds, all that was left was a line of pulpy dust and metal.

"What the–" started Gnately instinctively. She tried to catch the words before they escaped, but failed. Fear, thankfully, prevented her from completing her sentence.

"Now fetch me the map, deary. I'm too old to crawl around on my knees searching," said the woman. Her face seemed to contort into a reassuring smile, but to Gnately, that only made her more menacing.

Why wasn't I this scared of her back in Menshe, she asked herself? *Oh right! Because she didn't appear out of thin air and melt a door!*

Gnately hopped over the pile of debris at the doorway and ran to the back of the large table toward the shelves along the far wall. She grabbed a long wooden tube and checked inside to find that it was empty. Thankful to have the container, she then proceeded to grab every long roll of paper and every exposed map that she could find. She rolled each one as tightly as she could in a single pile and slid them all into the empty tube. After affixing the wooden cap and securing its leather straps, she walked over and extended the tube toward the old woman.

"Well done, lass," she said. They exchanged the tube of papers for five gold coins and the small, polished pebble.

Gnately looked down to put her reward in her purse, saying, "After this, I don't think I'm safe in Algo–" her words trailed off as the room brightened and dimmed, leaving an empty void where the woman had been standing. "Na," she said, finishing her sentence. "Guess I'll just find my own way out."

After making her way back through the Keep, she found herself at the huge exterior doors again. She got down on her hands and knees at the small hound door, and slowly pushed the door forward on its upper hinges. The crowd in the courtyard had apparently devolved into physical threats and bravado, leading them to encircle two of the men. The men paced around each other, sidestepping their way across the bit of open ground the crowd had left them, while cheers of support and boisterous taunts erupted from the throng.

Gnately pushed herself through the door and regained her feet. She checked her immediate surroundings to see that there was no one nearby, then made her way toward the stables.

"I ain't touched no Ulthran whores!" yelled one of the circling men defensively.

"That's all you do is dip your wick, you good for nothing liar!" returned the burly man from earlier.

Fists started flying, the sound of flesh impacting flesh cutting through the cheers of the crowd as she started to climb the outer wall of the stables. Her ascent was easy enough, considering the shoddy construction of the small structure, the many gaps in the wooden slats, and overdone exterior supports. She gave another glance at the crowd before moving to the back wall once she was on top.

She wasn't looking forward to the twelve-foot drop to the ground on the other side of the wall, but she knew there was no way she was getting past the soldiers amassed in the courtyard, or through the gates, with the drunken argument she'd inspired still raging. She turned around and slowly lowered herself down the wall as far as her arms would allow, then released her grip.

As she fell, she twisted in the air to face the open field, bent her knees slightly and braced for impact. The balls of her feet hit the ground first, and she allowed herself to crumple forward and roll. The force of the landing drove her knees upward and almost hyper-extended her hip. The wind was knocked out of her as her rotund belly gave way to her thighs, but other than that, she sustained no lasting damage from the fall.

With her ego a little worse for wear, she picked herself up and started jogging toward Menshe. After a few minutes, she stopped cold in her tracks. "They know damned well I came from Menshe in the company of Sir Ganreth. I can't go back. Soon as the commander heads upstairs, he'll see the melted doors and sound the alarm. Then they'll notice me missing and ride straight to Menshe and search for me. Fuck," she admonished herself. "Double fuck!"

She thought about where she was in relation to towns and fortifications. The road led southwest toward Menshe, where it met with another heading east to Gusarski Cove, or south toward the plateau. In the other direction, the road went back past Dereign, and then north in a meandering course toward the border of Ulthran and Algona, near Uldenheim. Most honest merchants used the Northern Byway, but that was several days' travel west, through woods she wasn't very familiar with.

My only options are Ulthran or Tellrindos, and both lie to the north, she sighed to herself. With a grunt of disagreement at the situation she'd left herself in, she crossed the road to the far side, and started north, hugging the trees to avoid detection by the soldiers in Dereign when she passed.

The night seemed to take an unbearably long time to transition into day. She spent half the night jogging, and the other half walking, all the while chastising herself and fighting to ignore her growing hunger. It wasn't like her to go more than a few hours without a meal, and there she was walking to far-off lands without supplies in the dead of night with winter in full swing.

"Well... at least it's not snowing," she muttered... just as a flake landed on her bulbous nose. "Figures..."

CHAPTER 7

ADVERSITY

Ris'Nammlil, Ahr'Antaerwyn 20th, 575 of the 1st Era

INATELY HAD walked for the better part of a week. After eating snow to get water, and handfuls of berries whenever she could find them, she was completely over the thought of traveling the wilds any further; especially without proper supplies. She was quite thankful, though, that the men from Dereign hadn't bothered to travel north in search of her. She wasn't sure she'd have been able to resist the urge to surrender just for the sake of obtaining a meal and a warm prison cell to sleep in.

On top of the lack of sustenance, she hadn't slept since the night before her adventure in Dereign. Exhaustion was getting the better of her, and she wasn't sure she could keep going for much longer. She stopped for a moment and leaned over to put her hands on her knees, burying her face nose deep in snow.

"Gods damn it!" she grunted as she stood back up. She pressed her hands into the small of her back and turned around. The trench she'd left in the snow behind her was almost enough to make her laugh, if she weren't so tired.

She stood for a moment and wondered just how far she'd made it. Mureketh was supposed to be a few days' walk north. While she freely admitted that at three and a half feet tall her stride wasn't very impressive, she was growing angry at the snow for having the nerve to fall and impede her progress. The ground cover had varied wildly during her journey, depending greatly upon the amount of canopy that stretched over the road, and how the wind was blowing. She'd tried the underbrush for a time, as there was decidedly less snow beneath the trees, but between the bushes, branches, brambles and other hazards, she'd made even less time amidst the wood; especially considering she wasn't tall enough to step over most of it.

"Why did I choose north? I don't like north," she sighed as she turned back around and resumed her walk. "My family moved north. I could have gone with them. 'No,' I said. 'I don't like the snow,' I said. Yet here I am, digging *trenches* in the snow, running north to avoid capture because I tried to make a little coin!"

Just as she uttered the word 'coin', the woods opened up into a field. The sun glaring off the snow was nearly blinding. She squinted and shielded her eyes with her right arm. Several brown buildings stood amidst the sea of white before her, thin lines of smoke rising into the sky above them.

"Oh thank the gods," she sighed.

She quickened her pace as best she could, leaving the expected trench behind her as she moved. *There won't be any hiding where I came from, that's for sure.*

AN HOUR later, Gnately found herself on the main street of a town named Mureketh. Small buildings lined the street on both sides, each serving a different purpose for local residents and weary travelers. The only one she cared about was the tavern just ahead on her left. The road was mostly clear of snow, having been swept away or trodden down by the passing of various feet and hooves.

Two horses stood tethered to the rail outside, the trough before them steaming slightly, having recently been filled with boiling water. They clopped their hooves into the ground as she approached, snorting in her general direction. She absentmindedly reached up and patted one on the snout as she went by, her only concern being reaching the hearth she could smell burning within the establishment.

The outer door of the Weeping Elk was quite exquisite for such a remote and insignificant town. Several panes of ornate stained glass made up its center, depicting a giant elk standing in a field with a single tear descending its cheek as two more of its kind lay slain just off in the distance.

"Well, that's a tad gruesome," she muttered as she reached up. The latch was at face level for her, and clearly designed for humans to use. As she pushed the door open, a subtle warmth washed over her, accompanied by the smells of fresh stew, roast potatoes, bread and yeast-laden ale.

She immediately crossed the room, weaving between chairs and tables, and proceeded directly to the roaring fire in the far right corner. With a wet plop, she dropped onto her bum next to the welcome inferno and went to work at removing her sopping wet boots.

"Oh, my dear! Did you walk all the way here?" asked a very kind older woman. She seemed to be the tavern's owner, or was at least working there in some capacity or another.

"Not by choice," said Gnately. "A moose spooked my pony as I was packing him up and he scampered off into the woods. Left me without food or bedding, hip-deep in snow and days from anywhere warm." Sometimes she couldn't help herself; the lies spilled out just as readily as an exhale.

"Oh, you poor thing! Let me help you," said the woman. She knelt and took over the task of unbuckling the little straps that held Gnately's boots fast. After a few moments, and a few soggy plops of clothing on stone later, Gnately's little gnomish feet were bare and pointed toward the fire.

"Thank you so much, my Lady."

"Oh, I'm no 'Lady'. My name's Francine, and you're welcome to my hearth," she said as she gave Gnately a reassuring pat on the head. "It's been many-a-year since we've had a gnome pass through town. You'll be quite the spectacle."

"Great," sighed Gnately. *Now when Dereign comes calling, everyone will remember me passing through.*

"I'll go get you something to eat. You get warm."

"Thank you, Francine. Name's Gnately, by the way. I can pay you once my hands warm up a bit. I'm still a little too chilled to go digging for coins just yet."

"Oh nonsense. You've been through enough. Besides, I cooked too much anyway. It'll just go to waste if you don't eat your fill," she said with a smile. Her face was slightly wrinkled and framed with gray hair. It lit up when she smiled and gave her a very warm and welcoming visage.

Gnately thought she looked dramatically young compared to Nightweaver. She suddenly felt like Francine was the nicest person she'd ever met. "Well, that's very kind of you."

Francine stood and went back to the kitchen without another word.

Gnately sat for a time, wiggling her toes intermittently as the fire slowly warmed her feet. The patrons of the Weeping Elk were lost in their own conversations, and seemingly hadn't noticed her arrival. That was until Francine returned with a wooden tray covered in food and delivered it to the hearth instead of a table. As she knelt and placed the food next to the fire, the tavern grew dead silent, just in time for Gnately's tiny voice to ring out as she said, "Thank you!"

"Someone bring their kid in here?" belted a man, followed by a round of laughter.

"Be nice, Brannik," retorted Francine. She stood and patted Gnately on the head again. "Pay them no mind. Eat up, your body needs it."

Gnately focused on the tray of food, ignoring the random jokes and insults being tossed into the air by Brannik, who was apparently a town favorite. Francine had prepared for her a small bowl of rabbit stew, an elk steak, two roast potatoes, and a hearty hunk of bread. To round out the meal, she'd also included a half pint of ale, served in a cup that was just the right width for Gnately's gnomish hands. Even the utensils had been presented thoughtfully, and were small enough for her to hold comfortably. *She must serve children here often. That, or she fancies gnomes a little too much.*

She wasn't sure if the cook was the best in the land, or if it was the fact that she hadn't had a meal in several days, but in either case she was having a hard time eating the meal slowly enough to swallow it properly. Everything she tasted was just about as perfect as she could've imagined, and she was very happy that she was eating alone. Otherwise, she was certain she'd have disgusted whoever was sitting across from her. *Manners be damned, this is amazing,* she groaned to herself.

Gnately had almost finished her meal when two young men walked over. They stood just off to her side and watched with eager grins as she grabbed the last hunk of her bread and tore a piece off with her teeth. She caught sight of them just as she began to chew the fluffy morsel, and promptly froze.

"Yes?" she asked through the food in her mouth.

"Told ya it were a gnome," said one of the men.

"I thought me pappy were crazy, talkin' of little folk livin' nearby. Ain't never seen one afore," said the other.

Gnately gulped her bread back without chewing it all the way in her rush to respond, causing more than a little pain in her throat. "I'm not an 'it'," she retorted.

"By the gods, it's a girl!"

Gnately grinned back at them. "What is this, some kind of sport? *'Tease the freezing Gnome who's trying not to die of frostbite?'*

Do you keep score? And if so, what's the over under, so I can place a bet?" she said, half angry, half intrigued.

"Oh, she's a feisty one!"

"Leave her be," said Francine from the bar with a sigh.

"She's fine, Francy," said one of the men.

"There you are!" came a new voice. It was distinctly higher pitched than the other men.

Gnately spun on her bum to see who had just arrived. Just behind the two men stood an elf with black skin and hair wearing black leather armor covered in straps with a small Algonan badge on his left breast; his brown eyes affixed firmly on her own.

"I was wondering when you'd arrive," said the elf. He pushed through the confused men and knelt beside Gnately. "Let me help with your things," he said as he picked up her boots and socks. "I've a table just over there." He nodded his head to the other side of the bar, where a second hearth was blazing.

She nodded at the elf in thanks, and quietly followed him past the rows of tables and their human occupants, all watching in stunned silence. Whispers sprang up around the room as they arrived at his table. He casually put his satchel on one of the chairs and bid her to sit. She climbed up and sat with her back to the hearth; her bum resting atop the soft contents of his satchel.

"Another round of ale?" the elf called to Francine. By the time their drinks were delivered, the tavern's patrons had returned to their private conversations and were no longer paying their gnomish guest any mind.

"Thank you. That was quite annoying." Gnately took a sip of her drink and gave the elf a smile, silently hoping he wasn't there to arrest her.

"I'm sorry I didn't notice you sooner. We both stand out like sore thumbs in a town like this, so I know how their reactions can be. Thankfully, they seem a little scared of me, so they keep their distance."

"Well, to be fair, you do kind of look like you're dressed to slit their throats and take their coin. That, or arrest them," she said with a wink.

"Arrest them... oh this?" he said, pointing to the badge. "Oh, no," he laughed. "I'm not with the Algonan guard. I bought this from them a few weeks back. To your other point, it's hard *not* to look like a ruffian when you're Dynar; at least in *their* eyes. In Quaan'Shala, we all dress this way. Well... except the day guard and farmers, they usually wear white or tan."

"I don't think I've ever heard of that place before, let alone know where it is," said Gnately.

"It's west of the Mythaeil Mountains in what the humans refer to as 'the Badlands'. We live at the edge of a savanna. Quaan'Shala is built mostly into the sides of several ravines over the forks of the Arashyvi River. Most of our people sleep through the day and work at night. Only those whose job requires the sun are awake during daylight hours... well, and the guard tasked with protecting them."

"That sounds so much better than what's outside right now. Well, it sounds warm, at least. What brings you to the north, of all places?" she asked, wrinkling her brow at the thought of leaving a savanna to come to a tundra.

"Poor life choices," he chuckled.

"Oh, I'll drink to that!" she agreed with a laugh. She raised her mug. He followed suit, and they drank to their mutual misfortune.

"Name's Tavyn," he said.

"Gnately," she answered with a smile.

"Was Mureketh your destination, or are you heading elsewhere?"

"I'm getting out of this town as soon as I get some sleep and find a pony."

"Sounds about right. I was going to head west and find my way through the Mythaeil pass, but from what I've been hearing, that journey is suicide," he said.

"Oh, aye! That trip would take you right through Toor lands, and trust me... you don't want that. Anyone wise avoids them."

"So I've been told. I would've caught a ship from Gusarski Cove, but Lord Vaelin closed the port. They received word of an impending attack from Gulthara, so they've been preparing for that. No ships in or out for the foreseeable future, and no trade vessels allowed to pass the coast."

"Which means you're land-locked with no route home," said Gnately.

"Precisely," said Tavyn. "Not that I'm specifically trying to head home, but it would be nice to know I had the option."

"Well, I'm headed further north; probably to Tellrindos. I don't *want* to keep trudging through the snow, but I don't have many options left. My people moved away a little while back, and I foolishly decided to stay behind and make my own way in Menshe; a town not much larger than this. Needless to say, it didn't quite work out. Maybe you could tag along? Port Gandraias isn't that far north of the border. You might be able to find a ship there."

"I just might do that. I hear there's a larger population of Dynar to the north, so I might not be as much a spectacle there. But I don't know how anyone's sailing south until Algona gives up on their blockade."

"You can catch a ship to Pelrigoss, I'm sure. Algona can't blockade the entire Hystari, surely."

"Only one way to find out," he said with a smile.

"Companions then?"

"For as long as you can tolerate me, or until I find a ship. Whichever comes first," he said, nodding.

"Well, I don't mean to be rude, but I haven't slept in almost a week. Part of me isn't even sure if you're real or a strange dream. So, I need to find a room."

"I have a room across the street behind the leather shop. I managed to bag an elk during my journey from Gusarski Cove, and brought a hide into town with me for trade. He offered me a place to sleep for a few nights while I got my bearings. There's a small wood stove in the back and a bedroll next to it with your name on it, if you're interested."

"What about you?"

"Elves don't really sleep once we reach adulthood. It's more a form of deep meditation. I can do that sitting along the wall. However, for tonight, I'll stay here so you can disrobe and dry those clothes."

"What about when the tavern closes?"

"It doesn't. Francine will leave eventually and her husband will take over and start preparing for dawnfry."

"Well, if that's the case, I need to get these boots back on and head over."

"Sleep as long as you need. I'll check around and see if anyone is selling mounts in the meantime," he said as he slid her his key.

"Thank you for everything."

"Think nothing of it. I'm just glad to meet a fellow outcast," he said with a chuckle. "It's nice to have someone to talk to that isn't automatically judgmental, even if they are almost two feet shorter than I," he added teasingly.

"Barely a foot and a half, you jerk!" she laughed.

With a smile and a nod of thanks, Gnately slid from her chair and retrieved her boots. She stepped into them haphazardly and excused herself from their table without another word, sleep the only thing on her mind.

TWO DAYS north of the town of Mureketh, Gnately and Tavyn found themselves confronted with a minor dilemma. They could either change direction, move further east into the field, and clear enough snow to make camp, or descend the hill to the west and introduce themselves to the large party already camped in that location.

"I hate clearing snow," moaned Gnately. "Can't we just ask to join their camp?"

"That means talking to strangers, and clenching our weapons all night in distrust," countered Tavyn.

"Does not! Who says we can't trust them?" asked Gnately, even though she already knew the answer.

"If we do this, I can't meditate because I'll need to spend all night watching to make sure you're safe. If we don't do this, I still can't meditate because I'd be worried all night that they'd sneak over to our *very obvious* campfire and steal from us. So, I lose with either choice. This really comes down to whether or not you want to answer stupid questions all night, and put up with them teasing you for being a gnome," he said.

"They already cleared snow for their camp," Gnately started, counting her points on the stubby little fingers of her left hand dramatically. "They already have a fire going. Someone's already stirring something in the pot hanging *over* that fire. Joining them means we don't have to do all that work ourselves, which saves us time now *and* in the morning, since we won't have to pack anything up. More importantly, I..." she paused for a moment, double-checking her fingers, "...forgot my last point, but you see where I'm going with this, yes?"

"Sure," said Tavyn with a smirk.

"They can call me all the names they want if they feed me and let me warm these frozen toes by that fire, especially if I don't have to do any of the work for it!" she stated determinedly.

"You are so unlike me. I don't know whether that fact is refreshing or frustrating, but I think I'm teetering between the two at the moment," he stated.

"Well, teeter your rump towards the one that gets me warm, fat and happy the quickest," she quipped as she snapped her pony's reins.

A few minutes later, one of the larger men from the camp stood and started closing the distance with long, determined strides. Gnately and Tavyn slowed their pace and tried to seem as harmless as possible, which wasn't easy when one of them was wearing black leather armor, and the other a mixture of chain, scale and leather. They seemed fit for war, or at least a minor scuffle.

"Ho there," called the man. He raised his left hand in greeting, but his right rested safely atop the pommel of his war axe.

"Well met, traveler," said Tavyn. "Might we join you for the night?" he asked as the three stopped a few feet from one another.

"We were about to select a campsite and saw the glow of your fire. Didn't seem right to camp right next to ya, or cast strange glances across the road all night," chuckled Gnately as awkwardly as she'd ever spoken.

"Aye, we've plenty of ground to spare, and might could spare some stew, if ya fancy it. S'long as ya stow those blades and keep your thievin' ways in check," said the man. His bushy brown beard and mustache shifted slightly as he curled his lips into a smile.

Gnately's tension eased at the realization he was teasing them. "S'long as you don't try to use that axe on our necks, we'd welcome your fire, and your food," she answered with a smile of her own.

"Come on down, then," he said with a wave of his hand as he turned. "Benry ain't the best cook 'round these parts, but it sure beats wasting away. And if it means I don't have to get my own hands dirty," he chuckled.

"I was literally just explaining that point to Tav, here," giggled Gnately.

As Tavyn shifted position to dismount, the human caught sight of the small Algonan badge on his chest and tensed. "We have papers for our goods," he said, his hand slipping from the pommel of his weapon to its haft.

Tavyn looked up at him and to his own chest rapidly, then said, "I don't need to see papers. I'm not actually with the Algonan guard, I just acquired a suit of their armor recently."

"Acquired?" challenged the man.

"Yes. Acquired. It came into my possession, and now I wear it. Best armor I've ever come by, if I'm being honest. Couldn't see the need to damage it by prying the badge off," said Tavyn.

"He's not a soldier, good sir. We're just travelers heading north," said Gnately.

"Fine," said the man with a nod. "I'll trust ye fer now."

As they arrived at the camp, the big man turned halfway toward them, propped one of his feet on a log next to the fire and leaned an elbow on his knee. "I'm Royce, and these are my boys. Benry's cookin' our dinner. The little guy there is Ferrin, and Ruan should be back any time now from his scoutin'."

"Well, I'm Gnately and my friend is named Tavyn. We're on the road from Mureketh, making our way to Lothenheim."

"That's a hell of a ride in the snow, lass," chirped Benry.

"It is!" she agreed. "I'm so exhausted," she added dramatically.

"Exhausted," chuckled Ferrin. "Shit, you barely just begun!"

"She's a bit over dramatic, at times," sighed Tavyn.

"Hey, Royce? Who are the rest of the guys, back there near your horses?" she asked, pointing.

Royce straightened up and returned his foot to the ground defensively. "Earnings."

"Earnings?" asked Gnately.

"They're none of our business," Tavyn stated with a nod to Royce. "They have papers, so he said. Everything is fine."

"Not gonna be a problem, is it?" asked Royce, taking a step forward, hand on pommel.

"Oh no, not at all. I was just wondering if they had names... you know, in case I had to kick one back in line," said Gnately in her toughest voice.

"There won't be any kicking the merchandise, lass. One o' them give you a problem, you talk to me," said Royce with a grunt.

"Well, that stew smells great," chirped Gnately as she slid from her saddle. She tossed Tavyn her reins without looking and calmly strode toward the big iron pot. "Could use a little something, though." She reached down and yanked up a handful of green off the freshly cleared and trod ground, knocked the snow and dirt off with her other hand, and presented the bundle to Benry.

"What'm I supposed to do with that?" he asked.

"It's wild onion, ya dolt. Spice things up a bit, will ya?" she teased.

"Oh, I like her," laughed Ferrin. "Been sayin' that for years, Benry! Ain't I Royce?"

Benry grabbed the handful of onion from her with a snarl of disapproval.

"Ya only just met the girl and you're already tryin' ta kiss her arse," sighed Royce as he turned back to the camp.

Gnately sat on the log and waited with a smile on her face while Tavyn secured their mounts and joined her. She didn't like what she was seeing, not in the slightest, but she decided it was wise to put on an act. As far as she was aware, everything was going according to plan... the plan they didn't have.

"What brings an odd pair like you together in the first place?" asked Royce. "I go years without seein' a single Gnome, then just last month we run into a whole family of 'em, and now we see another travelin' alongside a Dynar. Strange days in Algona."

"We just happened to meet each other in Mureketh," answered Tavyn.

"Outcasts gotta stick together, no?" said Gnately as Benry handed her a bowl of stew and a small wooden spoon.

"Aye. But why go from cold to colder? Why not head south?"

asked Royce as he accepted his own bowl of stew.

"Coin is hard to come by these days in the fiefdoms. We're trying to get out of this gods-forsaken land to somewhere we can turn a profit," said Gnately.

"Too right. These damned fiefdoms are so disorganized," said Royce in frustrated tones. "They hate each other so much, a man can't make a decent living on normal trade... or farming. Everything's too damned expensive. And if ya try to farm for yourself and live off your own land, they swoop in and tax you to death to starve you out!"

"Yep! Royce lost his farm that way!" belted Ferrin in agreement.

"I'm sure we've all got stories. Whole region is in shambles, all the while the soldiers celebrate their success and how 'peaceful' the lands are. It's a farce," said Gnately.

Ferrin and Benry talked over themselves, arguing about who had the best story they could share with their guests. Royce jumped in and tried to calm them down, but only made the situation worse for his efforts. As the noise level grew, Tavyn leaned over to Gnately and whispered, "We need to leave. Fast."

"What bout them?" whispered Gnately, jutting her thumb toward the slaves.

"You wanna become one? Because staying here is how you become one," whispered Tavyn.

"Let's give it a few minutes and see how drunk these guys get. Maybe we'll have an opp-" whispered Gnately.

"Hey, what's this about, then?" blurted Royce, raising his hand to silence his men. "We welcome you into our camp, offer you food, and have a nice, polite conversation, and you start scheming right in front of us? Don't give me that look of denial. I seen the way you thumbed toward our merchandise. Thinkin' of running off with our earnings, are ye?" He was on his feet in a flash as he spoke, axe in hand, before they could react.

"I was pointing at your wagon, actually, I-" started Gnately, trying to save herself.

"I'm sorry, Royce, but that's not how we carry ourselves. We aren't here to disrupt your business. I was just telling her I thought we should keep moving. I've no desire to be caught out here when a blizzard hits, and the sky's been hinting at one for days," said Tavyn.

"And I was telling him I would prefer to *stay* and have a few ales with you, if that's okay. It's been a while since we relaxed, and we've no idea when the opportunity will present itself again," she explained.

"Is that so?" asked Royce.

"Yes?" asked Gnately with a slight cringe. "Look... how can we prove it to you? Can we help in any way? Want me to go feed them? Or perhaps we have information that can help you avoid the Algonan guard?" she offered.

"What are you doing?" asked Tavyn.

"Making friends? What harm is there in helping them, so we can sleep safe tonight near their fire?" she asked.

"I'm not sayin' I don't trust you lot, but... actually, no... I am! You ride up out of nowhere, wearing Algonan armor, and start whisperin' and pointin' at our merchandise like we're too dumb to notice. Think we'll just be done with ya now and move camp," said Royce as he slowly advanced.

"Help! Please!" came a young girl's cry a short distance to the east.

Everyone turned at once to find the source of the call. A young human girl, no taller than Tavyn, was stumbling toward them through the snow, clutching her stomach in one hand, and dangling the other by her side lifelessly. The pale skin of her face, neck and arms was spattered with blood. The front of her pale blue tunic was similarly spattered, but soaked just under her arm and torn in several places. Her hair was clumped and matted on one side, periodically dripping as she stepped toward them.

Gnately jumped up faster than anyone else could respond and barreled across the snow toward her. "Oh my gods, young one, are you okay?" she yelled as she raced toward the girl, arms outstretched.

Royce, Ferrin and Tavyn followed shortly behind, forgetting completely about the argument they'd been having.

"I... I couldn't save him," the girl whimpered. "If I hadn't been wandering all alone, he'd still be alive!"

"Who, love? What happened?" asked Gnately as she latched on to the poor girl, and turned to help her walk the rest of the way to the campfire.

"Fetch some blankets!" Tavyn yelled toward Benry as the cook finally stood to come help.

"I just went for a walk. I didn't mean for anyone to get hurt. It's just," she started as Gnately helped her sit on the log. "I helped a tiny, scruffy-headed faun with a lute a few nights ago. He sang me a little song and vanished. All I wanted to do was see if he'd come back for a visit," she whimpered as she nearly doubled over in pain.

"Typical," scoffed Royce. "Runnin' out to play in the night, no care in the world... 'cept when someone has to rush in and save you, eh?"

"What attacked you?" asked Gnately.

"A bear! It was so big," she whimpered, her words trailing off. "But then he came out of nowhere and... and..."

"Who came?" asked Gnately.

"This man in scale armor, riding a horse. He rode up out of the darkness, jumped off his horse and went right after that bear with a big ole sword," she cried.

"That would be Ruan," said Royce with a nod. "Where is he?"

"After... after he killed the bear, the faun returned. He... he didn't much like that the man killed a forest creature, I guess, cause he got real angry, cast a spell and burned the man alive. I can still smell the stench!" she cried.

"What the actual fuck?" barked Royce.

"You're not helping!" yelled Gnately back at him. She focused on the girl again and asked, "What's your name, you poor thing?"

"Nadyra, my lady."

"Well, Nadyra, where do you live? Can I help you get home?" Gnately asked, wrapping her with the blankets Benry finally finished retrieving.

"You killed Ruan?" barked Royce, leaning in toward the girl.

"A faun did!" she cried, cowering.

"Sounds to me like he died saving her life," said Tavyn. "The man's a hero."

"I didn't fuckin ask you," growled Royce. "I've had about enough of this shit. First you two, now this? Supposed to be an empty fucking field, for Gnok's sake!"

"I think she should compensate us for his death, eh, Royce?" said Ferrin, tapping the side of a dagger on his left palm.

"Oh, I think that sounds grand, ole sport," said Royce, a wicked grin poking out from beneath his facial hair.

"It's you," said Nadyra. "It's you, isn't it?"

"If you mean your new master, yes! Yes, I am!" he answered.

Gnately stood between them, facing Royce, and spread her tiny arms out wide to protect the young girl. Tavyn stood and stepped to her side, hands at the small of his back.

"My father talked about a man that looked just like you. My mother wouldn't tell me the story, not until it was too late, but he knew. She told him everything the day they fell in love. He searched for you, you know? He visited every city in southern Tellrindos looking for your buyer. Big, burly man with a brown, bushy beard who didn't know what a comb was. Said he walked like an ogre and talked like an angry bear, but smelled terribly of sweat and stale piss," said Nadyra, her confidence growing more evident with every word.

"What the fuck did you just say to me?" belted Royce, spittle flying from his lips.

"Fourteen years ago, just west of Uldenheim. You attacked a caravan and assaulted a defenseless Afyr woman, then left her for dead!" yelled Nadyra as she stood, her arms tensed firmly at her sides. There was no wound on her stomach, and nothing was wrong with her arm. Her arrival had been a ruse.

"What the fuck of it?" growled Royce.

"So you're not even going to try to deny it?" asked Nadyra.

"Who gives a shit what I did fourteen fucking years ago? That's old news! Bitch spit in my eye. She deserved everything she got!"

"That *bitch* was her mother," came a new voice. A dark figure stepped into the light from the east, covered head to toe in black silk save for a featureless, white, pearlescent mask. She moved with an elegance that seemed impossible on the snow-covered, uneven terrain. As she calmly closed the distance between them, Royce and his men stood silent, as if in a trance.

Nadyra tugged on Gnately and Tavyn's arms. "You should back up. This isn't going to be pretty."

CHAPTER 8:
RECIPROCATION
Ris'Gaula, Ahr'Antaerwyn 22nd, 575 of the 1st Era

ROYCE LICKED his lips, his eyes full of desire. He tilted his head part of the way in Ferrin's direction, intent on keeping the strange, alluring woman in view. "Step back, lad. You don't know how to handle a woman like her."

"It's me she's looking at, old man. You ain't got the stamina to handle what she wants," retorted Ferrin.

"Yer both daft ta think a beauty like her wants anything to do with the likes of ya," groaned Benry as he pushed between them. "She wants a real man."

Nadyra led Tavyn and Gnately to the far side of the campfire. Once they were clear, she stepped in front of their line of sight, crossed her forearms for them to see, then pulled her arms apart dramatically and pointed to the slaves behind them. Both turned with a nod and set to work freeing the men's 'merchandise', while the strange woman in the mask took care of the slavers.

"You're a worthless fucking cook, Benry," Royce yelled, turning to face him. "Why don't you go make some more stew? I'll need to put something in my belly when I'm done with her!"

Ferrin jumped behind Royce, reached up, and put his dagger to the man's throat. "Back off, old man. I told you, I'm the one she wants!"

Benry took the opportunity to run past them both, stopping just a few feet in front of the alluring woman in silk. He slid to a stop with a look of deep longing, his arms out pleadingly by his sides. "Yes," he replied to an unasked question. "Of course." He turned around slowly and lowered himself to his knees, then looked skyward with his arms crossed in front of him. "Like this?" he asked as a look of wonder washed over his face.

"Yes," whispered the woman as she came to a stop behind him. She leaned forward just a bit so that her mask gently grazed the side of Benry's right cheek. "Just like this," she confirmed as her right hand crossed over his neck in a flash and drew back just as quickly. The dagger she'd been concealing split his throat wide open. Blood gushed forth, quickly spattering across his upper torso and arms as he fell forward, his eyes full of desire.

Ferrin glanced over his shoulder at the scene as Royce growled in protest. Upon seeing the woman dispose of half his competition, he took her act as a sign and followed through with ending Royce, though his blade was not as sharp.

Royce stumbled forward as Ferrin shoved the small of his back. He spun and twisted his axe through the air, burying it between two of Ferrin's ribs with a surprising amount of force. He grasped at his throat with his left hand, trying desperately to keep his own blood from spilling out. Small gasps and gurgles pushed their way through his beard as he fell to his knees, clinging desperately to what remained of his life.

Ferrin fell sideways as the twin-bladed axe slammed into his chest. A look of shock and loss washed over his visage, rather than pain. He couldn't believe he was about to lose his chance to let her have her way with him. He reached up for her as she passed, seeking at least a bit of her attention before he succumbed to the dark that reached for him. Both men expired in a pool of their own blood as the strange woman took a seat beside the fire and slowly removed her pearl mask.

Tavyn looked back at her as he freed the last of the slaves; a very large man wearing far too little to protect him from the cold. Her face was much like his own; dark-skinned and distinctly elvish. Her hair, though, was decidedly different from a member of the Dynar race, and seemed to glow in the dance of the campfire's light. He quickly got to his feet at the sight and raced over to the fire.

"So it is true? Dynar do live in the north!" he gasped.

"Half Dynar, but yes. I've heard of others in the larger cities of Tellrindos, but I've not personally seen them myself. We are few, to be certain, and not quite welcome in Ulthran or Algona, I fear." Her voice was as smooth as the black silk she wore. She was also noticeably younger than he.

"I am Tavyn of Quaan'Shala, first son of house Vexlarahn, Purifier of the Daxian Order," he said with a bow of respect.

"I am known as Sylk. However, I'm afraid I have no knowledge of your house or the Daxian Order. I have never been to our people's homeland of Quaan'Shala. I do hope to visit someday, but I have much business to attend to first. Besides, as a halfling, I question whether or not I'd even be accepted."

"You are part Afyr, yes?" he asked as he took a seat across from her. She nodded back. "There are many who come to us as outcasts from all around the world. Our society accepts them all, and they are treated as equals, for we are all considered outcasts. You would be quite welcome, I assure you."

"We've been watching these men for days," injected Nadyra as she joined them. "When you arrived, we were worried you'd be added to their stock, as it were," she said, jutting her thumb back toward the slaves.

Tavyn looked back at them for a moment. Most were at the slavers' carriage, pulling blankets and clothes out to warm themselves. The largest of them was slowly approaching with Gnately, and they were in deep conversation.

"Were you hunting them specifically, or do you just have a thing for killing slavers?" he asked with a smirk.

"A little of both, actually," answered Sylk with a smile. "Yes, we very much dislike slavers. I was, up until recently, a slave myself. We were also scouting this region for any sign of Nadyra's mother's assailant. The story she told was quite true. Just so happens, Royce loved to brag to his men."

"Over, and over, and over. More often than not, he retold the same three stories. I don't know how they tolerated him," sighed Nadyra.

"One of those stories was about how he took an Afyr woman. He was quite proud of the deed, it seems," said Sylk. She reached over and helped herself to Royce's abandoned bowl of stew.

"Sorry, um," interrupted Gnately. "This is Ainen, and he's asked if he could travel with us, Tav," she said, introducing the large man.

"I have no home. They killed my parents," said Ainen as he cautiously took a seat by the fire. He nearly cringed when Tavyn moved his hand toward him in greeting.

"It's good to meet you, Ainen. I'm Tavyn. I'm not sure you want to travel all the way north with us, I'm afraid. We don't have clothing big enough to fit you. Why don't you head to Uldenheim?" he suggested.

"Can't," answered Ainen, shaking his head.

"Care to elaborate?" asked Gnately as she handed him her bowl of stew.

"I'm wanted there. Killed a man by accident," answered Ainen.

"Lots of that goin' around," sighed Gnately with a sidelong glance at Tavyn.

"Sides... I don't mind the cold," said Ainen.

"Why are you headed north?" asked Sylk. "I could be wrong, but I wouldn't expect a resident of Quaan'Shala to be very fond of deep snow or frozen tundra."

"I'm not, but after what happened, I don't think I'd be welcome back home until I atone. As you said, Ulthran and Algona aren't overly welcoming to our kind, so I figured Tellrindos might be an option, and if nothing else they have sea ports I could utilize to get out of here," said Tavyn.

"We planned on stopping in Port Gandraias. Maybe resting a while, getting the lay of the land before we decided between Lothenheim or setting sail," added Gnately.

"You can't," said Nadyra.

"Why not?" asked Gnately.

"It's not there anymore," she answered.

Tavyn and Gnately exchanged confused glances.

"It's true?" asked Ainen.

"What? What's true?" gasped Gnately, growing frustrated. As much as she disliked gnomes, they at least got to the point. Sure, they'd have been overly colorful with the details, but at least she wouldn't have to ask a dozen questions to get a straight answer.

"Heard Royce and the others discussing where they could sell us. Some old lady stopped by camp a few weeks back; told em the port had been destroyed. So, they were trying to figure out where else they could take us," said Ainen.

"Must've been Nightweaver," said Sylk with a nod. "Saw her walking south a few weeks back, leaving the port. I was still a slave back then. She warned us not to go there, but my master went anyway. In a weird sort of way, that's how I ended up a free woman, and the owner of this equipment," she said, indicating her silken garb and the mask on her lap.

"Did you say Nightweaver?" gasped Gnately.

"Yes. Creepy old woman with ashy black robes that smelled of sulfur and skin that seemed barely able to cling to her bones?" explained Sylk.

"She paid me to steal a map from Dereign Hold about a week ago," explained Gnately. "She could somehow move through shadows and reappear wherever she wanted, in the blink of an eye.

Terrifying, really... but the pay was good," she shrugged.

"I think she's the one that destroyed Port Gandraias," said Sylk.

Gnately's face went stark white and her eyes opened wide. "She... what?"

"You're lucky to be alive," said Sylk with a wry smile.

Tavyn moved over next to Gnately and rubbed her back for reassurance. "She's not here, you know?"

"We should stop saying her name. She said she could hear when people said her name into the darkness. As far as I'm concerned, she's here, or could be if she wanted to. So let's change the subject, and all say a few little prayers to whatever gods you want. But pray. Please," gasped Gnately.

"I agree," said Ainen.

"Okay, fine. Let's change the subject," agreed Tavyn. He turned toward Sylk again. "You mentioned your equipment? Mind if I ask where you got it?"

"From a creature named Siscci. Nothing more need be said on the subject. Your friend is already terrified enough for one night," said Sylk.

"Trust me... you don't wanna know," added Nadyra.

"Well, how'd you make those men kill each other, then?" asked Tavyn.

"The mask gives me the ability to control people; force them to do things," she answered. He looked at her with more than a little disbelief. "It doesn't work on everyone; only those who have the ability to produce offspring. Very old men, women who can no longer bear children, or children themselves... it doesn't seem to work on them."

"That is fascinating," he gasped.

"I'm not sure how it really works. Some form of enchantment, obviously, but neither of us can cast spells, so," she ended with a shrug. "All I know is, it lets us seek a bit of revenge, and protect ourselves. I'm hoping to build my skills enough that I won't need it, but for now, it's all we've got."

"I could teach you combat, if you like," he said.

"What kind of combat?" she asked, intrigued.

"Knives, daggers, short swords, crossbows, quarterstaff and hand to hand. I was trained in the arts with the explicit purpose of hunting down and assassinating those deemed abominations in the eyes of Ishnu... Necromancers, and the like; those that raise the dead," he explained.

"Is that what you were doing in Haern?" asked Gnately.

"Yes. I killed a man that was kidnapping young girls, dragging them to his laboratory and turning them into undead. I read a bit of his journal on the ship during my voyage north. It seems he was trying to figure out how to make something called an 'Unliving', though he never quite pulled it off. My order hunts such creatures as well. They are considered to be the worst kind of abomination," he explained.

"You certainly have skills I need, but I lack the time to learn them from you... and the desire to travel with you into Tellrindos. We just left that Kingdom, and they're hunting for us thanks to our encounter with Siscci. In fact, being a strange Dynar, you may wish to avoid it as well, lest they confuse you for me," said Sylk.

"Well... if Gnately is fine with it, we could go somewhere more hospitable and spend a few weeks relaxing so I could teach you the basics. It's the least I could do for saving our asses, and helping us free the slaves," offered Tavyn.

"My folks' house would do," offered Ainen.

"Didn't you say they were dead?" asked Gnately.

"They are. They died trying to stop Royce from taking me," he explained.

"How the hell *did* they take you?" asked Tavyn, looking at the very large, very muscular man as if he'd grown two heads.

Ainen sat quietly. They waited for a short while, but he simply refused to speak on the subject.

"It's okay, Ainen. He meant no harm. We're just curious. You can tell us in your own time," said Gnately.

He nodded back to her.

"If you're okay going back to their cabin, knowing they won't be there, then we'll gladly go for a short while with Sylk," said Gnately.

"Is fine," said Ainen.

"His skills would help us with the rest of our plans," suggested Nadyra.

"Samuel has waited decades to experience the consequences of his actions. I guess he could wait a little longer," said Sylk with a smile. "Very well. Let's clear the camp and get some sleep. We'll leave in the morning. We'll take their draft horses. That should allow us to make decent time."

With nods all around, the group set to work dragging the corpses out of their way, and burying their blood in snow and dirt. By the time they were done, the rest of the slaves had left the camp headed northwest, and dawn was nearly upon them. They didn't sleep well that night, but what rest they did get felt very rewarding.

✦ ✦ ✦

AINEN COULDN'T help but check his wrists, over and over. He'd split the skin in several places, trying to break free of his bonds over the past several days. Riding along in silence at a painfully slow pace behind his companions' smaller, slower mounts gave him a lot of time to think, and his mind kept returning to the death of his parents and his time in bondage.

When he first took notice of the damage, his skin seemed raw and was speckled with blood. The pain was bearable, but evident every time he touched or moved the affected areas. That morning when he cleaned his wounds in the snow, however, all the wounds were gone. They'd been replaced by a very strange callus, seemingly overnight. The skin was much tougher than the calluses on his palm, worn thick by laboring on his family's farm for the past ten years. In fact, it seemed as hard as stone, and noticeably grayer than the rest of his normally tan flesh.

They stopped several times during their journey to allow their mounts to rest. Night became day, and passed into night again, yet they still hadn't reached the border of Tellrindos. Every time they picked a spot to rest, his companions immediately began gathering firewood, fistfuls of hay, and grass for their mounts. Their speed of action and attentiveness left him little to contribute to their camps. Instead, he focused on getting as much rest as he could. He hadn't slept well in weeks, having been chained up in a kneeling position for most of his captivity.

Each break was no more than a few hours, and Ainen had never done well taking naps. Though he might rest well in the moment, he was somehow worse for wear when they started moving again. There were no other options with their pattern of movement, however, and he was well aware that time was of the essence. Therefore, he resigned himself to sleeping in spurts, and being groggy for the entirety of their travels.

Gnately, on the other hand, seemed to be enjoying their pace. Every time they mounted up to leave a camp behind, she hummed a little song and smiled so widely he was sure her face would split in two and the top of her head would fold over. As each day stretched on, he came to realize she was a breath of fresh air in an otherwise dark and dreary set of circumstances.

He listened intently as they rode, learning as much as he could about his new companions; his saviors. As Tavyn shared his knowledge with Sylk, it became evident to them all just how much training the man had received. Little Gnately, meanwhile, often referred to herself as being in 'acquisitions'. She didn't strike him as being a bad person, just an opportunist who had little means of making honest coin. With her actions in saving him from slavery, and her constantly bright, cheerful demeanor, he decided she was worth giving a chance, even if he disagreed with her chosen profession.

Sylk, meanwhile, terrified him greatly. He appreciated what she and Nadyra had done to free himself and the rest of the slaves, but the way she dressed and carried herself gave him the distinct impression that he couldn't trust her. If it weren't for Tavyn and Gnately, he would have pretended to leave for Uldenheim when they set him free, and turned back toward Algona once Sylk was out of sight. His new friends seemed to trust her, so he decided to try his best, but he was determined to keep an eye on her all the same.

The group kept with the same routine for two days before they reached a large sign standing over the road, and what was left of a stone wall on either side. Large, white letters carved from wood indicated it was the border of Tellrindos, and the smaller signs affixed to the walls decreed several of their most important laws; most of which governed trade, and what goods were outlawed within their borders. Ainen was very familiar with the sign, because his family cabin was only a half day's ride northwest once they passed it. They were very tired, however, and something nearby had caught their attention.

Several merchant caravans were camped just east of the gates, their carts arranged in several concentric circles to deflect the wind. A large fire and several cooking spits sent smoke into the sky at their center. Intrigued and eager to buy a warm meal, the group dismounted and lashed their horses to a post at the rear of one of the carriages. With little hesitation, they made their way toward the fire to get warm. People of all shapes, sizes and colors were present, each completely reliant on whatever coin they could earn through trade with the north, and none seemed happy to have their travels stall on the snowy tundra.

"Hail and well met, travelers," called out an elderly man. He was dressed head to toe in expensive furs and seemed to be the wealthiest of those present. It was apparent by the looks of the others nearby that he was acting as camp leader. Out of respect, the group turned and walked directly toward him.

"Might we make use of your fire?" asked Tavyn.

"But of course! All are welcome who travel these roads," the man said, gesturing toward several carefully placed logs.

"Come here often?" noted Gnately, pointing toward the dramatic scale of their camp with a smirk.

"You have found us in the midst of a Convocation!" yelled the old man cheerfully.

"Nobody calls it that," muttered another merchant nearby. "Dramen gets a little too excited when we gather, that's all."

Gnately laughed. "What, might I ask, is a 'Convocation'?"

"Oh, it is a most splendid occasion when we members of the Southern Merchants' Alliance set aside our competitive ways to trade information, cut deals, and work toward a better mutual foothold in the north. All for the safety and prosperity of those in our profession! It is the most important of gatherings, and quite beneficial to those who take it seriously!" answered a very excited Dramen.

"When four or more of us encounter one another on the same road, heading toward the same destination, we stop for a time and chat. That's... that's basically it," said the other merchant. "It's not as big a deal as he makes it out to be. Happens a few times a year, usually at the gates to Tellrindos."

"Pay no attention to Thamin. He likes to devalue the Convocation. He can't see far beyond his next drink, and thinks our gatherings are nothing more than a party. The real conversations begin when those like him have drunk their fill and sought their bedrolls," said Dramen with a shrug.

The old man walked over and sat next to Gnately. "Are you merchants yourselves? New to the trade?"

"We are but weary travelers, headed north into Tellrindos in search of passage to other lands," she answered.

"We've heard distressing news of Port Gandraias, I'm afraid," said Dramen.

"I have seen it," said Sylk. "Nightweaver, the Night Witch, laid waste to it some weeks back."

All conversation around the fire ceased. Several men sat their ale to the side and leaned toward the halfling Dynar, listening intently.

Dramen sighed and shook his head. "That is trouble indeed. Most of us were bound for Port Gandraias; not only to sell our wares, but to retrieve goods for the south. If the port is gone, that hurts not only us, but also Tellrindos, and the people of the Fiefdoms."

"What about the port in Lothenheim?" asked Gnately.

"It is small, and dedicated primarily to the Kingdom's navy. Only two docks are open for trade, or passengers, and both are owned and operated by noble houses in Lothenheim. They don't barter with the likes of us. Goods we sell in Port Gandraias are sent north by Tellrindosian merchants, and we are usually welcomed no further into their lands," said Thamin.

"Why can't the merchant ships just be redirected to Lothenheim?" asked Gnately.

"They very well might be, but that's a challenge beyond the availability of their inadequate docks," said Dramen. "The waters are very treacherous further north. The Tellrindosian navy, for example, builds their ships to cut through small ice flows. The nobles pay mages to protect their own ships from damage, and cut through obstacles when necessary. Those vessels that normally dock in Port Gandraias have no such capabilities or enchantments."

"Damned Algonan blockade makes matters worse. If they weren't in the way, we could divert to Gusarski Cove and at least cut our losses," sighed Thamin.

"Johorr would have an answer," said a man across the fire.

"Aye, but nobody's seen him in months," said the man beside him.

"Prolly off somewhere cuttin' deals with Royce," said Thamin.

Gnately, Nadyra and Sylk traded concerned glances at the mention of Royce. Sylk seemed even more concerned at the mention of Johorr.

"We met a Royce a few days south," mentioned Tavyn hesitantly. "We shared his fire for the night. Last we saw, he was headed west, toward Uldenheim."

Thamin nodded. "Johorr's territory."

Sylk remained silent, deciding that the less they knew, the better.

"Well, if they aren't headed north, they must know something we don't," said a man.

"Aye. They know about Port Gandraias, and they're heading west," said Dramen. His brow wrinkled, deep in thought.

"Do you think they mean to trade with the Afyr?" asked Thamin.

"Nah, the Afyr don't trade in slaves," said another.

"Perhaps the Toor, but that's risky," said Dramen.

"Well, I ain't sellin' flour to no Toor," grunted a man.

"They'd just as likely kill ya as let ya speak, Marlen," laughed another man.

"All the same, Johorr and Royce have options we ain't got, is all I'm sayin'," said Marlen.

"Don't understand," sighed Ainen.

"What's that?" asked Dramen, studying the large man intently.

"Why not trade here? Let Tellrindos come to you? You've enough supplies," suggested Ainen, pointing at their carriages and the nearby forest.

"You *could* build a town," said Gnately, nodding. "I don't think Algonan law prevents it."

"I don't think whatever Lord owns this land would mind having more people to tax," added Tavyn.

Several men around the fire looked at each other as if to ask why none of them had thought of the idea themselves. Dramen raised an eyebrow, thought for a moment, then stood.

"Why don't we, indeed? Thamin, you're a timberman. Orwin, you're a carpenter. Gerand is a stonemason. Terrance is a wood burner. We already have supply lines for wool, cotton, linen, furs, flour, ale... we could build a market right over there atop the hill," he said, pointing past the rings of carriages. "We could each have a stall inside one big building, with fire pits and seating down the center."

"Serve a man ale, his purse strings loosen," added Thamin.

"Oh, my huge friend... what you have set in motion might well change the world," said Dramen gleefully. "We'll even build a guild hall! We can make our Convocations official!"

"We're not calling them that," snarled Thamin. "I hate that word."

"We look forward to seeing what your guild can build here, truly. However, we still plan on heading north. To that end, we need to feed ourselves—and our horses—then get some rest. Would any of you be willing to sell us some feed? Maybe rent us a tent?" asked Tavyn.

Dramen turned back to the group and smiled, his arms open wide. "You shall have whatever you need, fair travelers. Not only for the information you have shared, and the ideas you have given us, but for whatever coin you can spare to contribute to our new enterprise. Purely a donation, of course, no set amounts."

He turned away from the fire, toward one of the larger carriages. "Arilis, come!" he yelled. A few seconds later, a young girl emerged from his carriage and walked toward the fire. "See to these fine travelers' needs. They will be my guests this evening."

Dramen turned back to the group and bowed, his right arm leading toward Arilis. She stood in the distance waiting, a warm smile upon her olive face. Her fiery red hair was pulled back in a loose braid with several strands hanging in front of her sleek elvish ears.

"Is she your servant?" asked Sylk, her voice betraying a hint of distaste.

"Oh, no, no, no," answered Dramen as he stood. "She is well paid to care for me and help protect my goods, nothing more."

Sylk looked Arilis in the eyes. The woman nodded and smiled back at her.

"Very well," said Sylk.

Tavyn stood and waited for his companions to join him before walking toward Arilis.

"Thank you," said Gnately as they passed Dramen.

"The pleasure is ours, I assure you madame," answered Dramen with a smile.

THE CAMP grew quiet as midnight approached, and the merchants sought the safety, and warmth, of their shelters. Some of them slept in small, temporary buildings made from large swaths of fabric and precision cut wood, others simply unrolled a tent from the side of their carriage. Only the elves stayed awake and aware, tending the large fire they all encircled, and watching for signs of any intruders.

Tavyn had never seen such organization and preparedness from traveling merchants, or cooperation between what he could only assume to be competitors for their customers' coin. The merchants of the far south—those that traded with Haern and Quaan'Shala—were far more ruthless, and less apt to work together.

He lay for a time on one of the wider logs near the fire, staring up at the night sky and pondering the nature of the 'free lands', as Branforth had described them. Four would-be Kings ruling their territories in semi-autonomy, interwoven in their fates though they might wish to deny it; each carried on the backs of their people who—despite borders and ideological differences—had banded together *just enough* to make everything work. It was no wonder things hadn't changed in hundreds of years; no self-proclaimed King had been recognized as such by his peers, and nobody had successfully united the lands under one banner through force.

The citizens didn't seem to care about politics or claims to power. They wanted roofs over their heads, food in their mouths, and relative safety from war and outside influence. With so many of them finding ways to make their coin through methods that couldn't be properly tracked or prevented, it was no wonder tax earnings were low. This kept armies under-staffed and poorly equipped, while perpetuating their way of life regardless of what their Lords wanted.

He was still lost in thought when Arilis approached. She calmly, quietly placed a few fresh logs on the fire with a practiced grace; the result of many years living on the road with her employer. Even with his extensive training, and generally cautious and observant nature, he barely noticed the sound of her activity.

"Arilis?" he asked without turning to look.

"Sorry to have disturbed you, my Lord."

"I'm no Lord. You can call me Tavyn... and please, do whatever you wish. You aren't disturbing me."

"I used to lie under the stars nearly every night, staring up at their wonder, just like you are doing right now. I understand their appeal, and the peace such a view can bring," she said.

Tavyn sat up and patted the log next to him, inviting her to join him. She hesitated for a moment, then gathered her long fur robes around her hips and complied. The soothing smell of lilac and honey reached him moments before she sat, wafting subtly from the wispy hairs on her robe as she moved.

"I am Tavyn, from the southern Kingdom of Quaan'Shala. I've met several Tryn near my home, living in nomadic tribes. I have not, however, met one in a city... and certainly not in the frozen north."

"We exist, I assure you," she said with a giggle.

"What brought you into Dramen's service, if you don't mind me asking?" asked Tavyn.

"Oh, I don't mind at all. My father was a merchant and traveled to these lands often. I fell in love with the north. The purity of the snow, and how it seems to wipe the land clean every season. The burst of color as plants give way to seasonal death, only to be reborn each spring. The flowers that spring up as if thanking the sun and warm climes for returning. My homeland had no such diversity; it was always the same, all year round.

"I tired of it in my youth, and when my father finally succumbed to his age, I felt trapped; as if my escape from our lands had died with him. Years later, sir Dramen visited my people to trade rare goods, and I asked if he would hire me to work for him. Several decades later, I can say with certainty that I've never once regretted that decision."

She smiled at him as she told the story, clearly happy with how her life had progressed, and where she'd ended up. He hadn't met many people as confident in themselves. If it weren't for the nagging and pressing need to get out of the fiefdoms burning at the back of his mind, he might have leaned in to kiss her. In light of her happiness, and the reasons for it, he decided such an act would be in poor taste, and settled on returning her smile.

"Where is your homeland? It sounds dreadful. Even in Quaan'Shala, we have seasons. Not as extreme as here, I'll grant you, but our river valleys are quite divine in their own right," he said.

"Far west of here. Through the pass just north of Ekthri Wood, beyond the Mythaeil Mountains and the Scaled Lands after."

"The Eyshvari Wilds?" he gasped.

"Yes. Well... the central Wilds. The north and south are fairly dangerous."

"People say the Eyshvari is unlivable; a no-man's-land," said Tavyn.

"It's not as harsh as rumors make it sound. In truth, I tell most who ask that I'm from south of Quaan'Shala, since they can't tell the difference. I assumed you could, so I figured it was best to be honest."

"I just can't believe that anyone lives out there, or that Dramen made it all that way to trade with your people," said Tavyn.

"People live everywhere," she laughed. "Besides, he was much younger back then."

"Be that as it may, it is still quite surprising," he said, realizing how foolish he'd sounded. "Besides, I-"

A twig snapped north of camp, beyond the row of carriages. Several horses snorted and stomped, confirming that the sound hadn't been inside his head. He looked around for Sylk and caught a glimpse of her outfit as it disappeared over a carriage.

"Get to safety," he told Arilis as he stood, his daggers almost instantly in his hands.

"I was about to say the same to you," she retorted.

WHEN THEY arrived on the other side of the carriages, Sylk was slightly crouched and studying the treeline along the border.

"Goblins," she whispered. "Three or four, along the treeline. Probably more that I can't see."

Tavyn stood beside her, his daggers at the ready. He couldn't see any movement, or humanoid heat signatures as of yet, but he fully trusted Sylk when she said she'd seen potential enemies.

Arilis stopped beside them and removed a studded mace from beneath her coat. "They don't attack a convocation this large without numbers. If it's goblins, and they attack, we should expect thirty or more."

"If that's the case, we should wake the camp," suggested Tavyn.

"I've scared off worse," said Arilis.

"I haven't," said Sylk.

"I've never even fought a goblin," admitted Tavyn.

"The moment you turn back or start making noise to wake the camp, they'll charge across that field. We need to show them that we're not worth the trouble," said Arilis. "Last time this happened was many years ago, and I stood outside camp practicing my spells for a while. They never charged in, thank the gods, because I was out of spells in no time at all."

"Duel me," said Sylk, looking up at Tavyn.

"Pardon?" he asked.

"Duel me. You said you'd teach me, so let's get to work. Right out here in the open where they can see," she said.

"That's a brilliant idea!" gasped Arilis. "I'll bolster you both for battle. You'll fight faster and stronger than normal; really give them a show!"

With a nod, Tavyn turned toward Sylk, with his back to the trees, and took a few steps backward into the clearing. He waved his daggers, beckoning her to join him, and waited patiently in a defensive posture.

Sylk ran toward him as the first of Arilis's spells struck her back, sending a surge of energy through her muscles. She jumped in the air just before she arrived and spun in an attempt to surprise him with an extravagant maneuver. Her ploy did not work.

Tavyn took a single step backward, deflected her strike high, and punched toward her chest to knock her back. His fist passed through the space his eyes told him was occupied by her torso, but only managed to graze the outer surface of her silken garb and strike nothing but air. He resumed his defensive stance and looked at her with confusion in his eyes.

"Don't worry about hurting me," she said with a smile. "My clothing makes attackers miss."

"That's a tad unfair," he laughed.

"How do you think I survived this long without training?" she grinned.

Tavyn jabbed his offhand blade toward her heart, stepping into the strike as he moved. As his dagger once again struck air, he paid attention to the feeling of the silk as his attack went past her. The back side of his forearm was briefly graced with the soft fabric she wore, so as his attack flew by, he spun to his left while stepping through, tucked his right arm into his body, and drove his shoulder into her back.

Sylk stumbled forward and turned to face him, a bruise forming between her shoulder blades. "How the hells did you do that?" she asked, perplexed.

"Your outfit is splendid, but it won't keep you alive by itself. Any trained combatant who recognizes what it's doing to his perception can shift their focus to what they feel, rather than see, and all its defensive properties lose value," he explained. "Now attack me. And mean it, this time."

The pair went back and forth for several hours, with Arilis re-enchanting Sylk periodically so she could keep up with Tavyn. They traded blows while he explained techniques, and over the course of their duel she slowly gained control of what she was doing and was able to deflect a few of his attacks.

By the time they had tired of the activity, dawn was nearly upon them and Arilis had run out of spells. Tavyn congratulated Sylk on her progress, and sent her into the camp to have her fill of food and drink. When she departed, he turned to Arilis with a playful grin on his face.

"I noticed you didn't throw any of those spells my way," he said.

"Well, you didn't need them as much as she did," she said, ending with a firm nod.

"How would I know? I've never *been* enchanted. Maybe I wanted to know what it felt like?" he teased.

"Oh, well," she gasped dramatically. "Pardon *me* for protecting the young girl from the seasoned warrior."

"I know, I know," he sighed. "Believe it or not, that young girl saved our lives. Ainen owes her his freedom. She's not as incapable as she might seem."

"I noticed the marks on Ainen's wrists. Thankfully for you all, I don't think any of the merchants did, but I'd have him wear bracers until you part our company. It wouldn't do well for them to find out he was a freed slave."

"Are these men slavers?" asked Tavyn.

"Dramen and the boys?" gasped Arilis. "No, never. But they're friends with Johorr and Royce, who happen to be. Well... I say friends, but it's more like a respectful business arrangement. They help each other out, and in these parts, that means more than having honorable merchandise."

"Do you approve of Royce, or Johorr?" asked Tavyn. She looked at him as if she didn't know whether to be angry or confused. "I don't mean anything by it. I think it's an honest enough question, though."

"No, I don't approve. In truth, only a couple of these men do, but I think that's just because they knew Royce and Johorr before they started to sell what they do. They have a bond, and you can't convince them to change their minds. They're good men, other than some of the company they keep. As for me, no... I detest what they do," she explained.

"Well, I don't know who Johorr is, but what I *do* know is that up until a few nights ago, Ainen was Royce's slave, and Sylk was a slave until whatever happened in Port Gandraias," said Tavyn. "I'm only telling you this so that you know you can trust me. I trust that you won't share this information with the others."

"Oh my gods, why didn't I put that together myself? Sylk? Syl'Kara? Johorr had a slave girl named Syl'Kara; a little halfling girl... half Dynar, half Afyr. I felt so badly for her, but if I'd done anything to help, it would have caused so much trouble for everyone involved, if not cost me my own life," she sighed. "But if little Syl'Kara is free... that must mean Johorr is dead."

"Well, we killed Royce to free Ainen and his other slaves," said Tavyn.

"That's great news, on both counts... but we can't let the merchants find out. They're very protective of those they ally with, even if they're walking refuse," she said.

"I hadn't planned on telling anyone at all, if I'm being honest. You, though... there's something about you that I can't quite put my finger on. I just felt the urge to be upfront with you; to leave nothing hidden."

"Your instincts are sound. Who knows?" she started as she began walking back toward the center of camp. "Keep this up, and I might *give* you something to put your finger on," she finished with a smile over her shoulder.

CHAPTER 9:
DISCERNMENT

Ris'Anyu, Luthentyr 1st, 576 of the 1st Era

ADVAN STOOD in the doorway to Mina's bedchamber for several minutes before speaking. When he finally managed to voice the word, "Chancellor," a man burst past him with all the impatience of a hungry child, nearly shoving the old servant into the door frame on his way.

"You need a new houseman, Ahm, I've been waiting to be introduced for nearly an hour," growled the man in frustration.

"Hello, Threm. You've come to see me ten times in half as many weeks. My answer has not changed, and still you persist. Why do you insist on wasting my time?" challenged Ahm, refusing to take his eyes off Mina, tucked neatly into her bed. She hadn't woken up since the incident with the device, and had become the only thing that occupied his mind.

"The Queen demands you travel to Talaani and see to Lord Whun!" shouted the man with a stamp of his right foot for emphasis.

Ahm slowly stood and turned to face him, assuming the confident, powerful posture those who attended court knew to expect from him. "No one who knows Lord Whun is worried for his safety. The Queen just wants to know what he's up to; a detail your office should be capable of providing. The Queen demands nothing of me, or she'd be here herself. It is *you* who makes demands of my time, and you're too stupid to realize your station does not afford you the power to do so. A *wise* man would have known that before he bothered to speak. But you," he said, stepping closer to the man, "you insist on proving, time and time again, just how uneducated you are about how our system works, who has power over whom, and just how ineffective you truly are. And if you dare to so much as *touch* Advan again, I will personally flay your flesh from your bones and bind you to the waste Flute for all eternity!"

"Lord Whun hasn't reported in months. He is our ambassador! If something has happened to him, it is a matter for the Defense Ministry, which you govern!" barked the man as defiantly as he could muster. He wasn't fully capable of preventing his voice from quivering in fear, but Ahm had to give him credit for trying.

"Tell me, oh Chancellor, to what office do you report?" asked Ahm, far too calmly to put the man at ease.

"F... Foreign Affairs," he admitted with a gulp.

"Right, and did you somehow think that meant only keeping charge of the comings and goings at the docks while you line your pockets, pleasure yourself with drink, and pay for the company of women? Or perhaps you're just too ignorant to realize the Talaani Empire *is foreign?*"

"Of course it is," he said, his voice wavering. "But if something has happened-"

"If something has happened, then first you must prove it through investigation. Then you must try using the skills of diplomacy, which you clearly lack. Only when diplomacy fails would the Ministry of Defense be called to action. My job, lest you forget, is protecting our borders, and the sanctity of our cities and Kingdom... *not* traveling to Talaani to seek the fate of *your* agents because you'd rather not leave your favorite stool at The Ailing Wyrm. While they may indeed have the best ale in all of Dusk, you aren't, in fact, writing for the food and beverage column of the Duskian Gazette!" yelled Ahm. "Did you think I didn't know? Trust when I say, Mordessa certainly knows... for if I do, she does."

"I'll... I'll head out at once. Might I... ask for an escort? I've never been to their lands."

"That would be a question for Granforth, my Master at Arms. He manages troop assignments, a duty which includes delegate escorts. Unlike you, he's wise enough not to bother me with such trifling matters," growled Ahm. "Now begone, before I lose the last fragment of my patience!"

On his way out of the room, the man hesitated and looked back as if he was about to ask another question, but Ahm was already back at Mina's side, slowly stroking her cheek with the back of his hand.

A few minutes later, Advan said the word, "Threm," finishing the man's name, then turned and left the room as if he'd properly introduced him. Ahm realized it might be time to find Advan another purpose, no matter how much he didn't want to do so.

AINEN KNELT and studied the footprints for a short while in contemplative silence. Tavyn eventually came to his side and tapped him on the shoulder, saying, "Alright, big guy, I think it's time we keep moving."

"My parents were killed because of goblins. A group of them kept stealing our animals; one sheep here, two pigs there. My parents said not to chase them down, that it would only make things worse... but I was angry and wanted it to end. So I snuck out to track the bastards down. Before I knew, I was surrounded and my parents were running up the path trying to stop me.

"The slavers were nearby and heard the fighting," said Ainen, continuing his story as he stood. "If I hadn't disobeyed, they'd still be alive." A single tear streamed down his cheek, disappearing into the stubble along the ridge of his jaw. "I tried to save them, but I got knocked out. When I woke they were dead, and I was in chains."

"That's terrible, Ainen," said Tavyn, patting him on the back.

"It's not your fault," added Gnately.

"Could've happened to any of us," said Sylk.

"We didn't live far from here. These tracks could be from the same group of goblins-" started Ainen.

"They come back every night, but we can't know for certain if it's the same group every time," said Sylk.

"Look, we came out here to assess the threat to the convocation, not go on a hunt," said Tavyn. "There's no way we can know their exact number based on prints alone, but from what I can tell, they outnumber us. Besides, the tracks could lead miles away. We don't even know if they're at their camp, on their way here, or somewhere else entirely. What would happen if we tracked their camp down, only to find out they'd doubled back on us and killed everyone in the convocation during our absence?"

"Um, Tav, I get what you're saying, but... when did the convocation become our problem? We've been here for weeks," sighed Gnately.

"I told Arilis we'd give them one more week, just last night. We agreed I would train Sylk, did we not? That's what I've been doing.

Every single night," he said.

"Listen, I'm not trying to be cold-hearted here, but none of us are guards. They want to set up a little village and claim these lands, more power to them, but last I checked we were just a band of assassins and thieves trying to find a way to warmer climes," grunted Gnately, pointing at the snow she was standing in for dramatic effect. She wanted to be on the road. In fact, she wanted to be anywhere but standing hip deep in snow.

"Well, it might not be that simple anymore," sighed Tavyn. "Ainen is one of us now, and he's clearly going to need some resolution before we proceed with our previous plans."

"Fine. I'll do it for Ainen... but not these merchants," she growled.

"One more week, Ainen. If they haven't attacked us by then, we'll hunt them down ourselves before we head north, okay?" asked Tavyn.

They exited the treeline and surveyed the merchants' building efforts for a time before walking back toward the tents. Progress was coming along quickly, as far as any of them could tell. The town would soon have wooden walls to protect it, and the merchants could move their carriages inside and claim their land. The next time they passed through, they could expect to see a bustling business center, houses, taverns, and everything else a wandering soul might desire. Part of Gnately wanted to stay and ply her trade against those who came to partake of their offerings, but that would mean listening to a bunch of old men prattle endlessly about how strategic and wise Royce and Johorr were, revering slavers as the best among them. She didn't know if she could take much more of it, but she'd try for the sake of Ainen.

"How's Nadyra holding up?" asked Tavyn as he fell into step alongside Sylk.

"She's fine. Why wouldn't she be?" she responded.

"She's what, thirteen? Fourteen? I heard her telling Arilis the other night about her mother's death. I also saw her face at Royce's camp, watching those men tear each other apart," said Tavyn.

"What are you saying?" asked Sylk. She stopped and put an arm out to block him, then turned to face him.

"I'm saying she whimpers in her sleep, and I've seen her step out of her tent wiping tears from her eyes," said Tavyn.

"Nadyra will be fine. She's been through a lot," said Sylk. She turned away as she was talking, but Tavyn could clearly see the displeasure on her face just before she did.

"Sylk... I didn't mean anything by it, I'm just concerned for her," said Tavyn.

"And I'm not?" grunted Sylk over her shoulder.

"I wasn't saying that," sighed Tavyn.

"Well, Gnately can have her wish. You are hereby released from your obligations, Tavyn. We will take our leave this evening," said Sylk.

"Whoa! That isn't what anyone was suggesting!" said Tavyn.

Sylk spun on her heel and bowed with a flourish, her silken garb flowing in the wake of her gesture. "May Ishnu guide your path."

He stopped and watched in frustration as Sylk spun and jogged toward the camp. Gnately and Ainen were much further ahead, having left the two of them to their quarrel. He wasn't sure how things had gotten so far out of hand. All he was trying to do was express concern for the girl. He knew what it was like to struggle with tragic events. The necromancer's daughter still plagued him whenever he tried to meditate.

When he finally resumed walking, he noticed Gnately waiting for him outside the ring of carriages, hands on hips. Even in the well-trodden snow directly next to the camp, she seemed like she was about to be swallowed up by a wayward drift at any moment. She was right; she had no place in such a climate. Her attitude had changed dramatically during their stay at the camp, which he could only attribute to her patience wearing thin. Yet something else that was entirely his fault.

"I'm sorry, Gnat. We can leave in the morning. Sylk's done with me," he sighed as he arrived.

"Aye, she told me as she went by. I wasn't trying to cause trouble, Tav. I'm sorry. I just... hate this stuff," she growled as she kicked a bit of muddy snow.

"It's not your fault," he answered, reaching down to pat her shoulder. "I got caught up in teaching Sylk as a way to thank her for saving our asses and helping free Ainen. It didn't even dawn on me just how hard it was for someone of your stature to exist in this place."

"Right? And to think, my parents *wanted* to move north!" gasped Gnately, her hands spread wide in disbelief.

Tavyn chuckled. "I'm just glad you're here. First time in my life I wasn't the shortest adult around," he quipped.

"Hey!" she gasped, feigning insult playfully.

"That kid Nadyra has grown a full inch during our stay. She's what, thirteen? And already taller than me? It's just not fair!" he chimed playfully as they entered the camp.

"Try being three and a half feet tall, you ass!" gasped Gnately.

"I mean... are you short for a gnome, or just about right?" teased Tavyn.

"Just about right? What am I, a steak?" she growled.

"Ishnu, save me from this madness," he sighed with a smirk. "It's good to have you back, Gnat. I'm sorry we stayed here for so long. Hopefully, I'll find a way to repay your patience."

"Coin is always nice. Girls like coin," she said, nodding.

"I'll keep that in mind," he laughed.

THAT NIGHT, the outsiders made their own fire just outside camp. They wanted to speak freely without worrying about the merchants overhearing. As they were setting up, Dramen and Arilis approached with armloads of food for them to prepare.

"Worry not," belted Dramen as they drew near. "I am not here to interject or convince you to join us. I bring only gifts, so my favorite new friends will not die of hunger!"

"You didn't have to do this," sighed Tavyn.

"Oh, nonsense. You've held those goblins back night after night, and this food is the least we can do in thanks," he said as the group extracted the goods from his and Arilis's arms. "Did I hear correctly that you will not be training this evening?"

"Yes. Our sessions have concluded," answered Sylk. "Nadyra and I are leaving at dawn."

"As will we," said Tavyn.

"You aren't leaving together?" asked Arilis, one eyebrow raised.

"We aren't actually together," chuckled Gnately. "Our paths aligned for a short while, nothing more."

"Well, worry not about our encampment this evening. Thamin is organizing guard rotations as we speak. In fact, that was my motivation for making this little delivery. The less I'm involved, the more apt people will be to take part," he chuckled awkwardly.

"The city walls are coming together nicely," said Gnately as she prepared a spit for cooking. "You move fairly quickly, for an older lot."

"Thamin, Orwin and Terrance are all very experienced in felling trees. The rest of us just followed their instructions. We should have the first of our buildings going up in a matter of days, gods permitting," said Dramen.

"It'll be nice to move inside the walls tomorrow," said Arilis.

"Indeed, it will! Long gone will be the stress of camping in the open, and putting ourselves at risk!" said Dramen.

"You'll still need guards," said Tavyn. "Those goblins aren't going to just go away. Their numbers seem to be increasing, and they're persistent. They've returned every single night, watching and waiting."

"What do you think they're waiting for?" asked Dramen with a gulp.

"For you to not be ready," said Gnately. "The moment you let your guard down, they'll be on you."

"They hesitate now, but that won't last," said Ainen. "They will come for you."

"Let's get you back to camp," said Arilis, putting her hands on Dramen's hunched shoulders. "We've our own meal to consume, and these fine folks would like to have their night together before departing." She smiled and nodded toward Tavyn as she tugged him away.

"This was nice of them," said Nadyra as she massaged a bit of salt into a hunk of meat. "Not sure which one of them is a butcher, but they did a fine job aging their cuts. This would have cost my mother a full week's earnings back in Lothenheim." She drove the spit through the meat and then invited Ainen to heft it into its cradle over the fire.

"We won't be eating this good again for some time," said Tavyn with a nod.

As they settled atop piles of furs for the evening, Sylk started chopping vegetables. The rhythmic tap of her blade on the wood was so calming they sat in silence throughout the entire process. When she finally slid the chopped ingredients into an iron pan and placed it beneath the spit to simmer, she sat back and realized that all eyes had been on her for quite some time.

"It's just a flat stew. It'll form a small broth as the meat drips atop it, and the tomatoes render from the heat," she explained.

"Am I the only one here who doesn't know how to cook?" asked Gnately.

"I don't," said Ainen.

"Nor do I," admitted Tavyn.

"Wait... you mean the group I'm leaving with can't prepare food? Not one of us?" asked Gnately. Tavyn, Ainen, and Nadyra laughed. "Can I come with you instead?" she asked, leaning toward Sylk.

"We're heading south," said Sylk with a wry smile.

"Even better!" gasped Gnately.

"As fun as that sounds, I think Nady and I need to be alone for a while. We've business to attend," said Sylk.

"Fine. You're too tall anyway," said Gnately, sticking her tongue out for emphasis.

"I'm too tall?" gasped Sylk. "What of Ainen? He's got at least a foot and a half on me," she laughed.

"He doesn't count!" grunted Gnately.

"Why not?" asked Ainen, perking up.

"Because you're a human, person, thing. They're all tall. And besides, you rarely talk, so it's like you're not even here most times," she said.

"I talk," he lamented.

"Like when? Once a day?" giggled Gnately.

"In fairness, you talk enough for all of us," quipped Tavyn.

"A girl's gotta keep warm somehow," she said defiantly.

Nadyra chuckled.

"Don't encourage her," sighed Tavyn with a playful roll of his eyes.

"This is nice," said Nadyra. "I think we all needed this little break. But Sylk is right. We've got things we need to handle. Before long, we'll all be off somewhere, fighting our own battles. We can look back on this meal and think of these times," she said, her voice growing more somber with every word. "This is nice," she finished, tears welling up.

Sylk slid over and embraced her, kissing the top of her head as she pulled her in. "It'll pass. Just let it out." She rubbed her back for a moment and looked up at the rest of the group. "You were right, Tavyn. She isn't doing well, and it's really no surprise. The man that raised her died in my arms, her mother died in hers, and we just got vengeance on her very own father. It's going to take her time to come to terms with it all, and the best thing we can do is keep pushing forward. The longer we sit still in this camp, the more those thoughts are going to plague her."

"I understand. I'm haunted by visions of the lives I've taken, and that's not even personal loss, just regret. She's right, though, Nadyra, it does eventually pass," said Tavyn.

"No. You accept it. You live with it," said Ainen. "That's not the same."

"Just this morning you were nearly overcome with emotions at the loss of your parents," said Tavyn. "It just hasn't been long enough yet, is all. It takes time."

"They died almost a month ago," said Ainen. "It will not pass. Images of the man I killed did not pass. He died three years ago. I can still see his face. I live with it. I will soon live with their loss, too."

"How... how did you kill him? You said it was an accident, but," started Gnately hesitantly. She let her words trail off, unsure if she should push for answers.

"Was training with other boys. Uldenheim Guard insisted I join. Parents said give it a try, so I did. Evan was a jerk, always bullying smaller boys. I asked him to stop, and he did for a while. One day he pushed a boy to the ground, and I had enough. So I punched him. Once. His head bounced off the wall and cracked open. I tried to help, but he died in my hands. I didn't mean to kill him... but I couldn't take it back," explained Ainen calmly.

"Is that why your parents moved you to the middle of nowhere?" asked Gnately.

"Which got them killed, yes," said Ainen with a nod.

Gnately got up and walked around the fire to join Ainen. She went to kneel beside him and hug him, but stopped before committing, realizing she was far too small to pull it off. Instead, she changed position and stood behind him, and tried to hug him around his shoulders. However, her arms were too short to go around him, so she settled for wrapping her arms around his neck. "It's okay, Ainen. We still love you," she said in her best supportive voice.

"I'm fine," he sighed. He leaned forward mindlessly and reached for a stick at the edge of the fire with which to fidget. His change in position pulled her off the ground, her feet dangling down his back.

"Help!" she whimpered playfully. Nadyra giggled. Tavyn rolled his eyes and chuckled. Gnately grinned and slid off Ainen's back, then patted him, saying, "See? All better!" The faint smile on his face confirmed she'd accomplished her goal. Content, she settled back in to wait for their meal.

AHM HAD been pacing in his office for hours without realizing it. Threm's visits were an annoyance, but—until his most recent—hadn't given him much cause for worry. It hadn't occurred to him in that moment, but once Threm left Mina's room, he found his mind calculating the consequences of the imbecile mentioning what he'd seen to anyone of import. Had he said anything? Was he on his way to Talaani, too preoccupied to report his discovery? Was he even aware of what he'd seen? Ahm was a priest, after all, so perhaps Threm would assume he was just fulfilling his duties and helping a poor girl through an illness.

He needed answers, but couldn't fathom a way to seek those answers without raising suspicion through his own actions, thereby causing the very problems he was trying to avoid. It was a dangerous situation, no matter how he considered it. He shouldn't have let the man leave. He wasn't thinking clearly, and that was becoming more evident with each passing day. How long had she been unconscious? Was she going to wake up, and if so, when?

A single rap on his office door interrupted his thoughts. He composed himself briefly, then responded, "Enter," with a firm, authoritative tone.

A youthful elf entered, his gray tunic and insignia signifying he was one of the Ministry's agents. He knelt at the center of the room and looked up at Ahm with respect. "My lord, your suspicions were correct. The young boy, Eros, has indeed been snooping near the Cryx. He has been detained, per your request, and is waiting in interrogation room three."

Ahm nodded and made his way up the stairs. The rooms were located near the top of the stairs, close to the surface, but still far enough underground for interrogations to go unnoticed. They sat dormant for years at a time, only being required during times where threats emerged within Dusk's borders. Detaining Eros in one for questioning was unorthodox, and well beyond the purview of his duties, but the only persons aware of his overstep were Eros and himself. Considering recent events, he needed to make sure that knowledge went no further.

Each room contained only a single metal table and four metal chairs, all bolted firmly to the floor. They were uninviting, uncomfortable, and easily accomplished their primary task; to take their occupant off their game and weaken their resolve by inspiring an underlying feeling of unease. It was a small thing, but quite useful when dealing with beings of extended lifespan who had nothing but time on their hands, and thus were commonly considered overly patient.

When the door opened to room three, Eros jumped up from his chair and backed away to the far wall. The guard who'd opened it stepped back to allow Ahm's entry, then quietly closed it behind him. The boy was nearly in a state of panic, and Ahm's presence only served to heighten his anxiety.

"Sit," ordered Ahm, as he himself complied.

Eros hesitantly reached for the back of the chair and yanked, as if he were somehow going to move it toward him rather than getting any closer to the High Priest himself. Ahm was patient while the boy slowly came to terms with his predicament and succumbed to his authority, sliding into the chair across the table while nervously holding his breath.

"I know why you're here, and I have to admit it took a great deal of courage for you to take such an action," said Ahm, trying to put the boy at ease.

"What have you done with her? Where is she?" gasped Eros, seemingly unable to contain himself any longer.

"Straight to the point, eh? Fine. She is resting, nothing more. Rest assured, she will resume her visits with you near Bidlesh in due time. For now, she must focus on her duties, and I'm afraid those will keep her occupied for the near future," said Ahm.

"You can't keep her caged her whole life! She deserves her freedom! She's a beautiful, intelligent and strong woman, and she deserves a better life than this!" argued Eros. He regretted his words almost as soon as they escaped his lips. Clearly, he'd been bottling those emotions for far too long, and his subconscious could no longer contain them.

"I let her go to you, did I not? She is not a prisoner. I am simply protecting her," explained Ahm.

"From what? Who's protecting her from you?" growled Eros.

"You think I mean her harm?" laughed Ahm. "If it weren't for me, she would not exist, boy."

"That doesn't excuse your behavior. You may be Minister of Defense, but that doesn't give you the right to hold her against her will!"

"Actually, it does. In fact, I could have you killed right this minute for intruding in Ministry offices and disrupting official business," said Ahm bluntly. Eros's face drained of blood. "I won't, because I'm not that kind of Minister. I choose not to run my offices in that manner. You pass judgment on a situation you do not understand, and I sympathize with your point of view. That's why I won't punish you for your ill-advised actions."

"Can... can I see her? I just want to know that she's okay," Eros pleaded. "I haven't seen her in over a month. I can't help but worry about her, and I'm sure you can understand that I don't know what to trust about you and your relationship with her."

"Fair enough," agreed Ahm. "You seem genuinely concerned for her, so I must assume I can trust you not to divulge her existence, or her true nature, to anyone; not even my own agents."

"Her true nature?" asked Eros, concerned.

"I will take you to her, but make no mistake... once you know the truth, your fate will be forever bound to the looseness of your tongue," said Ahm.

Eros sat back for a moment and closed his eyes, considering what Ahm was suggesting. Without further hesitation, he leaned forward and simply nodded his acceptance of Ahm's offer.

"Very well," said Ahm as he got to his feet.

AHM BROUGHT Eros down to Mina's bedchamber without saying another word. The boy burst through the door and raced to the side of her bed so fast he nearly tripped over himself in the process. He grabbed Mina's hand between his own and looked back at Ahm, his eyes filled with tears.

"What happened to her?" he pleaded.

"She is helping me to test a device that will help defend our kingdom from the Talaani. There was an accident, and she was injured. Her powers have healed her, but her mind has not yet returned to the waking world," explained Ahm as calmly as he could manage.

"When will she wake up?" sobbed Eros, turned back toward her.

"Hopefully soon, but in truth, I have no way of knowing. We can't take her to anyone else for assistance, because they'd discover what she was. As much as that might make me seem to be a monster, there simply is no other way to handle the situation. We must wait," said Ahm. "You can stay with her, and help tend to her needs, if that pleases you, but the secrecy surrounding her is not up for debate."

"I... I don't understand. Why would anyone care that you have a daughter?" asked Eros through his tears.

"You see her as a simple, human girl. She is not. Her mother was Unliving, and father was Undead. Their union resulted in an impossible pregnancy, which I'm sure High Priest Delorain's teachings have conveyed through your studies. You should know very well what that makes her," he explained.

"No. That can't be. What you're suggesting isn't possible," argued Eros, shaking his head. He wiped the tears from his cheeks with the sleeve of his right arm, then returned his hand to hers.

"And yet you know it to be true. You've sensed it, or seen signs, surely," suggested Ahm.

"She... has these dreams; visions where she's connected to Queen Mordessa," admitted Eros. "They were simple at first, and neither of us knew what they were, but... they're getting worse, and the last time we were together she saw Mordessa kill a man in her antechamber."

"Please tell me I misunderstood you," gasped Ahm in disbelief. "Are you suggesting that her connection to the Aggripha has linked her, somehow, to our Queen?"

"If that's how it works, then sure. All I know is what she told me of her dreams," said Eros.

"Then things are far worse than I could have imagined," said Ahm.

✦ ✦ ✦

THE DARKNESS overwhelmed her again, swirling from the edge of her vision and replacing all she could see before dissolving once more into non-existence. She didn't know how long she'd been asleep, nor could she force herself to wake. Unlike her normal dreams, she felt fully aware of the fact she was seeing and that she was sleeping.

Once again she could see the crystal ball, standing upon its golden pedestal and the dark, red silk cloth draped across the table underneath. Mordessa's taloned hand waved in front of it, summoning yet another distant scene she could not see. The Queen spent seemingly countless hours studying the orb, searching for something she desperately feared. As far as Mina could tell, whatever Mordessa was searching for was very familiar, and represented a problem she was accustomed to revisiting at regular intervals.

That vision was the most common one she received from the Queen, interspersed with random interruptions from servants and officials. The only thing she was thankful for was she hadn't witnessed the Queen killing anyone else like she had on her last visit with Eros.

Just as the predictable fade to black began, the crystal ball pulsed a painfully bright, golden hue.

"Finally," said Mordessa, her voice much deeper inside her head than Mina remembered. "Now that I know where you are, I can see to your fate," she growled.

Who did she find? wondered Mina.

"Who are you? How did you do this?" asked Mordessa.

Me? Surely she can't mean me! gasped Mina.

"Mmmm, you reached me through the Aggripha, but how?" whispered Mordessa curiously.

A surge of power filled Mordessa, and thus Mina's mind. The feeling was simultaneously exhilarating and terrifying. As the energies reached a strength Mina had never felt, a sudden burst flooded her mind and pushed her violently away from Mordessa.

Mina woke, her hands shooting toward the sides of her bed to latch on. As far as her stomach was concerned, she was tumbling backward endlessly, and the pain in her head felt as if it were about to explode. She couldn't register the voices around her, and no matter how hard she tried, all she could see was darkness.

CHAPTER 10:
FOREBODING

Ris'Enliss, Luthentyr 6th, 576 of the 1st Era

AVYN, GNATELY, and Ainen set out the next morning, following the previous night's goblin tracks through several days of light snowfall. Their route was tedious to follow, since almost none of them seemed to walk in a straight line, or follow each other with any sense of organization. Now and then, they stumbled on the remnants of a squirrel, rabbit or other small woodland creature; splayed open or cut apart by bladed weaponry, half eaten and discarded.

The terrain along the path quickly became impassable for their mounts. After a brief discussion, they unanimously decided that since they sought boat travel anyway, it was better to return their mounts to the merchant camp, sell them off, and resume their journey on foot.

After returning to the forest, the trio traveled almost completely in silence, barring the few times Gnately had to be helped over an obstruction. By mid day, Ainen had fallen into a rhythm lifting Gnately up to assist her passage, and nothing needed to be said between them to instigate the maneuver.

The further they crossed into Tellrindos territory, the more frequently they ran across small gaps, or fissures, in the ground. Most of them appeared to be tiny chasms, as if the ground had sunk out from under a stretch of ground, but hadn't quite sunk far enough. They stopped late afternoon for a break next to one, and Gnately spent an inordinate amount of time inspecting it.

Ainen joined her after a time, asking, "Is something wrong?"

"What are these things? It's like... there are these tiny little gashes in the ground, like some great beast ran through and left claw marks for us to find. Please tell me it isn't a beast?" she said, curiously.

"There were some back home, not too far from here. My dad said caves and mines caused them," he answered.

"Great, so these things could just open up and swallow us at any point?" she gasped playfully.

"Hope not," said Ainen.

"Fat lot of reassurance you are," she giggled, rolling her eyes dramatically.

"Dad could have been wrong," Ainen shrugged.

"Gnat, you should probably rest up," suggested Tavyn. He was sitting against a tree, taking occasional bites of a hunk of bread and slowly sipping from a wineskin.

"Why, you gonna share?" she asked, pointing toward his drink.

"If you like. Arilis said this was a good way to keep warm," he answered, shrugging.

"Then why am I just finding out about it now?" she gasped.

"I didn't think about it?" answered Tavyn.

Gnately looked up at Ainen in feign disgust. "Can you believe this guy?" Ainen shrugged back at her and dramatically took a swig from his own wineskin. "It's a conspiracy!" she blurted, throwing her hands up in frustration. She turned and started dramatically, stomping her way back to the elf. "All this time you had the solution to my troubles and didn't share! The nerve! Here I am, freezing to death hip deep in snow, trudging through ankle deep mud, and fighting with chest high brambles. You lot get to drink wine, lithely glide over the terrain, and what... mock me the whole time?" she finished, yanking Tavyn's skin out of his outstretched hand and taking a long drag.

"I don't make you a gnome, you know," he laughed. "That was your parents' fault."

"I didn't make you a gnome, you know," she mocked, right as a twig snapped just outside of view.

The group went quiet, listening for anything that could give them a clue as to the source of the sound. A few seconds later, the distinct sound of metal clacking into tree bark pierced the silence.

Tavyn stood and drew his daggers. Gnately turned and stood back-to-rump with him, drawing her own. Ainen picked up a large, half-rotted branch and prepared himself for the worst.

"Have the defenders come to force us out?" asked a raspy voice.

"Not very nice," said another.

"We left you be, and still you came?" asked a third.

"Not very nice!" repeated the second.

Ainen tensed and took a few steps back toward his friends. Gnately's eyes darted around as she tried to find the voices among the trees.

"You scouted those merchants every single night! Why would you do that, if not to attack?" challenged Tavyn.

"He's so smart," taunted one of the voices sarcastically.

"He's a scholar!" hissed another.

Laughter broke out all around them. They were surrounded.

"Oh, look at them tremble!" called one of the voices.

"Not so brave without the elf girls to save you," laughed another.

"Did she teach you enough?" laughed yet another.

"I was teaching her!" barked Tavyn.

"Are you really arguing with a goblin?" sighed Gnately under her breath.

"I'm sure you were," mocked a much, much deeper voice. "Prove it!"

At his words, goblins rushed into their small clearing, jumping over underbrush and weaving between the trees. Their green skin, black hair and brown hide armor were the perfect combination for hiding in the forest. It was no wonder to Gnately why they hadn't been able to get an accurate count on previous nights.

Ainen sprang to life, charging at one of the larger goblins with a ferocious grunt. The goblin thrust its spiked mace toward him frantically, but Ainen's simultaneous attack slammed into his head, shattering the large man's branch and sending splinters flying in all directions.

Two goblins raced toward Tavyn, each flailing similar weapons in his direction. He deftly parried both attacks with his twin daggers, then dove between them, slicing outward as he crossed their threshold and went into a roll. Their necks spurted blood in thin streams along the wake of his weapons' passing. They backed away, frantically grasping at their wounds and dropped their weapons on the ground harmlessly.

Gnately ducked to her left as a goblin closed in from the other side, and dodged around the tree Tavyn had been leaning on. The beast's mace crashed into the ground behind her. It growled in displeasure and gave chase. She disappeared behind the tree briefly, stopped, and crouched low to the ground. As it rounded the tree trying to find her, she went completely unnoticed and took advantage of that fact to drive both of her daggers up along its outer thigh and into the soft tissue just above its hip. The creature lurched backward in shock and pain, taking her blades with it.

Ainen backed up, reached down and grabbed the maces Tavyn's kills discarded. He did his best to deflect the attacks of his two new opponents, but several hits slammed into his sides, gut, and chest in rapid succession. He grunted in pain with each blow, eventually crashing to his knees.

Tavyn turned and raced over to save Ainen. He approached from their left flank as quickly as he could, his blades whirling in a showy display, hoping to scare them into backing away from their current target. His ploy succeeded.

As they defended themselves from Tavyn's flourish, Gnately rounded her tree and came face to face with a very tall, very strong-looking hobgoblin. It was nearly as large as Ainen, wearing scale armor and brandishing a two-handed sword. Her weapons suddenly felt very inadequate in her hands. She squealed involuntarily at the sight and dove beneath his swinging blade, rolled between his legs, and got to her feet behind him. She tried to cut the tendons on the back of his ankles, but her blades glanced almost harmlessly off his armor. As he turned to face her, she ran toward the presumed safety of her friends.

Ainen got to his feet as Gnately approached, initially intent on helping Tavyn with the four goblins he now faced. Upon seeing who she was fleeing from, he turned instead toward the hobgoblin and charged toward it, maces braced to deflect an incoming blow, or so he hoped.

Tavyn dispatched one of the four goblins with a desperate thrust toward the creature's chest. As it fell backward, he stepped left to put the corpse between himself and the rest of his foes. Two attacks whizzed past him harmlessly, passing through air where he'd been standing. The third goblin redirected its attack at the last second, slamming into his right temple. As he fell to his knees, nearly succumbing to the beckoning darkness, he saw Gnately rushing up behind them. He did his best to growl and lash out with his blades, hoping to keep their attention.

Gnately rushed up behind the three goblins that were fighting Tavyn and jumped in the air just before she arrived. She buried both of her blades into the back of one of the goblins and let her weight pull her back toward the ground, carving two deep grooves in the creature's flesh, breaking several of his ribs, and sending blood all over her face, chest and arms.

She landed atop the fallen goblin and spun to face the two others just as Tavyn regained his feet and pretended to have his wits about him. The final two goblins turned and ran as fast as they could, desperate to get as far from the mad gnome as possible.

Ainen managed to deflect the first blow from the hobgoblin, which screamed down from the sky overhead with relentless ferocity. He wedged the blade between the hafts of his two weapons, but the horrid crack as it impacted made it clear his weapons were now useless. He shoved to his right with all his strength, sending the sword away, its tip glancing off the ground.

The hobgoblin pulled back on the hilt and turned toward Ainen's new position at the same time, dragging the blade across his body as he spun. The sword cut across Ainen's torso, leaving an inch deep gash in his stomach. He backed away, resisting the urge to double over in pain.

Gnately and Tavyn raced up behind the hobgoblin, drawing enough of its attention to make it hesitant to continue the assault on Ainen. As it turned to face the new threats, Ainen rushed him from his right flank and buried his shoulder under the creature's right arm, driving him to the ground with a violent crash.

The hobgoblin rolled with the blow, landing on his back as they crashed to the ground. In a flash, he reversed his left hand's grip on the sword and released it with his right. He then punched past Ainen's face with his left, rolling to his right simultaneously. The sword's quillons smashed into Ainen's cheek, crushing the bone within, and sending the large man rolling.

Just as that blow landed, Gnately dove on the hobgoblin's back and began stabbing at the back of its neck and head in rapid succession. Tavyn ran past the pair and dropped his blades as he came to Ainen's side.

The hobgoblin rolled over, causing Gnately to tumble to the ground by its side. Blood oozed onto the ground beneath its upper back and head, seeping out of a myriad of wounds caused by the angry gnome. He went to stand, but before he could, she was back atop him, straddling his neck with a dagger pointed toward each of his eyes.

"I think this is the part where you fuck off!" she growled as she pushed down on her blades, driving them deep into his skull.

"Ainen!" yelled Tavyn. "Hang in there!"

Gnately scrambled off the hobgoblin and over to her friends, sliding to a stop on her knees by the large human's shoulder. "Get your wine!"

"What?" asked Tavyn.

"Weren't you trained to treat wounds in the field? Get your

wine!" she repeated.

"No," gasped Tavyn as he scrambled toward the skin. "We're supposed to have a healer with us on field missions. Purifiers' only job is to kill," he finished as he returned to her side and handed her the skin.

She popped the cork and poured some into Ainen's wound. He wailed in response. "My mom used to pour stuff like this on our wounds when I was little. Ale, wine, brandy... whatever she had, if it could get her drunk, it could cleanse a wound. At least, that's what she claimed."

"We need to bandage him, at the very lea-" he started, but his words were cut off.

A strange wave of energy burst out of Ainen's face, nearly blinding the both of them. He screamed in pain and horror as the magics erupted from his wound so loudly that it hurt both their ears.

When the light faded and the noise subsided, they turned back to their friend to find out what had happened. His face's shape was back to normal, and the wound had closed completely. He looked up at them, confused, and asked, "What... what just happened?"

Neither of them could immediately find the words to describe what they'd seen, or the gray, hardened flesh that had taken the place of Ainen's injury.

WHUN DRIFTED into the Noktulians' prayer chamber, interrupting their service. He had news, and saw no reason to let them continue praying to their petrified draconic gods and delay his delivery of it. Prayers ceased almost immediately upon his entry, and all eyes turned toward him as he floated to the front of the room to address the head priest directly.

'I have found the Caier. It is hiding within a human in the lands of Gargoa. Each time he is wounded, his body repairs itself by turning that part of him to stone. The process is accompanied by a surge of primal energy that pulses through the weave briefly. I witnessed one such surge and tracked it down,' he thought to the priest.

"Assuming the curse has conveyed to his new host body, you have found the reincarnation of the Caier named Jaezyn," said the priest with more excitement than Whun had ever seen a Noktulian express.

'Have you prepared the spells you need to entice him to travel here?' asked Whun.

"From such a great distance? No. I am afraid our spells would not be strong enough to reach him in that way. We might, however, have a spell that would allow Jaezyn to speak with his host. His voice would grow stronger the closer he drew to our lands, and our relic," said the priest.

'I will return to the ritual chamber and watch for an opportunity to influence his travels myself, then. Gather whatever you need and join me. Be ready to cast your spell at me at a moment's notice, and I will channel it toward Jaezyn's host along with my own,' said Whun.

"How will you bring him here?" asked the priest.

'I have not watched him for long enough to know, as of yet. That is why I am returning to my visions, and telling you to be ready in an instant. From this moment onward, you and whomever you need to help you cast your spell are by my side. We will not rest until our task has been accomplished,' demanded Whun. He turned and floated away from the priest without another word.

"Very well, Lord Whun," said the priest.

MINA FRANTICALLY reached for something to hold on to. Her mind could barely comprehend that her back was touching a mattress. Everything told her she was tumbling uncontrollably and would soon crash into the ground. She could even feel air rushing past her face. Strange, rumbling noises came from her left and right. Unseen hands gripped her own in the darkness, holding fast and patting her forearms reassuringly.

Try as she might, she could not force herself to wake up. Panic had taken hold, and she couldn't shake it loose. She was about to die. She could feel it in every fiber of her being. The tears that ran down her face felt like molten lava, searing a path of destruction as they sought to destroy the last remnant of self within her.

EROS GRIPPED Mina's right hand as tightly as he could and gently patted her arm with his left. "Wake up! Mina, it's okay! Just wake up!" he pleaded. As Ahm raced to the other side of the bed, and her wailing grew in volume, he cried, "what's happening? Why won't she wake?"

Ahm grabbed her other hand and looked up at him, deep concern in his eyes. "She is awake."

"What?" cried Eros.

"This is a wailing curse. I've only seen it once before," said Ahm, so calm it sent a chill down Eros's spine.

"What do we do?" he pleaded.

"There is no cure for such a curse," sighed Ahm.

"You have to do something!" demanded Eros.

"I will," nodded Ahm. "Go and get Advan. Bring him with haste."

"Who?" he asked.

"The extremely old man we passed in the hall? Drag him here, if need be," said Ahm.

"What? Why?" asked Eros, his fear giving way to confusion.

"Either get him, or take his place, but I have to send this curse into a new host or she's dead!" yelled Ahm, his patience gone.

Eros nodded vigorously and wiped the tears from his cheeks as he scrambled to his feet and raced out the door. Ahm pressed his right palm firmly onto Mina's forehead and began reciting the spell he'd prepared centuries prior, just in case this curse ever befell someone he loved again.

He could barely remember his wife's face, she'd been gone so long. The years had fallen away in her absence, filled with mindless research and study, trying to discern what had happened to her on that fateful day. He'd sworn never to let it happen again.

After what seemed like decades, he'd discovered a curse that it was claimed could not be cast; that the casting of it required so much power, the caster couldn't survive the process. It was a curse of madness and physical torture that drove its victim's mind into killing their own body, slowly and painfully, as they wailed in pain and horror. There was no known cure, and countering it as one would a normal curse required him to be as powerful as the one who cast it upon her. In all his research, he'd only found a single alternative, and he'd spent years mastering the art on weaker ailments and curses.

Eros reentered the room, dragging a pair of large, booted feet. He made his way around the bed, gasping for breath as Ahm's chanting grew louder and more rhythmic. An involuntary gasp escaped his lips at the sight of Ahm's eyes, white flames dancing upon their surface.

Ahm slowly extended his left hand outward, reaching for something to grab. Eros assumed he meant Advan and lifted the man's hand toward Ahm's. The old servant's joints were stiff, and refused to cooperate without being forced. Eros readjusted his position and pushed Advan closer to Ahm to get a better angle. He lifted the man's arm again as Ahm's chanting intensified, but it lurched downward and fell from his grasp.

Frustrated, he got to his feet and straddled the old man's torso. Grunting under the strain, he lifted Advan's left arm as high as he could. Just as the man's hand was about to touch Ahm's, it lurched downward again. Eros's hands flew upward as the resistance on his muscles was removed, sending his left hand directly into Ahm's.

Ahm latched on, completely unaware of which hand he was holding. He completed one last cycle of the spell as the hand he held tugged and pulled frantically, trying to break free. As the spell completed, the flames atop his eyes faded and Mina's screaming abruptly ceased. His own consciousness faded slowly as the exhaustion caused by his spell overwhelmed him. Just as the darkness took hold, he could see and hear Eros falling backward to the floor, wailing uncontrollably.

MINA SHOT upright as screams breached the silence, and a hand slid free from her left hand with a thud. Eros was flailing on the floor against the far wall, laying half on top of Advan. As she swung her feet toward the side of the bed to slide off and go save him, she had to divert her movements to avoid stepping on Ahm's neck and chest.

"What the fuck is happening?" she cried. She spun around and climbed down on the other side of her bed and raced to Eros's side, cradling his head in her lap. "It's okay. It'll be okay. Just calm down," she pleaded as fresh tears rolled down her cheeks.

Mina watched helplessly as Eros twitched and screamed, experiencing the very horror she'd just awoken from. She held him for what felt like hours, gently stroking his hair, and cheek, with tears blurring her vision. Every time she reached up to wipe them away, Eros flailed and convulsed, as if the retraction of her hand was speeding his descent into madness, and death.

Though her perception said otherwise, only a few brief minutes passed before Eros's breathing shortened into quick gasps. The screaming ceased, replaced with his body's fight for breath and the accompanying lurch of his chest with each ineffective inhale. A few seconds later, his body fell fully onto the floor, and her lap, all tension gone from his muscles. As his head tipped sideways, lifeless and cold, she sobbed uncontrollably, angrily cursing Mordessa in her mind.

IT WAS hours before Ahm woke up. He found himself in a new position, laid out across Mina's bed with care, rather than crumpled on the floor. When he looked up, he saw Mina sitting beside him, head slumped sideways and gently snoring. He looked about the room, but neither Eros nor Advan were anywhere he could see.

"Mina?" he asked, pulling himself to a seated position beside her. He took her hand and gently stroked the back of it, joggling it to coax her back to the waking world.

She gasped for breath as she woke. "Ahm?" she asked, blinking the sleep from her eyes. "What happened?" she asked, her eyes filling with tears.

"I... I was about to ask you the same thing," he said.

"I woke up, you were crumpled on the floor and Eros was screaming and flailing, laying on top of Advan," she sobbed. "I think it's me who deserves an explanation."

"Eros was wailing?" gasped Ahm. "I thought that was a trick of my mind. I..." his words failed him. He didn't know what to say to fix the situation.

"What happened?" she yelled.

"Someone cast a Wailing Curse on you. Eros was helping me transfer it to Advan, but it must've somehow gone into him instead," said Ahm, realizing the truth of the situation. He suddenly realized what Mina must have gone through and looked up in sorrow, his stomach in knots. "Oh my dear Mina, I am so, so sorry. It wasn't supposed to happen that way. It was supposed to be Advan!"

"He died in my arms. I couldn't save him. His last act was screaming in pain and horror. I know what he was feeling. I know how horrible it was, because I felt it... and I had to watch him suffer through it!" she cried.

"Oh, my precious thing... I would do anything to take it back," cried Ahm, distraught. He couldn't fathom how to make the situation right, and was very uncomfortable in scenarios he had no way to control. The last thing he'd wanted to do was hurt her, and he'd done that very thing trying to save her life. "Where is he? Where is Advan?" he asked, looking around the room.

"Advan got up not long after Eros's screaming stopped, then dragged him out of the room. I... I didn't... I couldn't bear to look at Eros's twisted face any longer. I didn't want him to go, but I couldn't bring myself to stop Advan. When I finally calmed down enough, I got you onto the bed and waited for you to wake up, so you could explain what happened," she sobbed. "Why? Why did it have to be this way?"

A sinking feeling struck Ahm out of nowhere. He had a sudden inclination where Advan might have gone, and desperately hoped he was wrong. "We have to go. Now!" he barked as he got to his feet on the bed. He extended his hand to help her up. "Now!"

Mina wasn't sure what was going on, but a fresh wave of panic had washed over Ahm's face. Her pain replaced with fear, she accepted his hand and let him pull her to her feet. "What's going on?"

"I really hope I'm wrong. I'll explain on the way," he said as he pulled her along behind him.

The halls of Ahm's subterranean offices were always fairly dark. Natural light never found its way to their depths, and the occupants relied exclusively on torches, candles and glowing runes to help them see. That night the halls were especially dark, since Advan hadn't made his rounds to replenish extinguished flames, or recite the spells of illumination to light the runes along the ceiling.

"I think he took Eros to the Ascension chamber," said Ahm.

"But he's dead, he can't ascend," countered Mina.

"No, he can't... but that chamber manipulates souls. That's the basis of how it functions. Advan loves you. He helped raise you. Hell, he's older than I am. He used to help maintain that chamber, along with the Flute and everything else," explained Ahm.

"So you think he knows something about it we don't?" asked Mina, struggling to keep up with him. *When did Ahm learn to run so fast?*

"I can almost guarantee he does," said Ahm.

"Why wouldn't he have told you whatever it was, after all these years?" asked Mina.

"That man loved his secrets. He was full of them. Getting him to share was like pulling teeth with slippery fingers," sighed Ahm.

"No, I don't believe that for a second. He was always so open and kind," countered Mina.

"That's the Advan he wanted you to know," declared Ahm.

Mina tugged hard on Ahm's hand and planted her feet firmly on the floor, forcing Ahm to stop and face her. "I don't understand you one bit. First you're regaling me with tales of how smart and helpful Advan is, then you're claiming he was secretive and manipulative. One of those can't be true."

"I assure you, they can," argued Ahm.

"I don't understand, then! What the fuck is goi-"

"He's my father," interrupted Ahm. "I didn't meet him until I was already serving the Queen, but we've spent a great deal of time together since. Trust me, I know him better than anyone. He always kept little secrets from me, just so he could hold something over me. He always had to have that 'aha' moment tucked in his pocket, ready to pull out right when I'd given up."

"Wow, I... I don't know what to say," said Mina. She could completely understand how Ahm felt now that she knew Advan was his father. It was a familiar feeling she often felt toward Ahm himself. "Wait... you were going to sacrifice your father to save my life?" she gasped, suddenly realizing the weight of Ahm's actions. Tears filled her eyes again.

"I would sacrifice everything for you, Mina," said Ahm. "Now, can we please go find Advan and stop him from making a terrible mistake?"

Mina nodded and wiped away her tears. She ran behind Ahm as quickly as she could, but refused to hold his hand... she needed both hands to keep her eyes clear, and her cheeks dry. The situation was far more than she could handle, and her emotions were constantly at their maximum capacity. Running fast enough to keep up with Ahm just wasn't something she could accomplish while keeping them in check. One had to give.

AINEN SAT up before he could even open his eyes. As he blinked the sleep away, he peered around their camp, trying to figure out what had happened. Somehow he'd missed the end of their battle, the sunset, and his companions making camp for the night.

"What's going on?" he asked as he rubbed the final remnants of crust from his eyes.

"Ainen!" squealed Gnately as she barreled across the camp toward him. "Oh, you big oaf, it's so good to have you back," she finished as she jumped onto his lap and wrapped her arms around his neck.

"Okay?" he groaned, awkwardly patting her back. He looked at Tavyn, confused.

"You fell unconscious after our battle. She was *certain* you were never going to wake up, and we'd have to *carry* you everywhere," he explained.

"You wouldn't just leave me?" asked Ainen as he pushed Gnately back and peered into her eyes, slightly confused.

"Oh no, she wouldn't have that. Not at all. She was trying to figure out how to rig up a device to drag you around, so we didn't hurt our backs," laughed Tavyn.

"Why?" asked Ainen.

"Don't you like us?" gasped Gnately, pretending to be hurt.

"How?" Ainen asked, looking up at Tavyn. He reached for his cheek hesitantly, half expecting his hand to come away covered in blood.

"We're not sure, big guy. One second you're tackling the hobgoblin to the ground, and the next your face is crushed in, bleeding out all over the ground. We raced over and next thing we know, your face is glowing a blinding gold and when it faded, you were all healed up," explained Tavyn. He knelt beside his friend with a smile. "After that you blacked out, so we put a bedroll under your head and made camp."

"I just think he didn't wanna carry that hobgoblin. So he pretended to be asleep to make us do it," growled Gnately, furrowing her brow.

"I did no such thing," sighed Ainen.

"She's just teasing you, Ainen," smiled Tavyn as he returned to his feet. "Would you like some stew?"

"I'm quite hungry," he answered, as his stomach growled. The mention of food was enough to make him realize just how much he needed it.

"He was really heavy," whispered Gnately, pretending to still be angry.

"You're not," said Ainen with a slight smile, lifting her up on his hip as he got to his feet.

"Put me down!" she gasped, flailing at his chest with her tiny arms.

"Fine," he said with a smile, sliding her to the ground. "Better?"

"Just eat your stupid stew," she growled as she sat down in a huff on the other side of the fire.

"In all honesty, we were trying to figure out where to go next. We told you we'd handle the goblins, and we have. However, with Port Gandraias out of the picture, we need to find another way to get out of these gods forsaken lands. Lothenheim is an option, but walking there would take weeks, and the Tellrindosian guard are hunting for a Dynar, according to Sylk, so... we're kind of at a loss," said Tavyn.

Ainen sat for a minute, slurping the stew off his spoon, lost in thought. His mind kept trying to go back to the moment the hobgoblin bashed him in the face. Something about the event was tickling the back of his mind. Forcing himself back to the present, he looked up at Tavyn and said two words, "Fishing village."

"Thanks for the clarity," laughed Gnately.

"Is there one nearby?" asked Tavyn.

"Of sorts," he said, slurping more of the stew. "Three families, that way," he said, pointing east. "Two boats."

"Are they big boats? Seafaring vessels?" asked Tavyn.

"No," said Ainen. "Could catch a ride to one, though," he suggested.

"Oh, good idea!" chimed Gnately. "We could pay them to give us a ride to Lothenheim, or one of the larger vessels on the coast!"

Ainen nodded.

"Do you know these families?" asked Tavyn, wondering what their chances would be to convince them to help.

"Haimlesh family, no. They're rude. Mortdain family, yes. Friends of my parents. Culgrath family doesn't come west. Never met them," he explained.

"Great, so how do we get there?" asked Tavyn.

"Head east," said Ainen, shrugging.

"Is there a road?" asked Gnately.

Ainen shook his head as he slurped more stew.

"Then how do you know where they are?" asked Gnately.

"Hystari is east. Hystari has fish. They fish," answered Ainen with a shrug.

"Great, so we're headed east," shrugged Gnately. "So glad you woke up to tell us that," she laughed.

"Maybe it'll be more obvious when we get closer to the shore? No clue how we're going to pay for passage, but I guess that's a problem for when we arrive," said Tavyn.

"That's the easy part," shrugged Gnately. She held out her coin purse, released the tension on its cord and spread the top open for him to see. Several gold coins glimmered inside.

"How much do you have?" gasped Tavyn.

"About twenty-two gold, give or take a few silver. I've been saving up," she answered with a smile. It was obvious she was quite proud of herself.

"Didn't know I was traveling with nobility," teased Tavyn.

"Hey, you stop that right now! I earned every bit of this," she grunted playfully.

"Oh. Oh, I see," he responded, feigning an apologetic look.

"Well, whatever. I'll pay our way out of this snow, if you first promise me we'll never have to touch this stuff again, and second that you'll find a way to pay me back some day. This is my retirement money, after all," she said.

"Trust me, I want less to do with this fluffy white nonsense than you do. I grew up in a savanna, surrounded by sand. As to your second request, I will absolutely pay you back. I'll do whatever it takes, for however long it takes," he finished with a smile.

They sat for a time in silence while Ainen finished his meal. It was a pleasant evening, even if they considered the rotting corpses a few yards into the wood, and the vague sense of direction that governed their future.

After a while, Tavyn broke the silence with a question that had been burning in the back of his mind. "Gnat? What's that thing you fidget with whenever we're sitting around doing nothing?" He locked his eyes on her right hand, carefully and casually shifting something white and pink around in her palm.

"Oh, this?" she asked, presenting the small, oddly shaped, polished stone. "It was part of my payment from Nightweaver. She made it sound important, so I hung onto it. Don't know what it's for, though. Feels nice on my palm," she said somewhat sheepishly.

"Looks like an egg," said Ainen.

"An egg? It's just a pebble," laughed Gnately. She cut her laugh short, though, and studied the stone closer. *Is it an egg?*

"Can I see it?" asked Tavyn. "Don't worry, I'll be careful," he added, reaching his hand toward her.

She shrugged and handed it over. He studied it for a short while, then noticed Ainen reaching his own hand for it. Tavyn looked at Gnately to make sure it was okay. She nodded in response to his unasked question with a smile and a shrug.

As he placed the stone in Ainen's palm, it shook ever-so-slightly. It was as if something inside it was moving.

MINA AND Ahm had spent the past two hours running headlong through the wide open expanse of the Cryx. It was the one place in the whole of Dusk that she'd never been interested in exploring; a huge, dark void beneath the cathedral and political districts that lie at the center of the world's largest city, suspended in mid air by enormous iron chains.

She had an ingrained fear that somehow the gigantic mass of stone would fall and crush anyone underneath. Coupled with the knowledge that the Cryx-bound cast-offs—deemed no longer useful on the surface—performed their duties in the Cryx, and the sadness she usually felt in the presence of such tortured souls, she was as far out of her preferred element as she could stand. It took a great deal of effort to push onward, and only the thought that she was there to save Eros gave her the strength to accomplish it.

"We're here," declared Ahm, coming to a stop. "If my suspicions are correct, he'll be up there. If he's planning to resurrect Eros through the power of the Aggripha, we have to stop him. There's a law stating we must never allow such a thing. The law isn't clear about what could happen if we tried, but there are hints about the possible corruption of the person's soul."

Ahm pointed to a structure that seemed suspended beneath the bedrock of the upper city. Blue energy pulsed through a column that reached down from above, and seemed to spread into smaller beams of stone like a hand, gripping the top of an obsidian cube.

In each cardinal direction, a walkway stretched away from the cube. The ones to the north and south led to open iron stairs leading up to the city above. The ones to the east and west stretched down onto the floor of the Cryx below. On each of the northern and southern walkways, just before the stairs, was a small platform upon which sat a single iron chair. A figure was moving about on the southern landing, doing what appeared to be maintenance on the back of the chair.

"That's him!" gasped Mina.

"Probably, but we can't be sure until we draw closer," he answered, entering a jog. "Dozens of people ascend each day. So many, in fact, that there's usually a queue, and both chairs are almost always in use. At least, in normal times."

"Normal times?" asked Mina, trying to keep up. Her legs were almost at the point of failure. She wasn't sure how much longer she could go on.

"No one has ascended in almost six months, and each year there seems to be fewer than before," he confirmed.

"What? Why?" asked Mina.

"Every hundred years, the chambers are sealed and Ascension is forbidden until the Queen declares otherwise. After she does, everything resumes as if nothing happened," said Ahm.

"You never questioned that?" asked Mina, nearly out of breath again.

"Plenty have questioned it. Now ask how many are alive to know the answer," he suggested, giving her a quick glance over his shoulder.

They quieted as they ascended the western stairs. When they reached the top of the hundred foot ascent, Mina burst past Ahm and thundered toward the man in the chair with reckless abandon. It was indeed Eros, and working behind him with surprising fluidity was Advan.

"Eros!" gasped Mina as she arrived. Iron shackles barred his arms, legs, neck, waist, and forehead in place. He didn't appear to be breathing. "What are you doing?" she gasped toward Advan.

"Father, stop. You don't know what you're doing," said Ahm.

"You know nothing of what you speak," replied Advan, speaking clearer than he had in years.

"You can't bring him back!" gasped Ahm, stopping a few feet from the chair.

"Can't I? Centuries spent living in the Cryx, and you never bothered to find out what this place is or how it functions. Yet you stand here, declaring what can and cannot be done!" barked Advan in disbelief.

"How are you-" started Ahm.

"This place is so much more than you can imagine, poor Ahm. I only wish I'd known you in your youth. I could've taught you everything I know; everything I forgot. To think it only took my impending demise to show me just how much I failed you as a father," said Advan as he flipped a few switches, and pulled a pair of levers. "Did you never wonder what this all means? How it all came to be?"

"You can tell me later," said Ahm. "Just stop what you're doing."

"Aggriphaxxedon. The great prismatic dragon. Empress of the Talaani Empire. Her heart was ripped from her chest by Queen Mordessa and turned into the Aggripha, the crystalline heart that powers our Kingdom. With her latent magics and the Queen's enchantments, the heart became a Soulcairn. Everyone who ascends grants it access to their soul. Everyone who dies becomes a part of it. This Kingdom is trapped in an endless cycle of betrayal and death, all brought about by our terrible Queen.

"I only regret that it took my final act to show you the truth. I came here to save Eros; to save Mina the heartache you felt when Norrissa was taken from you by that same spell, cast by that same Queen. I tapped into the Aggripha to renew my strength; to sacrifice myself so I could accomplish this one task. Everything that I knew, all the memories I'd lost, flooded back all at once. It was then that I realized what had to be done. Resurrecting Eros is but the first step.

"The rest, I'm afraid, is up to you," he said, turning his attention toward Mina. "Now step back," Advan added, gently tugging on the final lever. She backed away as he continued to pull, and energies swirled to life atop Eros, dancing in and out of the chair. "Three souls were consumed to create Mordessa's curse of binding. Noktrusgodhen tried to break the curse, but failed," he said as the lever clicked fully into place. "Seek the prophecy of Korr!" he yelled as a wave of power rolled off the chair and crashed into him, rendering his body to ash in an instant.

The screams of a thousand souls burst forth from the surge of magic, echoing through the silence of the Cryx, and drawing a response from its many scattered, mindless workers. As the sound dissipated and the power ebbed Mina ran back to Eros's side, a small trickle of blood staining the side of her face just below her ear.

"Wha... where am I?" asked Eros as he woke.

Chapter 11:
Fate

Ris'Enliss, Luthentyr 6th, 576 of the 1st Era

MINA LOOKED back at Ahm, confused and terrified. "Get... get him out of this thing," she cried. "We should leave this place!"

Ahm didn't initially respond. He was stunned, unsure how to cope with what he'd just witnessed. "Why?" he uttered. "Why didn't I research the Aggripha?" he gasped.

"Who fucking cares? We can figure that out later! Help me!" she yelled.

"What's wrong?" asked Eros. "Why... why am I shackled to a chair?"

"I'm trying to get you out of it, just hold still," she sobbed as she struggled to release the pins that held them fast.

Ahm broke free of his trance and brought his mind back to reality. He turned toward the pair and hurried over. "Step back. I'll free him," he said. After a few seconds, the shackles swung clear, and he helped Eros out of the chair. "Can you walk?"

"I'll try," gasped Eros. His muscles felt as if he hadn't used them in years. "I'm so stiff," he said.

"It's ascension sickness. It'll pass," said Ahm.

"I ascended?" asked Eros as he leaned on Ahm for support.

"Not exactly," said Ahm. "Let's get you back to my compound. We'll figure this all out once we're rested and calmed down."

"Come on," chimed Mina, heading for the stairs.

DURING THEIR walk back through the Cryx, every echo of their footsteps drew cries from distressed voices in the distance. Mina had the distinct feeling they were being watched, which she could consciously reason away thanks to the nature of the place, and the millions of mindless citizens that worked in its depths. The feeling had not been present on their walk to the Aggripha, though, and something felt distinctly wrong during their return trip.

Even Ahm and Eros seemed troubled enough by the eeriness that surrounded them to remain silent during the journey, which was something else that struck Mina particularly odd. It wasn't like Ahm to remain silent when his mind was racing, trying to put the pieces of a puzzle together. Neither was it normal for Eros to keep his thoughts to himself, especially when stressed, concerned, or confused. To have both men silently following in her wake was more off-putting than she could have expected.

When they finally reached the outer doors to his office complex several hours later, she held the door for them to enter and slowly closed it once they'd passed. A wave of relief washed over her as soon as they were inside the walls of her home; her trap; the place she once resented more than anything.

"I know we're both thinking it," suggested Mina to Ahm as she caught up to him in the hall. "What in the gods' name is The Prophecy of Korr?"

"That would be the question of the millennium, it seems," he sighed.

"You said there were lots of prophecies and they were all madness," she said.

"No scholar worth their station puts any credence into prophecies. As far as I'm concerned, all of them were written by desperate people so fed up with their lot in life that they'd rather create hope through fantasy. In fact, that's pretty much how most of society views them. Pointless drivel meant to pull one out of their reality just long enough to give them an excuse for failing to overcome their own obstacles. 'Oh, I lost my business because So-and-so hasn't risen to overturn my tax debt', and the like," he explained.

"Clearly prophecies must get it right now and then, otherwise why would people believe them?" asked Mina as they entered his office. Eros pulled chairs over for them to sit across from Ahm.

"One can always look back at a thing that has happened and correlate it with a prophecy written prior, especially if they choose to ignore the details that disagree with them. Most prophecies are intentionally vague, specifically to leave them open for interpretation... a fact which further ruins their credibility," said Ahm, folding his hands in thought.

"Then who the hell is Korr, and why does *his* prophecy stand apart?" asked Mina.

"Korr... High Priest Delorain made mention of him once in a teaching about the folly of following one's own passion and ignoring the true calling of Ishnu... and the resulting impact it has on the Kingdom," mulled Eros.

"I have the same vague recollection, but not through being taught. Whoever Korr was, and whatever they did, it happened during my lifetime," said Ahm, leaning forward in contemplation.

"What does an ancient dissident have to do with Mina? Or me?" asked Eros.

"That's what we're trying to determine," said Mina.

"Before you brought me to Mina's bedchamber, before that... that... chair, you said Mina wasn't who, or what, I thought she was. Before you could explain, the curse befell her. Is that related to what happened? To whatever this prophecy is?" asked Eros.

Mina grew sullen, her gaze falling to the hands in her lap. Ahm remained silent, lost in his own thoughts.

"Would anyone care to explain?" asked Eros.

"When we spent our last evening together, you used a word to describe what Mordessa was. Do you remember?" asked Mina, looking back up at him with fear in her eyes.

"Yes, I said she was a Forsaken," he answered with a shrug.

"That's what I am; a Forsaken," she explained sheepishly. He looked back in disbelief. "My mother was Unliving, and my father Undead. Both had recently ascended, and had been forced into it by their families. They tried to flee, and in their flight—their passion—I was conceived. I shouldn't exist," she explained.

"How is that possible?" asked Eros, stunned.

"We don't know how. We just know it is a fact," said Ahm. "Additionally troubling is the way you were resurrected, Eros. In all my studies and experience regarding the Aggripha and its nature, I can't piece together how Advan made it happen. The laws hint it is possible, and warn never to pursue it. The act is punishable by death, in fact. Nothing about this sits well with me."

"And then there's the matter of the curse," said Mina.

"The Wailing Curse, cast upon you by someone far more powerful than I," he said.

"After the injury, I was trapped in a vision... watching the world through Mordessa's eyes. Unlike my dreams prior, I was a little in control of what I could see, and my thoughts were my own. She found whatever she was searching for in her crystal ball, and I remarked on it. She heard me," said Mina.

"You were having visions of Mordessa for over a month?" gasped Eros.

"I... I was unconscious for over a month?" gasped Mina.

"Yeah, we haven't had a good chance to explain that part yet," shrugged Ahm. "Quite a lot has happened since you woke, after all."

"Well, I woke because Mordessa threw me out of my dream state," stated Mina, more than a little concerned.

"She must've done so with the curse. Which means she was aware of what you are, more than likely," sighed Ahm. "Fuck."

"Maybe she thinks she killed her?" offered Eros.

"I don't think that's a safe assumption, but we don't have a way to prove otherwise. You two need to stay in this building—ideally on the lower levels—while I find out what I can about this 'Korr' and their prophecy. I'll send agents across the Kingdom to determine just how fucked we are. Until I have more information, I need you both to stay out of sight," said Ahm.

"Great," said Mina sarcastically. "Just what I wanted to hear," she sighed.

"Hey, at least I'll be here with you this time," said Eros, reaching for her hand.

Mina accepted his hand then looked up at Ahm in horror. "What... what happens next time I sleep? I always dream of Mordessa these days. Will she sense me again?" Panic washed across her face, and her skin went as white as the vellum on Ahm's desk.

"I'll move as quickly as I can. Eros... make sure she stays awake. Raid my bean stores and roast as much coffee as you need. Have her show you around. Do some research together... hells, why don't you show him the Raven? That'll keep you both busy," he suggested.

"Raven?" asked Eros.

"I... I won't try to fly it, but I can show him," she offered, calming slightly.

"Fly? Did you say fly?" gasped Eros.

"Go. Leave me to my research. This isn't going to be easy, and I need to focus," said Ahm.

As the couple exited his office, Ahm reached for the chest to his left, under the edge of his desk. It was Advan's chest, and he'd been meaning to go through it. The old man had been fading for years, but his decline had escalated in recent months. The magics that made an Unliving possible staved off rigor mortis and the following decay for centuries, sometimes longer, but they eventually caught up. Once rigor mortis eventually set in, it spelled the end of an Unliving's extended lifespan, and it was only a matter of time before they'd decay into mindlessness, and be sent into the dark depths of the Cryx to clean debris, or work the mines.

He'd put off going through his father's belongings for as long as he could. It was time to learn the last of the man's secrets.

GNATELY WAS quite tired of walking, though she was happy to know they were moving toward a goal; a goal that she hoped would lead to warmer climates and comfortable toes. That hope did nothing to ease the soreness in her knees, ankles, or thighs. As the smallest member of her group, she found herself constantly jogging—if not running—to keep up with her friends or catch up after falling behind.

"This totally isn't fair," she blurted.

"What?" asked Tavyn.

"Every time Ainen takes a step, I have to take like... twelve," she sighed.

"Four, but I get you. I average between one-and-a-half and two to his one, and I'm not enjoying it either," he said with a smile.

"Four? It's easily nineteen per one," she grumbled, rolling her eyes.

"I literally counted. You take four steps for each one of his," he said with a wry smile.

She hastened and shortened her steps, rapidly driving her feet into the ground while gaining as little forward momentum as possible. "See?"

"Twenty three! Impressive! And how'd that little demonstration make you feel?" he teased.

"Exhausted!" she gasped, dramatically throwing herself into Tavyn's arms.

"You know, if you wanted a break you could've just asked," laughed Tavyn.

She plopped her rump into the ground without another word and immediately extracted everyone's favorite polished stone from her pouch. Ainen heard the commotion and turned back to join them, sighing under his breath at their slowness. Tavyn set about gathering wood for a small fire.

"We're making camp?" asked Ainen.

"That was the plan. She's exhausted, Ainen. Can't really blame her. Look at the length of her legs compared to yours," said Tavyn.

"But... just over the hill-" started Ainen.

"-is more walking! I don't wanna!" moaned Gnately.

"Just over the-" started Ainen again.

"What's the harm in a little break?" asked Tavyn.

"Look!" demanded Ainen, pointing east.

Tavyn dropped his handful of sticks and twigs with a sigh and went to see what Ainen was pointing at. He pushed through a set of chest-high branches and found himself exposed to open air, standing atop a hill, looking down on a small cluster of buildings in the distance.

Shocked and humbled, he returned to Gnately's side and said, "Um... he's right. We've arrived."

"What?" she gasped.

"It's true," shrugged Tavyn. "Right over that ridge is a path down to three houses, a couple of outbuildings, and a fishing shed."

"Told you. East," said Ainen with a shrug.

"Fine," sighed Gnately. "Let's get this over with... but I'm leading," she grunted.

The next hour was very painful for Ainen. He'd never walked as slowly in his life. He had to check often to make sure they were even moving. How Gnomes successfully lived as nomads across Algona at a pace like that confused him greatly. It wasn't until they reached the bottom of the hill and saw the settlement's livestock that he remembered horses existed, and that Gnomes likely knew how to ride them.

A YOUNG boy and girl were playing in the field near the settlement. The girl stopped abruptly and pointed at the three travelers coming down the hill as they neared the bottom. Shortly afterward, the boy yelled, "Mom! Mom!" as he rounded the corner seeking the safety of his parents, the girl following closely behind.

The settlement was small, if not quaint. Each house faced a small well at the center, with various outhouses, sheds and barns sprawling behind them up the sides of hills, and leading down toward the shoreline. A dirt and gravel path led from the western hills, between the buildings, around the well, and split east toward the single dock, and north toward parts unknown.

All the buildings seemed to be constructed using the same techniques. Peaked roofs covered with brown clay shingles. Wooden slats covering their exterior, old white paint peeling away from old age. Stone footings made from dissimilar blocks of granite, held fast with old mortar that was slowly being worn away by the weather. All three houses even had similarly placed chimneys and thin streams of smoke rising into the sky.

Since they'd started their descent, the smell of burning wood and slow-cooked meats had filled the air with a faint undertone of wet hay and livestock. Pigs snorted happily nearby, accompanied occasionally by the familiar sounds of a cow speaking its mind, or a horse protesting the presence of flies.

Gnately wasn't sure the settlement's name, if it had one, or even which Kingdom it belonged to. The only thing she was certain of was that this small collection of homes nestled into a small clump of hills just south of Port Gandraias, but north of Algon Keep, was just about as cute a place as she could've imagined. Had it not been for the thin layer of snow on the ground, or the brisk, salty winds rolling in from the nearby ocean, she'd have asked to stay put, and slowly soak them of every coin she could manage... with a smile on her face, of course.

Two adults rounded the corner of the nearest home, accompanied by the small, excited children. "Hail, travelers," called the man. His clothes were distinctly home made, modest, and befitting a man that worked hard. A well-groomed beard adorned his chin, braided to protect it from the duties he performed, and accentuated by the bright white shirt behind it. The woman beside him was slightly better dressed, though her clothing was also handmade. Her bright blonde hair blew elegantly in the breeze, drawing both Ainen and Tavyn's eyes. If Gnately had to guess, she'd say the humans that approached had changed clothes before rushing out to meet their guests. The illusion had totally succeeded in the eyes of her companions.

"We're sorry to trespass; you've a wonderful settlement, and we don't wish to disrupt your lives. However, we find ourselves in need of assistance and, given the tragedy that recently befell Port Gandraias, were wondering if we might pay you for passage on board a fishing vessel?" asked Tavyn.

"Oh my," gasped the woman. "You're very well spoken for a man of the world," she added with a smile.

"Don't mind my wife, we don't get many visitors out this way," he said. "Name's Peter Culgrath, and this is my wife, Larissa."

"I am Tavyn. This is Gnately, and the big guy is Ainen," he said.

"You seem nice enough, but unfortunately, our boat is in desperate need of repairs. The Haimleshes don't really fancy outsiders," he said, pointing at their home across the street. "They're nice enough folk once you get to know them, and very good with livestock. But, they don't own a boat. The Mortdains over there," he said, pointing down the road, "have a fine vessel, but they've been out at sea for weeks. No idea when they'll return to the dock."

"What's wrong with your boat? Maybe we could help?" asked Tavyn.

"Well," sighed Peter, unsure if he should proceed.

"Hun, look at him!" said Larissa, pointing casually at Ainen. "We don't need Henry with a big man like that around!"

"She's right, I guess," admitted Peter. "What we need is muscle, and you seem to have plenty of it. Mast cracked in a storm a few days back. I barely made it back to shore. We've got a new one, but I can't lift it into place on my own. If you could help get me seaworthy again, I can see about taking you somewhere. Where did you need to go?"

Ainen answered, "North," at the same time Gnately said, "South."

Tavyn held his hands in front of his friends, signaling them to stop with a chuckle. "We were originally headed north to catch a ship back south, because Algona has shut Gusarski Cove down to prepare a blockade against Gulthara. Then we found out about the destruction of Port Gandraias, so we just assumed we'd have to head to Lothenheim, but... since we discovered your settlement was here, we hoped we'd be able to pay for an alternative, and save ourselves that walk."

"Wait, Gandraias was destroyed?" asked Peter.

"Yes, by an evil witch," said Gnately. "She's really old, and moves through shadows. I'd say her name, but I really think we shouldn't."

"Oh, no!" gasped Larissa. "Piya told me that's where the Mortdains were headed. Do you think they..." her words trailed off, her brow wrinkled with concern.

"Piya!" called the man over his shoulder.

A young girl exited the house, her curly red hair tied back, bouncing on her left shoulder as she jogged up to them. She was taller than Tavyn, but not by much, and wore a shirt, pants and boots very similar to Peter's, but had a leather apron over the top of her clothes. "Yes?" she said as she arrived.

"What route were your parents taking?" asked Peter.

"North along the shore to check the lobster cages, then south to Port Gandraias, where they planned to stay on vacation for a time, then out with the solstice tide to catch a marlin, then home, to cure the meat for winter," she answered.

"I am so sorry," said Gnately, her tiny voice barely doing the weight of her next statement justice. "I don't think your parents are going to make it home," she said. "A terrible tragedy destroyed Port Gandraias, and we believe all those who were in the city at the time."

The girl's face went stark white, her eyes filled with tears, and her bottom lip began to quiver. "Mo... momma? And papa?"

Larissa stepped toward the poor girl and pulled her into a hug. Gnately ran up and grabbed on to the poor girl's thighs, squeezing tightly.

"This is terrible," lamented Peter. "The Mortdains caught most of the fish we eat. That marlin was going to feed all three families for months."

"Don't you fish?" asked Tavyn.

"I mostly deal in shellfish, muscles, and the like; delicacies we sell in the ports. It's fine eating, but not the kind of eating we're accustomed to here. Our little community survives on trade. My wife makes our clothes, the coin I make brings in supplies from the south. The Mortdains provide most of our meat, and their coin covers the cost of materials we buy from the north. The Haimleshes handle the livestock and produce, giving us all dairy, vegetables, and eggs. So, yeah... this is going to hit our community quite hard. We just had to buy fresh brick to fix the Haimlesh's fireplace, and pipe for their wood stove so they wouldn't freeze during winter. We've no coin left to buy the food we need," said Peter.

"Well," started Gnately, backing away from Piya. "Ainen can help fix your boat, no problem. And I can help with coin. All we ask is you help us find a way to Pelrigoss." She opened her purse and revealed the gold within. It was more money than Peter or Larissa had ever seen in one place.

"How... how much are you willing to pay?" gasped Peter.

"Is five gold enough?" asked Gnately. She had no idea what ship passage cost.

"Gnately, is it?" asked Peter. Gnately nodded. "Ten gold would buy my boat outright. You could sail it anywhere you wanted. I'll even help you fix it before you go. That would let me replace my boat in spring, and still have enough left over to buy food for our community to get us through winter."

"Eight gold," said Gnately, stubbornly.

Larissa tugged on her husband's shirt. He turned back to her for a moment. She nodded at him, then resumed her attempts to comfort Piya.

"Okay, it's a deal. Eight gold," he said, sticking his hand out for her to shake. She counted eight gold out of her purse, and shook his hand with the coins sandwiched between their palms.

"Where is the mast?" asked Ainen, eager to get to work.

GNATELY AND Tavyn sat on the Culgrath's front porch while Peter and Ainen worked to fix the boat. Larissa brought them tea before heading to the Mortdain's with Piya, who was very distraught and having a hard time coming to grips with the news of Port Gandraias.

"Do you think things will go back to normal?" asked Gnately with a sigh.

"Do tell, what qualifies as normal in your eyes? And while you're at it, what about our circumstances *isn't* normal?" he asked with a chuckle.

"Well, see... *now* I need to know why you felt the need to ask that! What are you implying?" she retorted.

"As far as I'm aware, you grew up wandering the countryside with a band of miscreants, getting into trouble, and scrounging for food and coin. From where I sit, you're still wandering the countryside with a band of miscreants, getting into trouble, and scrounging for food and coin," he laughed.

"Fair point. But my question still stands," she stated calmly, then took a sip of her tea.

"How? How does your question still stand?" he gasped.

She shrugged.

"Are you just trying to sound intellectual because you *think* people should sound intellectual while sipping warm tea on a porch overlooking their community on a fine winter afternoon?" he asked.

She shrugged again and took another sip of tea with her pinky out.

"You are too much," he laughed.

They sat for a few moments in silence, sipping tea, while Gnately fidgeted with her pebble. She looked up at him and back at her stone a few times until he finally noticed what she was doing.

"Something troubling you?" he asked.

"Not really. It's just... you and Ainen said you felt Pebbly move, and I haven't yet. I mean, I know I've got chubby little hands, but you can still feel things through chubby," she sighed.

"What on Ayrelon are you-" started Tavyn.

"Well, it's like," she interrupted, then paused to think. "It's like, maybe it *is* an egg. And if it's an egg, and it's *my* egg, then why *shouldn't* I feel it move? You know? It'd be like if I was pregnant and *you* felt my baby kick through my tummy, but I didn't. Like... how would *that* be fair?"

"I don't know how it works, okay? Maybe Ainen and I are both delusional, and it's just a stupid rock like you said in the first place," he said. "Hell, you've seen what's going on with Ainen's skin. Maybe he's magical, and it only moves when it's near his magic?"

"What *is* going on with his skin? And why haven't we discussed that yet? Doesn't it seem a bit concerning?"

"You mean the fact that our friend, the former slave, who we really know nothing about, is somehow turning to stone whenever he gets wounded?" asked Tavyn. "I have trouble thinking of anything else, actually."

"You think he's really turning to stone?" asked Gnately as she slipped the pebble back into her pouch.

"While he was unconscious, I touched his cheek. It's very, very tough. Too tough. I tapped it with the tip of my dagger just to see and it clinked, just like stone. Something very strange is going on," he said.

"Well, have you talked to him about it?" she asked.

"He hasn't seen his own face yet, so I don't think he really knows what's going on. I've been trying to figure out how to bring it up, and I just keep putting it off," he said.

Gnately finished the rest of her tea and got up. She surveyed the area for a brief second, then turned toward Tavyn again. "I think we should go check on Ainen, see if we're going to set off tonight, or if we need to make camp somewhere."

"That's a good idea," said Tavyn, setting his tea aside.

As they walked down the path toward the docks, they could hear yelling coming from inside the Mortdain home. Ever the curious one, Gnately immediately ran for the door and listened. Tavyn slowly walked up behind her, much less curious, and more worried they were going to cause more harm than good.

"They were my parents! That makes this my home! Besides, you don't even know if they're dead! What if they come back tomorrow?" yelled Piya.

"This house belongs to the community, not your parents. If you want to be technical about it, the land-use deed registered with Lord Vaelin clearly states that all this land belongs to my husband! So, if your parents have passed, *and they have*, then this home returns to our control, and that includes everything inside!" yelled Larissa.

"You're going to kick me onto the street in the middle of winter because some *strangers* told you my parents died in an entirely different city? With no proof?" growled Piya.

Gnately finished picking the lock on the door and slowly pushed it open. Tavyn hadn't even noticed her doing it. She looked back at him and waved her hand toward the floor, asking him to sneak. He sighed and pushed past her, certain that sneaking was the last thing they should be doing.

"Did I just hear what I thought I heard?" asked Tavyn as he barged into the room.

"I was simply explaining to the girl that this house belongs to us now, not her. She's too young to manage property, run a fishing business and pay her portion of the taxes. We must take ownership of the home and rent it to someone more capable. It's a simple business matter, and none of your concern," said Larissa.

Tavyn reached up and brushed the dried mud off the insignia on his armor. It had been a convincing enough mark for Royce to mistake him for an Algonan soldier, so he hoped it would work on a woman such as Larissa. She took notice of the symbol and immediately backed away and calmed herself.

"I'm so sorry, my Lord. I didn't know," she said sheepishly, her head bowed.

"I'm sure Lord Vaelin will be interested to know what you're doing here. Forcing a young girl out on the streets to fend for herself, and laying false claim to her family home? I don't think he's overseen a case as scandalous as this in some time. You might even make the Gusarski Herald. You'll be famous," Gnately said, taking the lead. She walked up beside Tavyn with a wry smile, her small, pudgy arms crossed determinedly.

"Would you like to press charges, Piya?" Tavyn asked, following Gnately's lead.

"I most certainly would!" she yelled angrily.

"Keep it calm, keep it calm. There's no reason to let our emotions win the day," he said. "Is there, Mrs. Culgrath?"

"My lord, what can we do to make this whole thing go away?" asked Larissa, looking up toward him timidly.

"Are you trying to bribe me?" he quipped.

"Oh no, never. I wouldn't dare," said Larissa, bowing her head again.

"Gnately? Do you *really* want to travel all the way back to Gusarski right now?" he asked, his eyes still locked on Larissa.

"Not particularly. Seems like we just left. Hunted down that goblin horde like Vaelin asked, had our leisure time, and now we *should* be headed to Pelrigoss to gather intelligence on Gultharan activities... I'd hate to disappoint our liege," she answered.

"But if duty dictates we return, then we should return, yes? Even if we don't want to?" he asked.

"I mean... if the Culgraths saw fit to help us serve our Lord Vaelin, then perhaps their act would be enough to allow us to overlook *one* minor unsavory act," suggested Gnately.

"We'll give you back your gold. Keep the boat, and take your gold. That is fair, right?" gasped Larissa.

"Eight gold for a house, and what... five acres of land?" scoffed Gnately.

"Twenty acres, my Lady," said Piya.

"We don't have anything else!" cried Larissa.

"You have Algrim's armament!" said Piya. "It's sitting on full display in your smoking den. He wasn't much bigger than I am. It should fit just fine, with a little modification."

"Peter would never give up his father's armor or weapons!" argued Larissa.

"So he'd rather go to prison and lose his land?" asked Tavyn.

"Well... no," sighed Larissa. "I don't think he would."

"Is Algrim's armament fair trade for your parents' home, Piya?" asked Tavyn, crossing his arms.

"Yes. Not sure I'd want to come back here anyway, with this turn of attitude," said Piya.

"Fine. Gather your things. You'll come with us, and we'll help you find a new home after we return from our mission. As to you, Larissa, the house and land are yours, as you wished. Your payment is the armament, our gold, and the boat," said Tavyn. "Do this, and Lord Vaelin need never hear of your actions here. Instead, he will hear that you helped his agents in a mission of great importance."

"Yes, my lord," said Larissa and she sulked her way out of the house, defeated.

"I think I love you," gasped Piya. "Can we... can we go north and see if my parents are alive?"

"We certainly can, Piya," answered Gnately, drawing a stern look from Tavyn. "What? We can!"

"No, it's fine. I guess I'm just still adjusting to your version of 'normal', is all," he said.

"You love me. You know you do," she grinned.

Piya pointed to the kitchen. "We'll need food for the journey, won't we? Take what we need. They'll just steal it anyway," she sighed. "I'll be back down in a minute," she added as she bounded up the stairs.

"I like her," said Gnately. "She's like me, but human, and her parents are dead, and she grew up in a house instead of roaming a field, and her parents earned an honest income rather than teaching her the fine art of thievery."

"So she's not like you at all," said Tavyn, nodding, as he loaded a sack with dried goods.

"Precisely," said Gnately, nodding. "That's why I like her!"

"You're going to be the death of me," he laughed.

Gnately looked up at him and smiled, then nodded eagerly and exited the room, her arms wrapped around a very large round of cheese.

Piya joined them on the porch a half hour later, dragging two sacks. They waited patiently while Larissa brought Algrim's equipment, one piece after another, taking as much time as she could with the process.

By the time Peter and Ainen returned from the dock, all of Algrim's gear was lying on the Mortdain stoop, and Larissa was pacing frantically beside the well. Peter rushed over to her in a mild state of panic, then turned angrily toward the group and strode over. Tavyn watched, waiting for just such a response.

"Evening," said Tavyn, coldly.

"What the fuck is the meaning of this?" yelled Peter, pointing at his father's armor.

"Ask your wife," said Gnately.

"You waited for me to leave her side to throw Lord Vaelin's name around and steal our belongings? I'll have you hung!" bellowed the man.

"She tried to lay claim to the Mortdain estate, and we caught her. She was going to cast Piya out on the streets to starve, and die... in the cold... while you lived fat and happy on profits from renting this house out to someone new. So, if you want to talk about thieves, look to your own house first," said Tavyn, his hand moving to the small of his back just in case.

"Is this true?" Peter asked, swinging back around to face his wife. Instead of responding, she buried her face in her hands and ran back to their house.

"This equipment will go on to serve Lord Vaelin on our mission. It is a donation from your wife, in trade for the Mortdain estate. It will also ensure we have no motivation to tell Lord Vaelin about your wife's intentions of kicking Piya out into the wilds to fend for herself," said Tavyn.

"I... I didn't know she was doing that. She didn't tell me," he said, backpedaling slowly.

"Go home and reconsider the way you handle your affairs," said

Tavyn angrily.

Once he was gone, Tavyn asked Ainen to carry the armor to the boat, and they all made their way to the docks.

"What was that?" asked Ainen.

"They had to pay the asshole tax," said Gnately gruffly.

"Oh," said Ainen. After a moment, he asked, "that's real?"

Piya and Gnately laughed far too hard at his naivety.

"It should be, Ainen. It certainly should be," said Tavyn. "Otherwise the whole damned world will end up like Haern."

IT WAS obvious to all aboard that Tavyn had learned quite a bit about sailing during his trip north from Haern. The few things he didn't know were reinforced very quickly by a surprisingly knowledgeable Piya, who was more than happy to act as their captain, even without being asked.

Between the two of them, and Ainen's impressive strength, they were able to get The Cracked Clam into deeper waters and headed north along the coast. Piya guided them to a current her father often used, which ran northward at a considerable pace during the night. It followed a stream of air that raced up from Gulthara, and continued along the coast all the way to Lothenheim, where it turned east into the arctic waters of the northern Hystari.

By morning, Gandraias was within sight. Several ships were moored at its docks, many of which seemed damaged or partially sunken. Something powerful had ravaged them, and they were no longer seaworthy. On the farthest dock, Piya caught sight of her family's boat, The Timid Shark, and her heart sank instantly.

Seeing her sullen gaze, Gnately joined her on the bow and gently grabbed her hand. "Maybe they went overland to another city? Visiting someone in Lothenheim, perhaps?"

"I appreciate what you're trying to do. I really do. But we both know what I'm going to find," said Piya. "I have to look either way. It's going to eat me up inside if I don't."

Tavyn guided the boat to the same dock and Ainen worked to tie it off. They climbed onto the dock once everything was secure, and made their way to the Mortdain's boat. Its railing was slightly damaged from colliding with the footing of the dock, but the boat was so much lower in the water that its sides were not nearly as damaged as the other vessels nearby. The larger merchant ships hadn't fared as well, not even close. While the rest of the group searched the boat for clues, or anything useful, he walked toward the other end of the dock to take a look at what Sylk had told them about. As soon as the city came into view, he took an involuntary step back.

"By Ishnu's might, what happened here?" he gasped.

"What? What is it?" came Gnately's voice from the boat.

"You have to come see this!" yelled Tavyn.

Stretched out before the group was a blackened debris field, exactly where the center of the city should have been. Whole buildings had toppled, or simply vaporized, as a result of some explosion or magical outburst. They walked into the city out of sheer, morbid curiosity. All around them was ash drifts, rubble, and the odd piece of metal. No living soul remained; no corpses; no remnants of someone's meal; no animals. Everything and everyone had seemingly been obliterated in an instant.

"She described it to us, but I couldn't picture it in my mind. It's just... how does this happen? How is this even possible? All this was caused by one witch?" gasped Tavyn.

"I really regret stealing that map, now," said Gnately. "I shouldn't have helped her."

"How could you have known? I mean, you were sitting there with me when Sylk and Nadyra told us about this place. Did their description of the event register as anything remotely close to this?" asked Tavyn.

"No. How could it?" asked Gnately.

Piya, meanwhile, was in tears, walking behind them in silence. Ainen noticed and put his arm around her shoulders. She leaned into his embrace, seeking comfort. She didn't know how to process what was happening, or the fact that she was alone in the world, with no family left to care for her. It was too much. Finally at her limit, she fell to her knees and sobbed heavily into her hands.

Ainen looked up at the others and yelled, "Hey! We need to go! This is enough!" He knelt and whispered, "I'm going to pick you up now."

She nodded back, then he carried her back toward the docks. Their visit to Port Gandraias had gone just as badly as Tavyn anticipated.

ONCE THEY returned to the sea, Piya insisted they use the southern current several miles offshore, in choppier waters. The wind wasn't in their favor, given the inland storm fronts rolling west to east across their path. Regardless, she was able to guide them back toward their destination with greater success than they would have had without her knowledge.

She calmed over the next two days, and slowly came to grips with her new reality. The group was supportive during her bouts of depression, especially Gnately. They were a joy to be with during her more cheerful moments. Ainen looked after her like a big brother, taking special care to make sure she saw to her own needs, before letting her worry about the others. Tavyn remained stoic and focused, but she slowly learned from Gnately how to break him out of his shell with playful teasing.

At the end of the second day, she called everyone to the steerage with a few rings of the bell. She steeled herself for what she expected to be a heated debate while she waited for them to gather.

"We have reached the point of no return," she declared as they arrived.

"The what now?" asked Gnately.

"She's saying that if we turn to head for Pelrigoss, the currents and winds will prevent us from changing our mind and turning around very easily," explained Tavyn.

"That is correct. According to my father, when you cross this point," she said, pointing at the peaks of distant mountains to the southwest, and the strange dark clouds dotting the horizon to the southeast, "you must either go southwest and follow the current more toward Gargoa, thereby missing Pelrigoss entirely, or you head east into the sea and let the currents take you around Pelrigoss to Caierthor. If you come in from the south, you can cut across to Aegir or Drogna, the outer islands, but your path is more a half circle than a straight line, because you're fighting the currents to do it."

"So our choice is, travel west to Pelrigoss across the open ocean, many miles from shore, in a vessel that wasn't designed for such deep waters, or head back to Gargoa and come to shore somewhere around Gusarski Cove in hopes of paying for passage on a larger vessel," said Tavyn.

"With a blockade in place," added Gnately.

"Or risk trying to run the blockade, yes," teased Tavyn.

"That's not what I said!" gasped Gnately.

"I think we can make it to Pelrigoss," said Piya. "My father did once in The Timid Shark, but that was many years ago, during the summer... so there were fewer storms. However, this boat is the same size, so I think it's possible. We just keep our eyes on those dark clouds and steer as best we can toward them, keeping in mind the current will fight us if we stray too far."

"At least the winds are blowing the right direction," said Tavyn.

"They are," agreed Piya.

"How the hell do you aim for a cloud?" asked Gnately. "Won't it move?"

"Yes and no," said Piya with a smirk.

"Yeah, don't look at me," said Tavyn, throwing his hands up.

"That isn't a cloud so much as smog from Mount Skain. Unless the dwarves stop their forge, that smog will always be there, billowing up from the mountain like a beacon in the sky," she explained.

"And Skain is on Pelrigoss?" asked Gnately.

"Yes," answered Piya.

"It doesn't blow away?" asked Gnately.

"It does, but they're constantly making more, so it's always really dense near the mountain. Thus, it looks like it never moves, cause there's always more," she said, smiling.

"But it's so far away!" gasped Gnately, squinting and pinching at the air where the smog lined up in her vision.

"Pelrigoss is at least two weeks away. Well, Caierthor is. Then we need to sail around to Dagoh Bay to find a proper dock, if that's what we're after. This is a fishing boat, so we have a few more options than a seafaring merchant ship, but not too many. The vast majority of Pelrigoss's shoreline is dotted with jagged rocks and steep cliffs," she explained.

"You know a lot for a kid!" remarked Gnately.

"I like to read," said Piya with a smile. "Plus my dad was full of stories. He liked to talk about how Pelrigoss was once part of Gargoa, and the gods ripped large chunks of it into the sky. In other stories he claimed that the people of Pelrigoss were so vile the gods attempted to sink it. Both stories were used to explain the treacherous shores."

"We go to Pelrigoss," said Ainen with a nod.

"Aye, Pelrigoss," agreed Tavyn.

"I'm in," said Gnately. "What the hells, right?"

"Pelrigoss it is, then!" said Piya, happily. "I've always wanted to go there. I was worried I'd have to convince you!"

"Nah, lass, we're stupid. Didn't you know? If it's a dumb idea, we're all in," chuckled Tavyn.

"More fun that way," chimed Gnately with a grin.

Ris'Anyu, Luthentyr 19th, 576 of the 1st Era

THEY SPENT nine days at sea before land came into sight. The smog clouds over Skain had been growing in size with each passing day, from a barely perceptible series of dots to a block smudge much larger than the boat. Even so, they felt no closer to their destination. No storms had made an appearance, and for that they were thankful.

However, Tavyn was desperately afraid they'd run out of food before they arrived, and had limited their rations the very day they left the point of no return, which hadn't pleased the rest of them. As a result, Gnately was constantly hungry, and he'd caught her several times sneaking little bites of food or sips of water.

The waves had been fierce, and the roll of the open ocean was something none of them had ever had reason to grow accustomed to. It was a harsh environment, and they all had a newfound respect for those who lived upon the waves by choice. More than once, their tiny vessel had nearly capsized, and none of them were sure how much more they could withstand.

Each night, they gathered near the bow and told stories to keep themselves entertained. If the night was clear, they'd stare up at the stars and make up fantasies to explain how Provoss and Aygos were so far ahead in their path through the sky than their sibling Zathos. Piya even embellished her father's tales, saying that the gods had formed Zathos from chunks of Pelrigoss.

Just before nightfall on the tenth day, Ainen caught sight of a sliver of land to the southeast. "Land!" he yelled, more excited than he'd ever been.

"Do you think we can get there tomorrow?" asked Gnately, running up to join him. "I can't see! Pick me up!"

Ainen complied, hefting her weight and wedging her rump onto his shoulder between his head and right bicep.

"We can't use that stretch of land. It's too rocky. We have to go around to the eastern edge of the island, remember?" said Piya.

"But, but..." stammered Gnately.

"If the wind is in our favor, we should be able to touch dry land in two or three days. Right, Piya?" asked Tavyn.

"Right," she said with a nod.

"It's great that you saw land, Ainen. It means we're getting close. But we've still got time left at sea. The only good news here is we're closer to land, and that means things should be easier for The Cracked Clam to handle," said Tavyn.

"Right again!" chimed Piya.

Two days later, they rounded the eastern edge of Caierthor as dawn broke. It should have been an exciting occasion, except they weren't in a frame of mind to notice it. Instead, they were completely preoccupied by the dark clouds to the south, and the unnatural pace and direction they seemed to be moving.

"What is that?" gasped Gnately.

"A storm," answered Ainen.

"Storms don't move like that!" said Gnately.

"How do you mean?" asked Tavyn.

"It just turned toward us," she said. "It's heading north, against the wind."

"No, we turned south. It's an optical illusion," he countered.

"No, she's right," said Piya.

"Thank you!" grunted Gnately.

"The storm was headed west, and we east. When we turned south, it turned north. It's coming right for us," Piya explained.

"Are you certain?" asked Tavyn.

"Positive," said Piya.

"Can we make it to shore? Run aground and get to safety? Anything?" asked Tavyn.

"It's still not safe. There are rocks a few feet under the waves. We'd risk being torn to shreds," said Piya. "We're going to have to sail through it."

"We have to lower the sail and secure the rigging," suggested Tavyn.

"Right. Let's get to it," she said. "Ainen, open the hatch and help us stow the extra gear down below."

"Aye, Captain," said Ainen.

The storm was upon them in minutes. It moved with a speed that none of them could comprehend or understand. Purple lightning raced down from the sky all around them, lighting the world around them, and revealing a strange, disheartening fact. Just a few yards away, no matter which direction they looked, the sea was serene and calm. The storm was directly overhead, and was only affecting them.

The companions fought to stay on board as the ship rocked in phantom waves. Wind and rain thrashed them from all sides. It mixed with salt spray from the ocean, filling the air with the tinge of seawater. The only thing they could taste or smell was the ocean. Their skin was freezing and raw, and try as they might, none of them could keep sight of the land.

Two cracks rang out as the companions clung to the railing. The source of the first was unknown to them, but the second was instantly and horrifyingly obvious. As the mast fell to port, Ainen dove into its path to deflect it and save Gnately. Though she'd noticed its fall, she was chest deep in rolling water, and completely unable to gain her footing or force herself out of its path.

The rigging snapped under the weight of the mast, sending shudders throughout the deck. Ainen drove his shoulder into the large wooden pole as it continued its path portside, and managed to nudge it just enough so that it fell into the sea a few feet from Gnately's head, taking several feet of railing and a large chunk of the deck along with it.

As the mast crashed into the waves, the clouds overhead instantly dissipated, and the sea grew deathly calm. The companions looked around at one another in a state of shock and panic. Gnately couldn't help but weep out of both terror and frustration.

"What the fuck was that?" yelled Piya, her voice quivering.

"I... I can't believe what just happened," said Tavyn. "That had to be a magically created storm. There was nothing natural about it. Someone must have sent it to set us adrift," he gasped.

Piya made her way to steerage and tried the wheel. It was already spinning freely when she arrived. She tried it anyway, just to make sure, but there was no resistance; no response from the rudder. "Well, I found the source of that other snap we heard."

"Let me guess. The rudder?" asked Tavyn.

"Yep!" grunted Piya, dropping to the deck in frustration.

"No land," moaned Ainen. "It's gone."

Everyone raced astern to make sure he wasn't blind. He wasn't. Where the land had once been, it was no longer visible. It was nowhere to be seen on any side of the ship.

They had no way to steer, and no way to harness the wind for propulsion.

They were at the complete mercy of the Hystari.

AS THE immense powers dissipated from the room, Whun drifted out of the ritual circle toward a chair at the back of the room. Despite his normal remarks of needing no rest, casting a spell strong enough to send a magical storm halfway across the world had caused far more exhaustion than he'd felt since he had living flesh. He lowered himself into the chair without a word to the priests around the room, each struggling with their own side effects from the ritual.

"Is it done? We could not see what transpired," said their leader.

'It is done,' Whun confirmed. 'The storm has destroyed enough of *their boat that they are at the mercy of the Hystari. I have caused the currents to pull them toward Xxulrathia with haste. They should arrive in four or five weeks, depending on interference from natural weather phenomena, and if Mordessa finds them and manages to intercede.'*

"We must still find the other Caier," said the priest.

'I believe I know who another is. She is close by, so bringing her to the Talaani Empire was of lower priority,' thought Whun.

"We should bring her here!" gasped the priest.

'In time. We will also need her adoptive father. We cannot strip Mordessa's power without his assistance,' thought Whun.

"We should-" started the priest.

'I will handle them when the time comes. For now, you should start preparing your priests for another memory restoration,' thought Whun.

"That will take time. We must-" started the priest.

'You have until Jaezyn's host arrives,' thought Whun.

The priest nodded, realizing Whun was growing impatient with his demands and questions. When the Noktulians finally left the chamber, the ancient lich settled back into his chair, lost in thought.

CHAPTER 12

TREPIDATION

Ris'Enliss, Luthentyr 30th, 576 of the 1st Era

MINA SLID out from under the Raven as Eros entered the room. "I think I've figured it out," she chimed.

"Well, come over so I can replenish my blessings, then you can show me what you're talking about," he said with a smile.

They'd been hard at work in the laboratory since that terrible night in the Ascension chamber. Out of fear that Mordessa would sense Mina in her sleep, Eros had kept them both awake with spells he'd learned as part of his training at the Temple of Daahl, in the service of Ishnu. Meanwhile, they occupied their time trying to fix and adjust Ahm's flying machine.

Mina joined him at the table and waited patiently as his spells filled her with renewed stamina and a forced sense of alertness. He then directed her attention to the tray of fruit he'd brought with him. She grabbed an apple and took a hearty bite, smiling as widely as her mouth would allow around its contents as she chewed.

"You're going to make me ask, aren't you?" he sighed.

She nodded, swallowed, and smiled wider.

"Fine. What did you figure out?" he asked.

"Advan's diagrams! I can read them now," she chirped gleefully.

"Yeah, I don't believe that for a second," he said with a chuckle.

"Well, come look!" she said, standing abruptly and racing over to the workbench. She started explaining again before he even caught up with her. "See, we were thinking that we were supposed to lay these on top of each other and press them together, right? Then look through and see everything in layers?"

"Right?" he asked.

"That's not the case at all. See, each of these sheets is a different system, yes, but none of those systems are the same size when you try to find them inside the machine. See these gears?" she asked, pointing at two gears that were drawn the same size on two different sheets. "They aren't the same size in the machine. One is as big as my fist, but the other one is as small as the tip of my thumb."

"So they don't overlay to show the whole thing at once?" he asked.

"No. The red ink on each piece of paper includes those tiny little numbers, right? They correspond to one another, showing where they overlap or interact. So the twenty-three on sheet one matches the twenty-three on sheet four. However, while sheet one is drawn to scale, sheet four is five times the actual scale. He drew the smaller systems bigger to make them easier to understand," she explained.

"Okay, that tells us how each system works, but-" he started.

"Then there's the blue ink that we couldn't figure out the purpose of?" she said, pointing.

"Mmhm."

"Those markings correlate to entries in his journal," said Mina.

"Not the parts list, or the other diagrams?" asked Eros, perplexed.

"No! They were basically his way of saying, 'I need a spell here to make this part work,' but he didn't know yet what spell was going to be used. If you look at the journal, now and then you'll see an entry mention 'Marker fourteen', or whatever, and then go into detail about the spell Ahm or Whun used to solve the problem," said Mina.

"No wonder we couldn't figure it out. Every dead end we hit while tracing the rods and gears of the system wasn't a real dead end at all," he realized.

"Nope! It was just being handled by magic," she said. "In one of his journal entries he goes on and on for pages about how he wished they could make the parts smaller, lighter, and more flexible; that the rigidity and size of the frame were causing problems they hadn't anticipated. He even did a calculation about the size of gears they would need to lift a single wing, and lamented their inability to fit them into the body and drive them properly. Whenever he ran into something like that, he basically threw up his hands and said, 'well, I guess magic will solve this too,' and left a marker on the diagram. Then it was up to Ahm to find the spells they needed."

"That both solves and confuses a lot of things," said Eros.

"It solves things completely. We don't need to understand every little detail of how it all works. I wanted to fix the controls, right? Maybe move the levers around, or whatever we could do to make it easier to drive? Well, I think we can do that now. As long as our new controls move the same gears in the same way..." she explained, letting her words trail off for him to draw the conclusion.

"...then the same parts of the machine should respond in the same ways, no matter where the lever is fitted for you to use," he finished.

"Precisely," she said. "So we can stop worrying about wing this, and tail that, and focus on the levers, and where they're positioned. We don't have to bother with the rest. More importantly, all those connections we thought broke in the crash? They aren't broken, they were never physically connected."

"I still think it's odd that some old man was writing about this strange machine in his diary, instead of just redrawing the diagrams with full detail, or keeping them in some 'Raven Handbook', or something. Don't you?" he questioned.

"It's not a diary, it's his work log. He documented their progress every day for years. Reading it is like being there as they built it," she answered.

"And you've read the whole thing?" he asked, raising an eyebrow.

"Most of it," she said.

"We shouldn't have had the time for you to read the whole thing. I don't know how long we've been down here, but I know we should have had answers by now," he complained.

"Twenty-four days, eighteen hours and six minutes, give or take a few seconds," she chimed, looking over his shoulder.

"Well, that was a bit precise," he said in disbelief.

"The runes along the top of the wall. You didn't notice they changed?" she asked, pointing.

"Can't say I've been staring at the ceiling, no. Not quite *that* bored yet. I mean, we've been working on this, so..."

"Ahm asked Lord Whun to place the enchantments during a visit when I was young, since I couldn't see the sky, use the sundials that dot the city's squares, or even hear the church bells. I had no way to mark the passage of time, and he's a stickler for punctuality. So, Ahm had melrithium inlays placed into the engravings on the crown molding, and Whun enchanted them to glow with hovering sigils that changed based on the position of the sun, moons, and stars in relation to the Cryx. Once I learned to read them, I could always tell what time it was by simply looking up," she explained, smiling.

"That's a lot of trouble to go through for such a simple thing. He could have just let you breathe fresh air now and then," lamented Eros. He thought for a moment about whether he should say what was really on his mind. She could see the look of concern on his face, but still he hesitated. Without saying a word, she put a hand on his arm and leaned forward, staring deep into his eyes with that caring but inquisitive look she knew he couldn't resist. If he did, she'd end up badgering him until he admitted what was wrong anyway, and that was always worse.

"Are you okay?" she asked.

"I'm fine. Why don't you show me what your thoughts are about those controls?" he suggested, thumbing toward the device.

She smiled wide and skipped past him, grabbing his hand and guiding him to follow. He gladly moved to play along, but his body had other plans. He felt a sensation at the back of his head, like something intangible snapped and twisted, sending his mind spiraling, as if something had suddenly stripped away his ability to maintain balance. As his strength spilled out of his muscles, he collapsed onto his haunches, instinctively gripping the sides of his head to keep it steady.

"Oh my gods, what's wrong?" gasped Mina, turning and kneeling to tend to him.

"I don't know if it's because I'm not used to being underground for such long periods of time, or if it's the water, or something we ate... but I haven't been feeling very well," he explained.

"How so?" she asked.

"My heart seems to skip or add a beat now and then, completely at random. It feels like I'm trying to breathe through a wet rag. When I lay down, everything gets worse, which of course makes me very, very glad we've been using spells to avoid sleep. My brain feels like it's swimming. My muscles are slow to respond. My skin feels achy and dry. This is the worst I've ever felt in my life," he explained with a sigh, glad he finally put his feelings into words.

"Is it a side effect of the spells we've been using?" she asked.

"No. I used them for years during my studies, because I got a late start. Those were the first spells I learned, for the express purpose of working around the clock, so I'd be ready by the time my day of Ascension came. I never once felt as I do now. This is totally new, and it doesn't help that I can't stop thinking it might've been caused by however Advan brought me back," he said.

"Let's go talk to Ahm, okay?" she suggested, slipping her arm under his and lifting. "You're right, this doesn't sound normal, and I'm really hoping your suspicions are incorrect."

MINA LED Eros toward Ahm's office, stopping every ten or fifteen yards to let him rest. Their slow pace meant that she could hear Ahm pacing in his office, talking to himself for several minutes before they even got close enough to touch the door. She almost called out for his assistance, but something in the back of her mind encouraged her to wait, that she was being silly.

Just before she reached the handle, the door at the far end of the level, leading from the stairs to the surface, slammed shut with a ferocity that took her quite by surprise. What sounded like hooved feet and the horrid scrape of bone on marble echoed down the hall from around the corner, accentuated but a sound she could only assume was the tucking of leathery wings.

Mina's heart felt like it was about to burst. A warm sensation grew in the depths of her chest and spread quickly across her torso as a cold chill rippled across her flesh and up her spine. With her eyes wide in horror, and her breath caught in her throat, she whipped around toward Eros. Upon seeing her, he opened his mouth to respond, but it was almost instantly covered by her right hand as she shoved him backward with her left.

Every fiber of her being knew that she absolutely had to get out of that hallway. She had no desire to see what was coming, and even less of her wanted to be noticed. A rush of adrenaline flooded through her just as her mind consciously realized she had no choice but to escape. She wrapped her hands around Eros and half carried, half dragged him back down the hall and around a nearby corner. Returning her hand to his mouth, she pulled him to the ground and held him fast.

Eros's face drained of blood as he looked into Mina's eyes. She hadn't blinked since the door crashed at the end of the hall, and she was currently staring at him. Her eyes were so wide he thought they'd start bleeding, and she was trembling as she bit her lips, slowly shaking her head to ward off his questions.

The granite floor seemed to crack under the weight of the approaching creature. Each of its steps shook the hallway, even as far away as their hiding place. Between their impact, and the high-pitched scraping that accompanied them along the ceiling, Mina realized she could no longer hear Ahm speaking.

When the unseen force reached Ahm's office door, a loud crash echoed through the halls and chambers, followed by the sound of hooves on cracked wood, and a terrible, multi-layered voice.

"Threm sends his regards," Mordessa declared in sarcastic tones.

"Your Majesty!" gasped Ahm, falling to his knees.

"I knew I should have sent for you directly," she growled. "Clearly, Threm and his predecessor had no grasp of the urgency of our situation. Once again, I am forced to rely upon you to get the job done, where others have failed."

"Yes, your Majesty," he stated.

"I would say that Threm's failure and subsequent death stand as warning to you, but I know you do not care for the fate of such men. It's clear my threat would fall on deaf ears. Instead, I will make you a promise. Bring me Lord Whun, or find another world to inhabit. I made you who you are, and I will unmake you without hesitation," she growled.

"Aye, your Majesty. I will travel to Talaani immediately," he agreed, nodding.

She turned to leave, but hesitated. Looking back at him over her shoulder, she added, "While you are there, if you happen upon any strange, unknown visitors to their Empire who claim to come from distant lands... slay them. Do not hesitate. Do not think. Do not investigate, or seek to make sure of your targets. Slay them, and take whatever consequences the Talaani might impose. If that brings about your end, I will see that all of Dusk honors your sacrifice until the end of days."

"Whatever you ask, your Majesty, it will be done," he answered.

Mordessa ducked through the doorway she'd ripped from the ceiling, turned back down the hall and made her way out of the Cryx. Her exit was just as terrifying as her entry to Mina, save for the fact that once the sounds of her passing dissipated, it would mean she was no longer in their presence.

When Mina finally felt her fear fade enough to move, she quickly stood and raced into Ahm's office. He was more pale than she'd ever seen, and seemed genuinely shaken by their surprise visitor. They embraced to offer comfort to one another as they settled their hearts and calmed their breathing. Before either of them could speak about what had just happened, Eros stumbled into the room, crashing over the remnants of the door and barely maintaining his weak footing.

Mina went over and helped Eros to a chair, then pulled one alongside and joined him. Ahm watched, seemingly detached from reality for a short time, then sat behind his desk.

"I have to go to the Talaani Empire and search for Lord Whun.

He was stationed at our embassy in the Elonesti Dominion, and has apparently gone several months without reporting to Mordessa. She assigned Chancellor Threm to find him and he came here, instructing me to do it. However, you were in a coma and I didn't want to leave your side, so I blew him off. I shouldn't have done that," he sighed. "You don't want to be on Mordessa's bad side. That's never a good place to be."

"We heard," said Mina. "We're coming with you."

"This is not a vacation, or any other sort of leisurely outing. Talaanians despise our Kingdom. If Whun has gone missing, this trip is going to be exceedingly dangerous. I cannot allow you to accompany me," he said firmly. "If you indeed heard her, you also know I'm being sent as an assassin in addition to rescuing Whun, which puts me in very real danger."

"I am *not* staying locked up in the Cryx without you or Advan. Besides, staying here means using Eros's magic to stay awake so that she won't detect my presence. We've already been doing that for the past month. So, take this however you like, but *fuck* you. We're coming with!" she insisted.

"If you join me, then I need to find somewhere else to hide the Raven... that, or we have to find a way to transport it along with us. Neither of those sounds feasible to me in my current state of mind. Whun is the most powerful Lich in all of Dusk. If he's fallen victim to a Talaani plot..." he began, then shuddered and let his words trail off.

"Well, I've been studying Advan's journal regarding the device. He designed it to be disassembled. So, if we can take a Flute north to one of the farming villages outside the wall..." she started.

"Then we could load the parts into a carriage unseen and hide it somewhere outside of Baan'Sholaria," he finished.

"Exactly. Then nobody would find it," she said.

"Just make sure we take the journal and drawings with us," added Eros.

"And everything I've been researching about Korr. We don't want her finding that either," added Ahm.

"Do you have answers?" asked Mina, perking up.

"None you'll enjoy hearing," sighed Ahm. "I'll tell you on the way. For now, get back to the laboratory and dismantle the Raven. I'll send agents to procure shipping crates, and we'll make our way to a station. Eros, go pack clothes and supplies for the three of us while we handle the other tasks."

"Eros needs to rest," said Mina.

"Pardon?" asked Ahm.

"That's why we were in the hallway. She was bringing me to

come see you," said Eros. He explained the symptoms he'd been experiencing in recent days and waited patiently while Ahm fell silent, deep in thought.

"Provided your concern is accurate, removing you from the Aggripha's presence could be the solution. If you're wrong, though, and your symptoms get worse, we'll have to send you back to the Aggripha to await our return," said Ahm. "Otherwise, if this is just a simple illness, I can treat the symptoms with a few of my spells while we wait for it to pass. If we had more time, I could do a more thorough examination, but I fear we've precious little before Mordessa grows impatient."

"Oh, fuck! What happens if she scries us with her crystal ball?" gasped Mina.

"I can mask you from clairvoyance with a blessing. I can't mask your connection to the Aggripha, but I can at least prevent her seeing either of you when she spies on me to see my progress," said Ahm. What he didn't tell them was that he had every intention of leaving them inside whatever cave they stashed the Raven in for safekeeping. He had no desire to drag them into enemy territory.

THE STATION was eerily quiet the next morning. Mina wasn't sure if that was normal, considering she'd never ridden in any of the northbound tracks. However, she couldn't help but constantly check every shadow for signs of hooves, horns, and wings. Every other sound seemed to make her jump a little, and Ahm was slowly getting dragged into her anxiety just from witnessing it.

"Please calm yourself. You heard how much noise she makes when she travels. She can't possibly sneak up on us, and she can't see you through divination, either. You're safe," he reassured her.

"I can't help it. I need something to take my mind off her," she explained.

"Tell us what you found out about Korr?" suggested Eros, his voice weak and skin pale.

"If it will settle you down for a time," sighed Ahm. "I had hoped to find out more before sharing. Unfortunately, it seems that someone has cleansed almost every reference to Korr from our records. My agents had a troublesome time finding anything about the man or his prophecy. They found every other cryptic prediction you could imagine... but this one? This one was tricky.

"It seems Korr was a very special man. He was an apprentice to Advan, and helped maintain the Ascension chambers and Flute system, some two hundred and fifty years ago. This was back before I even discovered who Advan was, or his relationship with me.

However, Korr was also a Touched and could see spirits, like you can, Mina. He hid that fact well, but the more he was exposed to the power of the Aggripha, the more Advan noticed that something was off.

"Eventually, Advan turned Korr over to the Ministry of Internal Affairs, and they took him away. They rewarded Advan for reporting him, and as such his assistance was documented in the Ministry's archive, even though no other documents mention what Korr was actually charged with, or any trial that might have followed," explained Ahm. "After that, he wasn't mentioned again until his prophecy started spreading amongst the lower-class citizens. His writings were received by the masses as a fanciful tale, written by a very clever, but clearly insane author. Even though he wasn't being taken seriously, something about what he'd written must have struck a chord, because Mordessa herself had him hunted down. Shortly after his writings surfaced, he disappeared and was never heard from again. Anyone caught with a copy of his prophecy was arrested and fined. Even the printer who created the copies for publication disappeared, and his press mysteriously dismantled."

"Did you find a copy?" asked Mina.

Ahm slipped a hand into the satchel hanging over his shoulder and reached a leather-wrapped scroll of papyrus across the cart toward her. "We found just this portion. Ironically, it appears to be the most relevant to our current predicament. Mind the wind, that's the only copy known to exist."

Mina slid out of the seat onto the floor of the cart and carefully opened the front cover.

Aggriphaxxeddon did give her heart through ruptured chest.
Queen of Death and Hate did take that heart back to her nest.
Oh souls of three, an ancient troop, did come to abrupt end.
Sacrificed to forge the pact, so future souls would rend.
Sweet Aggripha now grants to thee a life of endlessness.
Yet Aggripha doth take from thee, thy soul as recompense.
Burn ye now, oh lifeless ones, for time is drawing nigh.
You'll see the omens come for thee, with fire in the sky.

Noktrusgodhen reached beyond the grave to end his curse.
He failed, but in his failure won small victory through rebirth.
Since dawn of pact, all souls were lost; sucked to the crystal heart.
Once fractured, one might be reborn, with destined goal, in part.
Oh souls of three, thou art now free, each century you birth.
Once come as three to Talaani, the curse of stone will burst.
Cower now, oh lifeless ones, as hubris come for thee.
Through dragon breath and thunderous ire, Talaani will be free.

✦ ✦ ✦

MINA RETURNED the scroll to its binding and handed it to Ahm as she regained her seat. She sat for a minute in contemplation, letting the words dance in her mind's eye. "So, Korr found out how the Aggripha was made, and discovered that it, what... rends the souls of those it grants eternal life to?" she asked.

"That's a little oversimplified," said Ahm. "When we make an Unliving, we rip their soul away from their body and reattach it, magically, in such a way that it preserves their flesh. The cost of that binding is that their body slowly eats away at their soul, extending their lifespan but ultimately ending their existence. When one's soul is fully consumed, they become mindless, and are sent to perform menial tasks until their body is no longer serviceable. Depending on the strength of the individual, and their attachment to some source of magic, that process can extend their life a hundredfold, or theoretically longer. What I think he's suggesting is that the Aggripha slowly takes some of that soul's power over time, eventually absorbing them. That would make it appear as if they'd been consumed by the expected process, and we'd have no reason to assume anything untoward had happened."

"Like a shopkeeper skimming coin on each sale. Effectively stealing from the business owner," suggested Eros.

"Precisely," said Ahm. "Furthermore, it seems that the Aggripha is the heart of the dragon that once ruled Talaani, and it was ripped from her chest by Mordessa. She then cast some curse to make it absorb, empower, and enchant souls, presumably at her whim, which seems to have crystallized the heart, making it what we know it to be today."

"Who is Nokrtusgodhen?" asked Mina. "Advan and the scroll both mentioned that name."

"If I'm not mistaken, he was the ancient dragon that ruled the Elonesti Dominion," said Ahm.

"The Dominion with the embassy that Lord Whun served in?" asked Eros.

"The very same. Their history isn't well documented in Baan'Sholaria's libraries or archives. Legend says there are no living dragons anywhere in Talaani. They do, however, worship gargantuan dragon statues, according to Whun's reports. It could be that Mordessa's curse petrified their draconic masters... which, if true, would explain why they've never once attempted to attack our Kingdom," said Ahm.

"So all this time we've been shifting resources to prepare for a war that Mordessa knew was never coming?" asked Eros.

"Trust me, I'm more upset about that prospect than anyone,"

said Ahm.

"We're going to have to go see for ourselves if we want to reveal the truth of Korr's writings," suggested Mina.

"Yes, that is true. It's the last passage that concerns me, though," said Ahm.

"The part about the souls of the three returning?" asked Mina. "Advan claimed that resurrecting Eros was the first step. What if, and this is a stretch, mind you... but what if he's one of the three souls, and the others are traveling to Talaani right now?"

"You mean the strange visitors Mordessa told me to look for and kill? Yes, I had considered that," said Ahm.

"Prophecies are birdshit, though, right?" asked Eros.

"That, apparently, remains to be seen," said Ahm.

GNATELY WAS hungry. Try as she might, she couldn't recall a time where she'd ever been as hungry as she'd been in recent days. Tavyn's insistence that they ration their food had been successful in perpetuating their lives, but no matter how much she tried, she couldn't make her body understand the logic of not eating her fill several times per day.

Ainen and Piya had resorted to fishing, which seemed to improve their moods. However, since they were stuck at sea on a wooden boat and the small galley had been completely destroyed by the storm, they had no way to cook their catch. If they eventually ran out of everything else, Gnately was sure she'd find a way to force herself to consume raw fish, but they hadn't hit that point just yet, and she desperately hoped they never would.

Oddly enough, drinking water hadn't become much of a concern. It had, of course, been their most pressing issue at first. However, after Piya found several buckets in the boat's tiny, leaking hold, their concerns had all but faded. Fate, it seemed, was being kind in at least one regard. Somehow, some way, a gentle rain fell every afternoon, directly over the boat and nowhere else, filling the buckets just enough that they wouldn't perish from dehydration.

"Thank the gods for small favors," said Gnately aloud, having meant to say it in her mind.

"What's that?" asked Tavyn from his seat next to her at steerage.

"Nothing," sighed Gnately, grimacing as she watched Ainen take another bite of his most recent catch. Her stomach growled loudly, as if arguing with her displeasure.

"I'm sure they'll share. They're catching fish for all of us, after all," said Tavyn.

"I want nothing to do with that horrid, disgusting mess. I'm just fine with stale bread, dried oats, nuts and cheese," she said.

Ainen took another bite. As he was chewing, he stopped and went completely still. After a few seconds, he uttered, "No. Just stop," under his breath, small flecks of raw meat spraying from his lips as he spoke.

"He's been doing that a lot lately," said Gnately.

"I noticed. I'm not sure what we can do about it. If we had a priest, I'd ask for them to step in, but we don't," lamented Tavyn.

"It's like he's talking to someone. But who?" asked Gnately.

"That's what worries me. Could be stress? Maybe he's talking to himself?" asked Tavyn.

"Or whatever keeps healing him and turning his wounds to stone has a voice we just can't hear," suggested Gnately.

"Or it's whoever caused the storm," muttered Tavyn, hesitant to even voice the words.

"Gods, I hope you're wrong," she said.

"So do I," he agreed.

CHAPTER 13:
TERNION

Ris'Anyu, Djacenta 1st, 576 of the 1st Era

ASCENDING THE steps of station three did little to ease Mina's mind. No longer in the Cryx, and free of the darkness that surrounded the subterranean rail of the Flute, she looked toward the sun for the very first time in her life. What she'd always imagined would be an exhilarating experience was ruined by the circumstances of her arrival at that moment, regardless of the sky's striking beauty. She squinted and looked away with a sigh as her heart sank just a little, threatening to pull her into a bout of sadness she had little time to confront. She'd never been in such luminous surroundings in her life. Even with the shadows cast by the surrounding buildings, the world seemed suddenly overwhelming.

Ahm left them standing near an alley while skeletal workers brought their crates to the surface on the cargo lift, one load at a time. He returned an hour later with two wagons, each being driven by a mindless, bound worker, and pulled by enchanted, half decayed horses. Behind them was another horse, tied loosely to the rear of the last wagon.

He instructed the lift workers to load both wagons with their cargo, while Mina and Eros watched on in silence. Mina was in no mood to talk; which was completely out of character, but understandable under the circumstances. Eros simply lacked the energy to press her into speaking. He had resigned himself to watching and waiting long before their ride on the Flute had ended.

When the cargo was secure, Ahm led Eros to the first wagon's bench, and signaled to Mina that she should ride on the other. He helped their ailing companion into his seat, then made his way toward her wagon afterward. As she waited, she realized a certain detachment from reality, as if she were watching the scene take place rather than experiencing it herself. The surreal nature of the feeling was both fascinating and unsettling.

"I will ride in the lead by myself," he explained as he arrived at her side. "Eros will follow me at a short distance, and you a short distance behind him. Stay far enough back that anyone watching would have to question whether we're all together, or just happen to be traveling in the same direction. That way, if she tries to scry me, she'll have no reason to suspect there's anyone with me."

Mina nodded several times as he spoke, while trying her best to bring herself back to the moment. He didn't know the odd sensations she was experiencing, and she felt it was best to pretend nothing was wrong. Pushing back the mixture of sadness and fear that threatened to bring her to tears, she calmly uttered, "Makes sense."

He spent a few more moments casting a blessing on her, then returned to the horse, untied it, and mounted. A few moments later, undead hooves clopped past on the cobblestone road, echoing off the buildings that surrounded them. Mina cringed involuntarily at each step, her mind threatening to force her to scream. She made a point of staring at Ahm's mount, trying to convince herself that fearing such a creature was senseless.

When their disconnected caravan finally set into motion, she stared for a time at her own wagon's horses. Her mind eventually eased enough to relax and take in the sights, but by then they had almost reached the outer wall. The sign at the gates indicated they were heading toward Arragesh, a farming village she'd read about, located on the northeastern border of Dusk.

The village's land owners were said to be reclusive, yet hospitable. They lived in relative seclusion, their farmhouses separated by miles of fertile fields. Harvesting, fertilizing, pest control and planting was mostly accomplished at the hands of skilled workers, most of whom lived in modest apartments and row houses at the center of Arragesh, or the edges of their master's land. It was said that the village grew much of the wheat, barley and hops used to produce some of Dusk's most popular ales.

As her wagon passed through the gates, seemingly endless fields came into view. They stretched for as far as her eyes could see in carefully cultivated rows across shallow valleys and rolling hills. A gentle breeze celebrated her arrival, carrying with it the faint smell of earth and vegetation, with a barely perceptible note of hops.

She had never imagined anything so beautiful. The sound of hooves on stone was replaced with gentle clops on earthen roads. The grind of banded wheels on cobble subsided, and in its place was the quieter, smoother, and softer flow of iron over dirt. Gone were the deep shadows cast by tall buildings across winding streets. No longer did she see hints of Mordessa's horrifying form dancing at the edge of her vision.

They rode for two days, each stopping to relieve themselves whenever necessary, then catch back up to the others. At regular intervals, Ahm slowed enough to toss them each a pear, apple or peach he'd blessed to prevent exhaustion. His tactic allowed them to continue without long breaks, and avoid the need to request beds from the residents of Arragesh.

While considered a village by Duskian standards, Arragesh was far from small as far as Mina was concerned. At the center of the village's territory stood a cluster of buildings, several rising five stories into the sky. She counted five taverns on the main street alone, along with grocers, clothing stores, tool shops, and far too many street vendors to seem reasonable. To her dismay, they did not stop to partake of the festivities or meet any of the locals. Before long, and without an opportunity to protest, Ahm led them through the other end of the main street and back into sweeping farmland.

Over the next three days, the village and its farms slowly faded into memory, while the mountains to the west loomed higher and higher into the sky. By the end of the fourth day, carefully cultivated vegetation had been replaced with rock-strewn fields, stoney hills, crags and boulders. Twin peaks rose into the sky above, each tipped white and disappearing at times into the clouds. A waterfall slowly grew louder as they approached, echoing through folds of the terrain from somewhere in the northwest.

By the time Ahm finally stopped their travels, they'd been on the road for nearly seven days. A rocky path led up the slopes to the west, straight into the foothills of the nearest mountain. There was no longer a road their wagons could traverse. Even though the thought of carrying the Raven's parts up that path by hand was daunting, the idea of turning around and heading back to Arragesh without a good, long rest was even worse.

"Is this our destination?" asked Mina as Ahm approached.

"Yes. This path leads to a ravine that cuts across the foothills toward the base of Mount Sulahn. There are caves not too far in that we can use to hide the Raven. The good news is I've already blessed us all to prevent clairvoyance, so we can safely work together. The bad news is, Eros is in no condition to help. So, it's up to the two of us to move everything inside," explained Ahm.

"He's worse?" gasped Mina, desperately concerned. She hadn't spoken to anyone, or been able to see Eros since they left Dusk. A sinking feeling settled into her gut.

"He appears so, yes. Once we load everything into the caves, I'll send him to the Aggripha," said Ahm, helping her down.

"Do you think that will work?" she asked.

"We have no way of knowing. However, it's clear he's getting worse. Whether that is from time or distance from the Aggripha, I cannot be certain. I will attempt to tend to him after we're done moving the parts, but I'm not expecting my efforts to make much of a difference. His ailment is like nothing I've ever seen," he said.

"Well, let's get this over with so we can find out, I guess," said Mina. "How did you know this was here?" she asked as she climbed down.

"Lord Whun and I did some research here once. An ancient tribe used to live in the caves. We came here to study them, but didn't find anything of note. I kept its location tucked in the back of my mind in case I ever needed it," he explained.

Mina hefted the first crate and started up the path. Everything seemed to weigh so much more after such a long journey.

AINEN SHOT upright, hitting his head on the sail they'd used to create a make-shift tent at the bow. He belted, "Caier," as he woke, in gasping, fearful tones. The pile of Algrim's armor he'd been leaning on settled into place behind him, giving him a small fright.

Gnately nearly jumped out of her skin at the sound, vaulting from her bedroll to her feet in such a hurry her eyes hadn't fully opened before she felt the leather-wrapped hilts of daggers in her hands. "Can you not?" she gasped. "You damned near gave me a heart attack!"

"I am sorry," said Ainen.

Tavyn stood from his position next to Piya, who was happily fishing off the port side, and joined the pair under the sail. "Is everything okay? What seems to be the trouble, big guy?"

"Yeah, we've heard you talking to yourself. What gives?" asked Gnately, returning her daggers to their sheaths.

"Voices. They keep saying, 'come to us,'" said Ainen.

"So when you were yelling 'no' the other day you were what, talking back to the voices in your head?" asked Gnately.

"Yes," said Ainen.

"You know they're not real, don't you?" she asked.

"They are," said Ainen.

"How can you be sure?" asked Tavyn.

"They made the storm," he answered.

"What?" asked Gnately and Piya in unison. Piya turned to face them, and nearly dropped her fishing pole for her efforts.

"They are descendents of the Caier. They speak to me all day, but when I sleep, I can see them. If they speak true, the Caier are older than the Toor," said Ainen.

"Which Toor? Older than who?" asked Gnately.

"All of them. Their race is older than the race of Toor," answered Ainen.

"Then why haven't we heard of them?" asked Tavyn.

"We kind of have," suggested Piya, coming to join them. "The eastern half of Pelrigoss is called Caierthor. I'm betting it was named after them."

"Do you know for certain?" asked Gnately.

"I'm not a historian, so no. It's just a guess," said Piya.

"Whether true or not, they say I was a Caier in a previous life," said Ainen.

"So you were reincarnated?" asked Gnately. "Right. That's not real."

"How do we know? None of us are priests, after all," said Piya. "We all saw the storm. It came from nowhere, moved directly toward us against the winds, and settled directly over the boat. That wasn't natural. We all know it."

"Meaning someone had to be behind it," agreed Tavyn.

"I wasn't hearing voices until after," added Ainen.

"Well then, where the fuck are they taking us?" asked Gnately.

"To join them," said Ainen.

"Why?" asked Gnately.

Ainen shrugged. Tired of their questions, he got to his knees and shuffled out from under the sail then stood.

"I doubt he's got the answers, Gnately. Why don't we try to find a way to help him cope with the problem instead? Just to get him through until we hit land, and can find help?" asked Tavyn.

Gnately nodded, walked past Tavyn, and hugged Ainen around his legs. "It's okay, big guy. We love you. We'll take care of you. We won't let no ancient Caier get their grips on you."

"Thank you," sighed Ainen. He extracted himself from Gnately's arms with a pat on her head and picked up Piya's fishing pole. He did his best to ignore his friends as they debated the various interpretations of his revelation, choosing instead to focus his mind on the gently rolling waves before him.

MINA AND Ahm spent the rest of the daylight hours opening crates, extracting parts and carrying everything into the largest cave. They left Eros to rest in a smaller cave nearby, atop a bedroll and a pile of blankets. He watched their progress as patiently as he could until exhaustion overcame him, succumbing to the aftermath of sustaining himself with prayers and blessings for nearly a month.

When all the parts and chests were transferred, Ahm instructed the wagon drivers to return to Dusk, then joined Mina in Eros's cave. "He may not wake for several days. The fruit I shared carried a second blessing with them that will send you both into a deep sleep while your body heals from all the damage not sleeping has done to you. It will also shut down digestive functions to prevent starvation, dehydration or any undesirable mess. When you wake, it should feel like any other morning, including the faint yearning for dawnfry," he finished with a smile.

"Well, it seems you thought of everything," she said, her eyes still locked on Eros. She was kneeling beside him when Ahm approached, holding his hand and watching him breathe.

"When he wakes, he needs to return to the Aggripha. The more I consider what Advan said, and the revelations about it in the scroll, the more I think his survival is linked to its power. We moved him to the laboratory very quickly when he was revived, and then brought him out here. The further away he gets, the worse his symptoms become. It's the only thing about his illness that makes sense," said Ahm.

"I don't know if he's going to agree to leave my side, and I can't go back there. I fear he's going to resist," she said.

"All we can do is encourage him to make the right choice," said Ahm. "I'm going to find a spot to get some sleep myself. You should consider doing the same. Once those spells wear off, exhaustion is going to hit you like a hammer."

Mina nodded and slipped under the blankets next to Eros. Ahm nodded his approval and left the cave without another word. She laid her head on his chest, just like she used to do at the Bidlesh Overlook, and quietly listened to his labored heart. Before she had a chance to acknowledge the urge to sleep, darkness washed over her consciousness like a wave.

AHM WAITED patiently for Mina to fall asleep, then quietly brought his undead horse to the opening in front of her cave. He retrieved a quill, inkwell and small piece of parchment from his satchel and quickly wrote her a note, then placed it a few feet inside the cave with a small rock on top to prevent it from blowing away.

Afterward, he gathered the rest of the supplies he would need, shouldered his satchel, and walked out of the ravine. As he headed north, he considered the damage his course of action might cause to his relationship with his adopted daughter. She was already full of trust issues when it came to his words and actions. He never wanted to make her feel that she couldn't trust him, but he hadn't been able to share everything with her openly for fear of causing further harm.

He had his reasons for keeping certain things from her; reasons he still felt confident were valid. Part of him regretted making those decisions and losing some of the bond they'd formed in her younger years. Leaving without her while she slept through a magically induced coma, which he had placed upon her, wasn't going to repair what they'd lost, and was likely to drive her even further away.

Regardless, he knew he was making the right decision, even if it pained him to do so. Where he was going was far from safe, even for someone as powerful as he'd become. Furthermore, if the prophecy was to be believed, and if there was any chance she was one of the three souls reincarnated, then taking her along would spell the end for Dusk.

He couldn't risk it.

MINA WASN'T sure how much time had passed since she fell asleep, but she hadn't moved at all in her sleep, and neither had Eros. As Ahm foretold, she woke with hunger pains and the urge to relieve herself of her last meal. She extracted herself from the bedroll and tucked Eros back in, then moved to go and remedy her needs.

The first thing that caught her eye was the horse Ahm had ridden on their trip through Arragesh, standing directly at the cave's entrance, unmoving, waiting patiently. A few feet away lay a small piece of paper with a rock carefully placed on top. Curious, she retrieved the paper, unfolded it and reviewed its contents.

> *Dearest Mina, I must apologize for what you are about to discover, but there was no other choice. Your safety demands that I leave you and proceed on my own to Talaani. Rest*

assured, I protected the caves from her sight, and you have plenty of supplies to last until my return. When Eros awakes, instruct him to mount my horse and say the word, 'Aggripha'. He will then be taken to it with haste.

Love, Ahm.

She couldn't believe what she'd just read. Angry beyond words, she growled and balled up the papyrus, then tossed it aside. After pacing for a short while with her hands balled into fists, she finally calmed enough to think clearly and was quickly reminded of her bodily needs. With a grunt of frustration, she exited the cave to comply with its unspoken requests.

Before she realized it, she found herself milling around mindlessly in the cave with all the parts, wondering when Eros would wake, if she should send him to the Aggripha, and if she should race off to join Ahm. With nothing better to spend her time on, she retrieved the drawings and journal from the chest and set to work reassembling the flying machine.

Maybe once Eros leaves for the Aggripha, I can use it to go find Ahm, she decided.

She worked through the rest of the day and most of the night, assembling the device piece by piece, and confirming everything she attached several times before moving on to the next. In fact, she was so enthralled in the process that she hadn't even realized how long she'd been at work until she stepped outside after completing it and saw the first few rays of light trying to breach the sky over the mountains.

Realizing in that moment that she hadn't eaten since she started working, she grabbed a waterskin and a few hunks of bread and cheese from the supplies Ahm brought with them and ate her fill next to the undead horse, who still hadn't moved. She mindlessly stroked the area where its mane should have been as she finished the last of her impromptu meal, staring at Eros and watching his shallow, infrequent breaths.

"Fuck it," she stated with determination.

She tucked the waterskin under one arm and wiped her hands free of crumbs as she approached Eros. Preparing herself mentally for what she was about to attempt, she set the skin aside and knelt beside him.

"Eros? I don't know if you can hear me, and I'm not sure if this is going to work, but I can't watch you waste away. Who knows if you'd even make it back to the Aggripha if I sent you anyway. So, since I'm bound to it, and have apparently healed myself many times through that connection... perhaps I can do the same for you. So, just in case this doesn't work and you wake up to find me dead beside you, just know that I love you."

Mina closed her eyes and placed her hands on his chest. She cast her mind back to the power she felt during her visions with Mordessa, and tried to feel that sensation in the world around her. Nothing happened. She couldn't feel anything. *No shock it didn't work the first time. I'll just try again,* she decided.

Determined to find a way, she settled back on her haunches and inched closer to Eros. She leaned toward him, carefully slipped one arm beneath him, and slid his upper body into her lap. Placing her hands on his chest, she tried to quiet her mind and push away all thoughts except the power she was searching for. As she drew closer to a meditative trance, she could feel something tickling the back of her mind, as if it were very distant.

Not knowing how to draw from or manipulate such powers, and unsure if the Aggripha even worked like spells would, she simply invited the power within her, and envisioned opening a door to her soul. She repeated the invitation, and the imagery, in her mind, several times, slowing her breathing with each repetition and exhaling each time she saw the door open.

She felt a warmth growing at the center of her chest.

Inspired by the feeling, she continued the process over and over. The warm sensation slowly grew into a ball of heat, and a tingling sensation radiated through her limbs, synchronized with her heartbeat. Now fully committed, she refocused her mind and imagined the power she felt was a rope, and that her hands were latching onto it. Once she was able to picture her hands holding fast, she pulled.

Power surged into her.

She pulled again.

The feeling grew so strong it sent pain radiating through her lower sides, spine, and shoulders. The faint sound of distant screams echoed through her mind.

She had touched the Aggripha.

Refocusing her mind one last time, she pushed with every fiber of her being, and pictured the power surging out of her, into Eros, and mending his broken body.

When the Aggripha's might flowed through her, a white, blinding brightness filled her vision. The rush of energy through her chest felt like the impact of a hammer larger than the room in which she sat, knocking the wind out of her and sending her backward toward the floor.

As she fell, the power raced through her arms, exited her hands, rushed through Eros and crashed into the stone below, sending tremors through the cave, and causing gravel and dust to fall from the freshly cracked ceiling.

Crashing back onto the rocky floor, darkness overtook her.

✦ ✦ ✦

WHITE, BLUE and yellow swirled across her vision, slowly dissipating and revealing a very familiar scene. She hadn't had a vision of Mordessa since the curse, and the sudden appearance of her crystal ball sent a small wave of panic through her.

Unlike her previous experiences, she could see the images glowing inside the magical sphere. She wasn't sure why, or how, it was happening but didn't want to do anything that would disrupt such a rare occurrence. Even though she knew she was sleeping, she instinctively held her breath so Mordessa wouldn't somehow hear it and become aware of her presence.

Glowing amidst the strange, swirling smoke inside the crystal was the scene of a great body of water. Floating in its midst was a boat that seemed too damaged to stay afloat. It was missing its mast and several chunks of its exterior walls, railing, and a large portion of the stern.

Several figures were standing or sitting on the boat, two beside its sail, which seemed to have been stretched out horizontally to make some form of shelter. The vision slowly moved closer until the face of one member of the crew came clearly into focus. He was a tall, muscular man with tan skin, brown hair, a scraggly brown beard, and a dark gray scar across his right cheek.

"I've finally found you. They couldn't hide you from me forever," said Mordessa.

The vision in the crystal ball seemed to back away, as if she were trying to discern their exact location. After a few seconds, when the boat was nothing more than a speck in the distance, land came into view.

"Well, isn't that convenient? You've nearly arrived! It looks like they're pulling you toward Uhldan. I can't have that. Let's see if I can't chan-" she started, but her words cut off abruptly.

The crystal ball went clear, its vision dismissed.

"You again?" she growled angrily.

You... can sense me, asked Mina in her mind?

"You're one of the Ternion, aren't you?" asked Mordessa. "Is that how you survived my curse?"

Mina fought the sudden urge to answer. The urge wasn't coming from her own mind. Mordessa was trying to pull the words out of her.

"No matter. Only one of you needs to die. As soon as I'm free of your intrusion and set my plans in motion, you'll be of no concern to me," growled Mordessa with confidence.

Mina's vision filled with purple hues as Mordessa's magic surged into her. She pushed back using the lingering power she felt from her attachment to the Aggripha, and her attempt to save Eros. As the two forces clashed, more power rushed through her, racing to her aid from her bond with the ancient, crystalline heart.

Just as her skin began to feel the sensation of fire dancing atop its surface, Mina woke. Before she could open her eyes, Eros's voice rang out, breaking the deafening silence.

"Mina? Mina! Wake up!" he shouted.

"I'm awake," she said, reaching for her eyes to rub the crust away.

"What happened? When I woke up, you were folded in half beside me, and moaning in your sleep like you were in pain," he said.

"I tried to heal you with the Aggripha, and the power knocked me out. I can try aga-" she started.

"No, it worked! I'm fine!" he reassured her.

"That's great!" she yelled happily, pulling him into a hug as she sat.

"What about Ahm? Where is he? When did you have time to assemble the Raven? What's going on?" he asked as he pushed her back to look into her eyes.

"We have to go!" she blurted, purpose filling her thoughts.

"What?" he gasped.

"If you sit behind me and hold on, I think the Raven can carry both of us while I drive," she said, rising to her feet.

"You're not making any sense!" he retorted.

"Mordessa is about to kill someone, and we need to stop her. They're out at sea, drifting toward Xulrathia, and they'll arrive any day now. If we aren't there to save them, and she wins, then all is lost. So, get your ass to the Raven and stop stalling me!" she commanded.

He got to his feet and fell in behind her as she strode determinedly toward Ahm's flying machine. "But you've never successfully flown it!"

"When I reassembled it, I put the levers closer to each other in a way that made sense to my brain. So, I should be able to handle it this time without frantically reaching around trying to figure out what I'm doing," she explained.

"But that doesn't-" he started.

"Just get the fuck up there, hang on to me, and if you're that nervous, use all that priestly training you've received and bless us to the afterlife and back!" she demanded.

199

"Fine," he sighed, climbing onto the Raven and sitting on its back behind her.

After he finished his blessings and grabbed onto her shoulders, she tilted her head back and reminded him, "Make sure you grip the sides as tightly as you can with your legs. I don't want you falling off."

"Actually, let me undo my belt and strap it to yours as well," he said.

"Great idea!" she answered.

Once he was set, she pushed the lever into place to connect the device to the Aggripha. As it lifted off the ground on a cushion of magic, it tipped forward and to the left ever so slightly, just as it had done on her first attempt.

She quickly pulled another lever slightly toward herself, and the Raven tipped back to the right. Continuing to ease that lever bit by bit, she used her other hand to move the center lever back as well. Over the next few minutes, she carefully nudged them as little as she could until the Raven seemed to stabilize and come to rest on top of the invisible force that held it aloft. She sent a smile back to Eros, quite happy with herself.

Eros sat patiently as she tested each of the levers, moving them so little he couldn't even tell they'd changed position. As each one caused the Raven to tilt or move in a direction, she adjusted it again to return to their previous stable position. Bit by bit, she practiced shifting the Raven around until she felt comfortable with how everything worked. After what seemed like hours, she finally checked the straps that held her in place and prepared herself to take the biggest risk she'd ever taken.

"Okay," she said. "Here we go!"

She pushed the center control forward, and the Raven tipped toward its beak. She then squeezed her legs together and pulled both outer levers back ever so slightly, which caused it to move forward at a slow pace, its wings moving down then up again at a barely perceptible pace.

Once they were clear of the cave, she manipulated the controls and caused the Raven to accelerate forward while rising up into the sky. As the wind rushed past them, Eros leaned toward her ear and yelled, "I am so fucking scared right now!"

"We only have a day or two to make the coast, and I barely know what I'm doing. So hang on!" she yelled back.

TAVYN CLIMBED up on the railing, holding onto the top of the prow to maintain his balance with the jostling caused by the waves. He wanted to be sure what he was seeing before he announced it to his friends. Once he was certain, he looked back at them and yelled, "Land! I see land!"

Everyone clamored over to the front of the boat to see for themselves. The boat was rising and falling; the shore disappearing periodically behind the waves. However, all of them were initially excited to see the end of their accidental journey approaching. It didn't take Piya long to realize that something was wrong.

"We are traveling way too fast," she said.

"What?" asked Gnately.

"We're moving way faster than we should be. Even if our mast was still intact and there was a strong wind in our sail, we'd be moving slower than this," she confirmed.

Tavyn looked down at the water, then back up towards the shore, which had grown noticeably larger. "She's right. When I look at the water, it's like we're barely moving, but it's some kind of illusion or trick of the eye."

"If we don't find a way to slow down, we're going to crash," said Piya.

"Storm," said Ainen, pointing south. Dark clouds were forming in a small cluster, similar to the strange storm that hit them near Pelrigoss.

"Oh, for fuck's sake!" yelled Gnately.

"Voices say 'listen to girl'," said Ainen.

"Yes! Listen to me. We need to put something in the water to create drag and slow us down. I'm not sure if the anchor will be en-" started Piya.

"Not you," said Ainen. "Her," he added, pointing into the sky to the west.

Everyone crowded around and looked down the line of his finger. A small, black speck was slowly growing on the horizon, and kept veering to the side as if trying to change course to correct for their movement. It looked like a bird, but the movement of its wings seemed shortened, as if it wasn't able to flap them properly.

Just as Gnately was about to tease Ainen, mostly out of frustration, for directing their attention to a 'stupid bird' and distracting them from Piya's plan, the bird-like object drew close enough that she could see what looked like two little dots riding atop its back.

"Are there... people riding that bird?" she gasped.

Several of them squinted, trying to make out more detail. The strange object was still flying directly toward them. It seemed to be coming down out of the sky and picking up speed as it went. After a few more seconds, Tavyn confirmed her suspicions. "Two riders, and I don't think that bird is natural. It looks to be metallic."

"So are we more afraid of the rocky shore we're racing toward, or the storm that just formed in the south and is closing in on us, or the metal bird flying straight at us like an oversized arrow?" asked Piya, unsure of how to proceed.

"Well, Ainen said to-" started Tavyn.

He was cut off by Gnately's shush, and her yanking on his arm.

Everyone on the boat grew silent, listening for whatever Gnately had heard.

"...off ...shore!" came a faint voice from the west.

"She's yelling instructions, I think," whispered Gnately.

"Jump off ...shore!" came the voice again, as the strange bird drew closer. They could clearly see one of the figures atop it waving their arms frantically, trying to get their attention.

"Jump off and swim to shore," said Tavyn, filling in the missing words himself.

Ainen jogged over to their makeshift tent and yanked the sail free of its ties. He shoved Algrim's armor on top of the fabric, grabbed the corners to form a bundle and dove into the water without further hesitation. He disappeared behind the boat far faster than anyone on board expected, and could be seen bobbing in the water behind the boat before disappearing behind the waves as little more than a speck.

"Did you see-" gasped Gnately, unable to finish.

"Jump! Jump now!" yelled Piya, her eyes locked on the fast-approaching shore.

Tavyn grabbed Gnately, who seemed too stunned to move, and jumped in with his arms wrapped around her. Piya jumped in tandem with them, terrified she'd be swept away, alone, and end up somehow lost at sea.

The boat raced away from them and collided ferociously with the waves produced by the magical storm. As before, the storm turned and traveled with the boat, following it for a time until they both crashed into jagged rocks jutting out of the water along the shore. The remnants of the boat disappeared from view before Tavyn could blink.

CHAPTER 14:
REVELATIONS

Ris'Kitthu, Djacenta 21st, 576 of the 1st Era

AFTER THE boat's passengers were in the water, Mina turned the Raven back toward shore to find a place to land. She was happy that they were able to arrive in time to save them, but concern crept in over the cost of doing so. Crossing the northern farmlands had been a big risk. Any of the citizens below could have looked up and seen them, and they'd have been none the wiser. How many had run to their temples and announced the strange object they'd seen in the skies above? How many priests had sent word to the Ebon Guard, seeking assistance, or attempting to alert the Queen?

While Eros's spells had been critical in staying awake, resisting the need to eat, and preventing the need to relieve themselves for the two days it had taken to arrive, they already knew what happened when the inevitable exhaustion caught up with them. Did she really want to risk sleeping, and linking with Mordessa's mind again so soon after spoiling the demonic Queen's plans?

As stressful as those thoughts were, they didn't account for her most immediate fear. The Raven had flown beautifully the entire journey, tilted slightly forward and racing through the sky at speeds she never could have imagined. However, all of that flying had been in a straight line. When they arrived over the ocean and spotted the ruined boat and its doomed crew, she had made the clear choice to slow the Raven down and get closer to the water so her warning could be heard.

During the descent, some of her controls had refused to respond. She'd meant to get much lower, and turn to follow alongside the boat as it raced across the artificially calm waters beneath its hull. The lever that allowed her to turn left hadn't responded. The one that made the Raven fly downward toward the ground stopped working during their dive. While those two control failures were concerning enough on their own, the center lever that controlled their forward movement kept sticking and seemingly refused to go all the way to its resting position.

"I fucked up," said Mina, cocking her face back toward Eros.

"No, no! You don't get to say something like that! Not now! Not while we're riding this thing!" he yelled.

"I'm trying to land, so hang on!" yelled Mina.

The Raven dipped to the right, spiraling slowly toward the ground. She pushed a few levers frantically and slowed the descent, but just as it seemed they might be pulling upward, a loud *clank* echoed from deep inside the Raven's body, and their spiraling fall resumed.

"What's going on?" yelled Eros, his voice trembling.

"I reconfigured the controls by crossing the beams so they'd come up through the body where I wanted them to," she answered. "I think they broke each other, or popped loose, or both," she explained, her voice overcome with sadness.

"How did you get us here, then?" gasped Eros.

"Literal magic? All I had to do was keep us in a straight line. I barely touched the controls at all!" she explained.

"But then-" started Eros.

"Hang on!" screamed Mina as the ground rushed up to greet them.

Chunks of dirt, tufts of grass, dust and rock scattered in all directions as the Raven violently slammed into the ground at the back of a hill, and skidded to a rest at its base. Bent metallic feathers tumbled to a rest around them as the Raven finally settled into the scarred earth. As the runes across its surface ebbed and darkened, the frame of the flying machine's body creaked and groaned, then collapsed a few inches inward.

Mina's legs were searing with pain. The skin of her inner thighs felt scraped and raw. Her calves and hamstrings ached from sustaining her grip as they hit the ground. She was certain she'd torn several muscles, and possibly the tendons in her hips and knees. Her back felt as if she'd been hit with a hammer in several places.

Eros hung loosely off the back of the Raven, moaning in pain and nearly unconscious. He was tilted to one side, dangling from the belts that bound him to Mina's back. His legs had lost their grip at the moment of impact, and he'd been jostled about with great ferocity during their slide and the eventual abrupt stop at the end. He reached up and released the buckle and let himself slide backward atop the wing, and down to the ground.

Mina released the straps then scrambled out of her seat as quickly as her injured lower extremities would allow. She slid down the wing to Eros's side and lifted him out of the position he landed in, head down in the dirt.

"Thank you," he moaned. "I... need to heal myself. Can you sit me up?"

"Of course," she said, her eyes starting to feel puffy and damp. She threaded her arms under his shoulders and pulled him atop her while leaning back, so his legs would straighten out between her own. Once he was settled, she nudged his shoulders forward and slipped her legs from around him, leaving him sitting on the wing, facing the ground.

He bowed his head and clasped his hands in prayer, speaking words of praise and thanks to Ishnu in soft, dulcet tones. An audible snap emanated from his back as his posture abruptly adjusted and the tension in his shoulders subsided. His prayers continued, yet changed ever so slightly. Shortly thereafter, his legs forcibly straightened, as if pulled by an unseen force. With a final word of thanks, the visible wounds on his arms, neck and face faded before Mina's eyes, and his skin returned to its natural youthful state.

"In all my years living with Ahm, I never once witnessed healing spells such as those," gasped Mina. "Do you think you could fix my legs while you're at it?"

"Certainly," he chimed. He reached out and grabbed her nearest ankle, then proceeded to repeat the second prayer he'd spoken to heal himself. After a few brief seconds, the pain in her legs faded away, and her muscles felt ready for whatever she could throw at them.

"That is amazing," she gasped.

"The Temple of Daahl specializes in the healing of muscle, bone, and tissue. Thanks to our brethren, the Xxrandites, we have countless scrolls documenting the inner workings of our bodies, and what injuries might look like from the inside. Daahl created spells to heal specific body parts long ago, and if one is talented enough to use them properly, they can heal anyone from just about any natural ailment," he explained proudly. "Unfortunately," he added, "I can only channel spells of that caliber through my body a few times per day, without risking severe injury to myself or death.

I may not be able to help our new friends if they arrive in poor condition."

"Crap!" exclaimed Mina, rising to her feet. She reached down mindlessly for Eros's hand, and tugged him up to join her when he complied. "Speaking of our 'new friends,' we need to go make sure they made it to shore!"

TAVYN STARTED to let go of Gnately so he could swim to shore. Kicking his legs with his arms wrapped around her was barely keeping them afloat. Her heart skipped a beat when she felt his arms loosen. Before he could respond, she lunged toward him and wrapped her arms around his neck.

"I can't swim," she whimpered.

"I'm not so good at it myself," he gasped.

Piya swam over to them and nodded her head to her gnomish friend. "Climb on my back."

Tavyn turned himself as best he could and grabbed Gnately around her waist. With some effort, and quite a bit of saltwater splashing into his mouth and nose, he managed to help Gnately over toward Piya. Once he was free of her weight, he fared far better in the rolling waves.

Gnately latched onto Piya's shoulders and lay flat up against her, belly to back. Piya turned and swam slowly toward shore, seeming quite at home in the water. None of them could see Ainen, or the strange metallic bird and its riders.

Piya led Tavyn toward a small stretch of beach just north of the rocky cliffs. Far in the north, a range of mountains stretched across the sky into the distant west. Tavyn found it easier to let the rolling waves crash into his upper back and carry him forward in surges, than attempt to paddle and kick along like Piya. He knew the principles of swimming, and had occasionally taken dips in the Arashyvi River back home, but he wasn't very good at it, and was content enough to avoid the watery depths.

After what felt like an hour, Piya's right hand brushed against a tuft of kelp during a stroke. Excited, she pushed ahead with all her strength. Once she was confident enough, she stopped and shifted to put her feet down, much to the chagrin of her Gnomish passenger.

"Eep!" squeaked Gnately.

"Don't worry, we're almost there," gasped Piya, more than a little exhausted.

A few minutes later, the trio had made it to dry sand. Piya stood watching the water, seeking signs of Ainen. Tavyn did his best to stand beside her, but resigned himself to leaning over, hands on knees. Somehow, swimming to shore had been more exhausting than scaling a building and clinging to its side for nearly an hour.

"There he is!" gasped Piya, setting off at a run.

Tavyn decided she didn't sound upset, so Ainen wasn't likely to be in trouble. Content to rest, he turned away from the sea and began lowering himself to the sand. Just as he turned, two figures came into view, rounding the corner of a sharp, rocky hill to the south.

"We've got company, Gnat," he said, reaching down to his distraught little friend's shoulder.

She got up and turned inland a moment later, and studied the pair that approached. A human woman with broad shoulders and of greater stature than would be average in Algona, followed closely by a human man with hips, shoulders and a slightly swishy swagger that she might have mistaken for a woman, if it weren't for his face and chest.

"Hail," said Tavyn. "Was it you who warned us, from the back of that... that..."

"Mechanical raven," answered Mina, "and yes."

"I'm Gnately."

"Nice to meet you, Gnately. I'm Mina, and this is Eros," she answered, pointing to the man.

"This is Tavyn. Our other two friends up the shore are Piya and Ainen," said Gnately.

"Does Ainen have a strange, gray scar on his face by any chance?" asked Mina.

"How did you know about that?" asked Tavyn, tensing.

"I saw it in a vision. In fact, that's what brought us out here to save you," answered Mina.

"Yeah, what was that, anyway? You saw the strange storm, right? And how fast we were moving?" asked Gnately.

Mina nodded. "Both things caused by Queen Mordessa to kill your friend, Ainen."

"Guys?" pleaded Piya, back near the water.

The group turned to see Piya desperately trying to block Ainen's path. He was pushing against her, staring off into the mountains, and churning his legs in the sand as if he were walking.

"What the hells?" blurted Tavyn as he sprang into action. He closed the distance and pulled on Ainen's hand, trying to grab the man's attention. When that didn't elicit a response, he shoved Ainen sideways with all his might. Ainen crashed to the ground, and immediately started to stand back up. Tavyn jumped atop him and pushed him flat on his back, using every ounce of strength he could muster. He looked back at the others, all standing in a ring around them. "Help me hold him still. We've got to wake him up."

Gnately dropped to her knees at Ainen's head while Piya and Mina assisted Tavyn. She gently stroked his cheek, calling his name in a calm tone for a few minutes. When that didn't work, she slapped him as hard as she could across his scar, sending pain through her own hand but seemingly doing nothing to wake the man out of his trance.

"Let me try something," offered Eros, kneeling beside her. While the others struggled to hold Ainen's arms and legs on the ground, he placed a hand on Ainen's forehead, closed his eyes, and recited a prayer. His spell seemed to do nothing.

"What was that?" asked Tavyn.

"I tried to heal his brain," said Eros, shrugging.

"He's been hearing voices," explained Tavyn. "He said they were calling him to join them."

"I could try blessing him to block outside influence?" suggested Eros.

"Do it!" barked Gnately.

When Eros completed his next prayer, Ainen seemed to grow oddly still. He looked up at the group of friends and strangers for a few moments, then asked, "Why are you on top of me?"

With a myriad of sighs and grunts, everyone climbed off of Ainen and let the man gain his feet. Mina and Eros quickly introduced themselves, and Ainen nodded in return.

"What were the voices saying this time?" asked Gnately.

"Not voices. One voice, but split in two," said Ainen.

"What? But I thought-" started Gnately.

"Voice is part mine, part not. Part of her is inside me, but the rest of her is far to the south. We are connected through something in the north. We're close to it," said Ainen. "I can feel her."

"Her?" asked Tavyn.

Ainen nodded. "She wants to be whole, but that is not her mission."

"What's her mission?" asked Gnately.

"To free them," said Ainen.

"Free who?" asked Eros.

Ainen shrugged. "She is barely strong enough to speak to me, and I have only just learned to listen."

"Well, as it so happens, we've got some bad news of our own, and it affects all of you," said Mina. "Let's go find a place to rest and talk. Eros and I will succumb to the side effects of his blessings soon, and will sleep deeply for an unknown length of time. I'd like it if you stayed with us."

"You saved our lives, so sure. But... why?" asked Tavyn.

"It will all make sense once we talk," said Mina.

"No, it won't," laughed Eros.

"Fine," sighed Mina. "It will be more terrifying, perhaps, and quite confusing, but you should have answers. Okay?"

Tavyn nodded and walked up the beach toward a small stand of trees. Gnately shrugged and joined him. Piya and Ainen followed quietly, seeming not to care one way or the other.

TAVYN AND Gnately set about making a camp without a word. While they worked, Ainen and Piya sat side by side. He seemed lost in thought. She didn't want to burden him, or make him feel uncomfortable, by asking what was wrong. Instead, she quietly placed her hand atop his and leaned her head on his shoulder.

Mina and Eros sat nearby, across the clearing. They hadn't had a chance to relax in quite some time, and hadn't been together under the stars in even longer. Mina silently hoped that the group's conversations would end peacefully, and quickly, so she could retire under the stars with her lover before more serious matters took over. Eros was secretly having the same thoughts, but resisted the urge to voice them out of fear Mina would think him selfish.

Tavyn dug a small hole in the center of camp and strategically arranged a few handfuls of dry reeds and small bits of driftwood at the base. He then placed three driftwood branches across the top of the hole in lines facing one direction, and three more atop them facing the other. Once he finished, he set a small bundle of dry brush in its own pile, and pulled a small piece of flint and a similar sized bar of steel from a pocket on his left thigh. After a few strikes, the brush caught ablaze at the center. He lifted the bundle, blew gently into the flame and watched as it grew and started to glow in the middle. Content with his accomplishment, he slipped the bundle between the branch grid, down onto the kindling at the bottom. Before long, the fire sprang to life, and he was able to sit back and relax.

Gnately, meanwhile, cleared areas for each of the companions to sleep, moving small rocks, leaves, dried bits of wood, and reeds off to one side. She then gathered a few tufts of long grass, and bundled them into soft little rings, for each of them to use as a pillow. Once she was done, she noticed the fire was burning brightly and joined Tavyn in the circle.

"As I said before, I am Mina. Mina Llanthor, adopted daughter of Ahm Stonehawk, the High Priest of Kesh, and Defense Minister of the Kingdom of Baan'Sholaria," she said.

"Why don't people have simple names anymore? Like, Tom?" interrupted Gnately.

Tavyn chuckled.

"I know, it's a lot. But it's also very important. The center of Baan'Sholaria is a city we call Dusk. It is extremely large, with a population of well over one-hundred-million," said Mina.

"No way," sighed Gnately with a roll of her eyes.

"I assure you, she is correct," said Eros.

"Then why haven't any of us heard of it before?" challenged Gnately, wrinkling her brow.

"That's almost two-hundred times as large as Amuer, in Haern. Something that big would be quite hard to hide," said Tavyn.

"We go to great lengths to hide our existence. Merchants from other lands only see our border colonies, and from that point of view, our Kingdom looks mostly like farms and small fishing villages. They are never permitted far enough inland to see our Kingdom's true size. That way, the outside world won't have reason to fear us, or seek to destroy us. That is what our leaders tell us, anyway," said Mina.

"Our citizens are servants of Ishnu and Xxrandus," added Eros.

Tavyn bowed his head, then looked up at him. "I thought I heard you say Ishnu's name in your prayers over Ainen, but you spoke very quietly; I couldn't be sure. As you are not Dynar, I dared not assume," he explained. Deep down, Tavyn was growing more and more fearful of their newfound companions. His order always warned its recruits never to travel to Xulrathia, but they'd offered no explanation for the rule.

"When our people reach adulthood, they are offered a chance to Ascend to a higher existence. Those who serve Ishnu can become an Unliving, and those who serve Xxrandus can become an Undead," explained Eros.

Tavyn noticeably and involuntarily tensed in response, his hand instinctively moving to the hilt of one of his blades.

"Fear not, sir Tavyn. Neither of us has taken Ascension. More importantly, our citizens bear you no ill will, and would not harm you. They live normal lives; working, playing, raising children, serving the Kingdom, and worshiping their god. Other than our clothes and the condition of our bodies, you would notice no difference between those living in Dusk and the citizens of any other city," explained Eros.

"Extending life spans through necromancy is against the will of Ishnu, and spits in the face of everything she stands for," growled Tavyn. "Ishnu values the cycle of life, and our contribution to the next generation upon our death. By becoming such abominations, your citizens disrupt that cycle, and harm all life that would follow."

"According to our teachings, it was Ishnu herself that taught our church how to perform the ritual of Ascension, so that we might act as guardians of the world, should the Talaani Empire ever rise from the ashes to threaten it," said Eros.

"That is not possible," said Tavyn forcefully.

"Our people do not travel to the rest of Ayrelon. We stay to ourselves. Once we accept Ascension, our laws prohibit us from ever leaving the Kingdom. This helps us prevent the spread of both our ideology and the knowledge of our existence. The only cycle of life we could disrupt is our own, and since the vast majority of our populace is not alive, by your definition, there is no cycle left to destroy," stated Eros.

"A Kingdom full of Unliving and Undead sounds both terrifying and intriguing," gasped Gnately. "Tell me more!"

Tavyn tightened his grip on his dagger. All of his training said that he'd landed on a continent that shouldn't exist, populated by Ishnu's most hated abominations. It took every ounce of his self-control to resist the urge to lash out or run for his life.

"Why is your friend so upset?" asked Eros, turning to Gnately.

"Well, that's where there might be a little problem," said Gnately. She turned to Tavyn for a moment, and caught his eyes. "It's not like you can hide it forever, and they seem nice enough," she suggested, shrugging. "Worst-case scenario, we find a way to leave, right?"

Tavyn did his best to seem as if he'd calmed down. He wanted to trust his friend. They'd been through many dangerous situations together, and she was the only person he'd met that hadn't judged him poorly once his profession came to light.

"Tavyn is a Purifier of the Daxian Order, from Quaan'Shala," said Gnately.

Eros stood and backed out of the circle.

"What's that?" asked Mina, grabbing Eros's hand before he could get too far away from her. She tugged, insisting he sit back down.

"I was trained to hunt all sources of Necromancy, including the Unliving and the Undead, for they are abominations in the eyes of Ishnu," said Tavyn, nearly growling.

"Well, we're both still living, and Eros is a priest, not a

Necromancer," reminded Mina. "In fact, I couldn't become an Unliving or Undead if I wanted to. I am Forsaken, and my soul was born already bound to the relic our churches use to perform the ceremonies. You are safe in my presence." She smiled at him reassuringly, then continued, "besides, I'm certain this Daxian Order is simply misinterpreting Ishnu's teachings."

"Or your people are," growled Tavyn.

"We can't associate with him, Mina," gulped Eros. "It is forbidden."

"What, are you saying Dusk knows about his Order?" asked Mina.

Eros nodded. "The Temple of Daahl has a copy of the Kingdom's most sacred laws. The most recent was added by the Queen almost two-hundred-fifty years ago. It is called the Dax'Vahr Provision. It decrees that any follower of Dax'Vahr should be put to death immediately, without trial, and that if Dax'Vahr himself returns to Xulrathia, or is found anywhere in the world, that he should have his soul destroyed for all time by Ishnu's strongest prayer."

"You know of Dax'Vahr?" asked Tavyn, growing confused.

"Dax'Vahr Ris'Klarran is the founder of your Order, is he not?" asked Eros.

"He is," said Tavyn, curious but still angry.

"The tome that mentions his name detailed his arrival in Dusk, near death on an abandoned ship ravaged by plague. He was taken in by the High Priest of Oltein against our laws. That priest, Anya Carafor, was curious, since she'd never met a Dynar in person. So, she did the only thing she could think of to save Dax'Vahr's life. She knew that Dynar served Ishnu, so she took it upon herself to Ascend the man under the assumption that all servants of Ishnu held the same beliefs as our church. That act was also against our laws. When he woke, she took him into her home and over time fell in love with him. When her actions were discovered, she was put to death for treason, and he was scheduled to die next. Before that could happen, he managed to escape and slew dozens of innocent citizens on his way to freedom.

"Worse still, since he couldn't find a way out of Dusk safely, he went on a rampage, apparently damaging many holy relics, and even invading the Void Spire above the Citadel of Xxrandus. Many phylacteries were destroyed that day, and thousands of our oldest, most valuable citizens lost their everlasting lives. Eventually, a young woman who feared Ascension helped him to escape, and he hasn't been seen since," explained Eros.

"None of that is true. His teachings make no mention of him being in Dusk. In fact, the only mention of this continent clearly states we should avoid it at all costs," retorted Tavyn. "Besides, if he was Unliving, as you claim, I would know. I can see spirits."

"You are a Touched?" asked Mina.

"You... know what that is?" asked Tavyn.

"I too am Touched. Our people have used that term for many, many centuries. Dax'Vahr likely learned that word from us, and brought it home to your people," said Mina.

"No, it's not possible. If he is Unliving, then he's been lying to us from the beginning. Unliving are the greatest abomination. They deny Ishnu's will, and disrupt the cycle of life. 'One shall not seek to live beyond their time,'" he finished, reciting a verse to prove his point.

"Did you ever meet Dax'Vahr in person?" asked Eros.

"Of course, I-" started Tavyn. He thought for a moment, then reconsidered. His face twisted in confusion as he came to the realization that Eros might be right, at least about one thing. "No, actually. I was supposed to be granted the honor of meeting him following my mission in Haern."

"So you have no proof to refute our archival documents which claim he is Unliving?" asked Eros, growing confident.

"No, I... I guess I don't," answered Tavyn.

"Do you concede that I knew his name without your mention of it?" asked Eros.

Tavyn loosened his grip on his hilt. "I... I do."

"How would I know his name, were it not written somewhere in our historical records? Pure luck?" asked Eros.

Mina put a hand on his arm, sensing he was growing a little too confident and proud. She bid him to sit and gave him a look that said, 'calm down.' He complied.

"I will admit that you could be telling the truth, but I will not accept your word as fact until I see proof, either from you or from a meeting with Lord Dax himself. For now, I will withhold action," said Tavyn, releasing the grip on his dagger.

"While this revelation certainly adds an unexpected challenge, it isn't what I wished to discuss with you," said Mina.

"Voices," said Ainen, nodding to her. "I wish to know about the voices."

"As far as we can tell, Queen Mordessa created a curse over a thousand years ago to thwart the Talaani Empire and prevent them from ever attacking Dusk. To enact that curse, she supposedly destroyed three souls and trapped them inside the enchantments that made an artifact we know as the Aggripha. A few hundred years ago, a man named Korr wrote a prophecy saying that those three spirits would reincarnate, or be reborn, into new hosts, and that eventually those new hosts would succeed in freeing the Talaani lands of her curse," said Mina.

"I sense one inside me," said Ainen.

Mina nodded. "Mordessa was searching for one in particular, and she was quite pleased when a sudden burst of magical energies drew her to you."

"The wound in the forest?" asked Gnately.

"After the goblins," agreed Tavyn, nodding.

"Can you explain what you mean?" asked Mina.

"Ainen took a nasty wound to the face, fighting off a bunch of goblins. We raced over to help, but this strange golden light burst out of his face and when it faded, he had that gray, stony flesh in its place," explained Gnately.

"Well, whether that was the event or not, she found you with her crystal ball. From that point onward, she sought a way to kill you in order to prevent you from reaching the Talaani Empire. And I think she's after me and Eros now, too... for the same reason," said Mina.

"You think you're the other two spirits?" asked Gnately.

"Eros was resurrected by the Aggripha under very strange circumstances, and I've been connected to it my whole life. I've been having visions of Mordessa by entering her mind when I sleep. Most recently, she yelled that I was one of the 'Ternion' while attempting to kick me out of her thoughts. In other words, one of the group of three," said Mina.

"Is that why you raced to save us on that flying contraption?" asked Gnately.

"It is. Mordessa yelled that only one of us had to die, and she was looking at the lot of you on that damaged boat when I entered the vision," said Mina.

"So it was Mordessa that sent the storms?" asked Tavyn. "Because Ainen is one of these spirits reborn?"

"As far as we can understand what's going on? Yes," said Mina.

"We aren't experts," admitted Eros.

"So then we just leave, right?" asked Gnately. "If we aren't on Xulrathia, we can't go to the Talaani Empire, and she'd have no reason to kill Ainen."

"Need I remind you, she searched for and found Ainen when he was nowhere near Xulrathia. To her, it doesn't seem to matter where you are. I was hidden by Ahm my entire life so that she would never know I existed, since I am Forsaken. She fears that a Forsaken might rise some day to challenge her power. So, my mere existence is a threat. The same goes for you. You might not be on Xulrathia in a given moment, but that does not mean you'd never come back," explained Mina.

"So what do we do?" asked Gnately.

"We can't go into Dusk," said Eros.

"Not with me in your company. I'm not sure how I'd handle being surrounded by the very thing I've been taught my entire life to hunt and destroy," said Tavyn.

"We're wanted, Eros and I. She knows who I am now, and she's hunting us down. She undoubtedly saw us arrive on the Raven and save you. In fact, she might even be watching us right this very moment," said Mina.

Gnately slid closer to Tavyn for safety.

"Only option is the Talaani Empire," said Ainen.

"She tried to kill us to stop something from happening... so let's go make it happen," said Piya.

"What if making it happen destroys their Kingdom? Kills everyone they know?" asked Gnately.

Tavyn shrugged, as if that was just fine with him.

Mina could feel Eros's spells wearing off and the inevitable exhaustion taking hold. "We'll have to discuss that again once we wake. Sorry, there's no fighting this off. I trust," she said, yawning. "I trust we're safe in your care?" she asked as she fell backward, unconscious.

Eros wasn't far behind her.

THOUGH HIS own situation was dire, Ahm's only concern was for Mina. Even locked in a magically sealed room by the Elonesti Guard, his mind kept racing back to the thought of her safety. Was she still in the cave? Had she set off on her own to follow him? Had she risked returning to the Aggripha with Eros? He'd anticipated a bit of worry invading his mind, but hadn't expected it to be prevalent to the point of distraction. While he certainly welcomed the diversion in his current predicament, he'd have preferred it was something other than fear for his adoptive daughter.

Without the ability to see the sun, he found it impossible to track time. During his walk to, and through, the Talaani Empire, he'd made sure to reapply Ishnu's blessings for endurance, sustenance and obfuscation every morning at sunrise. Without a way to know for certain, he found himself recasting the spells every time the thought occurred to him, just in case.

He wasn't certain how long he'd been trapped in the sealed room, but it had been at least two days, if not more, and yet they hadn't come back to interrogate or punish him. No threats had been tossed in his direction at all. In fact, the guard patrol that captured him hadn't attacked, threatened, harmed, or even spoken to him. When they'd run into one another, there was an immediate and unspoken understanding that he was going to be taken into custody. He'd complied out of a combination of exhaustion and sheer morbid curiosity. It was obvious they didn't know who he was, or that he was fully capable of escaping the room they'd locked him in.

'*You have done well. She has not seen you,*' came a familiar voice in his mind.

The stone door snapped into action, grinding along the floor as it was methodically, slowly cranked open by unseen hands. Floating in the twelve-foot entryway was Lord Whun. The robes of his position as ambassador had been replaced with the ancient attire he'd forged hundreds, if not thousands, of years prior from the hide of felled dragons. His pants, open shirt and exceedingly long robe were all made of supple, highly magical, and heavily enchanted black draconic leather. Gray and purple runes danced across its surface, intertwining and pulsing brightly whenever they collided and formed a nexus.

His bones had long since turned black, and bore glowing blue enchantments indicative of an undead who had long since lost their muscles and had to rely on magic to reanimate their joints. The open front of his shirt revealed the center of his ribcage, and the beating black heart within; each beat sending waves of power radiating through his core as purple and blue flames danced across its surface.

No longer able to use his legs, they hung akilter beneath his levitating torso, bent at the hip and knee at slightly different angles, his useless feet curled back on themselves feebly. Atop his head stood a two-foot-tall iron crown, etched with silvery runes and adorned with an exquisitely cut amethyst. Inside of the gem glowed a flaming eye, peering about the room of its own accord.

His jaw had long ago fallen off. Rather than re-attaching it through enchantment, he had chosen, instead, to fashion it into a relic that allowed him to speak with others through a form of forced telepathy, so long as he held the jaw in his possession. To that end, the jaw hung atop the exterior of his upper chest, held fast with the same bits of rusted barbed wire that suspended his heart.

Even though Ahm had known Whun for as long as he could remember, he found it impossible to be comfortable with the lich's appearance. Whun was unsettling even to Queen Mordessa, and that fact alone had resulted in his assignment to the Elonesti Embassy, to put him as far away from her presence as she could manage without drawing his ire.

"It's good to see you, old friend," said Ahm.

'You are as bad at lying as you ever were. One would think you'd have improved such skills as Minister of Defense these past centuries, but I suppose your lack of need to practice such techniques is to my benefit in these times,' answered Whun.

"We thought you were a prisoner," said Ahm.

'You and I both know that is impossible, as do the Elonesti,' said Whun.

"In truth, I bore little concern for your safety when you stopped reporting to Mordessa. She, however, seems rather concerned, and threatened my destruction if I didn't come to seek you out," said Ahm.

'I am aware of her... outbursts. It is not my safety which causes her concern, but rather her fear of what I might have learned,' said Whun.

"After what I've recently discovered, I'm sure I've got an inkling of what that might be," said Ahm, pacing.

'Of what do you speak?' asked Whun.

"The Prophecy of Korr," answered Ahm bluntly.

Whun laughed, his voice echoing in Ahm's mind as if it were a great cavern. 'Eloquent words. Shallow truths. Nay, I hid myself from Mordessa's view with the very spell of obfuscation I taught you so many centuries ago, and for very good reason,' said Whun.

"What reason might that be?" asked Ahm.

'I discovered the Talaani's greatest secret. After years of searching, and nearly being forced to destroy the Elonesti Dominion to prove its existence, I found what I was looking for, and learned a terrible truth,' said Whun.

He held his left hand out as if inviting someone to enter, then drifted slowly out of the way on unseen currents. A human entered wearing Baan'Sholarian robes usually reserved for noble family members, or persons of great importance. The sigil on his breast was of the Elonesti Dominion, but nothing else about him was Talaani in nature.

The man approached somewhat timidly, as if he was afraid to scare Ahm away, or worried Ahm might lash out when he spoke. When he got close enough to the pacing priest, the man extended his right hand in greeting, and said, "I am Korr. It is so nice I finally have a chance to meet the son of Advan."

CHAPTER 15:
PURPOSE

Ris'Uttyr, Djacenta 23rd, 576 of the 1st Era

W HEN MINA woke, the first thing she noticed was that she'd been moved. Her head was lying on someone's chest, and their arms were around her. Slightly panicked, but hopeful, she kept her eyes closed and listened intently.

The heartbeat beneath her was Eros.

Elated that her hope was reality, she relaxed and decided to savor the moment. The voices of their new companions rang out nearby as a burst of laughter filled the air. It was nice to hear others in good spirits, especially those who had been through such an ordeal.

She knew she couldn't lie in Eros's arms forever, even if that was what her heart desired. With a sigh, she extricated herself from his embrace with a kiss and got to her feet, smiling down at him. He'd passed out while holding her, and was blissfully unaware that she'd moved.

"No. I told you then, and I'll say it again now. I love fish, just not when it's bloody and still moving. You guys didn't even knock the scales off. You just... chomped down. I have no idea how you did it once, let alone several times a day for weeks," said Gnately.

"Are you saying you're happy we shipwrecked?" chuckled Tavyn.

"No?" said Gnately, trying to sound convincing.

"She is!" gasped Piya.

"My... my cheese wheel was gone. It ran'ded out," said Gnately with a pout.

"So you weren't upset we were trapped at sea, just that you were running out of cheese?" laughed Piya.

"Being as small as a mouse doesn't mean you have to eat like one," said Tavyn very plainly.

Mina enjoyed their banter as she walked across the beach to join them. A small fire roared at the center of their camp, and the wonderful aroma of burning wood and cooking fish was quite enticing. Her stomach growled painfully at the thought of a meal.

"Have room for one more?" she asked as she approached.

"Absolutely!" chirped Gnately, patting the ground beside her. "Careful, though, I apparently nibble random things and leave a trail of tiny pellets of poop behind me. Wouldn't want you to get sick," she laughed.

"It's okay. I love mice," said Mina, patting Gnately on the head as she sat.

Gnately groaned her disapproval. Piya couldn't help but laugh.

"Hungry?" asked Ainen, lifting a make-shift spit with a hunk of fish on the end.

"I am famished!" exclaimed Mina. "I haven't eaten in days."

"You slept through an entire day," said Tavyn as she reached for the stick Ainen offered.

"I expected we would. Eros used prayers to bless us with endurance and sustenance so we could fly across Xulrathia to save you. We traveled for two days at high speed without rest, covering a much greater distance than you could in a week on horseback. When blessings like that wear off, the lack of sleep catches up to you all at once," she answered. Without hesitation, she started picking chunks of meat off the fish and shoving it into her mouth with reckless abandon. She couldn't recall the last time she'd eaten seafood, and was immediately stricken with how wonderful it tasted. Its texture was far different from what she could remember; much more delicate and flakey than she could recall ever experiencing.

"We really do appreciate what you did. Without your intervention, we might not have noticed just how dire our circumstances were," said Tavyn.

"My only thought was slowing us down. Jumping off and swimming hadn't even dawned on me," admitted Piya.

"I can't swim, so I wouldn't have even suggested it," said Gnately.

"I don't like water," said Ainen.

"But you jumped in so fast," gasped Piya.

"Wanted to get it over with," said Ainen with a shrug. He picked up another stick from a small pile on his left and thrust the sharpened end into a scaled, gutted fish from the pile on his right, sitting on top of a blanket of leaves.

"Where did you get all the fish?" asked Mina.

"Piya was walking the beach and found some rope that washed ashore from our wreckage. She unraveled a few strands and tied them to some long sticks we found in that stand of trees," said Tavyn, obviously proud of his companion's ingenuity.

"I didn't do it all by myself. Gnately was kind enough to offer some of her lockpicks, and Tavyn helped bend them and sharpen the ends with his whetstone to make hooks. Then Ainen and I fished off the rocks atop that hill," she said, pointing, "for the rest of the day until we had enough to feed all of us. It was a team effort."

"You're all very resourceful. I'm impressed," said Mina between bites. "I don't think I would've thought to do any of that."

They sat in silence for a short while, watching Mina enjoy her meal. The sky was clear, and Zathos, the small, red moon, had entered the sky in the west. Provoss and Aygos had almost completed their journey to the east. There was so little vegetation nearby that it was absolutely silent, save for whatever noises their party made, and the gentle lap of nearby waves on the shore. The weather was just warm enough to bring the newcomers right to the edge of sweat, but a cool breeze frequently rushed up from the water to kiss them, and keep them cool. For many of the shipwrecked companions, it was the most perfect setting they could have imagined.

Tavyn chuckled again at the sight of Gnately wriggling her toes in the sand, kicked back and leaning on her palms, seemingly without a care in the world. He was glad she was finally warm, and had found her sandy beach, regardless of the circumstances that had brought them there.

"Did Eros wake and move me?" asked Mina.

"Aye. He woke for a time and seemed to wander around near the trees, talking to himself. Then he laid down next to you and pulled you into his arms before passing out again," said Gnately.

"He didn't come join you all? Did he eat?" asked Mina.

"No, and no. We didn't have all this set up at that time. Piya and Ainen were still fishing," Gnately answered.

"When he wakes, we need to get moving. It might even be wise to wake him now, get some food in his stomach and be on our way. If Mordessa watched what happened, she could have someone on their way to intercept us at this very moment. Thankfully, I didn't dream last night, but that also means I didn't have an opportunity to see what she was up to," said Mina.

"So, your visions occur when you sleep?" asked Tavyn.

"That's really a thing?" asked Gnately.

"Unfortunately, yes. It's a horrifying experience, but somehow also thrilling. I can feel the magic she has within her, and it's intoxicating. At the same time, though, she's absolutely frightening. However, those visions are also how I knew she was hunting you, so the experience *can* be quite useful," explained Mina.

"What's so frightening about a Queen?" chuckled Gnately. All she could picture were the nobles she'd seen in Algona. None of them seemed overly concerning in her eyes.

"Well, let's see," said Mina, picking a fishbone out of her teeth. "She's much taller than Ainen, but thin, sleek and muscular like Tavyn. Her legs are shaped more like a goat's than a human or elf, with thick, leathery skin on them and large cloven hooves. She has a massive pair of black wings, more like a bat than a bird. And let's not forget the giant black horns on her head, or the black talon-like nails on her fingers," described Mina. She looked around at the companions, each displaying a variation of shock, horror, or disgust. "Oh, and in one of my visions, I watched her simply clench her fist in the air, which made a man fold inside out and crush into a ball of goo because he said something she didn't like."

"Holy shit!" gasped Gnately.

"That thing is your Queen?" gasped Piya.

"She has been our Queen for as long as the Kingdom of Baan'Sholaria has existed," said Mina. "She united the two religious factions by common purpose, made the Aggripha, and built the enchantments that power our infrastructure. As far as anyone in Dusk is concerned, *she* is the reason we exist, and the only thing holding the Talaani Empire at bay."

"Why do you willingly serve her?" asked Piya.

"I don't. I was born here and raised in secret by Ahm because he recognized that I was Forsaken. I'm sure it was morbid curiosity that motivated him at first, but I think he came to care for me like a father fairly quickly. I don't recall ever feeling unwanted or unloved. I was *angry* at him for not letting me see the world I was reading and learning about, but now that I've seen what he was hiding me from... I just wish I could take my harsh words back, and thank him for putting his life in danger on my behalf," said Mina.

"Sacrificing ones' self for the sake of others is the noblest of traits. He sounds like an amazing man," said Tavyn.

"And yet you would attempt to kill him if you met. He is an Unliving. He is the High Priest of the Temple of Kesh; an Ishnite

Temple that teaches precisely what we explained to you last night," said Mina.

Tavyn leaned back, resting on his palms, conflicted.

"It's easy to judge someone from afar. I'm sure Dax'Vahr had plenty of justification for declaring our people were the enemy, but I'm afraid Dusk just isn't as simple as all that. We're normal people... who just happen to live very long lives through the power of a device that is blessed by both Ishnu and Xxrandus. Besides... if the legends are true? Our mutual goddess, Ishnu, is Mordessa's mother," said Mina, raising an eyebrow. "So whose to say it is not Baan'Sholaria that are right, and Quaan'Shala that are wrong?"

"I... I'd like to think what I've been taught my whole life was the truth. You're asking me to believe that everything I know is a lie. How would you take that information? Would it endear you to my cause?" asked Tavyn.

"There are plenty of lies beneath my truths. Not lies directed at you, but lies underlying the truths taught to the citizens of Dusk. The temples of both religions teach that the Aggripha is a blessing; a gift from Mordessa, granted to our people to provide us with eternal life. But that life is not eternal. In fact, we recently discovered that the Aggripha siphons our souls over time, starting the very day we accept Ascension as an Undead or Unliving through its power.

"Furthermore, something about how Mordessa created the device caused terrible consequences for the Talaani Empire, which I'm still not totally clear on. However, it was enough for one of their ancient dragons to reach out from beyond the grave with the help of his followers, the Elonesti Dominion, and attempt to break the Queen's curse. Apparently, it was his failed attempt to free his own people that led to the three souls being able to reincarnate, at least in part, in the hopes of completing his ritual, and some day freeing the Talaani from her oppression.

"What that all means, I have no idea. To your earlier point, I don't want to think what will happen to Dusk if we fulfill some ancient prophecy by seeing this through. However, Mordessa's only concern is stopping whatever she thinks we're meant to do, and after the lies I've seen revealed, and discovering that she's actually stealing power from all of Dusk's citizens, I'm certain that the proper course of action is to do whatever we can to thwart her.

"So, if I am willing to walk away from everything I know— everything I've been taught to believe—to right an ancient wrong and set a people free that I've never met, and have been conditioned my whole life to fear... then I'd hope you were willing to set aside Dax'Vahr's teachings for long enough to help us see this through," said Mina.

After taking a few moments to digest her words, Tavyn rose to his feet and bowed. "Very well. Let's wake and feed Eros. We've a mission to complete, and the sun will soon rise."

AHM TOOK a step back, confusion contorting his brow. "The Ministry of Internal Affairs declared you dead by the Queen's orders."

"It was two members of the ministry who helped me escape," laughed Korr. "Not all are as blind to the truth as the Queen thinks. After all, once I revealed that I had been speaking with the very souls Mordessa trapped to create the Aggripha, they were all too happy to see me to safety."

"So, you've been hiding here for what, two centuries?" gasped Ahm. "Why have we never discovered you until now?"

"I move from temple to temple, dominion to dominion. I particularly enjoy spending my winters among the Fiirnasi in the north. The Fiirnasi temple is surrounded by natural springs which draw warmth from the remnants of the ancient volcano that created the caldera; which they call Fulga. Well, I should say, those that are capable of speaking our tongue call it Fulga. They truly are a fascinating people," said Korr, barely able to prevent the grin on his face from splitting his head in two.

"So you've been traveling between the dominions and doing what? Preaching? Learning?" asked Ahm.

"Teaching, not preaching, but a great deal of learning as well. They accepted me into their society without hesitation, but that has a great deal to do with my skills as a conduit, and very little to do with my personality," he said, laughing. His disheveled, long brown hair somehow seemed to appear more frazzled at the mention of his demeanor.

"A conduit?" asked Ahm, growing intrigued. "Does this have anything to do with the scroll?"

"That old prophecy?" laughed Korr. "I wrote that to create a spark; to inspire the people of Dusk to question Mordessa's true motivations and stop following her blindly. That scroll inspired many, but most importantly for my own survival, it inspired two members of the Ministry of Internal Affairs to ask the right questions, and listen to my answers," he finished with a wink.

"So it wasn't true?" asked Ahm, growing slightly angry.

"Oh, it was, but I couldn't possibly convey the depth of the matter in such simple prose," said Korr, waving off the man's nonsense. "Had I tried, it would have ended up a several-volume saga stuck on the back shelf of some obscure back-alley library, ignored by the masses. No, I needed to reach the people, not fall into obscurity."

'We shall dine, and he shall explain,' said Whun in both their minds.

"Fine. Lead the way," said Ahm.

Korr happily snapped into action, scurrying from the room with his hands held before him, rapidly tapping the tips of his fingers together as he moved. A great stone hall stretched out in front of the room, with several large stone doors on either side. After a few minutes' walk, they entered a ninety foot long, eighty foot wide chamber with forty foot high ceilings. The walls were covered in tapestries depicting the rise in power of Elonesti priests over the centuries. Along the center of the room was a row of tables five feet high, eight feet wide, and twelve feet long. The chairs lining the sides of the banquet hall were clearly too large for a human. At the far end stood a massive stone, carved into an odd shape, with a thick bar of solid iron crossing it parallel to the ground.

As the three of them entered the room, Whun held his hands to the side, indicating that they should stop and wait. A pair of iron doors slowly began to open at the far end, floating on precisely engineered gears and wheels. Even though they were the same size as that entire wall of the chamber, they made no notable sound as they moved, revealing the care their builders had placed on precision and the importance of their maintenance to the workers in the temple.

Twelve foot tall, bipedal creatures began to file into the room as the doors reached their halfway point. To Ahm, they seemed like elves, but the sides of their necks, and several features of their faces, were scaled, like serpents, and they were far too tall. Their large eyes seemed to glimmer in the flitting light of the wall sconces, and their elongated, slit-like pupils appeared to widen as they entered the darker interior. They wore identical houppelandes made from a lustrous purple fabric that Ahm didn't recognize, which dragged the floor behind them. Even the tails that draped from their sleeves lighted upon the ground as they walked.

The elf-like creatures matched the simple descriptions he'd seen in the past of the Noktulians, but he'd never seen them in person. If the reports were correct, their ancestors had been made through a combination of Afyr, Velloth and draconic bloodlines, either through copulation or magical manipulation, far in the distant past. If he had to guess, he'd assume their dragon blood was derived from the Skalaani, considering their physique was said to be quite similar. However, as he'd never met a member of the species, he couldn't be certain.

Two by two, the Noktulians took their seats, leaving the three seats around the end of the table near the companions vacant for their use. After the procession had assumed their places, the doors snapped into their fully open position with the nearly deafening, deep clank of metal on metal. A great pair of wings could be heard outside, batting the air in a slow descent. Their owner was not immediately visible past the overwhelming brightness of the sunlight that poured in through the opening. Before long, enormous claws eerily scraped the marble courtyard, and the thud of a gigantic creature's weight echoed through the hall as it came to rest.

The doorway darkened as a figure filled its height and width, lowering its long neck to gain entry. After a few breathtaking seconds, Ahm's eyes were able to adjust, and the creature came into full view.

Hunched over, the creature nearly scraped the room's thirty-foot high ceiling as it moved. The horns atop its head and spikes that adorned the top of its fifteen-foot-long neck seemed to make its passage difficult. Its brown scales and bluish-white horns, spikes and teeth glimmered in the room's light, as sconce flames flitted and struggled to stay lit against the air currents stirred by the creature's movements.

It hunched further and pulled its massive wings tighter as it stepped over the giant stone carving at the far end of the table, rising onto the bar and gripping it with its powerful rear talons. Once perched, it tucked its leathery wings back and brought the hands at their dominant joints together in front of its chest. The trailing end of its wings fanned out behind it, blotting out the morning sun.

Ahm was so stunned he found it very difficult to convince his body to move. He'd never seen a wyvern in person. He hadn't even been certain they still existed. By all accounts, they should have died off with their dragon lords many thousands of years prior. To have one directly in front of him was a sight he never imagined he'd behold.

Before he could convince himself to move, the wyvern pressed a talisman that hung around its neck with the tip of one of its talons. A deep, horrifying voice filled the room, echoing off the walls despite the many tapestries that worked to deaden the sound. "Sit. Eat. You are our guest." A series of growls and hisses underlay the creature's voice, as if the talisman was translating what it said into the common tongue.

'I too was shocked to learn of their survival. They've done a wonderful job hiding their existence, have they not?' said Whun in his mind. 'Tuldaxx is but one of dozens of such majestic creatures, but most remain in hiding. Let us join her and dine. To refuse her offer would be an insult. She speaks truthfully; they do see you as a guest. Wyvern do not comprehend deceit,' explained Whun as he guided Ahm to his seat. 'Do not eat any of the meat, only the fruit and vegetables. I will explain later,' he finished.

Whun drifted to the end of the table, directly opposite Tuldaxx. Korr bowed to the great beast, then hopped into the seat across from Ahm. A few seconds later, seven-foot-tall human-like stone constructs poured into the room, each carrying a small silver tray bearing food. When they arrived at the table, their arms extended outward, sliding down the lengths of telescoping tubes within them so they could reach the center of the table without disturbing the diners. Once the trays had been placed, they retracted their arms and exited the room, leaving food and deafening silence in their wake.

Ahm looked to Whun, stunned at what he'd just witnessed. None of the lich's reports had detailed such extravagance, or magical prowess, to say nothing of the existence of living wyverns.

'All will be explained, in time,' said Whun, as if reading his mind.

"By Noktrusgodhen's favor, our bounty is provided. Eat, so that his glory might be upon thee," said Tuldaxx.

'So you've been living this way this whole time?' asked Ahm in his mind, hoping Whun would hear. He reached across to the tray at center and transferred a pile of roast asparagus, pan-seared potato, and a strange onion, mushroom and broccoli medley to his plate while specifically ignoring the tantalizing bits of bacon, sausage and bone-in chops that had also been provided.

'No. I had to earn their trust. For the first fifty years, I stayed in my tower, studying them from afar and only interacting with a few rare Noktulians. It wasn't until my gift of speech—that talisman adorning Tuldaxx's breast—that I gained enough favor to meet her in person. Prior to that meeting, she was nothing more than a name to me,' explained Whun.

'But you've been hiding it ever since? Why? How?' asked Ahm as he filled his mouth with food and chewed the savory morsels. The meal had been exquisitely seasoned.

'As for the how? Mordessa sees only what I wish her to see. It was I who suggested we create an embassy in the Talaani Empire in the first place. Maintaining peace, and giving us a chance to spy on them from within? Why would I not want these things? I never desired this position to be mine. She forced my hand out of petty fear that I might stand up to her in court. I am the one creature in all of Dusk that she cannot control.

'Since I was assigned against my will, my choices were to lash out and destroy the Kingdom I helped build, or resign myself to this post, and bow to her wishes. Ultimately, for the good of our people, I buried my own desires, and came here at her bidding, certain her true intent was for me to rend their empire to dust. However, what I discovered was not some great enemy that sought our destruction. Of course, there may be those among them that seek vengeance upon us, but that is justified, and you will soon learn why.

'As to the majority? They simply wish to be free. So, yes, I hid their true nature and their motivations. I did so because I've come to realize a great truth about their existence, and ours. A great truth which I will not share with you, but rather... allow you to realize for yourself,' said Whun.

'Why is that?' asked Ahm.

'Because I want your support to come willingly, of your own accord, not from some sense of duty, or blind faith in my words,' said Whun. 'We've had enough blind faith in our society already, and it has led us to a place where we no longer question the things that we should, and have fallen into a state of stagnant complacency. We've existed as a Kingdom for hundreds upon hundreds of years, as far as our citizens remember. I can say with confidence, it has, in fact, been thousands. Yet we sit idle, blindly accepting simple existence to be enough rather than seeking personal advancement or attempting to improve our Kingdom in any way. I ask you... why? Why do you think that is?' asked Whun.

'I have been asking the same questions, specifically in regard to our Kingdom's defenses,' thought Ahm. 'No one seems to take it seriously. We've indeed grown complacent, as you suggest. Why prepare for a war that will never come? Talking to the council and trying to convince them of the folly of their laziness is an effort in futility. I watched my predecessor pay the price for speaking out, so I have kept my tongue to myself during my tenure, and done what I could to prepare in secret,' finished Ahm as he swallowed the last of his food.

'You are of the right mind. Now listen to what Korr has to say,' said Whun, turning toward Korr and nodding.

Korr had been waiting patiently during their entire meal for Whun's signal, his hands fidgeting on the table in front of him. As soon as Whun turned toward him, his words burst forth as if his mind were erupting. "As I said earlier, I am a conduit. You said you found my scroll, which leads me to believe you discovered more about who I was? Perhaps you know I am a Touched?" asked Korr.

"I do," said Ahm.

"Well, being a Touched and working next to the Aggripha affords one a unique opportunity. You see, when in the relic's presence for a long enough period of time, a Touched can learn, quite instinctively, to see the individual souls swirling within its crystalline structure, and lighting upon its surface. That was the first clue, to me, that our Queen's gift wasn't what it appeared to be.

"After a time, I even started having brief conversations with the souls of the Ascended, as they were ascending! The Ishnites would place a man in the chair, start the ritual, and his soul would be ripped away, right?" asked Korr.

"That's how it works, yes," confirmed Ahm.

"But what happens when it's outside of the body during the ritual? Eh? I'll tell you! It drifts in and out of the Aggripha, screaming, and trying to get back to its host body! And sometimes... sometimes it gets tainted by other souls! Sometimes it grows powerful enough to break free of the Aggripha for a time, and speak! And if a Touched is nearby with the skills to hear, they can converse and share knowledge!" gasped Korr eagerly. It was clear he relished sharing the tale.

"And then what, it gets forced back into the Ascended, and nothing else ever takes place? We'd have noticed if corruption was occurring," said Ahm.

"Oh, but you have! Every hundred years it happens! It happened when I was young, right before my eyes. I had a brief conversation with a poor soul as he was Ascending, after he'd been tainted. I didn't understand it, so I kept it to myself. The Aggripha was shut down for a few months, and everything seemed to go back to normal. But then... a tiny little fragment of that tainted soul came to visit me. Just a teeny little piece, no bigger than my fist, but it was enough to give me a message," said Korr.

"And what message was that?" asked Ahm.

"Watch. That was it, just that one word. Watch. So I asked myself, 'watch what?' But I did what I thought I was being asked, and I kept working, and kept my eyes open. Then again, a hundred years later, *two* tainted souls Ascended before my very eyes. Two! And this time, I learned even more!" gasped Korr.

"Go on," suggested Ahm, growing intrigued.

"Those little tainted fragments are pieces of the Caier. Specifically, the last three Caier. Created by the Agthari long ago, right as they arrived on Ayrelon, long before the great war between the gods and the dragons! They were sacrificed by Mordessa so she could harvest their souls to create the Aggripha from Aggriphaxxedon's heart! But when Noktrusgodhen and his priests tried to break Mordessa's curse upon the Talaani, almost eight hundred years ago, they only partially succeeded... and part of that success gave the Caier the ability to send a fragment of their souls into the world, to attach to a newborn child, or the soul of one being Ascended, all in hopes of completing Noktrus's work and setting the Talaanian people free," gasped Korr.

"How did Noktrusgodhen do anything? Isn't he long dead?" asked Ahm.

"He sleeps," answered Tuldaxx. "You sit beneath his petrified body, trapped long ago by Caier Eloness to prevent Mordessa from slaying him. She was a master of earth and stone, and managed to perform one last spell with her dying breath, imprisoning the last of the great wyrms by turning their stone to flesh, to save them from your Queen's wrath."

"Eloness?" asked Ahm.

"The namesake of the Elonesti Dominion!" blurted Korr excitedly. "The Caier rise when they regain their strength, sending fragments of themselves into the world. They are only able to do this because Noktrus fractured the curse, and that was only possible because Eloness cursed Noktrus!" gasped Korr.

"If their petrification wasn't Mordessa's curse, what *did* her curse do?" asked Ahm, puzzled.

"All descendants of the Talaani empire, be they flesh or scale, are absorbed for all time by the Aggripha upon our death, which then consumes our souls to provide your Kingdom with power," said Tuldaxx.

"What?" blurted Ahm.

"Well, yes, it used to be that way, but Noktrus broke the cycle!" added Korr.

"Glory be to Noktrusgodhen," said Tuldaxx, bowing her massive head. The Noktulians bowed along with her.

"Dragons are naturally bound to the magical weave of Ayrelon. They're part of it, and it's part of them. Noktrusgodhen? Well, he was so old his blood was pure magic! When Eloness petrified him, his blood condensed into melrithium, and his soul bound with it like some form of enchantment. Over time, he learned to push his consciousness into his priests. He used that connection to empower them and teach them a powerful ritual. They performed it, but all died in its casting, since it required too much magic for them to withstand. Unfortunately, the knowledge of that ritual died with them and Noktrus has since become reluctant to put them at further risk, but they did succeed in freeing Talaanian souls from Mordessa's curse, in a way," explained Korr.

"We no longer fear the Aggripha, but we also cannot reach the afterlife. We cannot walk with our gods in paradise, or soar through the everlasting skies," said Tuldaxx.

"Now they reincarnate. In fact, that is the only time a Talaanian is not still born. Which means that while the curse was fractured, preventing their souls from being destroyed by Mordessa's magic, they caused another painful reality to take hold. No new life can be born in the Talaani empire. Only the souls of the previously deceased can enter their young," said Korr, full of sadness.

Tuldaxx bowed her head and closed her eyes. "Many cults have sprang forth across the land, sacrificing the elderly as the young become pregnant, so that their child might have a soul," she said.

"By Ishnu's might," gasped Ahm. "This cannot be!"

One of the Noktulians rose up from their chair and turned to face Ahm directly. "Lord Whun has shared with us his observations of you. When we sensed the return of Caier Xahn, it was accompanied by a burst of magic unlike any other. Whun sought the source of that event for us, and found Xahn in your company, as well as the one that we now believe carries Eloness."

"A burst of magic? Wait, you think Eros is Xahn, and what... that Mina is Eloness?" asked Ahm, astounded.

The being nodded. "We already knew of the other, and had sent a storm toward Pelrigoss to bring him to our Empire. He was born outside Mordessa's sphere of influence, far away on Gargoa. Caier Jaezyn is somehow able to cast his fragment farther than the others, and has done so on many iterations. We had already used the summoning ritual to cause a magical storm that would send him here before your Eros was resurrected by the Aggripha, waking Xahn."

"They don't always appear at the same time, you see," said Korr. "They've never succeeded in whatever must be done to break Mordessa's curse, and we think that's because Xahn, Eloness and Jaezyn have never returned to the Talaani Empire at the same time. It looked like this was going to be another failed iteration, and then whatever you did with Eros gave us hope."

"So you think they're fulfilling your prophecy?" asked Ahm.

"Prophecy? That was the result of a statistical calculation delivered in prose, not a prophecy! Given enough time, I knew the iterations of the three would eventually synchronize and provide a greater chance of success. I am an engineer and a mathematician, not some religious zealot!" gasped Korr defensively.

"So Jaezyn was on the way to Talaani. Advan resurrected Eros, which tainted his soul with that of Xahn, and somehow Mina's connection to the Aggripha is a result of the fragment of Eloness you believe she carries?" asked Ahm.

"She is connected to the Aggripha?" gasped Korr.

"Yes. It has healed her, and she has unwittingly used its powers," answered Ahm. "That is why I hid her from Mordessa all her life. She is a Forsaken, and would have been hunted down for simply existing."

"You think Forsaken is a title? A thing one can be? What has happened in Dusk since I fled?" laughed Korr.

"Care to explain?" asked Ahm.

"Mordessa is the daughter of Ishnu. She is called forsaken because she turned her back on her mother, and sought the love of Xxrandus! But when the gods waged war on the dragons, and Aggriphaxxeddon led them to victory, Xxrandus was driven out of our world, and Mordessa, his lover, was imprisoned in a magically reinforced obsidian tomb deep down in the Cryx, like she'd done to her sister centuries before.

"It was Lord Whun and his followers that found the black cube and freed her from it. He helped waged her war of vengeance that slew hundreds of dragons, and led to the death of Aggriphaxxeddon. She wooed him into her service, but never explained her motivations or told him the true story. Had he known the truth, he might not have helped her," said Korr.

'I cannot speak to what I would have done. Too much time has passed, and I am not the same creature I was back then. I sought power, and little else. However, Xxrandus's exile was ultimately her doing, and had I known that truth then, I might have slain her, rather than joining her cause. Regardless, all I can speak from is hindsight, and that is never the truth in the moment,' said Whun to everyone's minds.

"It was her sister Siscci's reemergence that drew our attention to Gargoa and led to our discovery of Jaezyn's new host. Most of the recent events that we've discovered are unprecedented in their own right. To have them all happening at once is an omen we cannot overlook," said the Noktulian.

"I'm sorry. It's not that I don't believe you. There have been a lot of strange occurrences lately that have forced me to question things, and this is a lot to take in all at once, especially in light of everything that's been happening in recent weeks. You'll have to give me time," said Ahm.

"We need you to convince your daughter to help us," said the being. "She trusts you like no other."

"Yeah, I'm not so sure about that," said Ahm. "I've failed her as a father."

"We will give you time to digest our words. Please know that you are safe among our people. We mean you no harm, and wish only to show you respect, Lord Ahm. You are critical to our survival," the being finished with a bow.

Ahm sat in silence as the Noktulians and Tuldaxx exited the chamber. He had too much to think about to be bothered with pleasantries and goodbyes.

THE FATED companions walked west for half a day before coming to a road. It approached from the west and turned south atop a hill before heading into the cliffs below Dusk's outer wall. Its placement seemed odd, and Mina couldn't recall seeing it from the sky during their previous journey. A small sign stood by the side of the road, but it could only be read if one was heading east toward the shore.

As the group rounded the sign, all equally curious what it might say, Mina read it aloud, just in case any of her new companions happened to be illiterate. "Port Uhldan, South," it says.

"But there was no port," said Eros. "It's just a beach."

"A very small beach with rocky cliffs to either side, and jagged rocks beneath the waves. It wouldn't be very safe to come ashore, let alone dock large ships there. Not that there were any docks, either," said Piya.

"You'd think we'd have seen them," said Gnately.

"Well, yes, but the road also heads south, into the cliffs. It doesn't even go toward the water," said Tavyn.

"I've heard the name Uhldan before. Mordessa mentioned it as she was watching you in her crystal ball," said Mina.

"If I'm not mistaken, Port Uhldan is where people who decline Ascension are taken to be sent into exile," said Eros. "I didn't pay strict attention to those details, because I wasn't considering it, but if I'm correct, then where's the port?"

"Exile?" asked Tavyn.

"Yes. The living can't stay within Dusk beyond adulthood. If their skills aren't needed in the border villages, they are sent to live elsewhere," explained Eros.

"Then why have none of us ever met someone who was exiled from Dusk?" asked Tavyn.

"They're told not to talk about it," said Eros nonchalantly.

"Everyone always talks eventually," said Tavyn, hand on hip.

"Should we see where the southern road leads?" asked Gnately. "Maybe the docks are further down, through a pass?"

"I'm game," said Tavyn with a shrug. He started walking without waiting for a response.

"Do we really have time for this?" asked Mina.

"Whether we do or not, I have to admit the lack of a port where one is supposed to be has piqued my curiosity. Clearly Mordessa lied to us about the Aggripha. What if she's lying about exile, too?" asked Eros.

Ainen shifted the makeshift sack of armor onto his other shoulder as he, Gnately and Piya turned and followed Tavyn. Eros shrugged at Mina and joined them.

"You have to admit," he yelled back to her, "it's not what Mordessa would expect us to do," he finished with a smile over his shoulder.

"Hells, it's not what I expected us to do either," she sighed, then fell in behind them.

A few hours later, they arrived at the base of a hundred foot tall cliff. Stretching out to either side was nothing but rock as far as the eye could see. Up above was a barely perceptible view of an ivy-covered wall. Directly in front of them was a cave, gently spiraling down to the right and out of view.

Tavyn moved close to the right side, and hugged the inner wall of the descent. Gnately, and the rest of the companions followed his example, and moved slowly, and as quietly as possible down the gravel ramp. Small signs dotted the outer walls, each confirming that Uhldan Port was just ahead, including the remaining distance a person might need to travel to reach it. Gnately watched as the distance on each sign got progressively shorter until they reached a final bend next to a sign that proudly claimed they had arrived.

The tunnel opened up after that bend into a chamber so large they couldn't see the far walls or ceiling. They found themselves on a ledge overlooking a vast expanse, small ladders leading down to the floor below, somewhere beneath the darkness. To the left was a walkway that led to two widely spaced doors.

Tavyn backed away just as soon as he stepped to the edge and peered over the railing, gasping in horror at whatever he'd seen. Gnately jumped at the sound, and started to tremble involuntarily. She'd never seen him afraid, and couldn't fathom what would cause him to react in such a manner.

"What did you see?" asked Mina.

"Corpses. Piles and piles of corpses, stretching as far as I could see. No flesh, just bone. Stripped bare and discarded. Thousands of skeletons, broken to pieces like so much refuse. Who would do such a thing?" he gasped, still backing away.

"Well, what's in there?" asked Piya, pointing at the doors.

"Let's check before we jump to any conclusions," suggested Mina, though her gut was sinking, and her mind had filled with worry.

Ainen put the sack of armor on the ground, walked to the first door and yanked it open, its hinges creaking wildly, echoing off the cavern walls like the shriek of a demon. The group peered into the room briefly, but only Tavyn could clearly see the room's contents. He pushed past the throng and grabbed a lantern off the wall and shook it, checking for oil. Upon hearing it slosh, he checked the exterior for a way to open it and found a small key sticking out of one side of the base. He raised his eyebrows at the novelty of seeing such an expensive lantern in such a place, and turned the key, striking the wick ablaze, and lighting the room for his friends.

At the center of the room was a pair of iron tables, complete with small grooves that ran to the edges and then down toward one end at a barely perceivable slope. Beneath that end of each table stood a single wooden bucket, resting atop a stone floor that was caked with dried blood. All along the walls were small wooden wheelbarrows with sharp hooks affixed at eye level above them. Sitting casually atop both tables were a collection of meat cleavers and battered wooden mallets.

Eros lost the forgotten remnants of his seafood breakfast onto the floor and stumbled backward. "It's... it's all a lie?"

"So they kill anyone who doesn't Ascend," said Mina, her words fading in volume, hardly able to believe what she was saying.

"Then what about their muscles? Skin? Hair? Clothing? Why are they just bones?" asked Gnately.

"They're butchering your people," Ainen said, looking at Mina.

"Are they... eating them?" gasped Gnately.

"They can't be!" belted Mina.

"They're probably... just... using the bits as animal feed?" guessed Eros, his voice wavering.

"Let's get out of here before we're forced to join them," suggested Tavyn angrily.

"Yeah. No more crazy adventures, please," said Gnately.

SIX HOURS later, they came to a stop beside the road next to a sign proclaiming that the village of Uhldan was just up ahead. They hadn't spoken at all since the cavern. None of them knew what to say, or how to say it. Mina and Eros felt both betrayed and horrified. They'd spent their lives growing up believing lies and couldn't comprehend what they'd just seen, let alone be certain they'd discovered all the horrible things Mordessa had done to their people. Tavyn, Gnately and Piya couldn't process the horror they'd found in Xulrathia. Ainen seemed to have detached from reality, and had simply followed mindlessly behind them.

Piya approached Mina as they stood by the sign, trying to decide whether to proceed. "I can't imagine what you're going through," she said. She wrapped her arms around Mina's waist and pressed her cheek to the woman's breast. "You've been through so much. This isn't fair to you, or Eros, or Tavyn, or Ainen."

Mina hugged her back, more than willing to accept small comforts whenever they presented themselves. She didn't know Piya, but could sense the young girl's concern was genuine. "Unfortunately, I think it's time we all set aside the afflictions of emotion and compassion. At least for a time," she said as she gently pressed Piya away. "It's clear to me that Mordessa has caused a great deal of pain in both the Talaani Empire and Baan'Sholaria. She threatened to kill my father. She tried to kill me... twice. Her magical storm almost killed Ainen. She's lied to over a hundred million people for hundreds of years; people that look to her for guidance and compassionate leadership.

"In all my visions of her, she doesn't think with compassion, and the only emotion she feels is hatred. Her actions have made it obvious that our only true choice is to stand against her and do the very thing she fears about us. If we're to succeed, I think we need to put any image of ourselves aside and assume the role we've been presented. Just like many of the parts of Ahm's flying Raven, we have become cogs in a greater machine. It's time we focus on that, and set that machine in motion.

"I say we go to Uhldan and find supplies. We need food, water, and some form of transportation. I didn't start this journey with a mind to cause harm to Dusk, but if that is our fate, may the gods protect anyone that stands in our way," Mina growled.

Tavyn extended his right arm toward her, as a swordsman might greet a fellow combatant. She was unsure how to respond, and reached for his hand gingerly. He smirked and stepped into her reach, grasping her forearm and using his other hand to press hers into his forearm as well.

"We may have been raised with conflicting interpretations on the teachings of Ishnu, but neither of us can deny the horrors we've witnessed, and the lies we've both unraveled. I will be your daggers, and strike down our opposition. We must put an end to the atrocities cast upon our people, and it is clear we share a common foe. I stand with you," he declared.

"Do you really think we stand a chance of bringing down Mordessa? She's the daughter of a god!" asked Eros.

"I will die trying, if need be," said Tavyn, staring deep into Mina's eyes.

Mina looked down at him with newfound respect. "I stand with you as well."

"Let's kick some demonic ass!" growled Gnately.

Piya looked at her as if she'd sprouted tails.

"What?" asked Gnately. "Her description sounded like a demon, didn't it? Am I the only one?"

"I am with you," said Ainen.

Piya mussed Gnately's hair and chuckled. "I'm with you too, Mina," she finished with a smile.

Night fell before they reached Uhldan. The road was lined on both sides by thick wooden fences enclosing large paddocks full of grazing cattle. The first few buildings that came into view were barns, followed by an extremely large slaughterhouse, and several smaller butcheries.

Taverns filled the next several blocks, their noise and aroma filling the streets. The streets behind the establishments were full of three-story and four-story buildings, each containing dozens of meager apartments for the many workers living inside city limits.

The streets were empty, save for the odd drunkard or two, who were far too intoxicated to take note of the strange travelers walking through their town. Tavyn kept an eye on any movement they saw, checking for signs of Undead or Unliving. He wasn't sure how he'd respond if he saw one, or how his companions would react if his first instinct was to kill them. The only thing he was certain of was he didn't want any surprises.

As they turned around a slight bend in the main street, they came across a cart on the right side of the road. On one side stood a slightly obese, thick-armed man wearing pants, a thick apron, and not much else. His hairy arms were fast at work chopping a large hunk of meat into smaller components, and tossing the chunks atop an iron grill to his right. Thick billows of smoke rose into the air, accompanied by the sizzle of fatty tissue, and the alluring smell of the food he was preparing.

In front of the cart was a small, ramshackle awning held up by thin poles that seemed inadequate to perform their duty. Next to the covered section was a small plank of wood, hastily painted with misspelled words that read, 'Frehs Meat'.

"You lucky bastards get the first bite!" he chimed as they approached. "Ain't often we get a surplus. In fact, it ain't happen'd since my grandpa's days. Come grab an Exile Steak while they last. Just two bits! Deal of the century!"

Just then, the butcher looked up and saw the motley group approaching. Mina, Eros, Ainen and Piya seemed like his typical clientele, but he'd never seen the likes of Tavyn or Gnately. He tensed almost instantly and stepped around the side of his cart, hefting a large cleaver in his right hand. "Who the fuck are you? How'd you get to Uhldan?"

Tavyn pulled his daggers without hesitation and strode directly toward the man, saying, "Why bother explaining?" Before any of his friends could intercede, he drove his left dagger deep into the man's right wrist, taking his cleaver out of the equation. He followed that strike with an upward slash from his other dagger, catching the man's jaw with the hook of its blade, and puncturing the top of his trachea. After yanking the blades free, he drew them back toward his chest, crossed his arms, and stepped toward the man as he hastily attempted to back away, blood gurgling in his throat. With a final slash, he ran both of his curved daggers through the front of the man's neck, then wiped the blades clean on the top of the butcher's apron as he fell to his knees. Re-sheathing his blades, he turned back to his friends... who were all staring at him in horror.

"You saw his reaction. We don't belong here," said Tavyn, pointing at Gnately and himself. "He was either going to attack us or call the guards. This was the only solution, and you know it."

"I'm glad you're on our side," said Eros.

"There had to be another way," said Mina, her face pale.

"There wasn't," said Tavyn determinedly. "Now, let's get through this city before we have more encounters like this one. Wouldn't want to coat your streets in blood, now would we? Remember, I don't see your people as innocent in the eyes of Ishnu. If someone gets in our way..."

"Right. Well, we need supplies, yes? To get moving and get out of here?" asked Gnately, trying to redirect their minds and break the tension.

Mina cleared her throat and looked down at her. "Yes. None of the shops are open, though. I was hoping one would still-" she started.

Gnately nodded halfway through her sentence and took off at a jog, straight for the door of a nearby shop. Before Mina could interject, the little gnome had bent over for a brief moment at the door, fiddled with the lock, and pushed the door open.

The companions started walking across the street to join their little friend. Before they could arrive, she exited the shop with a satchel full of goods hanging across her shoulders, and a wheel of cheese slightly larger than her own torso, which she was cradling in her arms as if it were her child.

"Okay. We're set. Let's get moving," said Gnately merrily.

"How did you-" started Mina.

"Tricks of the trade," Gnately interrupted with a smile.

Piya stepped in front of Mina and waved one hand to get her attention. "We should get off the main road, right?"

"The other end of this street should have a large building with stables and a shipping center. We flew over it on the way to the shore," said Mina.

"So, we should be able to acquire mounts," said Eros.

"Very well," said Tavyn. He turned on his heel and started down the street. The rest of the companions fell in behind him.

A few minutes later, they came to a bend in the main road. Ahead of them was an intersection. The road they were on ended at another that traveled north to south, right in front of a very important looking facility. The columned building had been made from expertly carved limestone, and covered in fine plaster. The entirety of its surface was white, despite the dirt-laden nature of the rest of the village. Tavyn could only assume it was a government building of some kind.

Gnately jumped forward, reached up and grabbed Tavyn's elbow, yanking him toward a nearby alley. "Let's get out of sight before they look this way," she gasped.

The group moved into the alley at her bidding. Tavyn and Mina peeked out to study the building, and the beings in front of it. Though several blocks away, they were standing in full view. Just in front of the building were a pair of guards, each wearing blackened plate armor with large horned helms. To Tavyn, and Mina, the guards glowed and shimmered, showing clear evidence they were Unliving; their souls had been stripped away and reattached through magical means, causing a magical shimmer in the eyes of the Touched as they slipped in and out of sync with their host body.

The pair were talking to a third creature, who was decidedly taller. Its lizard-like head was several feet above the guards, looking down at them inquisitively. It wore very little clothes atop its muscular, red scaled flesh. It seemed less concerned for its safety, or freedom, and more interested in whatever the guards were saying as they referred to something attached to a small board in one of their hands. They stepped to the rear of a wagon, which was barely within view from the group's vantage point, and pointed at its contents, and back to the board several times.

Tavyn mouthed the phrase, "Who are they?" to Mina.

"Two Ebon Guard," she whispered. "I think they're talking to a Skalaani, but I've never seen one in person."

Eros poked his head out to look then nodded in confirmation. "I've read extensively about the Skalaani. That has to be one," he whispered.

"You don't have them in Dusk?" whispered Gnately.

Mina and Eros shook their heads.

"So they're from the Talaani Empire?" whispered Gnately.

Mina and Eros both nodded.

"Then why are they meeting with your Ebon Guard?" whispered Gnately harshly.

"There's one way to find out," whispered Tavyn.

"No. We are not attacking two Ebon Guard. Besides, there are more inside. It's a government building," whispered Mina firmly.

"Then what the fuck are we doing here?" growled Tavyn, just barely above a whisper.

"Sneak north. Meet the Skalaani. Hitch a ride," said Ainen.

"What?" whispered Tavyn and Mina in unison.

"Voice says join him," said Ainen.

Piya looked at her friends for a moment. None seemed ready to make the first move, and all seemed conflicted on how to proceed. She sighed, stood, and started down an alley heading north. After a few yards she stopped, looked back at her friends and whispered, "Coming? You heard him!"

One by one, the companions succumbed to Ainen's guidance and followed Piya north.

Chapter 16:
Truth

Ris'Uttyr, Djacenta 23rd, 576 of the 1st Era

ROVOSS AND Aygos had completed nearly half their trek across the night sky before the wagon appeared in the distance. The group had decided to wait nearly a mile outside of Uhldan to avoid any chance of detection by the Ebon Guard. With no idea how long they'd have to wait, many of them had grown bored and were quietly whispering stories to one another.

Tavyn kept watch while his friends relaxed, his elven night vision giving him a distinct advantage, even if the night were clear and the area was fairly well illuminated. What he saw as the wagon came into view made him second guess their decision, and the sanity of Ainen's mysterious voice.

"What the fuck is that?" gasped Tavyn, ducking behind their hill.

"What? What is what?" asked Gnately, flustered.

"That wagon isn't being pulled by a horse. It's some kind of creature with four hind legs and two arms. It's bent in the middle with part of it upright. The rest stretched out along the ground, with a very, very long tail. It's holding the lead ropes in each hand and pulling the wagon along like it's just a thing it does, no problem at all," he gasped.

"Six appendages with two attached to shoulders at the top of a humanoid torso? An extended hind section with four legs, and a tail as long as its entire body? A distinctly lizard-like head, with long fangs and horns?" asked Eros excitedly.

"Yes! You know what it is?" asked Tavyn.

"I've seen sketches and read descriptions. There was this one tome that went into-" he started.

"Do you know what it is?" growled Tavyn as quietly as he could.

"Oh, yes! It's a Skaar. They're the strongest of the dragon kin, and do most of the empire's hard labor. They're supposed to be very intelligent, but prefer subservience," said Eros.

"Well, this one is pulling a loaded wagon, and its very large driver, like the weight doesn't matter at all," gasped Tavyn.

"Don't they have horses? Horses usually pull wagons, right?" asked Piya.

"If rumors are accurate, their empire doesn't employ mammals as labor," said Eros.

"Well, feel free to ask them if that's true just before they kill us," said Tavyn.

"I doubt they even speak our language," shrugged Eros.

"Tavyn?" asked Mina, interrupting their conversation. "We're traveling into an empire ruled by dragons. What did you think we'd find?"

"Sorry," he sighed. "I've just never seen anything like this."

"None of us have," said Mina, placing a hand on his shoulder. "We have to interact with creatures like this eventually, if we want answers. Why not now?"

"We shouldn't hide," interrupted Ainen.

"What do you mean?" asked Piya.

"What he means is," started Gnately, "how would you respond if a group of strange people suddenly popped out from behind a hill while you were just minding your own business on your way home through hostile lands?" She stood up and brushed herself off to look presentable, while everyone else tried to digest what she'd said.

"Valid point," said Tavyn.

The group gathered on the eastern side of the road and sat against the hill at Ainen's bidding. He then signaled for them to stay put, and walked south a few yards to intercept the wagon on his own. Tavyn was unsure of Ainen's plan, but let him take charge, since the voices that apparently instructed him seemed to know more than he and his friends.

As the wagon approached, the Skaar pulling it growled and hissed with its head tilting back toward the driver on the bench.

Both seemed to tense at the sight of a large human standing in the middle of the road, but they didn't stop, or seem to be planning an escape. As they drew within a few yards, the Skaar stopped abruptly, took a few hastened steps back and lowered its body to the ground in a strangely elegant bow, which it continued to hold. The wagon nearly ran the beast over, as its momentum continued to carry it forward a short distance.

The Skalaani hopped down from its seat with practiced grace and strode toward Ainen, holding a large piece of wood that seemed to serve as a club. As soon as it got close enough to see clearly, it too backed away and bowed its twelve foot tall, muscular frame in respect.

Tavyn and the others got to their feet and hesitantly approached, unsure what was going on. When they got within a few feet of Ainen's back, the Skalaani stood up, its muscles tensing apprehensively. Ainen signaled to his friends to wait.

"Do you understand me?" asked Ainen.

The Skalaani nodded.

"Do you recognize what is happening to me? Who I am?" asked Ainen.

It nodded again.

"Will you take us into the Talaani Empire to meet with your people?" asked Ainen.

The Skalaani nodded, turned sideways and stepped back, holding his right hand toward the wagon, inviting them to climb in. It waited patiently in that position until all had walked by, then casually took its place on the bench with a strange sense of pride on display in its posture.

Ainen tossed the armor into the wagon and climbed in. The rest of his companions followed hesitantly.

"Okay, what the fuck was that?" whispered Gnately aggressively as the wagon set into motion.

"My arrival is prophesied," said Ainen. "My stone skin is proof that part of me is a Caier reborn."

"So it's that easy?" gasped Gnately.

"If they follow their religion as much as Duskians do Ishnu and Xxrandus, then why not? I'm sure they're taught from a very young age to watch for signs of Caier arriving in their lands. In fact, they might even be hailed as heroes for delivering their promised ones," said Mina.

"I am so far out of my element," sighed Tavyn.

"Are you? You're religious. In fact, you were raised in a fanatical arm of the church of Ishnu by the Dynar; trained to kill those who oppose your views. How is your faith any different from theirs or ours?" challenged Mina.

"Religion isn't what I was referring to," sighed Tavyn. "A kingdom full of Unliving? Part of me probably could have dreamed that up as some fictional, final adversary according to the teachings of my order. Those citizens living normal lives? Wouldn't have even been an option in the back of my mind. A draconic empire, full of creatures like these? I mean, I've heard of dragons, of course, but everything we know back on Gargoa suggests they're extinct! Rumors of scaled creatures wandering the Scaled Lands north of Quaan'Shala are believed to be nothing more than myths and legends handed down to our children to keep them in line. Nobody goes out in search of them. Nothing like what I've seen here ever comes knocking on our doors. If I were to describe these two to anyone back home, they'd think I was making it up!"

"There's more to the world than what you were taught by the Daxian Order, and it's a far larger place than what you've seen of Gargoa," said Mina. "If you're going to travel the world, you'll need to open your mind."

"Oh, like you're some expert," laughed Piya.

"I wasn't saying I-" started Mina.

"Um, guys?" gasped Gnately, cutting her off. She held up the white and pink stone Nightweaver had given her. It was trembling in her palm, rocking side to side against the jostling of the wagon. "What's happening?"

Gnately's voice rose in volume as she spoke, ending in a yell. The driver looked back at the group, half turning in its seat, to see what the fuss was all about. When it caught sight of what the small Gnome was holding, it hissed at the Skaar and jumped out of the wagon without waiting for it to stop moving.

The group backed away as the driver came around to the back, and stuck its hands out, side by side, toward Gnately. When she didn't respond, it shook its hands briefly and bent its fingers in a flutter, as if saying, 'give it to me'. She looked at the rest of the group for support, and then sheepishly inched toward the creature's large, scaled hands. Pressing her eyes shut with all her might, she gingerly placed the stone in the nook between the creature's palms, and hastily backed away.

Without hesitation, the Skalaani turned away from the wagon and signaled to the Skaar. The two hissed back and forth for a few brief seconds, and the Skaar immediately hunched down and began gathering tufts of grass and forming a little nest. The driver carefully sat the trembling egg onto the ring of plants and backed away, while its companion raced off into the darkness.

The group climbed out, encouraged by the excited waving of the driver's hand, inviting them to come watch. One by one, they picked a spot and knelt down to watch whatever was about to happen. The Skaar returned a short while later and promptly placed a few small, dead field mice next to Gnately's knees, then patted her on the back with one of its massive front talons.

As their anticipation built, the egg suddenly cracked. A tiny pink snout broke just enough of the shell to lift a small flap and snort at them. Gnately giggled proudly. As the seconds went by, more and more of the shell cracked and peeled outward, revealing the miniature creature within. After what seemed like ages, a small creature tumbled out of the remnants of its shell, unable to hold its footing and squeaking for its first meal.

The Skalaani pointed at the pile of mice and signaled to Gnately that she should pick up the tiny life form and present it with its food. She reached down for the little thing happily, its tiny, silken wings unfurling as it stretched. Little paws extended from the largest joint in the wings, closing and opening, finger by finger, as the newborn tried to get a grip on her approaching digits. It wrapped its tiny tail around her thumb as she scooped it up, its stubby little legs unable to maintain footing as she lifted it toward her.

Pink scales glistened in the light of the moons as its worm-like neck extended its miniature head toward the carcass of the tiny mouse. As it chomped down and struggled to tear away little pieces of flesh, it seemed to purr in delight, sending Gnately into another flutter of giggles.

"Oh, my gods!" gasped Piya.

"What is that?" asked Mina.

"Is that a baby dragon?" asked Eros.

The driver shook its head. They raised one hand high up, and the other one lower down, both flat, palms facing one another, then dramatically brought its hands almost together, stopping a few inches apart.

"Tiny dragon?" asked Eros.

It shrugged as if to say, 'almost', and then shook its head again.

"Dragons have four legs, don't they?" asked Tavyn.

The driver nodded, then seemed to smile.

"Oh! Wyverns have only two, and talons attached to their wings!" gasped Eros.

It nodded again.

"So, this is a miniature wyvern?" asked Mina.

The driver nodded eagerly.

"I shall name her-" started Gnately.

The driver waved its hand at her, and shook its head. After a moment of thought, it pointed at Tavyn, then Ainen, then Eros, then back to the tiny wyvern.

"Are you saying it's a boy?" asked Gnately.

The driver nodded and smiled.

"Neat!" said Gnately, grinning ear to ear. "Then I shall name him Petree!"

The driver seemed to laugh along as Mina, Piya, and Eros chuckled. Tavyn could swear he saw the Skaar roll its eyes.

"Come, Petree!" she bellowed as she rose to her feet. "We have an Empire to save!"

Ainen hefted Gnately into the wagon so that she wouldn't have to use her hands. The rest of the group filed in after, taking seats in a circle around her. The Skalaani and Skaar resumed their positions and continued driving the wagon north, hissing back and forth to one another about what had just happened.

"So 'Pebbly' finally hatched, eh?" asked Tavyn.

"It was an egg this whole time!" gasped Gnately. "Ainen was right!"

"Odd how it waited until we were here to do it," stated Tavyn. "Petree could have hatched at any point in our journey, but he waited until now; right at the perfect time for us to have help from those experienced in such an event," he finished, indicating the Skalaani and Skaar with a wave of his hand.

"Well? You said it trembled before when it got closer to Ainen," she said, shrugging. "Maybe it had something to do with his connection to this place? Maybe it was waiting to get close to Talaani?"

"How would it know?" asked Tavyn.

"The curse?" suggested Mina. "Something about the magics that bind the Talaani? Whatever Mordessa did here, perhaps?"

"Maybe," admitted Tavyn. "I guess we'll have to see if anyone in the Talaani Empire can speak common well enough to explain it."

A few minutes later, Petree started craning his little neck, trying to reach past Gnately's hands at something down below. She lowered him down bit by bit, asking, "What are you after, little guy? Are my hands too warm? Do you want down?"

She placed him on the top of the crates they were sitting on and boxed him in with her hands, so he wouldn't go tumbling out the back of the wagon. No sooner did his little claws touch the wooden lid, than he began clawing at its surface, trying to get at whatever was inside.

"Um!" she blurted. "Mister driver? What's in these crates?"

The driver craned its head back and signaled to her, holding its right hand up and acting like it was putting food in its mouth.

"Petree eats meat, right? Does that mean this is meat?" asked Gnately.

The driver nodded its head.

"Is it 'Exile Steak'?" gasped Eros.

The driver nodded briefly, and then seemed to pause as it realized the reality of the situation. It called the Skaar to stop and immediately jumped out of the wagon, seeming to apologize with its gestures as it approached the back and bid them to exit. After a few panicked moments, the two Talaanians had emptied the crates onto the side of the road and bowed before the group, begging forgiveness.

"Thank you for doing that," said Mina. "We... only just found out our Kingdom was killing our own people for food. I'm sure you can sympathize with how we might feel about that."

"It's not like you knew you'd be picking us up. We're fine. It's fine," said Gnately with an uncomfortable shrug.

"Let's get going," said Ainen, holding his hand out to help his companions climb back into the wagon.

After a few minutes, the wagon was back underway. They spent the next few hours passing Petree between them, letting him get comfortable with each member of the group. He was the only thing any of them talked about for the rest of the night.

AFTER THE banquet, one of the magical constructs returned and showed Ahm to a very luxurious room on the third floor of the temple's residential wing. He hadn't been much in the mood for talking, and there had been far too much information thrown his way in a very short period. Maintaining himself through blessings alone had taken its toll, and he realized it was only a matter of time before it caught up to him. As curious as he was, he decided to go straight to bed and not worry about whatever scenery might lie beyond the curtained windows of his suite.

He lay awake for the next several hours, reviewing everything that Korr and Tuldaxx had told him, running the conversations through his mind several times, and focusing on each and every word. It wasn't clear how long he laid there, lost in thought, before his blessings expired and slumber took hold. He slept for nearly two days and woke to find a small group of constructs standing around his bed, holding a strange collection of devices.

Lord Whun was standing a few feet away, trying his best to assure the strange golems that Ahm was fine, and didn't need their medical assistance. As soon as Ahm sat up, and it became obvious that Whun was correct, they gathered themselves and shuffled out of the room, clacking scissors, twirling small knives, and cradling small bundles of magical potions, bandages, and sewing implements.

"Have they not seen a man sleep before?" asked Ahm.

'Sleep? Yes. Fall into a magically induced coma for two days? No,' said Whun.

"Well, I kept myself awake for days on end, traveling here and being held prisoner. That takes a toll," said Ahm.

'I am well aware. They were not holding you prisoner. I warned them you were coming, and they placed you in that room so I could watch to see if Mordessa was observing you. When I did not feel her presence, I opened the door, and we dined,' said Whun. 'Clearly that treatment is something you should have anticipated, considering your position.'

"If you recall, I arrived not knowing your fate. Had I been aware of your involvement, sure... it would have been clear," said Ahm as he climbed out of bed. He made his way to the window he'd avoided prior, and reached for the curtain.

'Careful, my friend. Once you see what lies beyond, you may not wish to return home,' stated Whun.

Ahm nodded once, then pulled the curtains open to both sides. A large window stood before him, spanning several feet in both directions and rising from floor to ceiling. He was immediately taken aback by the view that lay beyond.

Leading away from the temple, stretching as far as he could see, was a road paved with limestone, each block of which was larger than a wagon. It was five blocks wide, and graced at each junction with exquisitely carved arches that stretched over the intersecting roads and formed a peak at the center, with a small golden spire atop it reaching into the sky.

Buildings of all shapes and sizes lined each side of the road, each made from limestone, with granite columns and entablatures, or gold-inlaid domes. Marble statues stood in front of many ornate entrances, each depicting a draconic or elven figure, appointed with silver or melrithium engravings.

The city sprawled to either side of the road for what appeared to be several miles, rising and falling with the terrain like a sea of perfectly placed stones. Elves, dwarves, Noktulians, Skalaani and Skaar walked the streets, carrying on their daily business with magical constructs of various sizes following close behind.

Whun's insinuation had been correct. The Elonesti Dominion was nothing like Ahm expected, and he was sure he could spend centuries in such a place, learning from its residents and studying their way of life. He turned back to his friend, full of awe and questions. If the lich's face had been complete, Ahm would have seen him smirking back at him.

'It was not like this the last time we saw it... was it, friend?' asked Whun. 'While Dusk has expanded over the centuries, it was done out of necessity, in a very utilitarian fashion. Our population ran rampant, overtaking our ability to produce resources, and necessitating use of the Aggripha, just so we could avoid feeding half our population. What could have been a wondrous Kingdom full of power, and promise, quickly devolved into a pitiful example of complacent persistence. We survive, but that is all we do. Few stand up and think for themselves. Fewer still push for change. I knew you would come, and I knew you would see what I see. We are of like mind, you and I. You pushed the Queen to act in Dusk's defense, and not rest on her laurels. Did she so much as entertain your perspective?'

"No. Of course she didn't. She's all powerful in her mind, and nothing the Talaani Empire could ever do would ever stand a chance at unseating her. Even this prophecy is something she feels confident she can overcome, and she pursues that goal in solitary, unwilling to risk bringing anyone else into the fold to help her," said Ahm.

'That will be her undoing,' said Whun.

"You keep talking about a past I do not remember, though. You said this place was different the last time we were here, but I have no memory of that event. In fact, the last time I saw you, this place was a mystery to you as well," said Ahm. "What changed?"

'The Talaanian people changed. Over time,' said Whun.

"I don't understand," said Ahm, turning to face him.

'Every time they reincarnate, their souls pass through the Aggripha. There was a strange affliction placed upon the world some five-hundred-and-seventy-six years ago, which stripped us of our past. The Aggripha was not a living thing, and thus suffered none of the effects. Each time a soul is drawn into it, then reborn, it brings with it some of those lost memories. Over time, most of the people of Talaani have learned to piece that past back together.

'In fact, the Noktulians you met at the banquet are members of the Enclave of Ages. They are, in effect, the same people who lived here when Mordessa attacked and slew Aggriphaxxeddon. They remember everything that has happened in every generation since that time. Many of them performed Noktrusgodhen's ritual,' he explained. 'They saw value in my assistance, if they could convince me to help. So, Tuldaxx instructed them to offer to restore my memories. They made the offer, and I agreed, expecting it to fail, and knowing I would slaughter them after. Twenty members of the Enclave gave their lives to complete the ritual, and to their credit, it worked.

'If you wished your own memories restored, I'm certain they would gladly comply. They need your assistance with this matter, and *in their minds, no price is too great to pay,'* explained Whun.

"I wouldn't want twenty of them to die just to restore my memories," said Ahm.

'Ahm Braveck Stonehawk, son of Advan Tharam Stonehawk and Theresa Brynnaris Hohlm. Your mother died in childbirth, and your father left you for dead. I took you in as a runt, for I saw a spirit in you that I had long since lost. Like Dusk, I had grown complacent in my existence, but the passion I saw in you inspired me to see and do more. I took you in when you were seven years old, my adoptive son, and allowed you to remain a member of the church of Ishnu, because I chose to respect your wishes. It was the cause of many disagreements between us, but still I showed patience, because I knew the man you'd become. That was over eight-hundred years ago,' said Whun.

Ahm sat on the end of the bed, shaken by the revelation.

'Twas you and I that built Dusk, while Mordessa fought her war. You and I watched as the last of the half-Toor slaves, the Maithung, pulled Xur from the sky, placing it over the Cryx. I made sure you were the first Unliving when Mordessa brought the Aggripha to its cradle, her old prison. I also made sure your Ascension was pure, so that she could not take your soul from you. That is why you still thrive... and why she fears you.'

Ahm sat in contemplation for a time. Whun hovered nearby, patiently waiting. So much had happened in just a few days, and he felt as if his whole world was imploding around him.

"Do we know what caused the 'affliction' that took our memories?" asked Ahm.

'We do not, but we once met one who does,' answered Whun.

"How can you be certain?" asked Ahm.

'He foretold its coming. We made preparations,' answered Whun.

"We what?" asked Ahm.

'I will show you, but only after you have been restored,' said Whun.

"What we're asking the Noktulians to do," said Ahm, hesitant to accept his new reality.

'We are not asking. They have already offered,' said Whun.

"How does this work, exactly?" asked Ahm.

'They will take you to a crypt, far below Noktrusgodhen. There, they have preserved another crystalline piece of Aggriphaxxeddon; her brain. Their ritual forges a temporary connection between it and the Aggripha, and grants the ancient wyrm's soul access to your own. Through that connection, she peels back the veil, and grants you access to your past through her own,' said Whun.

"So this is only possible because of the Aggripha?" asked Ahm.

'Yes. If the prophecy is fulfilled, the Aggripha will be no more, and you will be the last restoration they ever perform,' said Whun.

Ahm's face went stark white. He looked into Whun's eyes, seeking any sense that the lich might be speaking in jest. As difficult a thing as that was to discern on the face of an ancient, reanimated corpse, the feeling struck Ahm all the same; Whun was not joking.

"You said nothing of destroying the Aggripha before," said Ahm.

'How else would we free our people, and the Talaani, from Mordessa's curses? She drains one of life, and the other of souls, while holding both halves of Xulrathia prisoner. Would you defend her now that you've learned the truth?' asked Whun.

"What will happen to the citizens of Dusk?" asked Ahm.

'There are over one-hundred-million citizens in Dusk. Some may come to harm through the course of events as we take these necessary actions. Furthermore, they will defend the only truths they know with their immortal lives, for they can't accept what we know. The harsh reality is, casualties are part of every war. The Talaani seek no specific harm to the people of Dusk. They care not for whether we extend our lives, or live as mortals. The only guaranteed side effect the loss of the Aggripha will bear is the resulting uselessness of the Flute, and a brief inability to perform Ascensions. You and I, however, can help them find a new way; a way that will not prematurely drain them of their souls, and will not harm the Talaani Empire.'

"You've given this a lot of thought," said Ahm, settling into the idea.

'I am three-thousand-nine-hundred-and-fifty-three years old, dear Ahm. I have fought countless wars, slain innumerable enemies, and risen to a level of power that would make even the most skilled wizard quake in fear. What do I have left to do with my time but think?'

"So we fight one more war, then," said Ahm.

'The first of many more, I am afraid,' said Whun. 'But they will all be necessary.'

"I will agree to be restored, but only if you answer one question first. As you are far older than our Kingdom, and have amassed such power... why? Why do you care about the fate of the people of Xulrathia, or anyone on Ayrelon, for that matter?" asked Ahm.

Whun nodded, as if he'd expected Ahm's question. 'I learned a long time ago that ruling others is unrewarding. I once yearned for titles and lands, but both left me wanting. Power became the only thing that mattered, but even the rewards from that are fleeting. I've nothing awaiting me on the other side of the veil. When I am destroyed, my soul will die with me. That leaves me only Ayrelon, and its people. In truth, I care not for the world, or this continent, or even *the random citizen that might flee at my approach.*

'While I crave no throne, what I will not abide is someone else conquering all, when I've seen fit to not do so myself. If I can resist the urge to impose my will upon others, then they will not be allowed to do so in my stead. Mordessa has overstepped, and her reign must be put to an end. She is my doing; I released her from her tomb. I will, therefore, take part in her downfall. After that, our next mission begins. The one that comes for Ayrelon is far beyond our combined strength, and we will have no help from the gods in our battles with him. Before you ask, no, I do not know his name. I was given visions of him and told the importance of our role. That is all that I know on the matter, but it should suffice to appease your curiosity.'

"Very well. I will accept the ritual, but know this. I am not convinced that destroying the Aggripha is the proper course of action. If my memories are restored, and I agree with your assessment, then we will proceed with your plans and bring Mordessa's rule to an abrupt and violent end. If the ritual fails, or my memories reveal another path, then know that I will do everything in my power to protect the Aggripha, and the benefits it provides to our Kingdom," said Ahm as he gained his feet.

'Then let us begin,' said Whun.

IMAGES, SOUNDS, and bursts of painful magic flooded into Ahm's mind. They tortured his conscious and subconscious, mending them, merging them together, then sundering them all at once. He had to break free from the onslaught, but he could not. The pain was greater than anything he'd ever experienced, even his Ascension. His Ascension! It was the key! The mere thought of it made visions coalesce, and the flood abated for a time.

He focused his mind on the Ascension his mind forgot. Strange scenes flooded past too rapidly to grab hold. A building. A field. A city floating in the sky. He grasped at the city, forcing its image to return. He latched on with every ounce of consciousness he could muster.

Sunlight burst past the floating city as it descended, each click of the massive chains sending tremors through the ground below as thousands of Toor workers pulled it out of the sky. None could remember why—or how—the land had been ripped asunder, only that the city had loomed over them for longer than their oldest residents' existence. When the Queen suggested pulling the city out of the sky by the enormous chains that held it down, none of them had known how to proceed. It had taken decades to build a system of gears in the Cryx below that could move the monolithic iron links. Now, after nearly a hundred years, the Queen's vision of a unified Kingdom was finally coming into focus, one day-long crank at a time.

Historians scrambled to the edge of the Cryx or the tops of nearby towers every evening, scrawling notes in a frenzy of excitement and wonder. No living soul had ever stepped foot on the floating isle, and hundreds of years of speculation were slowly being replaced with both facts and more questions. Who had built the great, dark stone city that was coming into view? Who had caused the land upon which it stood to float into the sky?

"She's right, you know," said Lord Whun, breaking Ahm from his thoughts. His jaw was intact. He stood upon the ground. This was a younger Whun than he recognized. His voice sounded hollow, as if his true self were many miles away. He was the oldest among them, and revered by many; though feared by most.

"How do you figure?" challenged Ahm, so young his voice sounded foreign.

"I can sense it drawing closer. The citadel is real, and its power is unmistakable," said Whun.

"I guess I should congratulate you, then. The church of Xxrandus is about to become our state religion," sighed Ahm, his youth granting him confidence he did not yet deserve.

"You misunderstand its purpose," said Whun.

"Then why don't you enlighten me? This whole thing has been a kingdom-wide project since before I was born, and quite frankly, I never saw the value in it. You Xxrandites wield all the power in Baan'Sholaria, and all I see happening is more of the same," grunted Ahm, displeased with his distant, self-proclaimed adoptive father.

Lord Whun had grown to respect him for his honesty, despite his youth and inexperience. "It has long been thought that the city we are pulling from the sky was once the home of Xxrandus himself, and as such, his citadel is directly bound to the primal forces from which he drew his power. Those forces are not the sole purvey of he and his worshipers. Or do you think a servant of Ishnu will be incapable of harnessing them? Do you think Ishnu to be weak?"

Ahm could barely hide the anger he felt at Whun's insinuation, regardless of the fact that the old lich spoke without any specific tone or inflection that would indicate his intent or motivations. His monotone delivery sounded as lifeless as he appeared, and often made Ahm far more angry than he should have been. "No," he sighed. "I don't think Ishnu is weak. I just don't see how this helps anyone but a Xxrandite."

"Both are gods of death. They draw their power from the same primal forces. Those forces are neither sentient, nor biased toward one religion or another. Either church may, therefore, use the citadel for their own means," said Whun.

Ahm sighed in frustration. "Yes, Ishnu is technically the goddess of death, but as we've discussed—at great length—she celebrates death as part of the circle of life. We are not alike, Whun, no matter how much you insist we are. You'll never find a servant of Ishnu who will willingly become the Undead; not like a Xxrandite. That's the whole point behind the struggle in Baan'Sholaria. That's why so many protest. Are you still so blind you refuse to see or admit that? Your church oppresses those who don't conform. How is this stupid floating city being pulled to the ground going to change that?"

Whun tilted his head toward Ahm and smiled, his decrepit skin peeling back horrifically. "There are other ways the Ishnites may become our equals; other ways to extend their lives to match, or exceed, the Xxrandites. The citadel is key to that effort, and is the true reason the Queen wishes the city pulled out of the sky; so that all might benefit from the powers held within. It is her vision that all within Baan'Sholaria would stand on equal footing, for we cannot hold out against the Empire to the north if we fight amongst ourselves."

"Great," grunted Ahm, still hesitant to believe his undead master. "So, in sixty days, when this giant hunk of rock is finally pulled back down into the crater below, we'll find the solution to all our problems. Good to know," he said sarcastically.

"This is but the first piece of her plan. She is in the north pursuing the other half as we speak," said Whun.

"She... she's in the Talaani Empire? Right now?" gasped Ahm.

"Is that so hard to believe? She takes this matter very seriously," assured Whun.

"So she's going to start that war we've been trying to avoid? That or she's going to get herself killed," sighed Ahm.

"No. It is true what they say about her," said Whun.

"What, that she's mad?" laughed Ahm.

"Your Queen is not mad, young Ahm, and you would do well to be careful with your words," insisted Whun.

"Yes, Lord," gulped Ahm.

"I first met Mordessa over five hundred years ago. She was trapped within one of the great pillars that once stood at the center of the Cryx. The Maithung were drawing her powers in the absence of the citadel, which they could no longer reach. Once I discovered her existence and set her free, we were able to push back the abominations and claim the lands for our people. To be trapped for thousands of years and still be alive is a feat of its own. To be capable of battle mere moments after being set free is another thing entirely," said Whun.

"So she won't die in the north. Got it," said Ahm.

"She draws her power from the same place as Ishnu and Xxrandus, young Ahm. She is the daughter of Ishnu, your goddess, and the lover of Xxrandus, my god. She was born to unify us. It is her purpose," said Whun.

"So the rumors say," scoffed Ahm. "You actually believe that nonsense?"

Whun turned and looked his mortal companion in the eyes. "I have seen it. I have felt her power. Walking in her presence is like standing before the gods themselves. She is the only reason the Church of Xxrandus has held back so long, and thus, the only reason you are allowed to exist."

"I see," said Ahm.

"No, you do not. But you soon will. As the most vocal Ishnite, and the only member of your church to earn my respect, I have chosen you as the first to ascend. Once our tasks are complete, you will become my equal, and will lead your church into a new era of peace," said Whun.

Ahm shrank back involuntarily at the tone in Whun's voice. It wasn't often the lich audibly expressed his feelings. It only happened when he was truly passionate about what he was saying. "Should... should I be grateful, or terrified?"

"Both," said Whun. "Mordessa has found a possible solution for the disparity between our factions... but-" started Whun.

"-but it's never been done before," realized Ahm.

"That is correct," said Whun.

"So I'm to be a test subject," said Ahm, a cold sweat beading on his forehead. He felt sick to his stomach.

"That is also correct. In reward for your constant insolence, you will be subjected to a process we know little about. Should you survive, you will be rewarded with a power to rival my own. If I were you, I would consider this a *fair trade, and worth the risk."*

"It's not you that's being risked!" challenged Ahm, *emboldened by his sense of hopelessness.*

"Once it is done, you will see as I do; as Queen Mordessa does. This is the way to save Baan'Sholaria, and protect us from all foreseeable futures," said Whun.

The cranks started moving again in the distance, filling the air with a deep, metallic moan. Four great chains shuddered as their lowest links were latched-onto and the day-long process of pulling them down began. Ahm recounted the remaining links as a tremor rolled through the ground beneath them.

Fifty-nine more days of this, he thought. Fifty-nine days until the end of my life, he sighed.

THE VISION ended, ripping from his sight with a violence that threatened to tear his mind in two. His life raced by, pouring into him, through him, and swirling his sense of self like a whirlpool into unknown depths. He grasped for something stable; another scene to latch onto. Fire. Heat. A forge. He grasped for the forge with every fiber of his being.

A strange visitor stood before them as the sound of nearby smiths rang out from all sides. The great forges of Mount Skain surrounded them, lit by the glow of its massive furnaces, yet cast in shadow by the enormous cauldrons that rode on great iron rails and chains overhead.

He studied the sword as Whun presented it, but refused to touch the wicked blade. A black heart was embedded in the surface of the man's chest, framed with an elaborate, blackened melrithium armor plate emblazoned with glowing purple runes. Black robes flowed out from the breastplate, embroidered with silver runes, and the sigil of some strange order. His silvery hair tied back like an elf, he was tall and pale and could have been mistaken for an Unliving in their homeland.

By appearance, he seemed the fitting wielder of the dark blade they'd forged. Yet, he insisted it was not for him to hold, nor brandish, in any war. He simply nodded his approval, and Whun sheathed the blade weapon, setting it aside so it wouldn't influence the man's words.

"You have done well; precisely as I instructed," said the strange wizard. "Strambáneur will serve your people well in

the coming war, but fret not when it is lost. When next it is needed, it will resurface, and you will know the Night Witch's plans have been set into motion."

"Should Mordessa overstep, this blade will be her undoing," said Ahm, much older and more familiar.

"As I said, yes. It is also much, much more than that, as you will discover in time," said the strange man.

"Very well. The pact is struck," said Whun. His jaw was starting to fail him, and would soon fall off. Much time had passed since the last vision, but how much? It was far too hard to tell.

"It has. You've been most helpful. In the near future, my past self will seek your permission to retrieve a very special ruby from deep within the Cryx, and you will let him and his assistant pass; the laws of Baan'Sholaria be damned. Remember, it is for the sake of Ayrelon's future that we've struck this accord," said the man.

"Agreed, Lord Mordechai," said Ahm.

"Then we are concluded, Lord Whun," said Mordechai with a bow of his head. As soon as the last word passed his lips, he was gone; vanished as if he'd never stood in their presence.

THE VISION ended, leaving Ahm feeling sick. He woke almost instantly and rolled to his side to release his stomach's contents, unaware he'd been lying on a raised stone slab. His eyes opened in fear as his gut clenched and air rushed past his face. He landed on his hands and knees with a thud, just as his stomach emptied a puddle of acid and bile onto the floor.

'The feeling will pass. Even I got sick when I was restored, and I had no stomach with which to appease the urges,' said Whun.

"So it's true. Every bit of it," said Ahm.

'Indeed,' said Whun.

"Where is Strambáneur?" asked Ahm, rising to his feet.

'You remember?' said Whun.

"Everything," answered Ahm. "You were tasked with hiding it, so where is it?"

'The last place anyone in Dusk would look. Inside this very temple, beneath Noktrusgodhen's feet,' said Whun.

"How the hell did you hide it there? We were at war!" gasped

Ahm.

'It took a great deal of effort, and cost a great many Noktulian and Skalaani their lives,' said Whun.

The pair exited the ritual chamber and climbed the marble stairs back to the main floor. As they entered the banquet hall above, a small door inset into the iron pair at the far end swung open with haste, and a lone Noktulian raced across the room, heading directly for them.

"Masters! I hope that the restoration was a success, and that your recovery is short. The vessels have arrived, and the time is nigh!" it gasped as it arrived.

Ahm looked at Whun and gave a single nod as the Lich turned to face him.

"It is time," he said.

CHAPTER 17:
INSURRECTION

Ris'Anyu, Brighanfjor 1st, 576 of the 1st Era

MINA, TAVYN, and the rest of their friends waited patiently outside the large temple. The shadow of an extremely large dragon statue lay across the courtyard, protecting them from the midday sun. They'd seen a great many wonders on their travels through the Empire, but their driver had kept them moving and thus they'd been unable to explore. Mina was particularly struck with its beauty considering the lifetime of teachings that described the land as desolate, and its inhabitants nothing but scaled savages.

Though many of the companions milled around, inspecting carvings in the stonework, or etchings beneath smaller statues, Ainen stood completely still, silently staring up at Noktrusgodhen. Some part of him knew that the stone dragon was not a statue, but the actual creature itself frozen for all time.

"What did you say the tall guy was, again?" asked Gnately, gently stroking Petree's tiny snout with her pinky.

"It is a Noktulian, and it is not a 'guy'. They are asexual," said Eros.

Gnately gave him a confused look.

"They reproduce without mating. At least that's what is written in our archives," explained Eros.

"You know a lot about this place," smiled Mina. "Were you planning on moving here?" She grabbed his hand and tugged, letting him know she was teasing.

"You can learn a lot about Dusk just by walking around. The Talaani Empire was a complete mystery. The only way I could learn anything about it was to read," he said, returning her smile.

"So, do they like... lay eggs?" asked Gnately, wrinkling her face.

"That's what I read, yes. I mean, it's fairly hard to be certain about anything regarding this place. So much of what we know appears to be lies, or at the very least, hiding the truth. For example, this city isn't supposed to exist. We certainly shouldn't have seen any settlements this large if the texts were accurate," said Eros.

"This is the fourth city we've seen that is this size," said Tavyn.

"Precisely what I mean! If we got that wrong, what else has eluded us?" gasped Eros.

"I think you missed your calling," giggled Mina. "You talk day after day about Ishnu and becoming a priest. I think you're more suited as a historian."

"Honestly, I never considered it," he shrugged.

An eerie silence fell over the group as the smaller door of the temple opened and a human stepped out. Mina and Eros seemed to recognize him and ran toward him without delay, her arms spread wide in preparation for an embrace. To Gnately, Piya and Ainen, there was nothing remarkable about the man, other than his white robe exterior and the red folds that revealed themselves when he moved.

To Tavyn, he seemed to shimmer, as if an echo of himself was slightly out of place, shifting into and out of the space he was occupying. Recognizing what the man was, Tavyn's right arm twitched as he fought the instinct to reach for his dagger. Open confrontation went against what he'd been taught, and he'd sworn to stand beside Mina through whatever was coming their way. The instinct to lash out and defend himself from what his mind instantly perceived as a threat was very hard to overcome.

Mina backed away from Ahm, smiling. "It's so good to see you. I was worried Mordessa's instructions would get you killed."

"They would, if I was foolish enough to follow them," said Ahm.

"Well, you know Eros," she said, pointing. "The little one is Gnately. Ainen is the huge one over there, staring up at the dragon. The young girl is their friend Piya, and the intimidating fellow back there in black leather is Tavyn."

"I am very pleased to meet all of you. I am Ahm Stonehawk, High

Priest of the Temple of Kesh, and former Minister of Defense to the Kingdom of Baan'Sholaria. We have much to discuss; a great deal more than you could have possibly anticipated, in fact. When we enter, the Enclave of Ages will provide us with a banquet. However, before we begin, I must prepare you for something you are about to see.

"Our majesty Queen Mordessa saw fit to send me to the Talaani Empire in search of our ambassador, Lord Whun, and to kill the lot of you. For reasons you're about to learn, I've decided not to do that. However, most importantly, I found Lord Whun quite safe, and working with the Empire in secret. He is one of our strongest allies in what must come, and so I must request that you treat him with respect and honor. Why do I say these things, you ask? You are neither residents of Dusk, nor natives to the Talaani Empire, and so I must assume you've had little opportunity to spend time in the company of an ancient lich, such as he. We wouldn't want his appearance to cause panic and something untoward to happen."

Tavyn's eyes went wide and his heart began to race. Nothing about his new circumstances felt right. His instincts insisted he flee or die fighting. He knew the proper course of action was to act normal, and show the support for his friends that he'd promised. Everything within him was torn by conflict. He didn't know what to do. In all their teachings, the Daxian Order had made one thing abundantly clear... a lich was something to be feared, and flight was always the proper course of action.

Gnately seemed intrigued by the idea that she'd get a chance to meet such a creature. Many scary stories told by her relatives around the campfire at night had included evil liches destroying kingdoms or killing heroic knights. Never in her life could she have imagined meeting one herself, let alone getting the chance to fight alongside one.

Ainen broke out of his trance and locked his eyes on Ahm, then nodded solemnly, as if to say he was perfectly fine with the idea. Piya looked to Ainen, seeking his strength. She had never heard of a lich, and her mind seemed to have lost touch with reality the moment they dove off the boat so many days prior. Nothing felt real, and it was as if she was still adrift in the ocean. Perhaps everything that had happened was a dream caused by exposure, and she was somewhere amidst the waves in the throes of dementia, dying from exhaustion and dehydration. She slid next to Ainen again, and pressed against his side, her shoulder wedged into his hip. He placed his hand on her upper back reassuringly without looking, but it was enough to bring ease to her mind.

"Tavyn is going to need a while to adjust, I'm afraid. He's a Purifier of the Daxian Order," said Mina calmly.

"Is that so?" asked Ahm, walking toward him.

Tavyn nodded, his apprehension rising.

"I knew the priest that saved Dax'Vahr's life. She actually came to me asking if she should go through with his ascension. When I told her no and warned against it, she got angry and stormed out. I think in some odd way she'd fallen in love with the man, though I couldn't understand why, considering he never had a chance to so much as speak before she thrust our beliefs onto him. Not only was what she did ill-advised according to Ishnu's teachings, she broke one of our Kingdom's most sacred laws.

"I offer you an apology on her behalf. She cannot give you one herself, for she was put to death for her actions. While I know you are not Dax, it would do me great honor if you would accept my apology in his stead. What was done to him was wrong, and we can not take that back," said Ahm.

At first, Tavyn didn't know how to respond. After a few moments of conflict, he reached his hand toward Ahm in greeting, and resigned himself to helping the group despite his personal misgivings. The Unliving were nothing like he'd been taught, and that gave him enough pause to consider the alternative; that they weren't abominations suited to be slaughtered, but rather normal people that were simply guided by a different interpretation of the same religion.

"I accept, though I'm certain Dax never would. It's becoming quickly apparent that things aren't as I was told. I admit having no comfort in the thought of working with a lich, but I promised Mina I would aid her in freeing your people from Mordessa's curse, and perhaps learning more of Ishnu's true will in the process. Perhaps one of our teachings is wrong, or we've both failed to interpret Ishnu properly. Either way, I agree to enter this convocation willingly, in the pursuit of our common goal, and a chance to learn more of our goddess," he said.

Ahm shook his hand with a smile, saying, "Convocation? That's an odd choice of words."

"Oh, don't mind him," said Gnately. "Some old merchant named Dramen threw that word in our faces a while back, and I think Tav's just been waiting for a reason to use it," she giggled. "So when do we get to meet ole lichy?"

Ahm chuckled. "It is good that you are of high spirits. Make sure you remember these moments in the days that come."

THE BANQUET hall had been cleared of all tables, save one positioned alone at the center of the enormous chamber. Lord Whun floated silently at the far end, waiting patiently for the new arrivals to take their seats. Each of the foreign companions involuntarily froze at the sight of him.

Gnately felt like one of the heroes from her father's favorite stories, entering a vile creature's tower and finally coming face to face with their enemy.

Ainen, who hadn't shown much of a response to anything since they came ashore, took a step back, but tripped over Piya and nearly tumbled to the ground.

Piya did her best to hide the rapid beating of her heart, and her breath catching in her chest, but she couldn't prevent a tear from rolling down her cheek, or the trembling of her hand when she reached up to wipe it away.

Tavyn's heart nearly stopped. The Daxian Order had provided extensive training in the power of liches. It was said that even Dax'Vahr himself preferred to avoid them at all costs, and that they should simply leave them to Ishnu's will. Floating on the other side of the room was a creature more powerful than any his order had described. Its magic was on full display, holding it several feet above the floor, and animating a skeleton so old it had no tissue remaining on its surface. Even the man's heart was on full display, and seemed to be alight with magical flames. Not once had any of those things been described as possibilities.

'Welcome, travelers. I mean you no harm,' said Whun in their minds.

"What the fuck?" yelled Tavyn.

"He casts his mind toward those he converses with, Tavyn. That is the only way he can communicate, since he has no muscles, no lungs, and no lower jaw," explained Mina. "I know it's off-putting, and I wish there was a better way. It must be a lot, all at once."

'We have neither the time to seek other means, nor to afford the delays while someone else speaks on my behalf. You will simply have to deal with this situation on your own terms. We've far too much to cover, and too little time to complete our goals before Mordessa discovers our plot,' said Whun.

"I'll be fine," grunted Tavyn, clearly displeased. He walked around the table to a random seat, drew his daggers, slammed them onto the stone table, and dropped into the chair in a huff.

'Will the rest of you please join us?' invited Whun.

As the companions gained their seats, Tavyn mindlessly spun one his curved daggers atop the table. Gnately and Petree sat on his left, and Mina to his right. They each reached toward him and motioned for him to hold their hands. He declined both with a wave of his hand, grasping his forehead with the other. "I'll be fine. Really," he sighed.

Gnately reached her hand back over, Petree in her palm fluttering his wings and snorting for the elf's attention. "But, but...

he loves you?" said Gnately in a sweet little voice.

Tavyn sighed again and let Petree crawl into his hand with a brief smile and a roll of his eyes. Gnately perked up as she returned her attention to the rest of the room, kicking her feet happily in her chair with her hands clasped together in her lap.

"First, we will discuss what is to come, and then we shall dine," stated Ahm. "All we ask for now is that you listen with an open mind. Most of you do not know our history or customs, so I apologize that some of the finer details might need to be skipped over for the sake of time. That said, Whun would like to begin."

'Mordessa has cursed these lands. She helped create the Kingdom of Baan'Sholaria, yes, but to solidify our power and secure our borders from the threat of a Talaanian invasion, she convinced us that the only way was to create the Aggripha. Doing so cursed the Talaani Empire into a cycle of reincarnation, where no new souls may enter their newborns, and their dead can never reach the afterlife,' explained Whun.

"What?" gasped Tavyn. "So-" he started.

"The cycle of life has been utterly obliterated in Talaani, in its purest form. While the bodies of the deceased can, indeed, be given back to Ayrelon, no new sentient life can emerge," said Ahm.

Tavyn's anger returned to his face. He carefully sat Petree on the table before him and adjusted his position in his chair, clenching his fists.

'Furthermore, her enchantments upon the Aggripha slowly steal the souls of everyone who ascends using its power, making it, and her, stronger,' said Whun.

"So that's how she's so strong," gasped Tavyn.

'That is but a small portion of where she draws her magic. The truth is something we've never shared, for we only just remembered it,' said Whun.

"Restoring what she stole from the world is the only way to weaken her enough to defeat her," added Ahm.

"What, precisely, are you referring to?" asked Mina. "How could you just remember something critical about where she draws magic? I mean, I thought it was the Aggripha too."

"The Noktulians have a way to restore the memories of those who lived before our recorded history; like Lord Whun and I. It costs them a great deal, and is not something they can perform often. It won't even be possible anymore if we succeed," said Ahm.

"So what did you remember?" asked Eros.

'Tavyn... you pray to Ishnu for guidance, yes?' asked Whun.

"I do," he answered.

'Eros, you pray for healing, blessings, and also guidance?' asked Whun.

"Yes, and so does Ahm," stated Eros. "What are you getting at?"

'It has never been Ishnu who answered your prayers,' said Whun.

"What is that supposed to mean?" asked Tavyn, confused.

'Thousands of years ago, Mordessa, and her sister Siscci, were brought to this world from another; a hellscape beyond your comprehension. They brought with them death and destruction, which inadvertently paved the way for their mother to join them. During their rampage across Ayrelon, Mordessa eventually discovered her sister's true motivations, and locked Siscci in a magical tomb; a cube of stone with no discernible opening.

'When Ishnu later arrived, and witnessed the horrors her daughters had been creating, she looked for them to put a stop to their reign of terror. Mordessa found out and sought protection from another god; Xxrandus. He fell in love with her and protected her from her mother's wrath. In time, their combined power became a threat to the ancient dragons living within the Talaani Empire. Aggriphaxxeddon led them into battle and, with the help of Ishnu, defeated Xxrandus and banished him from our world.

'Mordessa, however, managed to trick her mother and send her back to her home world, though their fight nearly ended her life. Fatally wounded, she drew upon her mother's power and put herself into a healing coma, inside a similar magical tomb. The people of the land feared her, sealed her inside the impregnable prison, and buried it at the bottom of what we now call the Cryx,' explained Whun.

"Mordessa caused Ishnu and Xxrandus to be banished from our world?" gasped Tavyn.

'Indeed. And in doing so, she became the only creature on Ayrelon who could touch upon their source of power, governing the raw essence that creates what you call 'life' and 'death'. It is through her connection that all who pray to Ishnu and Xxrandus are granted the power to channel their spells or blessings. It is through Mordessa that you are given guidance in your time of need,' said Whun. 'And with each prayer, she grows stronger. Such is the sacrament that governs gods and worshipers.'

"Okay, hold the fuck on!" gasped Eros. "Mordessa has been answering my prayers?"

"Not consciously or directly. In truth, her existence and attachment to that power is what unlocks our ability to access it and use it to cast spells. With Ishnu and Xxrandus no longer present on Ayrelon, were she to be slain, all priests of either religion would lose their abilities, and all access to such power would be lost... until the time another such entity took her place," explained Ahm.

"So you're saying a god, or goddess, is nothing more than a key? And the power they wield is some kind of ethereal thing that we can't touch, see, or use unless they are here to grant us access to it?" asked Mina.

"Yeah, and somehow us using those powers makes them stronger," said Eros in disbelief.

"There are many in Gargoa that worship Galrath, yes?" asked Ahm.

Gnately and Piya nodded.

"Galrath grants his worshipers access to the essences that govern Law and Chaos, War and Peace. He proclaims to be the god of Justice, no? His existence unlocks those essences for their use as tools, allowing them to cast spells in his name and sway those forces in our reality to their whim. The same is true of any god," said Ahm.

"What you're basically saying is we have to fight a god!" gasped Tavyn.

"No. I am saying we take that power from her, and *then* fight her," said Ahm.

'By calling Ishnu and Xxrandus back into this world, we will restore their power, giving them back what she stole,' said Whun.

"Great. Sounds easy," sighed Tavyn, throwing his hands up in frustration. "How the fuck do we do that? Anyone here summoned a god before?"

'It so *happens* that the gateway Mordessa used to exile Ishnu is still present, yet dormant. Once she is free, she can hopefully grant us the knowledge of how to bring Xxrandus back as well. The Noktulians have recovered the ritual necessary to open the gate. It simply requires a few very special elements which only now came into our possession,' said Whun.

"What might they be?" asked Mina.

"First, we needed knowledge of the spell. The Noktulian members of the Enclave of Ages have discovered that through the return of their memories. It took them several hundred years, but they've had plenty of lifetimes to accomplish it. Thanks to Mordessa, even their deaths barely impeded their progress because they constantly reincarnated. Once they grew old enough, they just rejoined their colleagues and kept pushing the research forward," said Ahm.

'Second, we needed a powerful servant of Ishnu, and another of Xxrandus. Ahm and I will fill those roles. We will be cornerstones in the ritual ceremony,' said Whun.

"Finally, we needed someone who was capable of wielding the key," said Ahm, turning his attention to Ainen.

"Me?" asked Ainen, calmly.

'You are host to a fragment of the Caier spirit named Jaezyn. One of his fragments was instrumental in helping Noktrusgodhen attempt to break Mordessa's curse nearly seven-hundred years ago. Part of their attempt was to transfer Eloness's curse of stone off of Noktrus and onto Jaezyn's host, and thus spirit, so that he could carry that burden on his lord's behalf. That is why your skin slowly turns to stone,' said Whun.

"The Caier were an extremely magical race. Their natural connection to the weave was second only to the dragons. The three that have risen, sending their fragments into you, were the most powerful of their kind. Jaezyn was certain that he could allow Eloness's curse to turn him to stone and remain alive," said Ahm.

'Becoming a wizard made from stone, if you will,' said Whun.

"A kind of sentient golem," said Ahm.

'We need but complete Ainen's conversion into stone, and he should be able to withstand the key's power, and resist the pull of the vortex when we open the gate,' said Whun.

"Great. Where's the key?" asked Ainen.

Ahm stood up and backed away, crossing his arms.

Whun raised his hands toward the ceiling and paused. The granite over the table seemed to shudder as thin streaks of purple lightning shot across its surface. The room shook. Whun clenched his skeletal hands into fists. Cracks erupted across the ceiling, creating a jagged oval around an area no larger than Tavyn. He then yanked his hands down to his sides with surprising speed.

The encircled chunk of granite broke free from the ceiling and fell atop the table with a violent crash. Following close behind, a black streak raced toward the table in a slow spin. It started horizontally and turned vertical before impact. With an ear-piercing clank, a black, two-handed sword buried itself quillon-deep in the slab and pulsed with dark energies.

Gasps and cries of alarm rang out around the room as several of the companions jumped clear of the event in a panic.

"I present to you, Strambáneur, the Render of Souls and Key to the Veil," said Ahm proudly.

'This sword was forged in the fires of Mount Skain and enchanted by some of Ayrelon's most powerful casters, under a magical shroud of secrecy that not even the gods could pierce,' said Whun.

"We made it almost six-hundred years ago, and it has remained hidden ever since; waiting for the day when all the pieces would come together," said Ahm.

"Right," said Tavyn, hesitantly approaching the table. "So when Ainen uses this thing to bring Ishnu back, Mordessa will be weakened and we can attack," he said, reaching for the blade.

'Do not touch it! Only Ainen can wield it, and only when the time is right to begin!' yelled Whun.

Tavyn jerked his hand back and sat with a sigh.

"There is still one more thing we must do," said Ahm. "Ishnu and Xxrandus are but the first step in our plan."

"Okay, so what's the rest?" asked Mina.

'If we succeed, we will next need to break the curse of stone, and free the dragons,' said Whun.

"What do we need to do for that? Make it rain emeralds?" laughed Tavyn.

"No," said Ahm sternly.

'Three of you are host to Caier fragments. Ainen, Mina and Eros. Never have all three reunited on Talaani soil. The Enclave of Ages will gather you and perform the Ritual of Remembrance one final time, gifting you each the memories of your Caier,' said Whun.

"Won't that destroy who we are?" asked Eros, concerned.

'It may change you, over time. However, we are not filling you with the soul of your Caier, or letting them take your place. Instead, we are going to give you their life experiences, and all they learned, so that you might act on their behalf,' said Whun.

"Think of it like Tavyn becoming a master of martial combat, then transferring all that knowledge and muscle-memory to you at the end of his days," said Ahm.

"So if my Caier was a powerful priest-" started Eros.

"Then you would have all the knowledge they ever gained. You wouldn't be able to access it all at once, and your body may not be able to withstand what they once could. Building tolerance and conditioning one's tissue for powerful spells takes time. You know this," said Ahm.

"I do," agreed Eros.

"However, they will have knowledge of the ritual necessary to reverse the curse of stone. Then our fight will be joined by Noktrusgodhen, Loshfurdahn, Buusfahrgeddon, Kaggahaaden, and Aashvukrier, the five ancient wyrms; rulers of the five dominions. The last remnants of Aggriphaxxeddon's brood," said Ahm.

'With Mordessa severely weakened, Ainen wielding Strambáneur, the three Caier granting you their knowledge, the might of the five wyrms, and the power of Ahm and I, we will be strong enough to lay waste to Mordessa's defenses and draw her attention away from the Aggripha,' said Whun.

Ahm nodded. "That is when Tavyn, Gnately and Piya will strike the fateful blow, destroying the enchantments upon the Aggripha, and breaking Mordessa's connection to the souls of one-hundred-million citizens across Baan'Sholaria. Only then can she be slain."

'And *only then by Strambáneur's edge*,' said Whun.

"How are they supposed to break the Aggripha?" asked Mina.

"That is the only piece of the puzzle we have not yet discovered," admitted Ahm.

"And how do we even get there? That's how far away?" asked Tavyn, sure he recalled Mina saying Dusk was hundreds of miles wide.

'*Tuldaxx*,' said Whun, '*The great wyvern of the Elonesti Dominion. She was still in her egg when the brood was petrified, and has been ruling the dominion in Noktrusgodhen's absence since she reached adulthood. When the battle starts, and all eyes are upon us, she will fly you to the Citadel of Xxrandus. From there, you will descend into the ascension chamber, gain access to the Aggripha, and break the spells that bind it.*'

"I should be there," said Mina.

"That is not possible," said Ahm.

"My soul is bound to the Aggripha. We are linked! If anyone is capable of destroying it, then it is I," she insisted.

'*She is correct*,' said Whun.

"No! Your connection to it puts you directly at risk! What if destroying it kills you?" retorted Ahm.

"So I'd be safer somewhere else? If destroying it kills me, will I not die here in the Talaani Empire just as well as in the Cryx?" she challenged.

'*She is going with them*,' said Whun.

"Um," said Piya. "Can I... stay here? I don't know how to fight, and I have no clue what most of this means," she said. Her voice was quivering, and her hand trembling.

"There, see? I'm taking her place!" insisted Mina.

"That is not what we agreed!" growled Ahm, turning to face Whun.

'*And yet it is what must be done*,' said Whun plainly. '*Did you think she would be spared risk?*'

Ahm growled and stormed off. Mina shrugged and turned back to Whun. "I'm going to the Aggripha. So, tell me how to destroy it."

'*Your Caier will know. You carry Eloness, the namesake of the Elonesti Dominion, the Talaani Empire's home of all that is pure magic*,' said Whun.

"Great! When do we begin?" asked Mina as she sat back down and crossed her arms defiantly.

"Why are you so insistent?" asked Eros.

"I was born to do this. Connected to the Aggripha since birth, and carrying a piece of the Caier who stood in defiance of Mordessa? It's obvious, is it not? This is my destiny!" she grunted. "Maybe once it's all said and done, I can finally be free to choose for myself, and go where I want to go!" she finished with a growl, her eyes welling up with tears of frustration.

'We begin on the morrow. For now, feast. This may very well be your last meal,' said Whun. 'Just... avoid the meat.'

As the ancient lich exited the chamber, wooden doors along the side opened and a series of humanoid automatons entered, carrying trays of food. They paused and sat them aside for a moment at the sight of the chunks of debris and the black sword atop the only table. A few moments later, a group of them returned with a new table and began preparing it for their guests.

Thanks in large part to the monumental nature of what lay ahead, none of the companions enjoyed their meal. However, after remembering what they'd seen in Uhldan, they made sure to heed Whun's advice.

AS THE group ate in silence, each contemplating the plan and their role in it, the Noktulian high priest entered the chamber quietly and approached Gnately. He stood in silence, seeming to smile down at her and the small wyvern perched on her shoulder. When she noticed his presence, she nearly jumped out of her skin.

"Can... can I help you?" she asked sheepishly.

"I mean you no harm, and didn't intend to frighten. It has been some time since we have seen a Wyvette, living and breathing. We thought them trapped by the same curse that sealed away our masters," it said.

"Wyvette? Is that what they're called?" said Gnately, wrinkling her brow. "I thought there would be a fancier name than that. With all the Magri-gaxx-eh-phax-eh-gedd-oh-don names and such, Wyvette just seems so... simple."

"Wyvette is what it happens to be, not what it is named. Have you given him a name?" it asked.

"Yes! Petree! Isn't it cute?" she said gleefully.

"Intriguingly, since I understand the egg was dormant until you arrived in our Empire, I should expect that young Petree is reincarnated, just as we. It seems he was waiting to receive a soul before he could hatch," said the priest.

"Really?" gasped Gnately.

"I could see no other reason for the delay. Wyvette eggs used to hatch within a matter of weeks. This one lasted hundreds of years, hidden away somewhere on Gargoa, where you're from," said the priest.

"Well, I got him on Gargoa, but I don't know where the previous owner acquired the egg," said Gnately.

"Fair enough," admitted the priest. "Take good care of him. He is the only Wyvette alive today, and may remain so if our plan fails. If our plan succeeds, he will be the only reincarnated Wyvette in existence, making him unique. In either case, he is something very special. However, keep care of your precious metals and stones. Wyvettes are known to covet shiny objects," said the priest with a wink.

"He's a thief?" gasped Gnately. The grin on her face couldn't have grown any wider.

"Indeed he is. Well, depending on who is inside him," added the priest.

"What do you mean?" asked Gnately.

"We do not know which soul he acquired. It could be a Noktulian, a Skaar, a Skalaani, an ancient Wyvette, or something completely different. If it is not a Wyvette, he may not grow to have their personality. Reincarnations usually occur within the same species, but since we've not had a Wyvette living in our presence since before Mordessa's curse, we can not assume Petree acquired a Wyvette soul," said the priest.

"Oh," said Gnately.

"When his memories return, you may even be able to learn his original name. If you do, please return here and tell us. We would love to perform our ritual of celebration with him some day, in honor of who he used to be, and what he has become," said the priest.

"I will! That sounds splendid!" said Gnately. As the priest walked away, she continued, "Did you hear that? You're someone special! I bet you were a full sized dragon. You may be small now, but trust me... great things come in small packages. I should know, because I'm just fabulous!"

MINA SAT staring through the window of her assigned bedchamber, watching as the sky grew dark and the streets below slowly emptied of the city's strange citizens. She'd requested sharing her room with Eros, but he hadn't come straight to the room with her. Instead, he chose to explore the city on his own, stating that it might be his last opportunity to see their world with his own eyes.

Too much had happened in recent weeks and months. With the visions of Mordessa escalating, the curse, the resurrection of Eros, the discoveries made reading Korr's prophecies, and everything since, she felt as if her whole world had been flipped over. Twice. Eros's sentiment about experiencing the Talaani with 'his own eyes' rang truer for her than she cared to admit. She wasn't sure she was the same as the last time she met with him under the stars, let alone what person she might become before everything that stood ahead of them came to pass.

She was still lost in those thoughts when the sound of her chamber door clicking shut caught her attention. There was no need for her to turn to see who it was. She could hear the familiar sounds of her guest approaching; the soft tap of leather soles, the gentle scrape of the edge of a silken robe. Ahm arrived at her side without a word of hello or any verbal acknowledgment by her.

When she was ready to talk, she turned on her rump atop the stool and shuffled her feet to her new angle. Looking up into his eyes, she could see the concern on display across every part of his face.

"I know," she said, acknowledging his unspoken protest about her decisions.

"You are, quite literally, the only person I care about," he sighed.

"I said I know," she repeated, lowering her head. "It's not like I asked for this burden."

"We can find another way," said Ahm. "I recommended sending the others because they were expendable. You aren't."

"They aren't either!" she retorted. "They're people! Living, breathing people that Mordessa was trying to kill, just to stop them from making it to the Talaani Empire. All so she could keep her precious little secrets and continue draining all our souls!"

"You're willing to throw your life away to save them?" he asked quietly, kneeling so that he could look her in the eye.

"I would've thought you'd do the same until all this started. I... I saw you differently," she said.

"Part of me has changed with the return of my memories, but I fear you've simply mistaken me for a man I've never been. You weren't around to witness my interactions as Minister of Defense. Every decision I've made over the past five centuries has been for the greater good of the people of Dusk, regardless of the consequences a small number of people might face. You are the only exception. I would cast the whole Kingdom into destruction if it meant saving your life," he said.

"Why? Why me? You dedicated your life to raising me and protecting me before you even knew me! Am I so special? How am I supposed to live up to whatever standards you've got in your head?" she growled, letting her frustration show.

"Look at me," he requested, placing a finger under her chin. A tear careened onto the surface of his digit as their skin met and left a small, but noticeable, wet streak down to his second knuckle. With her head lowered, he hadn't seen her start to cry. "From the moment I met you, I've loved you like a daughter. I can't explain why. I helped deliver you, right inside the Ministry, and watched as your mother was dragged away by the Ebon Guard.

"As you lay there, crying, my heart broke... realizing you'd never know your parents, just as I couldn't remember mine. I knew what my duty required. I knew why they brought your mother to me, instead of elsewhere. I just couldn't bring myself to go through with it. I had to know why, but I also had to protect you from the pain I knew.

"Is it so wrong of me to persist in those efforts? Protecting you, teaching you, watching you grow and flourish? You gave me purpose, beyond the monotony of Dusk. I'm just not willing to let that go," he said.

"All across Baan'Sholaria, young children are being born, raised, and indoctrinated into our lifestyle. Mordessa has doomed them all, not just me. Every single child of Dusk will die by her decree. Some just do it over the course of a few hundred years. You *had* to save me. Now I *have* to save them. They didn't ask for what she's doing to them. In fact, none of them even knows the truth. The last man that stood up to her and tried to tell them was ridiculed, hunted down and wiped from existence. And after that insane plan you and Whun were forced to devise just to have a chance against her, who else could possibly pull this off? It's up to us. It's up to *me* and no matter how I feel about it, I do not have a choice. This must be done," she cried.

"I... I understand," he sighed. He leaned in and kissed her on the forehead, then slowly stood and backed away. "I will leave you to collect your thoughts, and spend your night with Eros. Come morning, I will approach our tasks, and your role in them, as a strategist, and not a father. Just know that every part of my being is praying that you survive this ordeal, and remain true to yourself... even though I find it ironic Mordessa would be the conduit for answering those prayers, when my need for speaking them would be the pursuit of her demise," he finished with a wry smile.

Mina chuckled through her tears as he exited. She sniffed back her uncooperative sinuses and wiped her face on the sleeve of her shirt, hoping to be more presentable when Eros eventually returned.

A short while later, the door opened again and Eros burst

through with a huge grin on his face. He rushed straight over to her and presented a handful of strawberries while taking a seat on the bed. "We can't get these in Dusk anymore! My parents said they died off before I was born. They're quite sweet!" he chimed.

Mina picked one out of his hand and studied it briefly, then took a tiny bite of the tip. "Oh!" she gasped, then popped the entire thing into her mouth.

As she happily chewed, his eyebrows raised dramatically. "Oh! I almost forgot! Guess who I met when I went for my walk?"

"Who?" she asked through her food, trying her best to keep her mouth's contents inside.

"Korr! He's not dead!" he shouted happily.

She swallowed the remnants of the strawberry with a gulp and looked straight into his eyes, the back of her right hand preparing to wipe her lips. "Are you kidding?"

"Nope! He's a crazy old man, just like you probably imagined. I doubt he has an ounce of sanity left," laughed Eros.

"Did he say anything about what's going on?" she asked.

"Not much, just that he's very happy you're the one who's going to break the Aggripha," said Eros.

"Why would he say that?" she asked, more than a little surprised.

"Because you're the only one that can survive it," said Eros, smiling.

Still slightly confused, her heart skipped a beat and her mood instantly improved. She stood up from her stool, slightly hunched over, and promptly leaned over and pressed her lips to his. It was hard to tell, but she thought his muffled protest was in response to her haphazardly knocking the strawberries out of his hands and scattering them across the floor. That or he was thankful she was finally taking an action he'd only dreamed of. Since he didn't seem interested in pushing her away, and instead wrapped his arms around her when she pressed him against the mattress, she decided to ignore whatever protest his more-than-occupied mouth was attempting and enjoy their first night in bed with one another.

CHAPTER 18:
SACRAMENT
Ris'Nammlil, Brighanfjor 2nd, 576 of the 1st Era

THAT NEXT morning, a Noktulian awakened Mina, Eros and Ainen before sunrise. Dozens more waited in the hall to fall in behind the procession as they made their way towards the center of the temple. There, they were led past the debris-covered, sword-pierced dining table, through a door hidden behind the tapestries, and down a spiral stairway into the depths below the banquet hall.

Ahm and Whun were waiting when they arrived, positioned on either side of a large, crystalline brain. The strange relic glowed from an unseen source within, its ridges cycling through every color of the rainbow in no discernible pattern. The priests guided the ternion into specific positions in front of it by the shoulder, while the rest of the procession filed in to stand on sigils etched into the floor.

One of the Noktulians walked in front of them, up onto the dais that supported the relic. It walked behind the brain, raised its hands slightly as if presenting the strange device, and spoke in calming tones. "Like your Aggripha, this is a crystallized piece of our lost empress, Aggriphaxxeddon. The two are connected through a bond we cannot describe, for it is beyond our realm of understanding.

"Through their bond, we will invite her soul to merge, for a time, with the Caier fragments you carry within you. This will allow her to bring forth their knowledge, their memories, and their experiences, granting them to you, their host, as if you'd lived their former lives. The process will consume the fragment that you bear, and many of our Enclave as well. This sacrifice we make for you, so that you might bring about an end to Xulrathia's suffering; so our future children might know their gods, and live among them; so Dusk's children might live to their fullest, and no longer be sapped by an unjust Queen's pursuit of power.

"This process will not be pleasant, but we ask you to remain standing where you are for as long as possible. In the coming days, weeks, or months you may come to see Ayrelon anew as the Caier's lives become one with your own, but if you remain vigilant, you will keep hold of who you are, how you think, and those you now hold dear," the priest concluded.

"Eloness, are you ready?" asked the Noktulians in unison.

"I am," said Mina as something inside inspired her to respond.

"Xahn, are you ready?" they asked.

"I am," answered Eros.

"Jaezyn, are you ready?" they asked.

"I am," answered Ainen.

The priests lowered their heads in unison and reached their hands toward the relic, praying in a tongue the three of them had ever heard. Strands of white energy arced through the air, crackling like bolts of lightning, jumping from the crystalline brain to the chest of each member of the ternion. Involuntarily arching their backs, the three screamed in pain as the soul of a dragon passed into and through them.

Eros fell to his knees, power surging into him through bright pulses that moved down the lightning-like current, slamming into his chest, each escalating in ferocity. A priest nearby fell to the floor, skin shriveled and cold, as its life force erupted from its torso and streamed across the room toward the relic.

Another priest fell as the pulses raced toward Ainen, each impact on his chest sending small tremors through the floor. A third toppled over as the chanting intensified, drawing more power through to begin Mina's restoration.

Mina shrieked in pain and fell to her knees. Ahm panicked, but forcefully resisted the urge to run to her side. He prayed to Ishnu and brought forth a wave of healing magic, sending it throughout the room to heal the companions. Lord Whun reached one hand toward the ceiling and pointed the other toward the relic, then called a stream of magic down from the magical weave and channeled it into the ritual, to hasten the process and ease the burden on the priests. Eros tumbled to his side and began writhing on the ground, followed shortly thereafter by Mina and then Ainen.

Tears of white hot energy streaked down Mina's cheeks. The pain was too much. She had to save herself. There was no other choice. She reached out to the Aggripha, half driven by instinct, half by conscious thought. Her bond enhanced by the connection shared through the relic nearby, the Aggripha's power surged into her, then flooded the room with an unfathomable violence. A wave of blinding light struck the priests, Ahm, and Whun, knocking them to the ground and ending the ritual. The walls ruptured, sending fragments about the room, leaving large cracks along their surface and allowing the ceiling to sag in the absence of their strength. Six priests lay dead, lining the outer walls, the rest lie in heaps, with a myriad broken bones and torn flesh.

Ahm scrambled to his feet and hastened to Mina's side, his own injuries already healing through his subconscious prayers to Ishnu.

She was breathing.

Eros rolled to his stomach and forced himself to his hands and knees. Whun drifted over and reached down to help the boy to his feet.

Ainen, still on his knees, looked about the room in confusion, his skin almost completely turned to stone.

"I... I remember," said Eros, rising to his feet. "They were so beautiful; so graceful. They were our masters. They saved us from the Agthari, only to die at the hands of mortals, and the daughters of gods," he lamented, as he struggled to maintain his footing.

"Where am I?" asked Ainen, rising to his feet. "This... this wasn't supposed to happen," he stated, looking down at his hands in confusion.

"Mina? Are you okay?" asked Ahm.

She groaned in pain and rolled to her back. "My head! I can hear her speaking to me! I have her memories, but I don't think her fragment was removed," she gasped. "She... she's in pain."

"We'll figure this out," said Ahm, barely able to control his anxiety.

"Eros?" asked Mina, reaching a hand for him.

"I'm here, Mina," he said. He knelt beside her and placed her hand between both of his.

"Ainen?" she asked. There was no response. Ahm and Eros both looked toward him as Mina sat to see what was going on. "Ainen, are you okay?" she asked, her brow furrowed. The sight of his stone took a second to sink in, and she was fearful they'd lost their friend during the event.

"I am Jaezyn," said Ainen, his voice seeming to echo within himself. "I am afraid your friend is no more."

Ahm and Eros helped Mina to her feet. She cried for the loss of her friend, even though she'd only known him a short while. Ahm cried for the sadness he saw in her eyes.

Whun drifted over and inspected their large friend, while the remaining priests around the room gained their feet. He studied the stone-fleshed man for a few moments, then turned toward Mina. 'His soul has gone. The one present within him now has a different hue.'

"It seems our ritual was altered by your connection to the Aggripha," said the head priest as it approached Mina. "It is not your fault, child, it is ours. We should have anticipated such interference. I do not know what we would have done to compensate for it, but I apologize that we did not think of trying. Your friend Ainen's soul was destroyed by the event and replaced with the whole of Jaezyn's. It appears that you retained your fragment of Eloness, and it has grown in strength, since you say she can now communicate with you. Your friend Eros seems to be the only one who received his Caier's memories as intended."

"Did you say Jaezyn is completely inside Ainen's body now?" asked Ahm, perking up.

"We believe so, yes," said the priest.

"Weren't the Caier the three souls binding the enchantments onto the Aggripha?" Ahm asked, looking toward Whun.

'They were. Yes,' he answered.

"So it would stand to reason that the seal might have been weakened," said Ahm.

'Indeed, it would,' agreed Whun.

"So Ainen's sacrifice won't be in vain," said Mina.

"You needed his body to be fully stone, did you not?" asked Jaezyn. "To open the gate and bring the gods back to this world?"

"We would have preferred Ainen be present himself for the gate, but yes. We did need him to be living stone," said Ahm.

"The fact that I am stone also means the curse that binds Noktrusgodhen is nearly broken," said Jaezyn. "My petrification is a result of me bearing his curse... need I remind you?"

"How are you still able to move, then?" asked Mina.

'Because I taught him how to modify my curse, and he's had centuries to think on the matter,' answered Eloness in her mind.

"Eloness helped-" started Jaezyn.

"-you learn how to change the curse she put on the dragons," said Mina. "She just answered in my mind. Not only that, as soon as she did I saw the event through her memories. You were... communicating with one another while still bound to the Aggripha.

Should they have been able to do that?" she asked, turning to face Ahm.

"No. They're clearly more powerful than Mordessa anticipated," said Ahm.

"Let us make our way to the banquet hall," suggested the head priest. "It is best we vacate the ritual chamber, so that the Enclave can prepare it for another attempt."

"No. No more attempts," said Mina. "We've already lost too much."

"Very well," said the priest.

'I *like you*,' said Eloness in her mind.

The group made their way upstairs in silence, leaving Mina more time to think than she was comfortable with so soon after the ritual. It felt as if Eloness was exploring her mind, studying her life, and trying to decide if she liked her new host. Every time Mina thought the feeling was about to go away, another faint, '*Hmm!*' or '*Oh!*' would echo in the back of her mind.

At one point, near the top of the steps, Eloness yelled, '*No!*' at some memory or another, taking Mina by surprise and causing her to stumble. She reached out to her right as she fell, seeking the wall to save her footing. Seemingly at her bidding, part of the limestone wall broke free, jutted out and presented itself as a handhold for her to latch onto.

The priests following in behind came to a stop, startled by what they'd just seen.

Mina looked back at them, confused.

"You aren't meant to learn such skills so quickly," said one.

"What skills?" asked Mina.

"Eloness was a powerful spellcaster. She wielded the power to manipulate earth and stone. You just made the wall come to you, because you could not get to it fast enough to prevent your fall," said the priest.

"She what, now?" asked Ahm, turning to see what happened. He caught sight of the wall and looked at Mina with pride. "Our task gets easier still," he said with a smile.

"Don't get your hopes up too far. We still have to summon the gods and reanimate dragons for this to work," she chided.

Mina and Eros returned to their room after reaching the surface and promptly fell asleep.

Jaezyn joined the Noktulians in the temple's library to speak with them in private.

Ahm and Whun returned to the ritual chamber to study the relic.

+ + +

MINA LOOKED out across the desolate field. The dry, cracked ground stretched out in all directions, centered on her own feet. She raised her hands into view at the sight of her lower limbs, an overwhelming sense of unease rushing up to claim her. She was not herself.

Black, scaled skin glinted back at her, sparkling in the fleeting rays of sunlight that broke through the smoke caused by the strange event. The scales were much smaller than she'd ever seen and were silky under her fingertips. Her hands were unfamiliar as well. She still had five fingers, but the thumb and middle pair were much longer, and each was tipped with a sharp, thick red nail.

She pulled her hand away from her other arm as a cool breeze rushed by, sending an exhilarating, refreshing chill across her strange skin. The scales on her forearms lifted ever-so-slightly, as if attempting to stand on end as hairs on her human arm would. Bright red flesh peaked out at her from underneath, drinking in the cool air and passing the sensation deep into her core.

Mina spread her arms and looked down at her legs again. Her knees were much closer to her hip than they should have been, and the leg bent back underneath it to meet with a second. A spike made from red bone poked through the skin atop the lower knee, jutting into the space behind her leg protectively. Her leg bent forward again below that, stretching down to meet her ankles, and the elongated feet attached to them. She stood on the balls of her feet, her stunted toes tightly grouped at the tip, with thick, red nails at their ends.

She stood upright once more, rising to a height that seemed unnatural. It was hard to measure without something familiar nearby, but she was certain her body stood several feet taller than she remembered.

'*She comes,*' said Eloness, her voice resonating both in her mind, and in her chest. She was speaking inside her, and through her.

'*This is your body,*' said Mina, speaking both places as well.

'Yes,' answered Eloness.

A great dragon descended through the slowly dissipating smoke, lighting upon the ground with a surprisingly gentle touch. Its four legs were so thick she couldn't have wrapped her arms around them, and the body that stood above them was far larger than she could comprehend. Its thick scales were dark gray but seemed to shimmer with multi-colored magic, giving them a prismatic effect that she couldn't quite describe or even focus her eyes upon. The creature's neck extended upward for dozens of feet before arching back down to lower its head before her. Its black, leathery wings stretched out far beyond her peripheral vision, then tucked back, folding around its enormous body.

The beast's head came into view as Mina-Eloness backed away to get a better view. Two horns, each three times larger than she was tall, rose into the air above. Smaller horns reached up in clusters at the base of them, accompanied by rows of spikes that lined the ridges of the dragon's elongated face. Three vertical pupils glared back at her from each of its eyes, the center one larger than its companions.

"You have learned much," hissed the beast.

Eloness's ears could understand its language. Their shared heart skipped a beat and a sense of elation washed over them.

'I will be ready when she arrives. We will not fall,' said Mina-Eloness, both within and without.

"Though you may rend the ground in practice, you will find combat with a demon to be quite a different thing. I do not wish you to fight her face to face," said the dragon.

'What is it you wish of me, my Empress?' asked Mina-Eloness.

"If she defeats me in battle, she will seek out the great wyrms that govern the five Dominions. My brood must survive. If I fall, you must turn them to stone. They have been instructed to let this happen," said Aggriphaxxeddon.

'I do not wish to kill them, my Empress,' said Mina-Eloness. Their mind flooded with despair. Mina could feel the pain in her heart. It felt as if her whole world was being destroyed before her, and she was helpless to do anything about it.

"They will not be dead, only dormant. As their flesh petrifies, their blood will react accordingly. It will turn to melrithium, to which their essence can cling, and linger. In time they will awaken and darken the skies once more with their glory. If they are stone, she will not seek them. They will survive," said the dragon.

'What of you, my Empress?' asked Mina-Eloness.

"I will either kill her or be slain. Too many of our younger ones have died by her hands. I cannot let her campaign continue. She will not stop until we meet in battle. I fear that if she is robbed of the chance to fight me, she will take her anger out on my flock; my people. I cannot allow such an event to come to pass," she explained.

Aggriphaxxeddon extended her wings and thrust downward. A great gust of wind nearly knocked Mina-Eloness over as the beast rose into the sky. The dragon circled once before leaving, and called down a final message.

"The time is nearly upon us. Make yourself ready."

✦ ✦ ✦

MINA WOKE drenched in sweat. She climbed out of bed and walked to the window as she rubbed the sleep from her eyes. Eros's breathing continued rhythmically behind her, inviting her to return to his side. She pulled one of the curtains to the side and mindlessly stared at the city while her mind came to terms with what she'd seen.

Her last dream had been of Mordessa, back in the cave after healing Eros. Every time she'd gotten a chance to sleep since then had been complete darkness, with no memory of anything special upon waking. While the visions she frequently had of Mordessa were vivid, and often laced with a tinge of fear, or the extreme throes of panic, none had affected her as much as what she'd just witnessed.

Every ounce of her, down to her core, wanted nothing more than to climb back into the dream, see Aggriphaxxeddon fly, and feel the unwavering love that Eloness held for her. The despair she felt at the Empress's departure was the most visceral emotion she'd ever felt, and if pressed, she knew she'd fail at putting the experience into words.

'That was the worst day of my life,' said Eloness in her mind. 'I never saw her again after that.'

'I am so, so sorry. She cared for you. I could sense it,' replied Mina. Her heart ached just thinking about it.

'She loved us all deeply. We were all her children. But she never fully recovered from her war with the Agthari. I... I shouldn't have let her fly toward her death. I should have insisted she bring the Caier. Even though only three of us remained, we could have helped turn the tide,' said Eloness.

'She did what she thought was best to protect you. Just as Ahm did his best to protect me,' said Mina.

'I have seen your memories. He does seem to care for you, much to his own detriment. Like Aggriphaxxeddon, he puts himself in danger to protect you; to conceal your existence from that wretched Queen,' said Eloness.

'Are... are you here to stay? Will you fade over time?' asked Mina.

'I do not know. Prior to the ritual, my consciousness was with the Aggripha, and I could only send impressions of my thoughts to you through great effort. Now... I do not feel the Aggripha. I know that some of me still resides within its enchantments, but I can no longer touch that part of me,' said Eloness.

'If you can be free, I would wish you to be. If you cannot—if your fate is oblivion—I would rather you stay and share my life. I've now felt your love; your passion. We are very much alike, you and I, and *part of me already fears losing you,'* said Mina.

'What will be, will be. Fate is upon us, and there is nothing we can do to change that now. This is the last time the Caier will rise from the Aggripha. This is Talaani's last chance at freedom. Whether I survive is of no consequence. If I do, then so be it. If not, then I at least wish to see that wretched bitch die before I fade,' said Eloness.

Mina spent the rest of the night watching the stars move across the horizon, comforting Eloness in the back of her mind, just as Eloness sought to comfort her. As dawn crested the mountains to the east, and Zathos's red glow weakened, Eros stirred and joined the waking world.

She turned and walked toward him without saying a word. When she arrived at his side, she quietly bent down and pressed her lips to his forehead, then removed herself from their chamber. He looked up, confused, as she departed, but made no sounds of protest.

The companions joined Mina in the banquet hall as they awoke, each entering at various stages of awareness. Ahm and Whun ascended the stairs from the ritual chamber, arriving shortly after her, then left again to prepare for their morning. By the time Tavyn entered the hall, Ahm and Whun were returning with several tankards of steaming liquid floating in the space between them.

Ahm took them out of the air, one by one, and passed them around to the companions. They sat for a time in awkward silence, waiting for the Noktulians to arrive. When they finally did, they ushered the companions outside without a word, and directed them toward the lead wagons of a patiently waiting caravan.

The first ritual site was half a day's ride to the north. Gnately, Tavyn, and Piya, riding in the second wagon, talked among themselves during the journey, passing Petree between them and giggling at the things he was doing. Mina, Eros, and Jaezyn remained silent in the lead wagon, lost in thought. The final ten wagons carried a mix of Noktulians and several very pale elves, which they hadn't seen until that morning. Whun floated behind them, pulling the dark sword along through the air in his wake.

Standing atop a hill under the rays of the midday sun, two tall bone-like structures stretched skyward, rising over the horizon ominously as they approached. The pointed, pale columns were far enough apart that two wagons could park end-to-end between them, and were at least four times taller than a Noktulian. The outer edge of each spire was smooth, while the inner edge seemed to bear notches, or teeth. Between them was a flat expanse of granite, which seemed to have been scorched black in a pattern that burst from the center, extending several feet in all directions. A flat expanse of marble stretched out on the other side of the columns, etched with runes and sigils.

The caravan stopped in front of the pillars and allowed the passengers to climb down before the Skaar pulled the wagons a short distance away and parked them at the bottom of the hill. The Skalaani drivers then joined them and walked back up the hill, forming a defensive circle around the perimeter of a flat expanse of marble.

Whun floated between the spires and invited the rest to follow. The Noktulians and elves passed through without hesitation and formed up inside the ring of Skalaani and Skaar, each bowing their head when they reached their position. As they passed, Gnately looked at Tavyn and asked, "What kind of elves are they?"

"I'm not sure," answered Tavyn. "They're similar to Afyr, but as tall as a human. I've never seen their like. In a place like this, that somehow seems fitting, though."

"They are the Kysvali," said Eros. "When Mordessa breached into this world, they followed her here, trying to escape a great evil. Only a few hundred survived the journey, and less than three dozen remain to this day."

"The same ones? They're thousands of years old?" gasped Tavyn. "Elves don't live that long."

"They aren't of this world, Tavyn. Their kind were the first recipients of the Ritual of Restoration, as the Noktulians attempted to perfect it; long before they used it on Lord Whun," said Eros.

"How do you know this?" asked Tavyn.

"I know because Xahn knew. The Caier and Kysvali were quite close. Neither species could procreate on their own. Xahn never understood why, but he was proud of Eloness for her ingenuity in the matter," said Eros.

"What did she do?" asked Gnately.

"With help from Aggriphaxxeddon, she found a way to allow the two races to form a union successfully, which gave us the Noktulians," said Eros. "He didn't understand the minute details, only that a ritual was involved, and it could potentially be fatal to the participants. Most of the Caier died in the war with the Agthari, so only a few Noktulians were made through that process. The high priest of the Enclave was the first of them."

"But... that would make him thousands of years old!" gasped Gnately.

"His body is no more than thirty," answered Eros with a smile. "The Kysvali are the only living creatures on Xulrathia that were around when the wars happened. Everyone else is either Undead, Unliving or has reincarnated dozens—if not hundreds—of times."

"So, everyone in the Talaani Empire knows what happened?" asked Tavyn.

"That is true of some events, but not others. No one was around to see what happened between Mordessa, Ishnu and Xxrandus. All we have is speculation," said Eros.

Mina walked over to them, interrupting their conversation. "It's time." She led them between the spires to the platform and pointed to spots where they should stand. Gnately, Tavyn and Piya were sent a safe distance outside the circle, with little Petree perched firmly on his Gnomish mother's shoulder. Eros was instructed to stand on Jaezyn's left, with Mina on his right, all facing the space between the spires. Ahm stood behind Jaezyn, his arms extended in preparation. Jaezyn took a few steps forward and knelt, waiting for the start of the ritual.

Lord Whun drifted to the front of the gathering, the dark sword Strambáneur following in his wake. He waved his arm with a flourish and held his hand pointed toward Jaezyn. The sword floated across the space between them, slowly turning so the tip faced the ground. When it was within a foot of the stone man's lowered head, it dropped abruptly out of the air and buried itself halfway into the marble platform. Jaezyn stood and placed his right hand on the pommel, waiting for Whun's signal to proceed.

The ancient lich spun round to face the spires, raising his hands into the air. Black bolts streaked down from the cloudless sky, racing toward his outstretched palms in a constant stream. From horizon to horizon, the sky dimmed as a net made of lightning surged into view overhead. The bright blue of the normally invisible leylines that comprised Ayrelon's magical weave dimmed and went dark gray. The power sparking from their surface, twisting around them, and jumping between them in erratic patterns change hue, shifting to a vibrant purple.

As the magical forces poured into Whun, they radiated from his core. Before long, the power grew to such heights he could no longer contain it. With a crack of thunder, a thick stream of magic erupted from Whun's exposed, blackened heart. It exploded with ferocity as it hit an invisible barrier between the spires, spreading to the edges of the vertical plane.

He continued to channel the energies toward the gate for what seemed like an hour. Without warning, the weave faded from sight in the sky. The magical forces stopped flowing through him, and he fell to his hands and knees on the ground. The great lich could do no more.

The participants looked at the gate in awe, its surface rippling in small waves, as if wind blowing across a pond. The dark blacks, grays and purples had faded, leaving behind a silvery liquid that somehow hung suspended between the teeth of the spires.

Whun levitated back into the air, reclaiming his former stature. 'I have coalesced a fragment of our reality, creating an inert gate. Now it is up to the key-bearer to pierce the veil, so that we might *summon our gods back to Ayrelon,'* he explained. He drifted over toward the ternion and gave a simple nod to Jaezyn.

Once he was clear, the man gripped the sword's hilt in both hands and violently ripped it free from its marble scabbard. As he walked toward the gate, Ahm stepped forward into his position, placing a hand on both Mina's and Eros's shoulders.

Jaezyn stopped a few feet from the magical plane and lifted the sword to eye level, perpendicular to its surface. He pressed the tip into the liquid plane, causing ripples and sparks of energy to streak away from the point of impact. He pressed on, stepping closer, pushing with all his strength. The faint crackling of the magical field's resistance grew louder, filling the area with a rapid hissing atop a deep, resonating hum.

Mina felt the irresistible urge to chant. Eloness urged her to comply. Jaezyn and Eros joined in as she began, similarly driven by their memories of the ritual they'd discovered.

"Tsel le velo ichil kuxtal yéetel u kíimile', ka caminemos tu'ux ku k'ek'eno'. Crea jump'éel bej ichil le reino yéetel le kúuchil u mina'an u k'aaba'."

Gnately leaned over to Tavyn as the chanting rose in volume. "What language is that?"

"I've never heard it before," he said.

Piya slid behind him, grabbing his arm and shoulder for comfort. She was too scared to keep watching.

The Kysvali and Noktulians joined the chant, adding their own magic to the ritual, strengthening it further. Thin strands of energy became visible, streaming between the participants and the gate. The blade sank deeper into its surface as their chanting reached a crescendo. Jaezyn pushed harder, digging in his feet and thrusting with every fiber of his being.

The sword slammed quillon-deep into the surface of the gate, sending dark ripples throughout its surface. They stopped chanting as the gate's silvery surface slowly grew so dark it seemed to absorb any light nearby. Jaezyn shifted his grip and shoved the hilt toward the ground, cutting a slit in the center of the plane. The sword fell from his grasp and clanked to the ground several feet behind him, ejected from the gate by an unseen force. He took a step back, grunting in exhaustion and pain. The very second the sword was clear of the gate, Ahm started chanting the final portion of the ritual.

"Jay ka'ansaj u kuxtal, Ko'oten To'one'. Suut k lu'umil ka taase'ex Jets' óolal ti' k mentes. Concédenos santidad, utia'al u k tsa'ayal ten a ti' u kíimile'."

The Noktulian and Kysvali participants joined Ahm in his chant, their voices echoing across a great cavern they could not see. Dark magic spewed forth from the gash, colliding with Jaezyn. He maintained his footing, but the power was too strong. As he was pushed back by the force of the magical winds, his feet sliding across marble that was slowly being ground into dust, his body completed its petrification. As the burst of power ebbed, Jaezyn stood frozen in place, one hand extended toward the gate, the other attempting to guard his cringing face from the onslaught.

Before Mina or Eros could react, Ahm's portion of the chant changed, and a silvery sheen rippled away from the gash in the gate.

"Ishnu, come forth. I feel your presence. I know you are near. Return to Ayrelon, and help us put an end to the false goddess," prayed Ahm.

Two silver hands, each larger than Mina's torso, reached through the gash at an odd angle, as if their owner was crouching. They turned over, palms facing outward, and gripped the side of the gash like it was solid, then yanked outward with unbelievable force. The gash ripped into the sky with a horrible screech, reaching far higher than the top of the spires, disappearing out of their view.

What stepped through was something Mina could only describe as a titanic winged elf, with silver skin, white nails, white feathered wings, and white, flowing hair. Her distinctly feminine form was covered with an exquisite golden breastplate, layered metallic skirt, pauldrons, greaves, boots, and bracers. A thin golden crown adorned with a bright purple crystal floated several feet above her head. Mina was certain she stood at least twenty feet tall.

Every creature present knelt and bowed to the ground without hesitation.

"Oh, great Ishnu! Ayrelon has suffered for your absence!" gasped Ahm, his head pressed firmly to the marble platform.

"You have done well to restore me," said Ishnu, the whole of Xulrathia trembling at her words. Her voice was multi-layered, just like Mina remembered of Mordessa, as if several entities were speaking at once.

"Where is his eternal majesty, Xxrandus?" asked Whun, floating on his cloud of magic, resisting the urge to bow to a god he did not worship.

"I sent him back to the hell he created; to Melthax. That is why Mordessa sought my end," she answered, though all knew she owed him no answer.

"She has usurped your power, great Ishnu, and intercepted our prayers for her own gain," said Ahm.

"I am aware of her transgressions. Her access to the Sphere has been cut off by my return," said Ishnu.

"Will you help us defeat her?" asked Ahm.

"I cannot intervene," said Ishnu.

"Why not?" yelled Tavyn, rising to his feet at the edge of the clearing.

Ishnu turned to face him. She looked down at him with a hint of admiration and a faint smirk. "Sweet Tavyn. Ever passionate in your enforcement of my will. Do you wish to know what that truly is?" she asked.

Tavyn nodded, his eyes so wide he thought they'd bleed. He found it difficult to catch his breath.

"Simply live. Celebrate life, and mourn not those who have passed on. The cycle can tend to itself. The only true abominations in my eyes are those who find joy in the harm of others. If you truly wish to fight, fight for those who cannot. As for Mordessa, meddling in the affairs of mortals is what caused Xxrandus's downfall. The gods sent me to deal with him, and you can see for yourself the aftermath of those events. Though her actions brought her close to godhood, my daughter is mortal, and as such, must be dealt with by mortals."

She turned back toward Ahm and the rest of the congregation. She reached back with one hand toward the gate and yanked downward. All its power rushed into her palm and faded from existence. Her wings thrust downward, sending her into the sky, where she hovered briefly.

"Fret not. Bringing me back to Ayrelon was enough to secure your victory. She no longer has access to the Sphere, and even now suffers for its absence. Though I cannot intervene directly, know that you are all *blessed* so long as you stand in my favor."

As she faded from view amidst a swirl of purple magic, the crowd slowly got to their feet. Piya raced through them as quickly as she could, coming to rest beside the stone figure she'd once known as Ainen.

Torn between deep feelings of success and frustration, the crowd made their way back to the wagons. Gnately and Tavyn stayed behind for a while with Piya, eventually leading the poor girl down the path in tears. She'd grown close to Ainen, and his sacrifice would take time for her to overcome.

As the caravan made its way back down the hill, the roar of a distant dragon echoed throughout the caldera. Whun looked to the sky, the dark sword floating behind him, their impending victory the only thought in his mind.

HAVING LOST track of the Caier, and Whun, and Ahm, and Ahm's precious, secret daughter, Mordessa had let her rage consume her in recent weeks. She'd all but destroyed her own quarters, and the entirety of her ritual chamber. Her throne was in splinters scattered across the whole of her seldom-used audience chamber, and most of her servants had been ripped to shreds, or crushed, by her magical outbursts. The air in Dusk seemed to heave as she breathed, succumbing to her whims no matter the distance from her palace.

She was certain her staunchest supporter—Lord Whun—had turned against her. Though the thought had been prevalent before, she'd left room for her judgment to be in error. That room was no longer necessary. It had become clear. Not only was the hundred year cycle repeating, Whun seemed intent on forcing it to be the final iteration. No sooner had he vanished from her clairvoyance than everyone else of import started heading toward the Talaani Empire, and similarly disappearing from her sight.

In that moment, she decided it was time to fly to the Talaani Empire herself, and end their rebellion where it stood. She couldn't allow them to approach Baan'Sholaria, let alone enter the city of Dusk. As she plodded toward the exterior doors of her one beautiful palace, panic struck. Without warning, her attachment to the Sphere of Death disappeared. She could no longer feel the boundary between life and death, or the many souls that lie beyond the mortal world.

It was a power she'd felt for over a thousand years, and it was suddenly, inexplicably, no longer present. It felt as if a large part of who she was had been violently stripped away, and left in its wake was a void of nothingness; an empty vessel that was no longer sure of herself, who she was, and how she would maintain her position of authority or defeat the incoming threat.

The reality of her situation was far worse, and that thought did not escape her. Distraught as she might be for the loss of power, and the absence of those million screaming voices she'd grown so accustomed to hearing, it was nothing in comparison to the fear that was settling in. Her mother had returned to Ayrelon. Ishnu was free. Even if she overcame the rebels, and the Caier, and all that they planned to bring with them, she would have to face her mother in the coming days.

A cold chill ran down her spiked spine. She hadn't known panic, fear or anxiety in so long, the feeling was almost debilitating. Her muscles involuntarily tensed, and a knot formed in her throat. Her temples swelled, and the pressure inside her head caused every beat of her heart to send a wave of pain rushing through it. As she reached for her head, to massage the pain away, her hand trembled violently. No matter how hard she tried, she seemed incapable of forcing her hand to steady, and reach past her face normally.

Anger swelled up within her, quickly overcoming her fear. No...

it will not end like this, she thought with as much determination as she could muster. Though it felt like she'd just been sent back twelve hundred years in her progress, one thought tickled at the back of her mind that gave her hope; one simple fact, one source of power, that she hadn't had at her disposal during her original conflict with Ishnu. She was Queen of Baan'Sholaria; creator and master of the Aggripha. She might not be able to call upon the fabric of existence and leverage the powers of life and death, but she could draw her strength from over one hundred million souls all across her Kingdom.

With renewed vigor, she leaned into her anger and stood tall in defiance of her enemies; ready to face them, and show the true power of their Queen.

Let them come.

NOKTRUSGODHEN CROSSED paths with the caravan less than an hour after they got underway. He dove from the sky amidst cheers from the Talaanians, extending his wings at the last second before impact to catch the air and cease his fall, sending a rush of wind through the procession. He released a small metal cage from one of his talons and landed off to the side, then peered at the small creatures, searching for the one he needed.

With a series of hisses and growls, Noktrus told his servants to bring the woman forth. Several Noktulians ran to Mina's wagon and reached for her without warning. She backed away instinctively.

'*It is me he's searching for. You must go with him,*' assured Eloness. '*All will be fine. With my power, you can release the rest of the wyrms from their curse. Four Noktulians will come with us, to carry their burden of stone.*'

'*You mean die as I transfer your petrification curse to them,*' corrected Mina.

'*Yes. Precisely as they wish. They gladly give their lives in service to their masters, just as you, I'm sure, would gladly give your life to save Ahm, or Eros,*' said Eloness.

Mina stood and climbed off the wagon. She shrugged off the hands of the Noktulians that reached for her and made her way toward the dragon. It seemed nearly as large as her vision of Aggriphaxxeddon, with deep blue scales instead of prismatic. She reached out to touch the great creature. Sensing her desire, Noktrus lowered his maw, placing it just within reach of her. She ran her finger along the crease between the scales near its nostril, then retracted her arm with a nod.

"I will come with you. Eloness assures me that you mean me no harm," said Mina. She looked at the cage for a moment, concern rising at the back of her mind.

'You cannot ride on his back, if that's what you were expecting. He's far too large for you to maintain your grip. You would fall to your death. The cage is large enough for you and the Noktulians to ride in safety. He will grip and carry it while he flies,' explained Eloness.

With one final nod, she walked into the cage and sat on a metal bench along its side. Four Noktulians entered with her, the last closing the door behind them. Once all were seated, Noktrus rose up on his hind legs, grabbed the cage with his left talon, and jumped into the air, thrusting his wings downward as he cleared the ground.

Though he tried to hold the cage as steadily as possible, its occupants were still jostled quite a bit as he took off. Their ride seemed to smooth out quite nicely once he was airborne. Mina reveled in the feeling of the cool wind rushing past her face and through her hair. The world below seemed tiny and insignificant as they flew over. Her joy was short-lived; interrupted by Eloness's flood of instructions on which spell to use, and how to cast it without dying.

PIYA LOOKED at the rest of the group after Mina departed. She was tired of crying, and tired of being scared. Her parents, the storm, being lost at sea, the shipwreck, the horrid piles of skeletons in Uhldan, the loss of Ainen's soul, his petrification, a god climbing out of a magical field, and now a dragon taking one of her friends away without an explanation; it was all too much. She was supposed to be learning to operate her own fishing boat and manage a crew. Her father had promised her a boat of her own when she turned eighteen, and it was almost her birthday.

She couldn't contain herself any longer. Fresh tears joined the dried ones on her cheek, and she let herself fall sideways into Tavyn's lap. He looked down at her as she landed, and slowly began rubbing her back, unsure what else he could do. Gnately came to her side, tears of her own on her cheeks.

"It's almost over, Piya. We'll get you back to Gargoa soon enough, and take your family's home back for you. Everything will go back to normal soon," said Gnately.

"There is no normal. My parents are gone. If I go back to our house, I'll be all by myself. Ainen was going to join me when this was-" she started, but her sobbing got the better of her.

"Well... then, we'll figure something else out. Maybe we can go somewhere new, like the Shattered Coast?" suggested Gnately.

"That's an excellent idea," said Tavyn, patting Piya on the back. "There's a great fishing industry down there, and no winter weather to contend with. I mean, I don't know if that's what you're after, but there's plenty to do and see if you like hot weather and salty air."

"Maybe," sighed Piya.

"That's all we need, a maybe!" chimed Gnately.

"I think I'm going to look for Sylk after this is done. Her work aligns quite nicely with my new understanding of Ishnu's will. Besides, I think she could use a little more training," he laughed.

"I have a job for you, Piya," said Gnately.

Piya looked up, her curiosity breaking her out of depression momentarily.

"Will you watch Petree while we go after the Aggripha? It'll be safe here, in the Elonesti Dominion, and I'd rather he be here with you than in danger with us, in some deep, dark chamber," said Gnately.

Piya nodded and sat up, reaching her hands toward the tiny wyvern. Petree crawled into her palms, then licked them with his tiny forked tongue. The tickling sensation caused Piya to chuckle, and significantly brightened her mood. She looked up at Gnately and smiled in thanks. The three of them sat in a little clump on one side of the wagon for the rest of the journey, playing with Petree and trying their best to keep Piya's mind off her anxieties.

Eros spent the rest of the trip back to the temple watching the sky, hoping to catch another glimpse of a dragon.

CHAPTER 19:
WAR

Ris'Gaula, Brighanfjor 4th, 576 of the 1st Era

VERYONE RAN outside when Tuldaxx roared, signaling the approach of the five ancient wyrms. Aggriphaxxeddon's brood had finally been restored to its former glory, and they approached from the north in a spectacle unlike anything they'd ever seen. Even the residents of the capital city ran out of their homes, or climbed onto roofs, to watch their silhouettes grow in the sky.

Eros ran across the courtyard as Noktrus placed the cage on the ground and flew up to his roost above the temple. Mina was the only passenger that remained. He helped her out of the cage amidst cheers of celebration, and led her through the sea of onlookers toward the banquet within.

Streams of fire shot through the sky behind them as the dragons celebrated their return. Torches and lanterns sprang to life across the city. No citizen would rest that night. Tavyn, Gnately and Piya fought back against their desire to join in, and left the celebration to join their companions inside.

The hall had been filled with three long rows of tables, joined end to end. Though the hall was empty of guests, the sheer volume of chairs made it troublesome to traverse. The tables were covered in trays of all sizes, each bearing various dishes or piles of food. Eros led her to their seats at the far end of the hall, around a table that ran perpendicular to the rest. She dropped into a chair with such a thud as he turned toward his that he nearly twisted an ankle, spinning back around to check on her.

"I'm fine," she sighed. "Eloness's magic is extremely taxing, and very dangerous. According to her constant barrage in my mind, it took me 'six times as long' to channel the same powers as she used to be able to handle. She was definitely surprised that I survived, though, and I did get a bit better with each casting."

"We're just glad you made it back in one piece," said Tavyn as the rest of the friends took their seats.

"Eloness credits my success with my lifelong attachment to the Aggripha. She says that had I not been absorbing its power my entire life, building up my resistance to such strong forces over time, that I would have 'melted from the inside out' the moment I tapped into Primal Earth," sighed Mina as she reached for a pear.

"Primal Earth?" gasped Eros.

"Yep. That's where she drew most of her advanced magic from, whatever that is," said Mina.

"Wizards struggle their whole lives to touch the primal elements without dying to their power. In fact, just last year, more than twenty liches completely destroyed their bodies trying to harness one primal element or another. I don't even know if Lord Whun can pull it off," gasped Eros.

"I wouldn't say I pulled much off, to be honest. I just followed Eloness's instructions, and leaned on what I could salvage from her memories," said Mina. "I certainly didn't know what I was doing."

"Either way, the fact that you touched such magical energies and survived is something to be celebrated," said Eros, raising his mug in toast.

Mina wrinkled her brow at him. "Drinking ale? Tonight? We have a war to wage tomorrow," she grunted.

"Exactly! This might be our last chance to celebrate," he grinned, holding his mug even closer to her.

"I'm in!" yelled Gnately, waking Petree from his nap as she jumped onto the table with her mug. Eros and Mina shot her a questioning glance. "What? I can't reach, otherwise!"

"I'll join the celebration too," said Tavyn, lifting his own mug.

"I could use a night of fun. Might not get another one for a while," said Piya, shrugging. Her face was puffy from crying all day. Her heart wasn't really in the mood to celebrate, but the alternatives were far less appealing.

294   *Ris'Gaula, Brighanfjor 4th, 576 of the 1st Era*

Their celebration continued into the long hours of the night. Ahm even joined in when he returned with Lord Whun.

THE NEXT morning, the companions were awakened by the roar of a very impatient wyvern. Tuldaxx stood waiting at the center of the courtyard. Four of the wyrms were perched delicately atop nearby buildings. Noktrus watched from his roost atop the temple. Ahm and Whun walked ahead and joined Tuldaxx at the front, then signaled for the companions to gather before them.

"The time has come," said Ahm. "We will commence our attack within the hour. Tavyn, Gnately and Mina will ride in the cage carried by Tuldaxx. Lord Whun will be carried by Aashvukrier, and I will be carried by Loshfurdahn.

"As we pass over Arragesh, Tuldaxx will hang back and create distance from us. When we cross the outer walls, Losh and Aash will drop Lord Whun and I near the Ministry of Internal Affairs' northern headquarters. There we will lay waste to every Ebon Guard in sight, and anyone else who rises up to stand in our way. Once we attack, the wyrms will seek out official buildings all across Dusk and burn them to the ground.

"Make no mistake, there will be resistance. Many members of the Ebon Guard are casters in their own right, and they will not hesitate to attempt to pull the dragons from the sky. The longer they linger above the city, the more danger they are in. However, Tuldaxx can *not* start the next phase of the attack until Mordessa is drawn out of hiding and joins the fray," said Ahm.

"This all sounds like a lot of Dusk's citizens are going to die just to draw her out of hiding," said Mina.

'They *will*,' answered Whun.

"They didn't do anything wrong! They're just living their lives," said Mina.

'They are unwitting puppets, but also her most extensive source of power. The fewer of them, the weaker she shall be. Besides, you can't honestly believe they'll survive this encounter. Many will die. They are all acceptable losses,' said Whun.

"But-" started Mina, frustrated and concerned.

'This is the only way. I will lay waste to the entirety of Dusk to take Mordessa down; their lives matter not,' said Whun.

Ahm watched for a moment as Mina grew angrier, but she chose to remain silent. When he was certain the argument had concluded, he continued his instructions. "Once she has been seen, the wyrms will cry out for Tuldaxx. At that point in time, she will approach the center of the city and take the three of you to the Citadel of Xxrandus, then the rest is up to you. Once you destroy the Aggripha, Mordessa will weaken, and we can deliver the fatal blow."

"You said the sword was the only way to kill her, but Ainen—I mean Jaezyn—is petrified. So who will wield it?" asked Tavyn.

"Eros will have to," he replied.

"I thought you said we couldn't?" asked Eros.

"More to the point, you shouldn't. However, we have no other options. I cannot touch it, because I am Unliving. Whun cannot, because he is a Lich. You are the only one here who isn't headed for the Aggripha that can touch Strambáneur without having your soul disrupted, or destroyed," said Ahm.

'We do not make this decision lightly. This is not ideal,' said Whun.

"So what will happen to Eros?" asked Mina.

"We do not know," said Ahm.

"With my healing spells, I would have expected to travel with Mina," said Eros.

"Were Jaezyn still with us, that plan would make sense," said Ahm. "As things stand, we're out of options."

"I'll take his place," said Piya, exiting the temple. The group spun in shock, not expecting her to be there. "You were quite loud leaving your rooms, and woke me up. I'd say I was offended that you didn't invite me, but I understand."

"You are not skilled in wielding blades, and have no magical training," said Ahm.

'If either of us can keep Mordessa engaged, she could easily sneak up behind her and strike the fatal blow,' said Whun.

"All I have to do is stab her once, right?" asked Piya.

"Fine," agreed Ahm.

"So I'm going with Mina, then," said Eros.

"Wait a damned minute. If anyone's going to wield such a weapon, it should be me. Why put her in harm's way?" demanded Tavyn.

"Do you think the Aggripha will be unguarded? Or the citadel, for that matter?" asked Ahm. "You are a trained assassin. I need you to get the party to their target."

Tavyn grunted in frustration.

"I can do this, Tav," said Piya confidently. "Besides, if the Noktulians have a blacksmith, I have Algrim's armor. I could wear that for protection."

'I *will alter it with my magic so it fits you*,' thought Whun with a nod.

"Then it's settled," said Piya.

The wyrms hissed in unison. Tuldaxx reached a talon up and pressed the talisman around her neck. "The brood agrees to this plan."

Whun left for Piya's quarters and returned a few minutes later with Algrim's armor floating in the air behind him, glowing and slightly modified. Tavyn spent a few minutes helping her put it on, then turned to the group and indicated they were ready.

"Piya, you're with Lord Whun," said Ahm without delay.

The group climbed into their assigned cages and held on tight as their winged allies carried them into the sky. None of them could manage to break free enough of their anxiety to enjoy the flight that followed.

PROVOSS AND Aygos began their ascent, ready to cast light upon another peaceful evening. Though tens of thousands of guards were stationed in thousands of towers all along the wall at Dusk's northern border, few were watching the sky, and fewer still took notice of the six approaching specks on the horizon. Many of them had been members of the Ebon Guard since before they could remember, serving hundreds of years in defense of Her Majesty's people. Not once had they been attacked. Not once had there been reason for concern.

Five-hundred-seventy-six years of boredom had conditioned them to pay those specks no mind. Dice were thrown, cards were dealt, and ale was withdrawn from old wooden casks; all serving as a means to distract them from the tedium of a long night on watch. Even the citizens of the northern districts went about their nightly routines with no reason to question the sanctity of their city's defenses or look toward the sky.

By the time alarm bells rang out in distress, streams of fire had already begun to rain down from above. The tops of five towers filled with jets of fiery liquid, pouring in through their windows with horrific precision. Panic filled the streets as the Ebon Guard rushed into action, unsure where their enemy was, and in total disarray.

An unfamiliar sound echoed through the streets at thunderous volume as air was thrust downward through the repeated flapping of enormous leathery wings. The chaos rippled through the city in the wake of their passage, guards springing into action long after they'd gone, and citizens pouring into the streets to flee the roaring blaze.

Losh and Aash lowered their cages to the ground a few hours later, placing them in a large courtyard before a great domed building. Ahm, Whun, and Piya climbed out of their cages as the pair returned to the air and joined the rest of their brood. The sky glowed orange all around them. The city was ablaze. Cries of thousands of panicked citizens echoed through the streets.

Lord Whun rode his magical currents six feet into the air. Purple fire sprang forth at the center of his chest, enveloping his entire body in a terrifying display. *'Thy end is nigh!'* he shouted, sending his message into the minds of everyone in a three-mile radius, accompanied by a crack of thunder that seemed to echo across the whole of Dusk.

Ahm strode determinedly toward the Ministry headquarters, looking back once to insist Piya keep up. She reached down and grabbed Whun's sword by the scabbard, hefting its weight with trembling hands. She wrapped her arms around its three-foot blade, cradling it in the crook of her elbow and pressing it against her chest as she entered a jog.

Purple lightning shot down from the sky, striking dozens of members of the Ebon Guard with horrifying precision as they raced toward Lord Whun, their minds full of duty, and panic in their eyes. Jets of flaming liquid rained down on the streets in a half circle behind the domed structure as Ahm and Piya approached.

The Eternal Watcher, broken free of his trance by Whun's decree, rose from his desk, his joints creaking from disuse. His crystal ball went clear, his mental focus disrupted. Drawn by the sounds of chaos, he could not resume spying on the citizens of Dusk until he found the source of the disturbance. He strode from his chamber full of anger, sure that someone had botched their duties, ready to hand them the ultimate price for their insolence.

A dozen guards poured past his central office, down the open stairwell a dozen feet in front of his door, and out into the streets beyond. He followed closely behind, as the sound of their screams echoed through the shattered windows at the front of his building. As the cries faded, and the thuds of their armored bodies falling lifelessly to the ground came to an end, he completed his descent and peered across the lobby, through the windows, seeking their assailant.

"You have made a terrible mistake," said the lich as it exited through the doors.

Standing a few feet away was the High Priest of Kesh, his white and red robes spattered with the black blood of the guard, which lie crumpled in a ring around him. The Eternal Watcher jutted his right arm toward the mad priest, clenched his fist and uttered a single word in an attempt to end the man's life in a single spell.

Ahm thrust his own hand at the same time, a golden burst of

energy filling the air between them, and dissipating the lich's spell harmlessly. He ran toward the Watcher, taking advantage of his greater mobility, and slammed into the creature before it could react. He grabbed the Watcher's robes in his left hand, and its jaw in his right, just as the blinding light of his own spell faded.

Hooking his fingers into the skeleton's mouth, Ahm yanked downward with magically enhanced strength, and ripped the lich's jaw from its head. The Eternal Watcher shrieked in pain, its black tongue flailing uselessly about its neck.

"Cremare!" yelled Ahm as blue flame burst out of his left palm, directly into the chest of the creature. He stepped back as the flames overtook the ancient lich, rendering it to dust in a few short seconds.

Piya ran to Ahm's side as guards swarmed up from behind them. She ducked behind as he turned and sent a magical shield into the air, deflecting spouts of magical flame and a barrage of crossbow bolts.

Lord Whun floated into position behind them, lowered his hands toward the ground, clenched his fists and yanked upward. The ground beneath their feet ruptured, chunks of all sizes bursting several feet into the air. He slammed his palms back toward the ground half a second later, driving the debris down atop the guards, crushing them and ending their attack. Whun nodded at Ahm and spun back to face the main road.

"What now?" whimpered Piya, trying her best to sound brave.

"Now we hold this position until Mordessa comes to stop us," said Ahm.

"I really hope that's soon," she cried, barely able to voice the words.

"No. No, you don't," stated Ahm plainly as he surveyed the courtyard.

LIGHTNING SHOT from the sky, narrowly missing Noktrusgodhen's wings. He spiraled down, seeking his attackers. Six figures stood atop a small building south of the Ministry's headquarters, waving their hands and chanting phrases. He dove as his eyes caught sight of them, intent on cutting their spells short.

Just before crashing into them, he turned skyward and thrust his wings down, ceasing his descent and buffeting them with a wind gust that knocked them off their feet. Before they could stand, he spewed fire onto the building, setting them all ablaze. As he slowly pushed back into the sky, a feeble barrage of arrows streaked toward him, bouncing harmlessly off the scales on his right side. He continued to flap his wings to hover in position, looked toward the source, and growled.

Noktrus raised his right talon toward the archers standing atop a row of buildings nearby. He clenched his fist and yanked his talon toward his chest, then took flight. An unseen force violently ripped the archers through the air, sending them over the sides of their buildings and down into the streets below.

Three miles away, Aashvukrier was hit in the back by a bolt of lightning, and her chest by six balls of pure magic. The impact knocked the wind out of her lungs, sending a wave of pain through her body. She dropped from the sky for a moment, unable to flex her wings. Just before hitting the ground, she regained her control and caught herself on the wind, gliding over a crowded intersection where her attackers stood waiting.

Bolts careened off her red scales as she soared overhead, sapping the last vestiges of her patience. She tucked her wings, rolled and landed on her hind legs facing the intersection, straddling across three fractured, crumbling buildings destroyed by her impact. She rose to her full height and issued three short growls in laughter, sending tremors through the ground.

She hissed a short phrase and wove her front talons in a quick series of symbols, then spread her arms to the side. The streets beneath her attackers cracked, steam escaping from the openings. She smiled down at them as the stone glowed red, melted into magma beneath them, and their horrified screams echoed through the streets. She took flight again, feeling vindicated, as the streets melted and crumbled into a newly formed fissure in her wake.

A BLACK-WINGED figure approached from the south. It flew through the sky like a silvery streak, faster than the nearest dragon could fathom. Buusfahrgeddon dove toward it, intent on intercepting what it recognized as the Queen of Death. Only once had it seen her in battle, and that memory was all too vivid in its mind. Aggriphaxxeddon had forbidden him from fighting her then, but she was no longer around to prevent his assault.

Buus opened his maw, intent on catching the demon and biting her in half. As he closed the distance, she tucked her wings and went into a spiral, decreasing her altitude just enough to avoid his gnashing teeth. She extended her right hand as she crossed under his neck and raked her claws down his torso, peeling away several bright blue scales and ripping the flesh underneath. Once clear of his legs, she rolled face down and spread her wings, soaring back to higher altitude in a matter of seconds.

Ris'Anyu, Brighanfjor 7th, 576 of the 1st Era

The great dragon twisted its body in pain and extended its wings perpendicular to the ground, causing enough resistance in the air to come to a near stop. He hissed a few words and twisted his foretalons in quick gestures, causing a sphere of water to coalesce in the air in front of Mordessa. She slammed into the strange phenomenon with a violent splash, and stalled to a stop at the center of the dense liquid. With one final phrase as he began to fall backward, Buus turned the water to ice, then rolled over and used his wings to halt his descent.

Larger than a building, the ice fell from the sky. It smashed into the streets below, scattering frozen debris between the buildings in all directions. Mordessa twisted in the split second between the ice's impact and her own, managing to land on all fours and slide to a stop, aided by her talons.

She jumped into the air again and sought the wretched beast. Buus tipped into a turn at a wide arc, grasping at his wounds with his front talons, seeking a safe place to land so he could focus on healing magics. Intent on his death, she sped toward him, thrusting herself through the air with amazing strength. She was so focused on Buus; she missed the arrival of Loshfurdahn entirely.

Losh swooped down from the clouds above, using her descent to hasten her approach. She reached her mind toward the space beneath Mordessa and hissed a quick spell of her own. The air beneath the demon's wings all but vanished, sucked into nothingness by Losh's magic. With no pressure to keep her aloft, Mordessa tumbled and fell, as if an unseen vortex had pulled her toward the ground.

Mordessa glared up at Losh as she tumbled, straightened her body and pushed with her mind, sending a wave of magic beneath her, lowering her to the ground without harm. Losh growled in frustration and turned back toward the Ministry, realizing that drawing the Queen toward Ahm and Whun was the wisest course of action. She cried out to the rest of the dragons that the next phase of their plan should begin.

NOKTRUSGODHEN ROARED, shattering windows and rupturing the eardrums of many nearby Unliving. All four of his brood responded from their positions, and began their flight back toward the Ministry. Hearing their signal, Tuldaxx dove from her position in the clouds to gain speed, soaring toward the Void Spire with haste.

Tavyn, Gnately, Eros and Mina clung to the bars of their cage, eager to put an end to the destruction they'd been witnessing. Petree bit down on Gnately's left earlobe in a panic, trying frantically not to be blown from her shoulder. She reached up for him with one hand and pulled him down to her chest, saying, "It's okay, little buddy. It'll be over soon."

The Void Spire slowly came into view, its dark surfaces difficult to see against the pitch black of the night sky, save for the purple magic that illuminated its many pinnacles and buttresses. It stood three hundred feet above the citadel, which itself was nearly one hundred feet tall. Made from a strange black stone, and decorated with dark gray features, it was as ominous a place as they could have imagined. Less than a foot wide at the top, but over thirty feet wide at its base, the spire was nothing short of breathtaking to behold as they drew near.

To Tavyn and Mina's eyes, the spire's entire surface seemed to writhe with the spirits of those who'd died beneath its halls.

Tuldaxx slowly circled the spire, scouting for any signs of potential resistance below. When she didn't immediately see any, she lowered to the ground in the great, black courtyard before the citadel. A titanic pair of iron doors loomed over the group as they exited the cage, standing not less than sixty feet tall. Its entire surface was adorned with iron bars shaped into leafs, thorns and vines, stretching up and joining to curve beneath the front wall's peaked arch.

The sound of a dozen booted feet approached from their rear. Tuldaxx hopped and twisted, landing with her back to the group, her tail whipping around and barely clearing their heads. They backed away as she jumped toward the attackers, lashing out with her rear talons, and shredding two of the Ebon Guards' chests, their armor all but useless. As the others rushed forward, she buffed her wings, sending them backward, then blasted the remaining soldiers with a spray of molten flame. As they burned at her feet, she craned her neck back toward the companions, pressed the talisman on her chest, and told them, "Get moving!" With no hesitation, she sent herself aloft and began circling the courtyard, intent on keeping their rear flank secured.

Tavyn quickly studied the exterior of the citadel, looking for a way in. Eros rushed past him, toward a small stone awning along the far left side, already aware of how to gain entry. Tavyn, Mina and Gnately rushed to keep up.

The door led directly into the narthex and another set of titanic doors made of dark oak and iron, hanging slightly ajar. They crossed the large, square room and passed through the inner doors into the citadel's oval central chamber. The domed ceiling stood ninety feet overhead, held aloft by a series of flying buttresses attached to nine-foot-wide columns. The center of the ceiling opened directly into the base of the spire, leading up into the darkness several hundred feet beyond.

Sitting at the center of the room was a twenty foot high throne carved from a single piece of obsidian. To its left, a twelve foot long bladed mace stood on its head, resting on a circular dais. To its right was the perfectly preserved skeleton of a Skaar, its bones singed red at the joints by some ancient magical event many eons prior.

All along the walls, continuing up into the spire, were countless tiny alcoves, each holding a small gem, vial, pot, or ornate container. All glowed to horrifying effect in the eyes of the Touched. Eros saw the expression on his companions' faces and remarked, "The alcoves hold phylacteries containing the souls of hundreds of thousands of Undead all across Dusk."

"Great," sighed Tavyn, resisting the urge to break them all. "How do we find our way down to the Aggripha?"

"The entrance to the Ascension chamber is behind the throne, set into the back wall," said Eros.

"Let's get going," said Mina as she went into a run.

MORDESSA QUICKLY gained on Losh, closing the distance with frightening speed. Her smaller body and sleeker physique made her much more nimble in the air than the dragon had anticipated. She growled in protest and dove to gain speed. The dome of the Ministry was in sight. All she had to do was make it there in one piece.

Buildings raced by, narrowly missing her talons, as she pulled up just before impact. She could feel her speed decreasing, her proximity to the various obstructions on the ground changing the air pressure beneath her wings, and threatening to force her to seek higher elevations. Her heart raced as she closed on the dome, thrusting her wings back as hard as she could.

As Losh burst through the space above the courtyard, Mordessa nearly upon her, Whun reached up with both hands, grabbed hold of something unseen, and yanked down toward the buildings on his right. Mordessa was torn from the sky by a ball of purple energy. Columns broke and tumbled into the courtyard as her body slammed through them, black blood spurting into the air in her wake.

She climbed to her feet with a great deal of effort, power rolling through her and healing most of her minor injuries as she moved. Her left wing remained broken, hanging limply to the side.

"You have sealed your own fate," she growled, her many voices echoing through the courtyard, freezing Piya in horror.

'*You have betrayed our Kingdom, and shall now pay the price,*' retorted Whun for all to hear.

"I built this Kingdom! It is mine to do with as I please!" she growled.

'We *built this Kingdom, and it will live on without you,*' hissed Whun.

Ahm stepped forward, a pulse of golden light issuing from his outstretched hands.

Mordessa raised an arm to block her face and growled in pain as Ishnu's holy flames seared into her flesh. She thrust her other hand toward him in retaliation, sending a bolt of raw magic racing straight into the center of his chest, throwing him back, and crashing him into the side of the Ministry.

Whun took advantage of her distraction and tore the ground beneath her feet, pulling her down into the stone, burying her up to her knees.

She ripped her legs free in a surprising display of strength, chunks of debris scattering across the ground all around her. Her eyes erupted in blue flame as she yanked her arms back, pulling the wall behind Whun off the building, and crashing it to the ground atop him.

Noktrusgodhen landed atop the dome and sent a stream of magic-laced fire in her direction, casting a spell upon his fierce breath as he called it forth. She rolled out of the way just in time, the stone where she stood rending to molten slag in an instant.

Whun burst out of the rubble in a blaze of purple flame, as Ahm regained his feet and started casting his next attack. Noktrus, Losh and Buus began their own spells atop the buildings surrounding the courtyard.

Mordessa's eyes surveyed the scene quickly. The odds were not in her favor. She summoned forth a surge of power from the Aggripha in an instant; an ability she'd honed through hundreds of years of practice. A wave of raw power surged forth, rushing in all directions from her core. The buildings erupted, causing the dragons to fall, while Ahm and Whun tumbled backward, disrupting their spells.

Piya, already lying prone, whimpered in fear, as fresh tears caught the dust that blew past her face, painting her gray.

TAVYN LED the group down several flights of stairs, their journey occasionally interrupted with tremors caused by the distant battle. After descending for what seemed like hundreds of feet, they passed into the open air of the Cryx onto the final flight of steps suspended above the void.

A large black cube hung from the rock ceiling, walkways leading to and around it below the steps. Eight guards were stationed next to the cube, two standing at each side. Unlike the Ebon Guard they'd seen on the surface, the ones below them wore full suits of black plate armor, including great horned helms, and all of them were shimmering in Tavyn and Mina's eyes. Each of them had a sword on their hip and a gold-trimmed, gold-emblazoned kite shield strapped to their left forearm.

As the group came into view of the chamber, the guards sprang to life, drawing their swords and barreling toward the stairs with practiced ferocity. Tavyn drew his blades and yelled, "Fuck!"

"They're Unliving, not Undead. You can injure them!" belted Mina.

"I can try channeling one of Xahn's spells if you keep them off me!" yelled Eros as the first two knights reached the bottom step.

Gnately drew her daggers and jumped to Tavyn's side. Mina filled the gap on the end, completing the line of companions, and blocking the guards' path up to Eros.

Tavyn sprang to life as the first knights arrived, parrying a downward strike from the one on the right with his crossed blades, then driving his shoulder into the shield of the one on the left.

Eros began chanting. His companions felt a tingle wash through the surface of their skin.

Gnately ducked sideways as the knight on the right attempted to bash her with his shield while turning to face Tavyn. Petree jumped toward the knight's face, intent on pecking out its eyes, while Gnately slipped low and to her right, then down a step, stopping behind the knight's knees. The leather behind his joints allowed his leg to bend, but offered little in the way of protection. She stabbed both of his legs simultaneously, and yanked her daggers free as he howled in pain, his voice echoing in his own helmet. Petree fluttered back to Gnately's shoulder as the knight fell backward.

As Gnately's knight tumbled down the steps, knocking others down in his wake, Mina focused her mind on Eloness's powers, searching her memories for a spell that might help them win the battle. As Tavyn parried blow after blow from the only remaining knight nearby, Mina selected a distant memory where Eloness had accidentally altered a cavern's structure, and nearly killed the other Caier.

'Nice choice!' yelled Eloness in her mind.

She focused her eyes on the stone overhead, then closed them and imagined her desired outcome. Power surged through her, permeating her flesh and filling the air nearby with the scent of wet earth. Suddenly the ceiling grew downward, forming stalactites within seconds, shooting toward the knights to horrid effect.

Before the knights below could respond, spikes extruded from the stone ceiling above, impaling most of them and trapping the others in a cage. The one fighting Tavyn panicked, and lost his focus. Gnately had made her way around behind him while Mina was casting, and signaled up to Tavyn, accompanied by a squeak from a very excited Petree.

Tavyn took note of her position, locked the soldier's sword in place with his daggers, and shoved the man back with all his might. Gnately drove her daggers into the back of his knees and lifted as he toppled, using his momentum against him. The knight nearly flipped head over heel before landing hard on the steps, cracking his neck and rendering him lifeless.

Mina turned and patted Eros on the shoulder, signaling that he could stop casting his spell. He looked around and saw the horrific scene below, many of the men still wailing in the throes of death, or crying to be freed.

"Your doing?" he gasped.

She nodded.

"That was splendid!" remarked Tavyn.

"Yeah, but how do we get down?" asked Gnately, pointing out the fact that Mina's spell had blocked the stairs entirely.

"Just make the steps wider on one side," suggested Eros.

"Pardon?" asked Mina, raising an eyebrow.

"The ceiling was stone. The steps are stone. Make them grow sideways," he clarified.

"Oh!" gasped Mina with a smile.

She turned back to the stairs and focused on his idea. A few moments later, all that was left to do was climb over the railing and descend, carefully, to the other side of the stalactite cage.

MORDESSA REACHED her mind deep into the Aggripha, pulling on the millions of threads that lay at the edge of its grasp. "Enough!" she yelled, her voice echoing through the whole of Dusk. The muscles beneath her skin began to glow in a swirl of purple, green, and orange hues. She lifted into the air on a current of magic as the power at the end of those threads passed through the ancient dragon's heart and filled her completely.

Raw magic rolled off her flesh in waves, rippling across the ground, through the buildings, and into every creature nearby.

Three-hundred-thousand Undead and Unliving across Dusk fell dead every second as the remainder of their leashed souls were sucked into their Queen.

Bolts of white lightning shot out of Mordessa's horned crown, piercing each of the five wyrms and seizing their bodily functions. She rose higher by the second on the currents of her overwhelming power as Lord Whun and Ahm were struck by similar bolts.

All of her attackers slowly rose into the sky behind her, pulled up by the streams of magic that ripped through their flesh.

Piya looked up in horror at the display, clutching the dark sword to her breast, fearing that all hope was lost.

WAILING FILLED the Cryx as its mindless denizens felt the rest of their souls pulled away, and their lifeless bodies fell to the rocky floor. The group searched the black stone cube, ignoring the din as best as they could manage. No entrance was apparent.

"I don't see a door, or any other way in," said Tavyn.

"Can you open it with your new magic?" asked Eros.

"Maybe? I'm not even sure this is made from natural stone," said Mina, rubbing her hand along its surface.

"We don't have any other options, right?" asked Gnately. "What do we have to lose?"

"Right," sighed Mina.

She focused again on the powers she'd acquired from Eloness, and reached out with her mind to the strange material. Try as she might, she could feel no connection to it like she could with the rocky ceiling or the stairs.

"That's not going to work," she sighed.

"Well, how does Mordessa get in? She put it in there, right?" asked Eros.

"Hmm," sighed Mina. She placed her hand on the box and closed her eyes, reaching out to the Aggripha, pulling some of its power into herself. When she sent the power into the material, it shuddered, as if trying to move. Her anticipation piqued, she repeated the process with all the power she could obtain.

The great crypt opened.

Hovering above the center of its floor was a crystalline heart, still beating and swirling in blinding magical energies. Mine and Tavyn saw a stream of souls ripping through the air, into and through the heart, racing to some far off destination. They looked at each other knowingly, as a new wave of panic set in.

With no more hesitation, Mina jumped into the box and wrapped her arms around the Aggripha in an attempt to yank it free. The screams of millions of souls filled her mind in an instant, threatening to fracture her psyche and send her into fits of madness. She jumped back, shaking in fear and pain, grasping at her temples frantically.

"What happened?" pleaded Eros, rushing to her aid.

"She's draining everyone in Dusk to fight Ahm, Whun and the brood," gasped Mina.

"She's what?" yelled Tavyn.

"I have to stop her," said Mina.

"But you could barely touch it!" yelled Eros.

'The enchantments that bind the Aggripha are nearly broken. Jaezyn is gone, and most of me is within you. That leaves only Xahn and a small fragment of me to bind it,' said Eloness.

'What does that mean?' asked Mina.

'That means it can be broken. Pull Aggriphaxxeddon into yourself and unleash the both of us toward the seal, just as Mordessa consumes the souls of Dusk to defend herself,' said Eloness.

'I will try,' said Mina. She turned to Eros one last time. "Eloness has a plan. Do what you can to calm my mind and heal me with your spells. This may very well kill me," she said.

Eros jumped forward and pulled her into a kiss. He didn't know if any of them could survive what she was about to do, but the one thing he was certain of was that he didn't want to leave the world without expressing his love for her one final time. After a kiss that was far too brief for his liking, he gave her a nod, stepped back and searched Xahn's memories for the best spell to use. When he started chanting, and she felt the power light upon her skin, she turned back to the Aggripha and focused her mind.

No sooner had Mina's mind reached out to the heart with purpose than Aggriphaxxeddon rushed to her aid. She sent herself through Mina without stopping to fill her, knowing her power was too much for the human to hold. She'd been waiting centuries for just such an opportunity; for someone to direct her power at the enchantments that held her fast.

The power poured into the heart with blinding ferocity. Tavyn and Gnately backed away as quickly as they could, unable to withstand the heat the spell was generating. Eros's magic struggled to keep Mina standing, her flesh peeling away and reforming before his eyes under the barrage of Aggriphaxxeddon's assault.

After seconds that seemed like hours, the last vestiges of Mordessa's magical bonds shattered, sending a ripple through the

Cryx, rupturing the surface of the cavern's ceiling in its wake. As the last of Aggriphaxxeddon's power dissipated, and Mina's mind was freed, she stumbled back a few steps and fell into Tavyn's dexterous arms.

Streams of power still rushed through the heart, drawn to the horrid Queen. As Mina regained her feet, she looked at her friends. Tavyn's face grew grim as he gave her a knowing nod.

"There is one more thing that must be done, but you cannot be here when I do it, or you will be destroyed," said Mina firmly.

"What? No!" gasped Eros.

"I have to destroy it! I can survive this, but you can't! She's killing millions of our people to power her spell, and do gods know what to Ahm, Whun, and the dragons. We cannot let her win. This is what Whun was talking about when he sent us here. The Aggripha must be destroyed," said Mina. She walked to him and pulled him into a hug. "I'll be fine," she lied. She had no idea if she would survive. The only thing she was certain of was they would not. "Get to the surface. I'll join you shortly."

Eros leaned in and kissed her again. He didn't know whether to believe her bravado, but he knew she was right; the Aggripha couldn't be left intact. The group looked back one more time from the top of the stairs, then started to run.

Mina gave them a few seconds to get to the surface, then walked up to the Aggripha. She didn't know if breaking it would end all lives in Dusk. She didn't know if she was going to survive the aftermath of what she had to do. She could no longer sense Eloness's presence, and couldn't ask for advice. The only thing she knew for certain was she had no other choice.

With conflict filling her mind, she reached for the crystal heart and placed a hand on either side. It came away freely from the center of the cube as her body surged with its power. Unrestrained by the enchantments that had bound it, she could no longer control how much of its magic she allowed to pass through her. She was all at once exhilarated and overwhelmed with searing pain.

Lifting the Aggripha high above her head, she threw it over the railing and watched it fall into the void. A mere second later, it shattered on the floor and a column of raw power shot through her, through the ground above, and through the Void Spire beyond.

THE MAGICAL floating isle of Xur had once been a simple, natural mountain on the southern plains of Xulrathia. Xxrandus, in all his might, had ripped it into the sky, flipped it over, and claimed it for his home. For the next thousand years, his constructs created a vast city in his honor, and a citadel to house his throne. A millennium later, his fate was sealed and mortals pulled it from the sky, binding it to the ground with great iron chains.

On that fateful day, the magic that had held it aloft beyond recorded history was destroyed. The once glorious city of Xur fell into the Cryx at that moment, and sent quakes throughout the city of Dusk, destroying more than half of the Kingdom of Baan'Sholaria.

TERROR AND denial filled Mordessa's eyes as all the Aggripha's power was stripped away from her. She and her potential victims fell to the ground in an eerie silence, as a wave of destruction slowly approached from the south.

Buildings, streets and walls all across dusk trembled, crumbled or fell as fissures and sinkholes ripped across the land, spreading outward from Xur as it fell. Tens of millions lay dead in its wake, either slain by Mordessa's greed, or the quake's indiscriminate destruction.

In the chaos, a young girl hefted a dark blade. She strode up to the horrid Queen, her body shattered on the ground, barely clinging to life. The girl slid the weapon free of its blackened melrithium scabbard, clasped its hilt in both hands and drove the sword downward.

No more tears would she cry. She had none left to give. Whoever she'd been when she arrived in Dusk had perished in a night of horror. As the blade drank the vile demon's soul, it fed it to her, twisting her, and cursing her with a portion of the Queen's knowledge and power. Dark wings burst through the skin and armor on her back, and horns broke through skull. Her legs contorted and grew longer, and her skin grew pale with a silvery shimmer.

She turned her blackened eyes toward the ruins of Dusk, the proud priest, the ancient lich, and the great wyrms struggling to gain their bearings. Without remorse or regret, she leapt into the sky, leaving the continent and its people to their fate.

TAVYN, EROS, and Gnately had made it to the surface just in time. They felt the ground drop out from beneath their feet and landed hard on the floor of the citadel as Xur crashed into the Cryx. Phylacteries toppled out of their alcoves and smashed into the ground. A column of power was surging up from below, passing around the throne and up through the center of the spire.

Eros looked back at the stairwell, but upon seeing it had collapsed, he led the charge around the throne, toward the exit, deftly dodging falling debris as best he could with his eyes full of tears.

Once they reached the courtyard, Tuldaxx swooped down and prepared to retrieve them. As they moved to enter the cage, the column of power abated, and a strange noise came from within the citadel. Eros turned on his heel and ran back, hoping beyond hope.

As Eros entered, Mina came into view. She was riding a magic current as the stone melted away to create a path for her ascent. As her feet reached the floor in front of the throne, the ground sealed behind her, leaving no trace of her passing.

Her eyes were alight with gray flames, and her skin was radiating a light blue aura of magic.

CHAPTER 20:
AFTERMATH

Ris'Anyu, Brighanfjor 7th, 576 of the 1st Era

INA AND Eros embraced, their hearts racing with love, uncertainty, and the echoes of their fear. "You're alive," he gasped, his eyes filling with tears despite the smile on his face.

"I told you I'd be up shortly," she said with a wry smile, her voice seeming to echo within her.

Tavyn and Gnately raced into the room and joined them, very excited to see she had survived.

"We should go find Ahm and see if Mordessa-" started Tavyn.

"She has been slain. I felt her die," said Mina.

"You-" started Gnately.

"Yes, I felt her die. Her grip on the people of Dusk relinquished in an instant, and a very powerful soul surged into the world, just beyond my grasp, tickling at the edges of my senses. But, then it was gone. I can feel all of Dusk's citizens now, and all of you... somehow. I think the Aggripha became a part of me," she said.

"Well, that's great news then, isn't it?" asked Gnately excitedly.

"Yes, but somehow no," said Mina.

"Care to explain?" asked Eros. "I thought her death was what we wanted?"

"Tens of millions of our citizens died. The Aggripha is destroyed, so we cannot perform ascension as we have for hundreds of years. We are in a new era for Dusk, with no clear direction on how to proceed; a fact our citizens don't even know yet. That is not to mention the death of tens of millions, and the quake that destroyed so much of our city. Plus... there's something else; something tickling at the back of my mind that I can't quite grasp," said Mina.

"Well, I-" started Eros, but he was interrupted by a streak of purple lightning striking the ground a few feet away.

Lord Whun drifted out of the point of impact, emerging from thin air as if he'd simply always been there. The area seemed to darken in his presence, as if the sun's light simply refused to get involved in the lich's actions.

'The Kingdom is yours,' said Whun for all to hear, though his eyes were locked firmly upon Mina.

"I beg your pardon?" said Mina.

'You care for them... you tend them. They are yours to herd, for they are most certainly sheep. Mordessa is slain, and neither Ahm or myself have any desire to rule this wretched place. That leaves only you,' said Whun.

"But I... no! I don't want to rule! I never wanted to be Queen! I didn't even know I wanted Mordessa dead until all this began. How can I rule fifty million people, when I never learned how to do the job?" gasped Mina.

'Your lack of training will make you a better leader. They need what Mordessa never gave them. Guidance. Empathy. Inspiration. I do not have the patience to lower myself to their level, and make them a better people,' said Whun.

"Lower yourself to their level?" challenged Gnately.

'Do you not think I am beyond their petty lives? If I were to rule, they would become my subjects... is that what you truly wish? You wish to give me a legion of undead to command? Who shall I conquer next? Haern? Tellrindos? The whole of Gargoa? Perhaps I shall conquer the world, and teach all mortals the pathetic reality of their brief and meager subsistence,' laughed Whun.

"I knew it. Never trust a Lich," said Tavyn through gritted teeth.

'I never claimed to support your cause, or values. Our goals aligned for a time. Nothing more. My question still stands, Mina,' he thought, turning back to face her. 'Do you really wish me to rule Dusk?' asked Whun.

"No," she answered, her face drained of blood. She'd somehow always known Whun was more than he let people believe, but hadn't quite known the scope of his convictions.

'People of Dusk! Hear me! Your wretched Queen has been slain and the Talaani Empire has awakened. However, worry not. Your Queen's great power has passed to another, and she has already earned the respect of the great dragons to the north. Queen Mina Llanthor will address you all in the coming days. She will help you rebuild, and you will see a greater peace than Dusk has ever known,' thought Whun, pushing his mind across the whole of Baan'Sholaria. Focusing back on the group before him, he added, *'It is done. You are Queen.'*

"But-" started Mina, too shocked to say much else.

Just as he'd arrived, Whun vanished in a flash of lightning, leaving nothing more than the stench of his ancient rot in his wake.

"He's not the only Lich that will see her death as an opportunity," lamented Eros.

"You're right. This is going to be a battle. We may have created a tenuous peace with the Talaani thanks to waking their dragon lords, but we won't have peace within Dusk for quite some time," said Mina. Her face grew grim at the thought.

"What can we do to help?" asked Gnately.

"Nothing. This isn't your battle," said Mina.

"But-" started Gnately.

Tavyn interrupted before Mina could respond. "I need to find new purpose. My whole life has been forged around misinterpretations of a simple, honest truth. It's going to take time for me to come to terms with what I've learned, and what I've seen here. I think that path leads me toward Sylk, and the cause she professes to champion. I don't know for certain, except that it means leaving Dusk. Not sure how long I could stomach being around undead and unliving anyway. It's best for me, and your people, if I'm elsewhere."

Mina placed her hand on Tavyn's shoulder and nodded. "Thank you for your help with all this. None of what happened here was your responsibility. You are an honorable man. I'm sure you will find your purpose in this world."

"Well, if you're leaving to help Sylk, and I can't stay in Dusk, where does that leave me?" asked Gnately with tears in her eyes.

"I'll travel with you back to Pelrigoss, or Gargoa; wherever you want to go. After that, you can choose to stay with me, or find your own path. We'll always be friends, and you can always count on me for help when you need it," said Tavyn. He knelt down and kissed her on the forehead, then mussed her hair.

Gnately furrowed her brow in response. "Fine. We need to collect Piya, then, and find our way out of this field of bones and debris, yeah?"

"She's with Ahm, isn't she?" asked Eros, looking toward Mina.

Mina closed her eyes and focused. She felt for Ahm's familiarness among the sea of disconnected, distraught voices tickling at the back of her mind; countless souls crying out for answers, or help. Ahm was distant, but seemed in good health; at the very least his soul seemed intact, and unburdened. Piya was nowhere to be found.

"I can sense Ahm, but not your young friend. They know where we are. We can wait here in this courtyard. Ahm's first act will be to come find me and make sure I'm safe," said Mina with a smile.

AS THE hours passed, more and more citizens of Dusk came to the ruined temple courtyard seeking answers. The first to enter their presence was a group of twelve Ebon Guard. Upon seeing them, Tuldaxx prepared herself for battle, rising back into the air from her perch atop a pile of rubble. No sooner had they entered, than they knelt in honor of Mina and promised their allegiance to her. They then encircled the courtyard and carefully controlled who was allowed to enter and address Mina, all without being asked.

"Why are they so quick to accept me? How did they know who I was? I've remained in hiding my entire life!" said Mina.

"You're glowing with soul magic. It's seeping from your pores," said Eros.

"Really?" gasped Mina. She looked at her arms for a brief moment and finally noticed what Eros was referring to. Not only had she absorbed part of the Aggripha's power, she had apparently taken on some of its appearance. Her skin was shimmering with magic, shifting between opaque and semi-translucent in seemingly erratic splotches. Blue energy seemed to be rolling off her in waves, dispersing into the air around her like a barely-perceptible blue smoke, with an underlying distortion near her skin, as if she were also radiating heat. "Well, that explains much," she said with a roll of her eyes, wondering if the effect would be permanent.

"Your eyes are also alight with gray flames," said Tavyn. "Not that you can see that yourself, but I figured you should know."

"Well that's just splendid," she laughed. "Just what I always wanted!"

The crowd continued to grow as the hours passed. Citizens entered, one by one, knelt or bowed before her, and were shuffled off by her newly acquired guards to the side of the courtyard. Eros grew concerned as the procession grew in volume, and eventually found himself unable to contain his worry.

"Notice something?" he asked, leaning in toward Mina's ear but keeping his eye on their visitors.

"What's that?" she asked in return.

"Not a single undead among them. They're all unliving," he said.

"It makes sense. The Temple of Xxrandus was destroyed, and most of the undead's phylacteries were inside," she said.

"So we'll be left to contend with a few dozen liches who were all strong enough to ascend through their own power, and didn't need help from the Aggripha," said Eros.

"It looks that way," she agreed.

"Meanwhile Ishnites outnumber them millions to one," added Eros.

"True. They'll likely feel outnumbered, and unfairly represented. After centuries of balance between the factions, this could quickly devolve into civil unrest, if not outright war. However, there is one thing to keep in mind that just might help us cut that war off before it begins," she said.

"What's that?" asked Eros.

"We can't make more Unliving. This is it. The surviving citizens are the last. They relied exclusively on the Aggripha to ascend. Meanwhile, any Xxrandite can grow strong enough in their magic to become new liches," she said.

"Hopefully that'll be enough to convince them to hold back. They crave power, and from where I stand this looks like they just lost all of it," said Eros.

"There's nothing we can do about it at the moment," said Mina.

Five silhouettes were sighted in the sky, flying in from the north. Dozens of bystanders screamed and panicked at the sight, interrupting their conversation. Mina turned, saw the brood's approach, and returned her attention to the citizens that had come to her side.

"Worry not. It is they who helped us free ourselves of Mordessa's horrid curse. She is no longer draining your souls, secretly shortening your lives, and feeding you the flesh of your deceased brethren. We have them to thank for our freedom, and they have us to thank for theirs," she declared.

"You didn't just dump that information on them like that, did you? Did I hear that correctly?" gasped Eros.

"They have to learn it eventually," she answered with a shrug. "One thing they'll learn real fast... I don't plan to hide anything from them. Full transparency will be my policy. We've had enough deceit to last thousands of years. It's time we all stood on equal footing."

"Let's hope that works," said Eros. As the dragons began landing at the back of the courtyard, Mina shot him a puzzled, somewhat frustrated look. "I'm not trying to be a downer, I just don't know if everyone is ready to learn the truth so quickly after such a big event."

"They'll be fine," she said as she turned to approach the cage Ahm was riding in, just as Noktrusgodhen set it down.

Ahm exited the cage so quickly he nearly tripped. He raced over to Mina and pulled her into a hug faster than the Ebon Guard could respond, seeming not to notice her glowing skin or flaming eyes.

"Okay, okay," she gasped. "I'm fine!"

"I held out hope you'd survive the destruction of the Aggripha, but part of me was certain I'd seen the last of you," he said. He moved his hands to her shoulders and took a step back to get a look at her, finally taking notice of her physical changes. "I told you to *destroy* the Aggripha, not *become* the Aggripha," he teased.

"What? Am I grounded? Should I head to the Cryx?" she teased in return.

"Our dynamic has certainly changed, has it not?" he laughed. "It's good this is finally over. We're finally free."

"I just want to know... why didn't you want to rule Baan'Sholaria? Why leave it to me; a seventeen year old girl? It's not like you raised me to be nobility, or attend court," she asked.

Ahm removed his hands and took a step back. "That's... that's complicated."

"Well then, un-complicate it," she demanded.

"As bad as Mordessa was, someone much more terrible is trying to breach our dimension and gain a foothold on Ayrelon. I have far too much research to do, and too many preparations to make, to be tied to a throne," he explained.

"What? Who?" asked Mina, confused.

"I can't explain. I barely understand it myself. It was all part of a revelation buried deep in my memories from before Baan'Sholaria was founded. Whun and I were warned of his arrival, and of a coming war. We are to play a critical role in Ayrelon's defenses. That must be our focus," he said.

"You didn't answer my question," she said.

"I cannot, for I do not possess the answers," he said plainly.

"Then how do you-" she started.

"I just know. The man who helped Whun and I to create Strambáneur told us just enough to set our wheels in motion,

318   *Ris'Anyu, Brighanfjor 7th, 576 of the 1st Era*

nothing more. For now, I will wait within Dusk and help you rebuild. When the time comes, I will take my leave and join that fight. Until then, all my free time will be spent researching and preparing," he explained.

"Very well. How much time will we have together?" she asked. Her eyes attempted to water, but her tears were burned away by the gray flames atop her eyes before they could grace her cheeks.

"We will have enough, I assure you. I will not depart until she comes to recruit me for the Circle of Nine. According to The Timewalker, that will not transpire for at least a hundred years," he said, as reassuringly as he could muster.

"Pardon," said Gnately, walking up and interrupting. "Where's Piya?"

"I am sorry, Gnately," said Ahm, growing somber. "She succeeded in slaying Mordessa, but Strambaneur transferred some of the Queen's power to the girl. I regret to say, she is no longer the Piya you knew, and has left of her own accord."

"What? Why didn't you stop her?" gasped Gnately.

"Well, for one thing, I was too injured to pursue her. I was barely cognizant enough to witness her transformation. For the other... I cannot fly," he said.

"She... she flew?" asked Gnately in disbelief.

"As I said, she is no longer the Piya you knew," he said.

"I'm sure *that* won't come back to haunt us," remarked Eros.

"Yet another thing we can do nothing about at the moment," sighed Mina.

"Indeed," said Ahm.

"Well," said Gnately, turning to Tavyn. Her face was growing puffy and red, and her eyes were full of tears. "I guess we can leave?" she finished with a sniffle.

Tavyn pulled her into a hug and rubbed her back. "Let's go find a new life, shall we?"

She pulled herself deeper into his embrace and nodded her head against his belly with a whimper, refusing to let go. Petree climbed onto his chest, clinging to the various leather straps, to escape her disappearing shoulder.

"What's the best way out of here?" he asked, raising his eyes to meet Ahm's.

"I'm sure Tuldaxx would be willing to carry you to Bidlesh village along the southwest coast. It's a small fishing town. They have a few trading vessels that make the trip to Pelrigoss a few times per year," said Ahm.

"Oh... um... have Tuldaxx drop them off on the overlook. They can work their way down the path from there, and then she won't terrify the citizens flying in all of a sudden," suggested Mina.

"Yeah, they don't know what happened here. They'd panic pretty much instantly," laughed Eros.

"Here," said Ahm, reaching into his pocket for a small scroll, quill and ink pot. "Thankfully for you, I have to be ready at a moment's notice, as Minister of Defense." He scrawled a quick note on the scroll and handed it to Tavyn. "This will identify you as guests of the Ministry. Take it to the quartermaster near the docks. He'll pay you for your assistance in our uprising, and secure your passage."

Tavyn took a quick glance at the scroll and slipped it into his belt pouch. "Thank you, Ahm. Payment was unnecessary, but it will certainly help."

The group spent a few moments exchanging handshakes and hugs before Tavyn and Gnately climbed into the cage Ahm had arrived in. A few moments later, Tuldaxx picked up the cage and lifted them into the sky.

"How much did he pay us?" asked Gnately, settling into the idea of forging a new life.

"Two platinum each," said Tavyn. "Pelrigossian coins," he clarified.

"Platinum? Did you say, platinum?" gasped Gnately.

"Yes. I know it's more than a gold, but I'm not current on conversion ra-" started Tavyn.

"They're five hundred gold per coin, Tavyn. He just paid us a thousand gold each! And in Pelrigoss, a gold is worth... um... three hundred silver each. That's three hundred thousand silver for each of us!" she yelled.

"Holy shit!" gasped Tavyn.

"I know what I'm doing with my half," she said gleefully.

"What's that?"

"I'm going to honor Piya and the Mortdains by buying a ship!" she chirped.

"All that time we were stuck at sea, and you want to *live* out there?"

"It'll be different this time. I'll have a full *crew* and a real *kitchen* and as many cheese wheels as I want!" she exclaimed.

"That sounds delightful," he said with a smile.

Pronunciation Guide

Aashvukrier	-	ä-sh-voo-krēr
Aggripha	-	a-grĭff-ä
Aggriphaxxeddon	-	a-grĭff-ax-eh-don
Buusfahrgeddon	-	booss-fär-geh-don
Kaggahaaden	-	kä-gä-hä-dĭn
Loshfurdahn	-	losh-fur-dän
Noktrusgodhen	-	näk-truss-gäd-hĭn
Siscci	-	sĭssy
Tuldaxx	-	tool-da-x
Whun	-	woon

Months

1	Luthentyr	-	loo-thĭn-tēr	Winter
2	Djacenta	-	d-jä-sĭn-tä	Winter
3	Brighanfjor	-	brĭg-än-f-yor	Winter/Spring
4	Nyevantyr	-	nyev-än-tēr	Winter/Spring
5	Caer'Nuun	-	k-air-noon	Spring
6	Gwyddinfyr	-	g-wĭd-dĭn-fēr	Spring
7	Bloedden'Vasche	-	blud-ĭn-vä-sh	Spring/Summer
8	Aiengust	-	aīn-gust	Summer
9	Danufyr	-	dănoo-fēr	Summer
10	Oghenfall	-	ôg-ĭn-fall	Summer/Fall
11	Arran'Hael	-	air-ran-hāl	Fall
12	Amaethur	-	ä-mā-thur	Fall
13	Ahr'Antaerwyn	-	ärr-änt-air-wĭn	Fall/Winter

Days of Week

1	Ris'Anyu	-	rĭss-än-yoo
2	Ris'Nammlil	-	rĭss-näm-lĭl
3	Ris'Kitthu	-	rĭss-kĭt-thoo
4	Ris'Gaula	-	rĭss-gä-oo-lä
5	Ris'Uttyr	-	rĭss-oo-tēr
6	Ris'Enliss	-	rĭss-ĭnlĭss

Made in the USA
Columbia, SC
20 November 2022

a5993c1d-9597-470b-a68c-2e1c803850e4R01